THE SIGN OF
ONE

THE SiGN OF ONE

EUGENE LAMBERT

First published in Great Britain in 2016 by Electric Monkey,
an imprint of Egmont UK Limited
The Yellow Building, 1 Nicholas Road, London W11 4AN

Text copyright © 2016 Eugene Lambert

The moral rights of the author have been asserted

ISBN 978 1 4052 7735 8

59774/1

www.egmont.co.uk

Typeset in Perpetua by Avon DataSet Ltd, Bidford on Avon, Warwickshire
Printed and bound in Great Britain by the CPI Group

To Martin
who shares my DNA
and my dreams

PART ONE
PEACE FAIR

1
GIRL WITH DARK GREEN EYES

The Cutting was yesterday. We missed it. Soon as we hit the trail out of our valley, I knew we would. I've seen dirtworms slither faster than some of our lot walk. Three boggin' days it's taken us to get to Deep Six. On my own I could hike it in one, but that was never going to happen. Out here in the Barrenlands, you go mob-handed and in dayshine or you don't go at all. Our wildlife's too nasty and there's always the chance of running into Reapers. It's a curse, missing the Cutting, but at least we've made it to the Peace Fair in time for tomorrow's Unwrapping.

'C'mon, Kyle,' Nash says to me. 'You done yet?'

Our men have cleared off to do some catch-up drinking, the women and the girls to check out the merchants' stalls. Nash and me, we've been left behind with the wagons, stuck with setting up camp and finding fodder for our fourhorns. Now we're supposed to sit tight and look after everything. Don't think so.

I hammer the last guy rope in. 'All done.'

We head towards the roars of delight from the nearby fairground. I feel sick with excitement and sweat pours off me. See, this is my first Fair.

'I'm going to tell them,' says Nash.

He's only a year older than me, but he's been to loads of Fairs already. We both know I could be flogged for not attending sooner. Once you're ten, the Saviour's law says you *must* go, at least once every three years.

'Give us a break, Nash.'

He sniggers. He's such a gommer.

It's Rona's fault. She won't say why, but she *never* attends the Fair. She gets away with it because she's the only healer in Freshwater. Which is fine, I guess, and none of my business. Except every year she comes up with some excuse why I can't go neither. Last year, I kicked up. Told her I was going, no matter what. Next thing I know, I'm flat on my back with swamp pox, the only dose in the three valleys. Rona denies it, course she does, but I swear she gave it to me deliberate. And you can die easy from the swamp pox. It's a miracle I wasn't scarred for life.

Well, she might be my mother, but I'm sixteen now.

At the gate, we hand over credits and flash our ID tags. I worry the gate man will figure out mine is fake, but this is the Barrenlands — he couldn't care less.

Nash keeps his poisonous little mouth shut, for once.

We hurry through a dark tunnel to emerge blinking back into evenshine, halfway up some stone-built terraces, which curve round to form an immense arena. The size of the crowd rips the breath out of my lungs — I'd no idea there were this many people on Wrath, let alone in the Barrenlands. Stalls and show tents stand out like brightly painted islands in a boiling sea of bodies. It's fierce loud. A madhouse of hoots and rough laughter and merchants yelling their wares.

'Are those the idents in the cages?' I ask.

'What do *you* think?' says Nash.

At the far side of the fairground is a stage, loads of cages stacked like crates around the back of it. Even from here I can see each cage has two child prisoners inside. So it's true. We get to gawp at them between Cutting and Unwrapping. They can't mess with their wounds without someone seeing.

Nash dives into the crowd. I follow him to a food stall.

Surprise, I end up paying for both of us. A credit buys a beer each and steaming bogbuck steaks wrapped in purple leaf. While I wolf the meat, I stare at the faces around me. Most are thick-fingered grubbers like us, but I see plenty of hunter and scavenger folk too. The locals are easy to spot, their pale miner faces scrunched up against the sun. Nearly as many women wander around as men, many with straw still plaited into their hair, to celebrate the recent harvest.

'You don't eat the leaf, you donk,' says Nash.

'Oh,' I say. It *was* chewy.

I watch him as he takes a long pull from his beaker. His eyes water, but he doesn't drop dead or anything, so I sip mine. It's fierce strong beer and tastes foul, but he's watching me back. I smack my lips and pretend to like it.

'Rona'd kill me if she saw me drinking this.'

'Rona ain't here.'

After I finish it, I feel floaty. Can't stop smiling, even at strangers. It's like the hoots and yells and laughter get louder too. The crowd's excitement is more catching than swamp pox. My heart starts pounding.

Why was Rona so worried about me coming here?

We bump into some girls from our valley then – Vijay, Mary and her little sister, Cassie. They tag along, which is no hardship. After a while, we end up near the stage and its wall of cages. Nash and the girls push on to watch jugglers, but I see two pale faces peering from the nearest cage and hang back.

Hairs stand up on the nape of my neck.

Both these girls have exactly the same long red hair, the same blue eyes, the same lips pulled down at the corners. One face two times. Twin sisters. Despite the muggy air, I shiver. I bet even their own mother couldn't tell them apart.

Identical. But one is a monster.

I make the Sign of One. Our sign against evil.

'Oh, come on,' says Nash, back at my elbow. 'Don't go all pious on us.'

Mary and Vijay snigger, safe behind him.

I shake my head, feeling stupid. The cage looks solid enough and is covered in wire mesh. Both girls have iron leg shackles. They're going nowhere.

And the thing is, neither looks evil to me, only scared.

'Never seen idents before,' I say. 'That's all.'

'Not even baby ones?' says Mary. 'Doesn't Rona heal them?'

I shrug. 'She does, but always goes on her own. To spare the families.'

Even back in Freshwater, so tiny compared to this great big mining town, we have five families now cursed with ident babies. Rona's helped deliver all of them, but won't do the marking. Says chopping fingers off infants is no job for a healer. Sometimes I've heard these babies crying as I passed by, but I've never seen any of them. The shame is so great and guys like Nash would throw stones, so the unfortunate families raise them inside, behind bolted doors. Four long years of despair and misery before Slayers take them away to the ident camps.

What must it be like to be their parents? Just cruel.

And yet where would we be without the Saviour's law to protect us?

'Hey, see the bandages?' says Nash, pointing.

Further along, two ident boys stand in their cage, gripping the bars. I see their forearms, bandaged from the Cutting. I see too that both bear the telltale mark of the ident, the little finger hacked from their left hand. Sick but clever that. Word is, back in the early days of the Saviour's law, desperate parents would hide their ident offspring by splitting them up. No way to hide a missing finger though.

I look back at the redheads, but they see me staring.

Although I've paid good money to be here, I have to look away. Okay, so I know these girls are freaks, but it still feels wrong to gawp. Just does.

'C'mon,' says Nash, making to head off, 'I'll show you something better.'

'Wait,' I say. 'Those girls.'

Nash stops and stares, obviously not bothered in the slightest that they can see him looking. 'Yeah. Cute, but not my type. What about them?'

'Which do you think is the evil one?'

Nash frowns at me, like I'm some kind of drooling idiot.

'Well, my money's on the redhead. Oh wait – they're both redheads!' He slaps his forehead, and this sends Vijay and Mary into fits of laughter. 'Look, we'll find out tomorrow at the

Unwrapping. Now are you coming or what?'

I let him drag me away.

But the look on those girls' faces, it dents my mood.

Don't get me wrong, I'm still buzzing, but I'm not so dazzled now by everything I see. Maybe that's why I start noticing faces in the crowd that aren't red and shiny with having a good time. I nudge Mary and point out one such woman. She's got a little boy by the hand. To look at her long, grey face, you'd think she was at a funeral, not a fair. Her brat looks fed up to the back teeth too.

'You can't please some people,' I say.

Mary winces, surprising me. 'The Saviour giveth, the Saviour taketh away,' she says, quoting Freshwater's preacher, old Fod. 'Even idents have families.'

Cassie catches up and grabs my hand. She's shaking.

'Hey, what's up?' I ask her.

'I'm glad there's only one of me,' she whispers.

'You wait till you see this thing,' says Nash, with a weird laugh.

'Is it scary?' squeaks Cassie, her brown eyes wide.

Nash leads us out of the crowd, towards an alcove set deep into the stone wall of the arena. As we get closer, I see wrist-thick iron bars sealing this space off and turning it into another cage. A torn canvas awning flaps above it, filling the alcove with scuttling shadows. Off to one side, a sun-scorched old man sits cross-legged on a mat, watching us. Sharp-eyed kids are hanging about.

'Is it some wild animal?' I ask Nash.

'Wait and see.'

One brat is slow clearing out of our way. Nash shoves her aside. I expect screeching and swearing, but the girl hardly notices. She just keeps staring at the cage, her grubby face a muddle of fright and teeth-bared anticipation.

Weird. All I can see is a heap of rags and bones.

Until the rags and bones move.

The rags *are* rags, but those bones still have skin on them. As my eyes adjust, I see a mottled hand clutching the rags around a filthy wasted body.

A skull-like head slowly lifts to regard us.

'Oh – my – Saviour!' I make the Sign of One again.

I've never seen a real-live twist before and my guts tie themselves into cold knots. Idents I expected to see, wanted to see. But this monster with twisted blood – this I'm not ready for. I take several steps back despite myself.

Cassie pulls free, turns and runs. Don't blame her.

Nash sneers, but I'm not fooled. He can act tough, but he's eyeing those bars same as me, gauging their strength. He's scared too. Who wouldn't be?

The bane of Wrath, a devil in human form.

Those iron bars are the only reason we still have throats.

I force myself forward. A breeze shifts the awning and shadows scatter. I see the mad hatred in the creature's bloodshot eyes as it watches me. I'm so close now its stink shoves up my nose. The twist's skin is covered in muck and a rash of angry red scars, its waist-length hair filthy and matted. I thought *I* was a bit skinny, but this thing's nothing but skin and bone. Male or female? Impossible to say. It hisses at me like a rock viper and shows me its teeth, all filed to sharp points.

Nash elbows me, scaring the crap out of me. 'They always have one here.'

I nod, not trusting myself to speak.

Behave — or the twist will come in the night and get you!

It's what grumpy old folk like to growl at naughty little children to scare them. Seeing this disgusting monster is like having my worst nightmares made flesh. It's horrible to think one of those redhead ident girls will end up like this.

But that's why we have the Cutting and Unwrapping.

'You scared, boy?' asks the twist's keeper, the old bloke.

'Not me,' I say, grimacing.

'Y'ought to be.' He cackles, pulls a leather cosh from his belt and rasps it along the cage.

The twist lets out this blood-curdling scream, bounds to its feet and hurls itself at him. Its skeletal arm shoots out between the bars, bony fingers clawing for the man's throat. Only just in time, he steps back out of range.

It happens so fast — inhumanly fast.

Behind me, I hear children's delighted shrieks.

'See what I mean?' says the man. He spits into the dust at my feet, then looks at me, unblinking and seemingly uncaring, as the twist thrashes to reach him. 'Some folks, they don't believe in evil; they gotta see for themselves.'

Mary tugs my sleeve. 'You got a credit?'

The man elbows her out of the way. His breath stinks as bad as the twist. 'A credit and you can make it dance.'

'Do what?' I say.

'Just pay the man,' says Nash, shoving me.

They're all sneering at me now, so I toss the man a credit.

He makes a big show of biting the coin, then fetches this long pole with an insulated grip at one end. A thick cable snakes away from it through the dirt, towards an ancient power pack. On the grip is a crude trigger.

'Done this before?'

I've no idea what he's on about and shake my head.

The twist sees the pole; it howls and flings itself to the back of the alcove. The man presses the trigger and I hear an electric whine. Casually, he touches the pole's tip against one of the bars. *BANG!* There's a blinding flash. Showers of yellow sparks make us all duck and I smell the familiar hot stench of arc welding.

The iron bar glows red where the tip touched it.

Oh my Saviour. The twist's skin, all those wounds. I know why now.

'Have fun,' says the man, handing me the pole. 'You got one minute. And don't get too close. If the twist tags you, that's *your* problem not mine.'

I think I'm going to puke, but Nash's face is a mask, stretched taut with anticipation. He licks his lips and pushes me forward.

'You heard him – make it dance.'

'I don't want to,' I moan. 'Somebody else do it.'

This is sick. In my head I see Rona's *I told you so* face.

'You big, soft gom,' growls Nash. 'The thing's not human. Doesn't matter how bad you burn it, it'll be okay tomorrow. These monsters heal so fast.'

Not human. But it was once, wasn't it?

I stare in horror at the twist as it grovels and whimpers at the back of its cage. Okay, so maybe it *is* a monster now, like they keep telling us. What do I know? I'm a nobody from the arse end of the Barrens. But it sounds human.

'Come on,' says Vijay. 'Don't be a wimp.'

I look at Mary, but her lip curls.

'Stop wetting yourself. Get stuck in!' shouts Nash.

The old man wants the business too. He thrusts his face real close.

'Y'ain't no stinking twist-lover, are ya?'

Faces in the crowd are staring now. My skin crawls, but what can I do? Nothing. I know – we all know – what happens to twist-lovers, those fools who preach the heresy that twists aren't evil, just another human species. They end up hanging from trees, their eyes pecked out. I grit my teeth, step up to the bars.

Only for my legs to be kicked out from under me.

The ground leaps up and smashes into my back. For several seconds all I can do is lie there groaning, struggling to catch my breath. Too late I remember the pole I'm holding is a weapon, before a booted foot grinds that hand into the soil. I look up to see my attacker standing over me – a little guy with white dreads, shabby leather overalls, eyes hidden by mirrored sunglasses. In each lens, I see my shocked face, gob open, gasping for air. Two me's, like I'm an ident too.

He pushes the shades up into his dreads and he . . . is a girl.

A girl with death in her dark green eyes.

'So you like torturing twists, do you?' she hisses.

'Drop dead,' I say, wheezing.

Big mistake. I see now what she's pointing at me – a snub-nosed flamer, a weapon so lethal it's banned even on dump worlds.

She leans down and presses the flamer's barrel into my forehead.

'Wrong answer.'

The gun's a blur, so I focus on the girl's face. Pale, tough-looking, about my age. Black thumb-thick bars painted across her cheekbones. Teardrop tattoo dripping from her left eye. Those long, greasy dreads, bleached white.

And she looks mad as hell.

'No, wait!' I say. 'I –'

A bald guy in matching leathers and face paint hauls the girl off me. He's massive, double ugly and looks even meaner than she is. I like him already.

'What the hell are you doing, Sky?'

He wrenches the flamer from the girl's hand and shoves her away. She glares at him like she'll argue, but settles for making a gun shape with her hand and pretend-shooting me.

She stalks off then, limping badly.

Baldy waves her flamer at us. 'Anybody see what happened?'

Nobody wants to die so nobody answers.

The man grunts with obvious satisfaction. 'Good. You keep it that way.'

He pockets the gun and follows the girl towards the exit. Our stunned silence is broken by a slow, leathery slapping sound. The twist is sitting up at the back of its cage now and it's clapping.

Slowly, miserably, I pick myself up.

'Wow, Kyle,' says Nash, poking me with his finger. 'You just got your head kicked in by some gimp windjammer girl.'

'That right?' I say.

He opens his mouth to make another smart-arse comment.

I don't give him the chance.

All my life I've been scared of thugs like Nash, but it's like I'm suddenly possessed by rage. Or maybe it's shame. I snap his head back with a punch. He staggers and goes down. When he gets back up, he's clutching his mouth and cursing me, blood dribbling thick and red between his fingers.

'You so had that coming, Nash,' I say.

2
HIGH SLAYER

It's not like I want to go, after everything that happened. I volunteer to look after our campsite. But Clayton, who's as close to a leader as we've got, and no fool, says I go to the Unwrapping and Nash stays as punishment for fighting. So here I am the next day, wedged inside the arena again, ten rows or so back from the stage. We've been here for hours already. Today's another hot one, and I see storm clouds gathering out west on the horizon. The mood is serious now. Apart from a few stalls selling spiced meat snacks, the merchants are gone. The bars are all closed too.

Clayton says we're here to witness, not be entertained. He's warned us to be on our best behaviour.

I'm standing with the Reeve family, including a squirming Cassie. Since I took the girl's hand yesterday, she's attached herself to me like one of those nasty little suckerfish you get in our lakes. On the stage, men are covering an altar with crimson cloth. Suspended over the cages at the back, a massive vid-screen made from loads of little screens shows our glorious leader, the Saviour himself.

He stares down at us, magnified a thousand times.

Me, I've only seen him on faded posters before, where he looks old and severe. Here on the screen though I see he's still barrel-chested, strong and vigorous for a man his age. A mane of thick grey hair falls over his broad shoulders and he's got a mouthful of the whitest teeth I've ever seen. We get to see a lot of them too, with him smiling as he does his famous 'reaching out to the people' pose that Rona hates so much. Like he's a father figure, not the dictator she's always saying he is.

It'd be confusing if I could be bothered thinking about it.

I stop watching him and look out instead for that scowling girl with the white dreads and the flamer. In this crowd it'd be easy for her to sneak up behind me and slide a knife between my ribs without anyone seeing.

Turns out Nash was right. The leathers and those marks on the girl's face means she's windjammer crew. Me, I've never seen a windjammer, but like all kids, I know about these ridge-running glider transports. Cobbled together from the scrapped orbit-to-surface dropships that dumped us here back in the day, they're crude enough flying machines, but as hi-tech as it gets here. Worlds like Wrath are where whoever runs the galaxy disposes of criminals, and that's a locked-down, marooned and forgotten kind of deal. We're left to fend for ourselves.

So folk say anyway, but what do I know?

I've wanted to be a windjammer pilot since forever.

Down on sleep after a bad night, I yawn. Whenever I closed my eyes, I kept seeing that flamer. But that wasn't the worst thing – I wish I'd had the guts to tell Nash and that old man to drop dead. I should never have picked up that pole thing. Okay, so the twist looked nasty, but – *and I know this is heresy* – wouldn't being tortured and tormented, day in, day out, turn anyone into a monster?

A trumpet sounds. At least, I think it's a trumpet. We don't go in much for music in the Barrenlands – it's nice, but you can't eat it.

'What's happenin'?' squeals Cassie.

People file on to the stage. I can tell straight off they're important because they're sleek and fat and wear rich-looking clothes. You have to be a big deal on Wrath to be fat. One by one they waddle along and crush their seats.

'They look down, we look up,' somebody hisses.

The crowd starts muttering now.

I'm twisted round, trying to hear what's being said, when I hear gasps. I look back and have a gasp sucked out of me too. A raven-haired young woman stalks across the stage, swaying her hips, a long brown cloak draped over her shoulders. Under this she wears a fancy black-leather uniform, trimmed with shimmering nightrunner fur, cut tight and clinging to show off her figure. She stops at the altar, turns and faces us. Even from here I see her fingers clenching and unclenching. She reminds me of a spider – all long, spindly arms and legs, waiting to pounce. Trumpets blast, then fade away. Cassie kicks me in the shin.

'All right!' I hoist her on to my shoulders.

The people behind us moan, but I ignore them. Cassie's thrilled. I'm not – she stinks. She also thinks it's okay to hold on to my ears.

'Who's the tall skinny woman?'

'A High Slayer.'

I'm pretty sure, seeing how much gilt she's got on her uniform.

The only Slayers I've seen before are those who come for our idents, when it's time to cart them off to the camps. Everybody always turns out to watch because, let's face it, nothing else happens in Freshwater. Rona says they're stone-cold killers, the Saviour's special forces from the war. They've got some other fancy names too, like Preservers of Human Purity, but I like Slayer better.

'What's her name?' Cassie asks me.

'How should I know?'

'Commandant Morana,' whispers Mary, Cassie's sister. 'High Slayer for the Barrenlands.'

'Nasty piece of work,' adds Mary's mother, quiet-like, out of the side of her mouth. 'Eats babies for breakfast.'

I shudder, and try to imagine what babies might taste like. Disgusting, if Cassie is anything to go by.

The Saviour fades away and the big screen zooms in on the woman's face. She *is* beautiful, but there's a harshness stamped into her features no creams or powders can hide. Her eyes stare back at us, so cold and bleak I shiver, even though I'm hot. And when she starts talking, her voice is impossibly loud. Her words crash around the arena, like thunder echoes around our hills. I'm gobsmacked, until I see the microphone clipped to her collar and the speakers up on poles.

'Good afternoon, citizens of the Barrenlands,' she booms. 'Welcome to Deep Six on this, the last day of this year's Peace Fair. It is . . . gratifying to see how many of you have chosen to make the difficult journey here.'

I can't help sniffing. Chosen? Okay, so *I* chose, but it's the law.

'I would like to begin,' she continues, 'by asking you all to show your appreciation for our hosts, the loyal and industrious mining community of Deep Six, who once again have made this year's Fair such a success.'

The bigdeals haul themselves up from their chairs and the crowd starts clapping. Hardly deafening though – nobody will be going home with blisters on their hands. And this lack of enthusiasm isn't lost on Morana. Magnified on the screen above her, she stiffens and her scowling face lifts to look behind us. *Uh-oh.* Turns out that she isn't the only Slayer in Deep Six today. When I look, I see loads more have spread out behind us around the rear wall of the arena. Some are only carrying non-lethal shockers, but most are armed with pulse rifles.

The clapping gets louder – some creeps even cheer.

Deep Six's Elder, a red-faced woman with a whiny voice, makes a speech. She thanks the High Slayer, then bangs on for boring ages about new productivity records for the iron-ore mines. It's worse than studying maths, so I'm glad when she eventually sits down and Morana returns to the centre of the stage.

The crowd, which had started muttering again, quiets.

'We are gathered here today,' Morana announces, 'to celebrate thirty years of the Saviour's peace. A peace which has allowed us to rebuild our shattered world and raise new generations of pureblood singleton children. A peace which sees us looking forward from our dark past towards an ever brighter future.'

She pauses. The speakers blast out the first verse of 'All Hail the Saviour'.

We chant it back, like good little citizens.

What follows is a history lesson from her that makes me sigh. I mean, as if I haven't had this drummed into my head a thousand times already by our preacher, Fod, back in Freshwater. Anyway, Morana reminds us how the outbreak of ident births was first considered a blessing as we struggled to survive in those early days after being dumped here and needed all the strong hands we could get, to clear the fields and labour in them. Then the realisation that only one twin was pureblood human, the other a less-than-human twist. And yet still we tolerated them. Only for our generosity to be rewarded by the Twist War, when the twists showed their true monster faces by rising up against us purebloods and almost wiping us out, being faster and stronger and entirely without pity. How we purebloods survived only because one man among us would not be beaten: the glorious leader we are now pleased to call our Saviour, who saved us from our doom.

Yeah, yeah. I've heard it *all* before.

The whole time she's talking, the screen shows grainy footage from the war. Seen that before too. Women and children torn limb from limb by half-naked soldiers, who look human, but aren't. Slayers leading regular troops in devastating counter-attacks. It looks staged to me. Why was somebody filming it instead of blasting away with a pulse rifle? But like I said before, what do I know?

Cassie buries her face in my hair. 'It's horrible.'

The crowd starts getting twitchy and excited now. Most people will have been to Fairs before. They will know what's coming after the speeches.

'Yet today is not only a celebration,' Morana says, at last. 'Today serves another, far more important purpose. We are gathered here . . . for the Unwrapping.'

'*Un-wrapping!*' roars the crowd.

The screen cuts to Morana's half-smile, half-sneer.

'For we must never relax our guard against the bane of Wrath.'

'*The bane of Wrath!*'

She glares at us and I, like everyone else, stick my believer face on.

'There are some who claim not to believe in the curse.' Her voice becomes menacing now, a stern mother explaining something for the very last time to a witless child. 'To those doubters I say – BEHOLD THE BANE OF WRATH!'

There's a disturbance at the rear of the stage, where a gap in the stacked cages forms a tunnel. Using long chains attached to a collar around its neck, four muscular guards drag out the twist we saw yesterday. They fasten the chains to anchors in the stage floor then step back, panting and sweating.

And the crowd goes mental.

'*The bane of Wrath! The bane of Wrath!*'

The stark-naked twist raves and claws at its collar. It *is* a monster, I do see that now. Even so, I can hardly watch – it's too cruel. But the effect it has on the crowd is as shocking. It's like I blink and suddenly I'm drowning in a sea of contorted red faces, eyes bulging, mouths gaping as they bay for the twist's blood.

Even Mary, always so precious, screams her head off.

'What's wrong with it?' asks Cassie.

'It's possessed,' I explain, wincing. 'Taken over by demons.'

Morana strolls towards it. The creature screams and hurls itself to meet her, skeletal arms outstretched, fingers like talons – only for the chains to snap taut, jerking its head back. The High Slayer doesn't flinch, but stands just out of reach at a red line painted on the floor. She shakes her head as if disgusted and holds up one black-gloved hand. A guard steps forward with a disruptor tube. There's a blue-white flash and the twist freezes, mid-snarl. On the screen I see it's still twitching, its mad eyes full of hate, but that's all it can do now.

'Hard to believe,' booms Morana, 'that this evil, this monster, could once have passed for human. Yet I assure you it did. This is why these foul caricatures of humanity are such an insidious enemy. Why we must always remain vigilant and work so tirelessly to preserve the blessed purity of our human bloodline.'

'*Un-wrapp-ing!*' howls the crowd, growing impatient.

'What's *insidyus* mean?' asks Cassie.

'Dunno,' I say. 'Something bad. Shut up, will you?'

Morana raises her voice, so loud it hurts. 'Let the Unwrapping begin!'

3
UNWRAPPING

More blaring trumpets. Morana takes her place on a seat behind the altar. A tall man in a cloak, nose and mouth hidden by a black mask, emerges from the cage-tunnel and stalks centre stage, his boots thumping the wood. I overhear someone behind me telling a buddy that this guy does the Unwrapping. The masked man fumbles under his cloak and a screech of feedback almost takes our heads off.

One fool laughs out loud – he must be drunk.

'Bring forth the first subjects!'

Subjects. I wondered what he'd call them. We try not to say words like 'double', or 'couple', or 'two' here on Wrath. It's bad luck. There's a rhyme we're taught as kids: *One, three or four, that's the score.* More than four is greedy.

Now some more guards emerge from the tunnel.

Held between them, ankles shackled so they can only hobble, are the first idents to be unwrapped. Skinny brothers, stiff with fright, both wearing a sort of sleeveless white smock, which covers them down to their knees. Thick leather belts go round their waists. If they're any older than ten, I'd be amazed.

Scared little boys, who happen to be spitting images.

'The family Anderson,' declares the man in the mask, and now he turns towards the steps at the front of the stage, as if he's expecting something.

'What's he waiting for?' I ask Mary.

'The parents.'

Oh yeah. I see a man and a woman climbing the steps now, grubbers like us, from their round shoulders and farm clothes. They bow stiffly, before shuffling to the side of the stage, away from the still-frozen twist. A murmur spreads through the crowd, which sounds like sympathy. On the screen, the mother sobs. And I see now what the belts are for – each boy has his right arm, the unbandaged arm, bound behind his back to a loop in the leather. Nobody's taking any chances.

One of these idents may be a lot stronger than he looks.

A man with a camera scurries forward to get close to the action as the guards force the boys to kneel facing each other, either side of the altar. The boys hold their bandaged arms out, palm down on the cloth. The big screen switches to a view looking down from above. It zooms in nice and tight so we can see the bloodstained dressings on their puny, hairless forearms, then tracks along to show us their hands.

Only four fingers, of course. Little finger gone.

Bile fills my mouth. Guess I see now why they use a red altar cloth.

'My money's on leftie,' whispers Mary.

'You what?'

Stunned, I hear whispered wagers and watch as credits change hands around me.

'Five says it's the left one. He looks meaner.'

'I'll take that. Check out the eyes of the one on the right.'

On the stage, the masked man steps up to the altar. He pulls a curved knife from his robes and brandishes it for our inspection. Steel glints in the bright dayshine. And the crowd roars, nearly deafening me. '*Un-wrapp-ing!*'

The man turns, his cloak swirling, and bends over the altar. His back is to us, but the screen shows us what he's doing. I watch, cringing, as he slips the blade under each boy's bandage and slashes it loose. With a practised flourish, he rips both bandages off at the same time, then leans in and inspects. After he steps aside, the camera lingers, teasing, then zooms in. Both boys have a single bloody slit across their forearm. An ugly, still-open wound. No signs of any healing.

The crowd sighs with obvious disappointment.

Thank the Saviour, I think, biting my lip.

'First-timers,' says Mary. 'They hardly ever manifest that young.'

'What's that mean?' a voice says in my ear.

I'd almost forgotten Cassie who's still on my shoulders; she's been so quiet. 'It means we can't tell which one is evil yet.'

'Why can't we?'

Quick as I can, I tell her how twists are sneaky – exactly the same as us purebloods when they're little, so impossible to tell apart, but how when they're older they start to show signs of the monsters they will one day turn into.

'Like being faster and stronger than us?' says Cassie.

'Yup. And they heal quicker too. Impossibly fast. That's how we tell.'

She shuts up at last, seemingly satisfied.

I catch myself rubbing my forearm as the parents are led away, both sobbing. They aren't allowed to visit their children in the camps, so this is the one time they get to see them every year. How must this feel? Relief that both their children are spared for another year, or regret they don't get one son back today? Or just despair at the whole proceedings? Despair – it's got to be.

'Bo-ring!' sings Cassie.

That does it – heartless little maggot. I yank her off my shoulders.

She complains loudly, like I care. I fend her off as she tries to clamber back up again. In the relative hush, this makes quite a commotion. When I look up, my heart pounds. I hold my breath and freeze. Morana is looking towards our section of the crowd. I can't be sure, but it seems like she's staring straight at me.

Cassie kicks me again, but I hardly notice.

The High Slayer looks away and I breathe again.

The guards drag both boys to the front of the stage. They parade them around together now, holding their arms up to the crowd, making sure we all get a solid look at their unhealed wounds before they pull them offstage, back through the tunnel, back to their cage and another year in the ident camps.

Next up, two much older boys are hauled out for their unwrapping.

'The family Bachmann.'

I crane over the heads of the people in front of me, but this time there's nothing to see. No slope-shouldered, sad-eyed parents haul themselves on to the stage. Which makes me wonder – do these idents have no parents, or have their parents chosen to stay away? I'll never know. But, for some reason, it matters.

Me, I'd have thought it impossible to look defiant in leg irons, dragged along by four brute men to be tested for evil. I'm scared half to death just watching them, safe out here in the crowd. But these lads manage it. Where the Andersons were white-faced and petrified, these idents hold their heads high and meet the curious gaze of the crowd. I stare up at the expressions on their identical faces, magnified massively on the big screen. I shouldn't be impressed, but I can't help it. I see scorn and contempt, but not a flicker of fear.

'*One good, two e-vil, one good, two e-vil,*' chants the crowd.

The ident on the left, just before he's forced on to his knees before the altar, pulls away from his guard and sends a big gob of spit into the front row of the crowd. The people there don't appreciate it. They howl and throw stuff at him.

The guards drag him back to the altar.

Mary's dad grins at me. 'A credit says it's the spitter.'

'You're on,' I say. What else can I do? I can't look like I feel sorry for twists.

The masked man wields his knife again. When he steps back, we have a winner. Or a loser, I should say. And I'm shiny, up a credit. The kid who spat has five scars and one open wound. His brother – or the twist pretending to be – only has five scars. A big yellow crust comes away, stuck to the bandage. Where the cut would have been is smooth, pink skin. A deep cut healed overnight.

Don't need to be a healer's son to know that's unnatural.

The arena erupts. A thousand little fingers slash the air with the Sign of One. All around me, people jump up and down, emptying their lungs in an orgy of hysterical shouting and screaming. I scream too. I yell nonsense until my throat is raw from yelling. It's impossible not to – fear needs a way out.

Suddenly, the crowd starts chanting something new.

'*Pu-ri-fy! Pu-ri-fy!*'

Now what? This time, only the twist is paraded. On the screen, I see his brother watching, mouth turned down, as a guard removes his leg irons. They push him towards a fire basket, but he struggles so they have to force him.

'If I was *him*,' I say, 'I'd be jumping for joy that my blood isn't twisted.'

'You don't have a brother, do you?' says Mary's mother.

'He's not a *real* brother,' says Mary.

Her father scowls and hands over my credit. Mary winks at me, obviously delighted, maybe hoping I'll spend it on something for her later. She'll be lucky. Up on the stage, one guard holds the innocent youth. Another, leather gloved and aproned, pulls an iron rod from the hot coals. Without any hesitation, he plants the glowing tip on to the boy's left bicep. I wince, seeing smoke curl and hearing the amplified hiss. The boy staggers, but doesn't cry out.

'*Scabb-er!*' chants the crowd now.

Scab. That's what we call the pureblood ident. The lucky one.

'Why'd they burn him?' asks Cassie, as guards haul the boy off the stage.

I let go a breath I hadn't known I was holding. 'Now they're sure he's pureblood, they brand him with a big P. Like your dad brands fourhorns.'

'So they can tell who owns him?'

'Nobody owns him.' I sigh. 'It's so he can prove he's pureblood.

He gets his life back today, but if we didn't mark him people would see his missing little finger and think maybe he's an ident on the run. This way, he can just roll his sleeve up, show his brand and you know he's all right. Now do you get it?'

'But won't the mark heal and go away?'

I scowl down at her. 'It won't, mud for brains. You saw him unwrapped. Only twists can heal a scar away. That mark'll be on him till the day he dies.'

Cassie sucks her thumb doubtfully.

'What will he do with no family to go to?' I ask Mary.

'Who cares?' She laughs. 'It's what happens now that makes it worth dragging ourselves all this way. You get to see what the Peace Fair is all about!'

Even as she says this, a tall frame hisses up from the floor of the stage. I stop wondering when I see the noose hanging down from the cross member. It's a gallows. The guards drag twist-boy over, both his hands bound behind his back now. He struggles, his bare feet hammering the stage, but they stand him up, slip the rope round his neck and give it a vicious tug to tighten it.

No way – I'm going to witness an execution.

'*Pu-ri-fy! Pu-ri-fy! Pu-ri-fy!*'

Desperate to see, Cassie starts climbing up me, but I push her away.

Commandant Morana stands. She holds her fist out, palm down. The crowd shuts up in a heartbeat. After the uproar, the silence is so empty, I feel like I'm teetering on the edge of a cliff. A lammerjay caws high overhead.

She opens her hand.

Thunnkkk! A trapdoor opens in the stage.

The boy drops like a stone into the dark hole and out of sight. The rope jerks iron-bar taut, then twitches and swings as he kicks his life away. I want to look away, but I can't. The crowd around me hoots and applauds.

Twists are fighters, I'll say that. It's a minute before the rope goes still.

In the Barrenlands nobody dies from old age, so I've seen plenty of death. Like that old guy gored by a bull blackbuck, who died screaming, still trying to shove his guts back in. Or my mate Keane, after they pulled his fish-gobbled body out of the lake. I thought I was used to death, but this is just so . . . cold-blooded. Sweat stings my eyes. I can't stop my legs shaking.

This I did *not* see coming.

Maybe I should've done. Twists are the bane of Wrath. If we take our foot off their necks, they'll gang up again to slaughter us. I do get that. That's why the Saviour's law demands we mark idents and cage them and test them when they're old enough. All this, when the simplest thing would be to kill both. Proof of the Saviour's infinite benevolence, Fod likes to preach. A system put in place to protect us, while sparing the innocent. Harsh and cruel perhaps, but merciful.

I knew all this before I handed over my credits.

But knowing is one thing; seeing the grim limits of the Saviour's mercy another. I swallow hard, grateful at least for not having to watch the twist thrashing at the rope end. Why the hell hadn't Rona told me about this Purification?

'What's with you?' says Mary, eyeing me. 'The thing was evil.'

'Yeah, I know,' I say. 'Sure.'

My eyes stray to the back of the stage. The idents are making some kind of fingers-crossed salute to the dead kid through the bars of their cages. Slayer guards are rushing up and down, clubbing at them with their rifles to stop them.

The crowd sees and jeers even louder. All part of the fun.

But the screen shows none of this. It sticks with the bigdeals on stage clapping their delicate hands, then pans to Morana, hiding a yawn with her gloved hand. Over the next hour, twenty more pairs of idents are unwrapped. Seven more twists test positive and make the drop into the trapdoor, three of them girls. The youngest, a girl with a face full of freckles, looks about eleven. Even she gets a cheer from the crowd when she drops. The scabs are branded, but only four are claimed by their families. Mary, enjoying herself hugely, pulls my leg about my long face. Cassie stuffs her face with sweets and pesters me to try one as Maskman summons the Lynch family. The crowd has a big laugh at the unfortunate surname, but I can't join in. The Lynches are those redhead ident girls I saw yesterday. A woman, an older image of the girls, hauls herself on to the stage, but collapses. Last time I saw these girls they were petrified, but now they look calm and resigned. It's the loving look they give each other as they're forced to kneel at the altar that undoes me. I can't watch any more – just can't. I've had it with the Unwrapping.

I peer round at the Slayers, wondering if they'll blast me if I make a run for it back to camp. I don't care what people think. I have to get out of here, away from this madness. And that's when Cassie's greed does me a favour.

She pukes her guts up, all down her front.

'Oh, Cassie, no!' says her mother.

'No bother,' I say, hastily. 'I'll take her back and clean her up.'

4
THE ROAD BACK

Such a nice young man. That's what Cassie's mother is telling everyone, ever since I hauled her puking daughter out of the arena for her. I reckon she's got her eye on me as a match for her Mary. Well, one person who disagrees is Nash.

Surprise, surprise – he isn't taking his split lip well.

It's three days after the Peace Fair and we're almost back to Freshwater. Five klicks back, we crested the pass through the foothills. Nash is still picking on me every chance he gets, which is loads. Thing is, the few men with enough spine to tell him to leave me be are out on the trail, scouting ahead for trouble.

I'm looking forward to seeing my girl Jude. Okay, she might not be quite so pretty as Mary, but she likes a good time and I can talk to her about anything. She'll kill herself laughing when I tell her about the windjammer girl.

I wonder, does she miss me like I miss her?

The trail drops down, following the bank of a tumbling peaty river through forests of hash-willow. By midday, we're less than ten klicks out. Even the fourhorns hauling our wagons – the dumbest animals on Wrath – sense this and pick their pace up without me prodding. Best of all, the sun comes out at last. These past days we've been battered by storms; now we can put our rain gear away.

I sniff the air. 'Do you smell that?' I ask the Zielinski woman. She says she doesn't.

A musky stink, but it's gone now. Animal maybe?

Apart from this, the forest smells fresh after its scrubbing by hail and rain. There's plenty of shade here too, so we don't go from cold to boiling hot. The hash-willow leaves look incredibly yellow. Wildflowers sway in the ever-present breeze. Reds and pinks and whites and blues. I even recognise some of them too, the ones Rona grinds into her healing pastes. I don't know their names, but they look so bright and cheerful you'd swear some kid's been at them with a brush.

I'm not going to sing or anything, but I'm cheering up.

And I need to. I picture our isolated little shack, tucked away under the trees, and me walking through the door with a long face on. Soon as she sees this, Rona will launch straight into one of her *I told you so* routines. *You won't listen to me, what do you expect?* On and on. I mean, as mothers go, Rona and I get along pretty well, way better than most, but still. I'll never hear the bogging end of it.

That's not what's been dragging me down though.

I've always been a bit of a loner – I guess because of all that moving about we did when I was younger – but now I feel even more left out and alone than usual. It's like I don't know these guys any more, even the ones I'd almost call friends. I watch them as they walk or ride the trail, happy and laughing, teeth flashing as they chat away. Okay, so everyone's keeping a wary eye out too, but it's been like this ever since we left Deep Six. Even when the hail was rattling down, everyone was banging on about the Fair and how good this or that was. Hey, look, see what I bought? The food was crappy this year, wasn't it?

Blah, blah, blah. And – I – just – don't – get – it.

See, I couldn't give a toss what the fishcakes were like, or what such-and-such might make from that reel of synth-cotton she bought. How can they laugh and joke so soon after seeing such horrors? Am I the only one here who wants to talk about what *really* happened? Am I the only one still feeling sick to my stomach?

I was freaked out by what I saw at the Fair, but they loved it.

Maybe Nash is right – maybe I'm the weirdo.

I know what he'd say. We live on a dump world. Life is hard, get over it.

And speak of the devil . . .

'What's the matter, Kyle?' says Nash, sidling up to me where I'm leading the fourhorns hauling one of our wagons. 'Missing your girlfriend?'

I ignore him. Best way with bullies, Rona says.

Tell the truth, I'm not so scared of Nash and his thug mates now, after the Fair. I know they'll give me a kicking and I know it'll hurt. But here's the thing, I feel kind of numb about it. What's a few bruises compared to a hanging?

'Took you apart, didn't she?' he says.

Oh right – he means that psycho windjammer girl with the dreads. I taste bile again, remembering being sure I was going to die. I'll be glad if I never see *her* again.

And there it is again on the breeze, that weird musky smell.

'You wait,' says Nash. 'We're going to give you such a beating. You'll still be sucking your food through a straw when the snows come.'

I stare at the hash-willows by the trail. Did something move there?

'You hear me?' he says.

'No,' I say, distracted. 'Something's not right.'

That's when I hear Clayton shout, his voice high and scared. *'Rea-pers!'*

Next thing, I hear the *thump, thump, thump* of our scouts' pulse rifles rapid-firing in the woods high to our left, and glimpse several bright acid-green flashes through the trees. A woman screams from somewhere up front.

Nash clutches my arm. Not such a tough guy now.

The Reapers leap up from hiding places in bushes and drop down from branches overhanging the trail. Everywhere I look I see more, loping towards us like human wolves, howling and shaking their spears and long knives. I'm rooted to the spot by the sight of their half-naked bodies, plastered in filth and twigs and swirling blue tattoos, their savage Reaper faces all twisted with bloodlust.

Too many – I see that straight away. We're screwed.

'Don't run. Fight!' roars Clayton.

I can't do either. I can't even breathe. It's like I've been zapped by that Slayer muscle-lock. All I can do is stand here, gawping like a fool as Clayton leaps down from his wagon. He drops to one knee, aims his pulse rifle and snaps three thumping shots off before an arrow gets him in the throat, toppling him sideways into the mud. With a curse, Nash knocks me aside and sprints forward along the trail. He snatches up Clayton's pulse rifle, throws himself down behind our leader's crumpled body and starts shooting. *Thump! Thump!* One Reaper, almost on him, flies backwards, a huge hole in his chest.

'Ammo!' screams Nash.

He fires again and again into the charging Reapers. One goes down. Another spins round and screams, half his arm gone. Other men are firing now, but the Reapers are on top of us. My muscles unknot themselves. I gulp a huge, sobbing lungful of air. Every nerve in my body screams at me to run, but I swear and dash back to the wagon. If a gommer like Nash can fight, I have to help him. Spare pulse-rifle magazines should be in a box by the bench seat. I clamber up, straight-arming the panicking Zielinski woman out of my way. But I can't open the box. Some idiot has padlocked it. I plant my feet and howl curses and pull like crazy, ignoring the pain in my fingers. The hasp gives way in a shower of splinters.

No mags in the box, only dirty grey bugwebs.

I look up, just in time, as a Reaper spear flashes towards me. How I twist myself out of the way I'll never know, but it hisses past. I throw myself across the seat, drop down on the far side of the wagon and pull my hunting knife out. It looks so small in my hand – a child's toy compared to that Reaper spear.

Sweat pours down my face and screws with my seeing.

The shouts and screams suddenly get louder. I can hear the desperate grunts and scuffles of hand-to-hand fighting now. Something else too, which makes me pant with disbelief – the bang and crackle of a blaster. I grovel in the dirt for a look under the wagon. Through the wheel spokes, I see a man's boots staggering backwards, surrounded by bare Reaper feet. The boots lift and hang quivering in mid-air. I hear his death shriek, then his body falls to the ground.

It's Nash I think — or what's left of him.

The wagon bounces on its springs as something lands on it. A shadow flickers over me and I hear a splash as feet land in the mud behind. I whip round, wheezing with fear, and I'm face to face with a Reaper.

Once, I electrocuted myself. Got careless hooking up a live fuel cell. This feels like that as a jolt of pure terror rips through me. I stagger to my feet, meaning to run, only to find my legs are rubbery and useless.

'Stay away from me!' I shout.

This Reaper is short and scrawny, not much older than I am, although it's hard to tell, he's so plastered with mud and feathers. He comes at me, leading with his knife. I twist out of the way and he cuts my side, but not serious. I grab his wrist before he can have another go. We pant into each other and wrestle back and forth. He's way stronger than he looks, however, and fights dirty too. When we end up face to face, he rocks back and headbutts me. I stagger and drop my hands.

What saves me is that Reaper boy's a gloater.

He steps back, grinning from one filthy ear to the other. And I feel that terrible ferocity shudder through me again, same as when I punched Nash. When he struts back in to finish me, I'm not just ready — I'm looking forward to it.

If I die, then so does he!

I look into his bloodshot eyes and hurl myself at him.

Next thing I know, I'm shaking and down on my hands and

knees. Reaper boy is on his back in front of me, legs kicking as he tries to slide further away. The bloody hilt of my knife is sticking out of his chest. Not a killing wound, but he looks as shocked as I am. His knife is beside me. I grab it, the handle slick and warm, and scramble up. His face goes rigid – he must think I'm going to finish him.

I should . . . but I can't. It's just not in me.

On the far side of the wagon, the fighting sounds almost over. I gulp air and try to think what to do. Behind me is the fast-flowing brawl of the river. I don't swim too good, so that's no use. But I'm the fastest runner in the three valleys. If I can get past their spears, I reckon no half-starved Reaper will catch me. The forest is *their* world, so it's the trail or nothing.

But how to get past their spears?

I scramble to the front of the wagon. On the trail, I glimpse hell. Swarming Reapers. Bodies everywhere. A woman screams as she's dragged away by her hair into the trees. Behind me, Reaper boy starts yelling. I hold my breath and dodge between the rearing, plunging fourhorns. Somehow, their lashing hooves miss me as I reach up and slash their trace ropes. I hack at their flanks. The stink of blood and Reaper does the rest. The maddened fourhorns, free from their harness, red-eyed and frantic with terror, stampede. Reapers scatter. I see one tossed into the air, but daren't stop to watch. I slip along to the front of the leading wagon, pull my head down into my shoulders and take off running like I've never run before.

I make it past the spears, only to trip over a root.

Soon as I hit the ground, I know I'm hurt bad. I scramble up, but my ankle won't take my weight and I cry out as Reapers come running. I limp backwards and they follow me. They're in no great rush now, seeing I'm hurt.

It hits me then, like a knife in the guts.

I'm dead.

Something clobbers the back of my knees and sits me down hard. It's a shelf of rock above the river. I haul myself backwards up on to it, sobbing, staring in horror at the red smears my hands leave on the limestone. My blood, or Reaper blood, or fourhorn blood? Guess I'll never know.

I think about throwing myself into the water. But I can't.

'Not much meat on *this* one.'

I look into their hateful Reaper eyes. And I don't know what shocks me more – that Reapers can speak, same as you and me, or that this is the end. Reaper boy struggles up to join them, grinning, my hunting knife in his hand.

At least I left my mark on him. That's something.

I loved that knife. It's about the only thing Rona ever gave me, apart from that dose of swamp pox. Slowly, painfully, I haul myself to my feet.

The sky's so blue – not a cloud in it.

Biggest Reaper points a blaster at me and pulls the trigger.

5
AWAKENING

Agony. Raging and cruel, sinking its razor-sharp fangs into my jaw, neck and shoulder. Tormenting me. Dragging me down, deeper and deeper into the cold, wet darkness. Whispering *give up, Kyle, time to die* . . .

I scream and scream, but the pain shows no mercy.

A long darkness.

Maybe I come to. Or maybe I just open my eyes.

Either way, I'm staring at feet, sliding free of rushing green water. One booted, one naked, white and shrivelled. My boot. My foot. My legs attached. Dimly, in the small part of my mind that isn't roaring red with hurt, I realise I'm still alive and someone is hauling me backwards out of a river.

I squeeze my eyes shut again.

Put my hand to my jaw and feel bone, slick and wet.

Shouting. Lots of shouting. And someone calling out my name.

'Kyle! Can you hear me?'

I try to answer, but all that comes out is spit and groans. I'm cold – so cold.

All I want to do is sleep, but the shouters won't let me. They lay me on my back on to something hard. When they pick me up, the agony comes scuttling back. It leaps on to my chest, hot and heavy, much more alive than I am, crushing me so I can't breathe, tearing at my flesh again.

After that, I only remember bits and pieces.

The sky bouncing around.

Crying out as they drop me, seeing the old door that's my stretcher.

A crash as they kick a gate open.

Hard hands lifting me, putting me carefully down. Whispers and curses.

A man's voice, strained: 'Where the hell *is* she then?'

Somebody running out.

Rona rushing in and gasping as she sees it's me, dripping gore all over her clean kitchen table. Next thing I know, she's pushing a needle into my arm. A wonderful soothing warmth as whatever stuff she's pumped into me trickles its way through my veins. The room spinning round and round my head.

I sob with relief as the drugs chase the agony away.

'Am I going to die?' I ask her later. I don't sound like me. I don't even sound human. My voice is this weird, paper-thin rasp. It's only because Rona's leaning over me, cutting off the remains of my shirt, that she hears.

'Don't try to talk, Kyle,' she says. Her healer voice wobbles.

Someone lifts my head gently on to a pillow. The way I'm lying now, I can see how messed up I am. Blaster spatter has caught me high across my chest, collarbone and jaw. The skin is mostly burnt away, the flesh below red and white and ugly yellow, charred to hard black in a few places. There's a finger-wide crack where the swollen flesh has burst apart. Everything's wet and oozing stuff. All around the edges are these huge, angry red blisters and there's blood everywhere.

I groan. I knew I was hurt bad, but –

'I'm surprised he can talk at all,' a man says.

Rona steps aside. Vaguely, I watch the ceiling fan's blades swish round, until two blurry faces lean in and stare down at me. One is old Fod, Freshwater's preacher. His gaunt face looks more suspicious than sympathetic. The other face, wide-eyed and nervous, belongs to my girlfriend Jude.

I think it's Jude squeezing my hand.

'Does it hurt?' she asks. Then her hand flies to her mouth.

'What-do-*you*-think?' I manage.

Rona shoves her roughly out of the way. 'Apart from the blaster wounds, he's in shock, he's been stabbed, he's got some broken ribs and I'm worried his skull might be fractured. Of course it bloody well hurts, Jude.'

She slides another stinging needle into my arm.

Out of the corner of my eye, I think I see faces. It's torture, but I roll my head to look. Some must be the men who carried me here. The rest are our neighbours – the Clancys, the whole Ferguson brood, some of the Smiths. The men stand there, shuffling their feet and scrunching their hats, as if they're in chapel. The women wince, look mournful and swap whispered remarks. The children fidget, nudge each other and gaze at me curiously, their eyes like saucers.

Even though I'm struggling to keep my eyes open now, I get it. They're here to pay their last respects.

*

When I come to my senses again, Rona has kicked everybody out, except for Jude. It's dark outside, but I'm warm and dry and propped up in my bed. A tube snakes from the needle in my left arm to a bottle hanging on a hook. I can't see my wounds now – they're smothered in lime-green dressings, which stink of those powerful herbs Rona calls painsuckers. I've got to say, they're doing the job. The pain still gnaws at me, but I don't feel like screaming the whole time now. Rona is rooting through her battered old medchest. Jude sits cross-legged on the floor beside her, as if she's waiting to be handed stuff. She's chewing her fingernails.

Both are way too preoccupied to notice I'm awake.

'I'm so sick of searching for thirty-year-out-of-date miracles in here,' Rona says, sounding tired and cross. 'No antibiotics. No synth-skin. Nothing useful at all. It's like being back on Earth during the Dark Ages.'

Jude spits a nail. 'Can I help?'

Rona glares at her. 'Can you change the fact we're on a dump world?'

'Just asking.'

'Hey, what's going on?' I sound almost like me again.

Jude's freckled face lights up with pleasure and relief. She jumps up and hurries over. I flinch, half thinking she's going to give me an agonising squeeze, but she stops at the foot of the bed and hugs herself instead.

'Rona's been wagging her finger at me.'

'Um,' I say, not surprised. 'How long have I been out?'

'Best part of a day. Rona says the danger now is infection.

If I hug you or kiss you, I could kill you. Then she'll have to kill me too.'

'Sometimes you have to be cruel to be kind,' says Rona. She holds a packet of stuff up to the light and squints at the label on it, before cursing and slinging it back into the medchest. 'Are you feeling more comfortable now?'

I nod. Big mistake. Even with the soothing painsuckers and injections, the stab of agony in my neck leaves me gasping and wheezing. Through an eyeful of tears, I see Jude start chewing her fingernails again.

'It's only a scratch,' I tell her. 'Honest. I feel better already.'

Rona scowls, like I've said something stupid.

Jude tries to smile. 'Trust you to get shot in the gob.'

I try to return her smile, but only the left side of my face seems to work. 'Was that you holding my hand before?'

'No, it was Fod.'

She darts a glance at Rona, then comes closer and takes my hand. My eyes go blurry again – but not from hurting. I want to tell Jude how badly I've missed her, to thank her for being here and trying to cheer me up, but I can't, not with Rona around. Instead, I blurt out the question that's been tap-tap-tapping away at the back of my mind. 'How come I'm not dead?'

'You've the luck of the devil, that's how,' Rona says, with a frown. 'I don't know much about blasters, but either it misfired or was low on power. Probably old and half-broke, like everything else on this godforsaken planet. The cold river water probably helped too – with the burns, I mean.'

'Who found me?'

'Cal Ferguson. You were tangled up in a fallen tree, close to the bank. He fished you out. How you didn't drown or bash your brains out drifting down through the rapids, we'll never know. I didn't think you could swim.'

'I can't hardly.'

'You don't remember going into the water?'

'All I remember is the blaster.'

Rona takes her glasses off and rubs her eyes. In the dim light from the glowtubes, I see how tightly the wind-burnt skin on her face is stretched. Her eyes are dark pits from lack of sleep. She turns away to the sink and starts rinsing what look like soiled bandages. Jude hops up on to the bed beside me and plants a kiss on my forehead. Even this hurts, but I'm not complaining.

She reeks of soap and strong antiseptic.

'We were hanging about,' she says, 'twiddling our thumbs until you got back, when we heard the pulse rifles. Some men grabbed guns and rode out straight away. I wanted to go too, but they wouldn't have it. You should've heard me screaming and swearing – but I'm glad now. They say there was nothing anybody could do. By the time they got there, the Reapers were long gone, but it was an awful sight. Bodies everywhere, torn to pieces. Carts stripped clean. Cal was on his way back here to fetch help when he spotted you in the water.'

Reapers. The word makes me shiver, even though I'm safe now.

'Any others survive?'

'Uh huh. Four. Although young Meg Zielinski and Todd Patenaude are both hurt bad. Rona's doing what she can for them, but –'

She shuts up as I have a coughing fit. I feel like I'm suffocating again. Rona hurries over, shoos Jude off the bed and tries her best to soothe me. She manages to pour a mouthful of some sweet drink into me and that helps.

'I told you. You shouldn't talk,' she says.

'What about Clayton?' I croak. 'I saw him get an arrow in the throat.'

Rona shakes her head. 'They didn't find his body.'

We all know what that means – we've heard the stories. I shudder as I remember that dreadful hungry look I saw on the Reapers' faces.

'What did they look like?' Jude whispers later, behind Rona's back.

'The Reapers?'

She shivers. 'I've never seen one.'

'Be glad then.' In between coughs, I describe them to her.

'Human though, same as you and me?'

More carefully this time, I nod. 'Only more savage.'

I don't blame Jude for asking. I'd always wondered about Reapers too. Out here in the back of beyond, our handful of farmsteads scattered around the freshwater lake, a lot of what you hear is ignorance and superstition. That's what Rona says anyway. Like some folk swear Reapers are half-men, who've bred with Wrath animals. Others say they're mutants, turned weird and mad by radiation, whatever that is. Rona, always so sensible, says nobody on Wrath knows for sure what Reapers are, only that they're out there and fierce dangerous.

There's not many like me who've seen Reapers and lived.

Rona comes back and clicks her tongue. 'Look, don't just stand there moping, Judith. You're getting in my way and Kyle won't shut up while you're still here. He needs to rest.

You can visit him tomorrow, when he's feeling better.'

'See you later then,' says Jude. She squeezes my hand.

The door shuts behind her and I close my eyes. For a long while, all I hear are the small sounds of Rona faffing and the hiss and rattle of my breathing.

I clutch at what Rona told Jude. The danger now is infection. So does that mean I'm *not* going to die?

When I open my eyes, Rona is staring down at me. She has this weird look on her face – like she's looking at me, but seeing a ghost.

'What's the matter?' I say.

She starts. Gives her eyes a rub again, but says nothing.

Whatever Rona keeps pumping into me knocks me out all right, but fills my head with nightmares. I'd have thought they'd be about Reapers, but instead I'm back at the Peace Fair. Only now I'm looking *down* at the jostling crowd. I'm on the stage and I see the fear and hate in people's eyes as they stare up at me.

They hoot and jeer and make the Sign of One.

Suddenly, I'm on my knees, the altar digging into my chest. Vice-like fingers hold me down, crush the side of my face into the blood-red cloth. I see my bandaged arm, stretched out in front of me. It itches, itches like crazy.

Across the altar, another me stares back.

The same lopsided face. The same greasy brown hair flopping over his forehead and falling into his eyes, the same gap between his teeth.

His arm is stretched out and bandaged too.

'Who *are* you?' I ask him.

He smiles — a sneery smile — like he knows something I don't. They cut his bandage off and his wound is deep and gushing blood. He winks at me.

Strong hands pick me up, haul me towards the gallows.

'No!' I scream. 'You're making a mistake!'

The crowd goes crazy as the executioner drops the noose over my head. A hatch bangs open under my feet and I plunge into the darkness and —

And wake up, choking and clawing at my throat.

The glowtubes flick-flicker on. Rona comes running. She holds me down until I stop thrashing, then gathers me in her strong arms and rubs my back, like she used to when I was very little. She looks all crumpled and baggy-eyed.

'You're all right, Kyle. You had a bad dream, that's all.'

'I wish I'd never gone to that stupid Peace Fair,' I say, when I can talk.

'Well, I *did* tell you,' she sighs.

I pull away. 'Why didn't you tell me they killed them?'

'And if I *had* told you?'

I shift uneasily. 'Everybody else goes. I'm sick of being the odd one out.'

Rona smiles at me sadly. 'What's done is done, I suppose. But you could have been killed; it's a miracle you weren't.'

'That's hardly *my* fault.'

'No, of course it isn't,' she says slowly, 'but you've no idea what the consequences will be. How *impossible* this makes things.' She reaches over, checks my dressings are secure, touches my cheek.

'Impossible?' I say, not sure I heard right.

Rona gives herself a tired little shake and stands up. 'Look, it's the middle of the night and I'm bone-tired. We'll talk about this tomorrow.'

She goes and fetches me a glass filled with some cloudy-looking liquid.

'Drink this. It'll knock out a fourhorn.'

She makes sure I swallow it all, then goes back to bed.

But I don't go back to sleep. I'm too scared to. I toss and turn, staring up into the darkness, my wounds itching like crazy under their dressings.

Itching, just like my arm did in the dream . . .

6
NEVER SAY THAT WORD

The next day, I'm itching so bad, I nearly go out of my mind. Rona has to bind my hands to stop me tearing at my wounds. She tries all her ointments to soothe me, but nothing works. And she can't even knock me out – it's like my body goes all hyper and won't shut down. I howl like a baby, even in front of Jude, but Rona says that if she gives me anything stronger she's scared I won't wake up.

She reckons itching is good – a sign of healing.

But if so, why's she so cranky? She bites Jude's head off so many times that Jude storms off. She doesn't come back either. Anyway, the day after, I finally do get some sleep. When I wake up, the itch is gone. The pain too. I can lift my right arm and move my head without whining. Rona gets some of my favourite grilled tubenose fish inside me and I even manage to chew. I feel tired and incredibly stiff, like Nash and his mates have kicked the crap out of me, but that's about it.

If I moan, it's about wanting to see Jude. Only Rona isn't listening and Jude stays away the whole day. I stop worrying about dying and start worrying how bad my scars will be.

No girl wants someone who looks like a monster.

The third day since they brought me in with half my face and shoulder blown off, I wake up feeling almost strong again. A bit fed up with Jude though, for not standing up to Rona and coming to visit me, but otherwise good.

'When can I get up?' I ask for the hundredth time.

'When I say so. Don't ask me again!'

Rona's extra cross because she's caught me out of bed once already. Okay, so maybe I should do what she says – she's the healer after all. But my legs are twitching with all this lying about and I'm sick of pissing into bottles. Somehow I'm still alive. I want to see the sun and breathe fresh air again.

'But I feel so much better,' I say, yawning.

Crash! The sound of glass shattering pulls my head round. I see Rona has dropped one of her ingredients bottles. An oily pool at her feet bubbles and smokes on the wood floor, but she's staring at me, wide-eyed.

My mouth goes dry. 'What?'

She frowns, then purses her lips. I call this her decision face.

'You really don't know, do you, Kyle?'

'Know what?'

She sighs, such a big sigh it's like she shrinks letting that much breath go.

'Right,' she says. 'This has gone on long enough.'

I watch, amazed, as she bolts the shack door and closes all the shutters. The glowtubes flicker on automatically.

'Do you feel well enough to travel?' she asks me.

Before Jude stopped coming to visit, she told me the gossip that's going around. Freshwater is history – we're going to have to hit the road and find someplace new. Folks are sweating that with so many killed we're way too few now to bring in the harvest, look after all the animals *and* fight off Reaper attacks.

'Think so,' I say, not wanting us to be left behind.

I struggle up, but she shakes her head and gently pushes me back down. She fetches her curved bandage scissors and holds them up so I see.

'Stay still,' she says, grimacing. 'This might hurt.'

I cringe as she slides the cold blade under the dressing on my neck and starts snipping through the layers of gauze, but it's not so bad. When she peels it off, I hear a nasty sucking sound, but it doesn't hurt. She hands me a mirror.

'I'm so sorry, Kyle. I should have told you.'

Her face is whiter than the bleached bedsheets. I hesitate, but I have to see the damage some time, so I bite my lip and hold the mirror up, fingers trembling.

I tilt it back and forth, searching for the wound.

Only . . . there is no wound.

'What's going on?'

I take another look. All I see is the livid pink flesh of my nightmares, bits of crusty yellow scab hanging off and a smear of green painsucker. No scorched flesh, no pus-filled blisters. By some miracle, I'm almost completely healed.

Then I get it – this is no miracle.

No. This can't be happening. Not to me! I'm no ident!

I leap out of the bed and rip my other dressings off, careless of any pain. Rona tries to stop me, but I lash out and send her flying. And my chest and shoulder are the same – pink and shiny, no sign of a scar even. My jaw still looks all ugly and raw, but there's flesh over the bone now, which wasn't there four days ago.

I tear at myself, but the healing is part of me.

'Stop that!' shouts Rona.

In the end, I just stand there, panting and sobbing, my head thumping. 'What *am* I?' I hear myself say.

Rona grabs me by my wrists, shakes me until I look at her.

'You're human, Kyle. As human as I am.'

'How can I be? Look at me. Only a twist can heal so —'

'Never say that word!'

She slaps me across the face. So hard it stings.

I'm so shocked, all I can do is stare at her. She's never hit me before. In her bloodshot eyes, hiding behind all that anger, I see guilt now.

'You knew all along, didn't you?' I say.

She lets go and crumples into the chair by my bed. In the dim spill of glowtube light, her face looks old and exhausted. 'Yes. No. I mean, there was always a chance it was you.' She dries her eyes with the heels of her hands. 'I suspected it last year, when you recovered so fast from that swamp pox. Look, I know you don't understand. How could you? There's so much I need to tell —'

She stops. Footsteps crunch across the dry grass outside our shack.

A second later somebody hammers on our door. The latch lifts and rattles; the door shudders in its frame as whoever's outside tries to open it. We both hear a man's loud grunt of surprise at finding the door bolted.

'Hello-o-o! Is anybody there?'

It's Fod's gravelly voice, our self-appointed preacher, the

very man who'll put the rope around my neck if he finds out I'm a twist.

'One minute!' shouts my mother. 'I'm changing Kyle's dressings!'

The next few seconds are frantic. I dive back into bed. Rona scuttles around, picking up the dressings I ripped off. She tapes them all roughly back into place. When she's done, she pulls the sheet up so only my eyes show.

'Remember when you were bad with the swamp pox?' she whispers.

I get it. Look like I'm out of it.

Rona gives me one last urgent check to make sure no healed skin is showing, then opens the door. Through half-closed eyes I see Fod bustle inside. With his stoop, long-nosed, wrinkly face and straggly hair, he looks like one of those giant wader birds as he twitches his narrow-eyed, suspicious gaze around the room.

He looks at me. I do some moaning and squirming.

'What's the meaning of this?' he demands.

'This?' says Rona, all raised eyebrows and innocence.

'Your door was bolted, your shutters closed.'

'And is there a law against that? Can't you see I'm busy here?'

He stiffens – even with my eyes half closed, I can see he's not best pleased. He's more used to people bowing and scraping to him than talking back. Rona will get into trouble if she keeps on like this. I fake a louder groan, to distract him.

'I'm simply doing my rounds,' he growls through gritted teeth. 'Checking on my flock at this difficult time, to offer my prayers and support.'

Rona scowls. 'And I thank you, Preacher. But I was changing

my son's dressings and didn't want to be disturbed. Can't you understand that?'

They face off against each other.

Even with his stoop, he towers over her, but Rona bristles right back at him.

'Of course,' he says at last, in that stiff way people have of saying things they don't mean. And now he stalks over to my bedside, twitches the sheet away from my face and stares down at me. 'Kyle, will you join me in prayer?'

I squeeze my eyes shut and groan. I can only hope my scared face looks sick enough, and that Fod is every bit the idiot people whisper he is. Rona's only slapped my old dressings back on. How won't he see that they are far from fresh?

'He can't hear you,' Rona says. 'I've done all I can for him, but —'

The sheet lands back on me. I risk a peek and Fod is staring at Rona, who's got this mournful-but-trying-to-be-brave look on her face. Her chin trembles.

She's good. I worry for a second that I *am* dying.

'You can't save him?' says Fod.

'Not with a few herbs, I can't. All I can do is ease his passing.'

I moan again, extra loud and pitiful.

'I'm sorry,' he says. 'I'll pray for you both.'

'It'd be more useful if you helped me bathe him,' says Rona. 'He's fouled himself again — he can't help it, the state he's in. Perhaps you could spare us a minute or three of your valuable time?'

I groan for real this time, but Rona knows what she's doing.

'Any other time, I'd be glad to help,' Fod says quickly. 'But I'm in a rush. Many more people to visit; the day's getting shorter. I'd better be leaving now.'

'Of course.' Rona's voice could curdle milk.

I wait until I hear the door slam and bolts going home before I open my eyes. Rona glares at me, her back against the door, a finger pressed to her lips. We listen to Fod's crunching footsteps as they almost run from the shack.

Rona puts her hands to her mouth. Me, I feel like laughing *and* crying.

'What d'you want to tell Fod that for?' I ask Rona as she peers through the shutters, making sure he's gone. I sit up and start gingerly pulling the dressings off.

'Tell him what?' she says, obviously only half listening.

'That I'm dying.'

'I had to, to get him to bugger off.'

'But now he'll go and tell everybody I'm dying. And I'm not.'

Rona eases the shutter closed and comes over to sit by me on the bed.

'Listen,' she says, 'we got lucky just now, but sooner or later someone will get a good look at you. Like your Jude. Especially if we have to up sticks and trek someplace else. They'll realise your healing is . . . unusual.'

She sighs and shakes her head.

I stare down at my new skin again. Impossibly smooth and pink, glowing with health where only days ago I saw sickening wounds. Unnatural healing. The manifestation of evil.

My head is spinning, like I've stood up too fast.

'But can't we say you healed me?'

'Won't work. Those men who carried you back here, they all saw how bad your injuries were. Even if they could maybe believe I pulled you through, they'd expect you to be badly scarred. They'd soon figure it out. And then —'

I suck my teeth. Rona doesn't have to paint me a picture. A real live twist found hiding in their midst — that would explain Freshwater's run of evil luck. We'd both be dragged to the nearest tree and hung. The whole settlement would gather to watch us swing. I kind of doubt Fod would call the Slayers in to deal with us. When it comes to idents and twists, blame has a way of sticking too widely.

My flesh, new and old, tries to crawl off my bones.

'We have to get out of here,' I moan.

'We will, but you'll have to die first,' says Rona. When she sees my stunned look, she dredges up a sad smile. 'Not *really* die. We fake it. If everybody thinks you're dead, they don't miss you and they don't come looking. See?'

'Everybody?' I say, thinking of Jude.

'Everybody.'

I grimace. 'But won't they expect to see my dead body?'

My mother's eyes go narrow and cunning. 'Oh, these old wooden shacks with their home-made log burners — accidents waiting to happen. What with the Reaper attack and everything else, I can't see anyone poking through the ashes.'

'We burn this place down?' I say, shocked.

A ghost of a smile haunts her lips. 'Got a better idea?'

7
A BAD DECISION

'Don't just sit there. Get dressed and give me a hand moving this,' says Rona. She pulls at our cast-iron log burner, but can't move it on her own.

The enormity of what's happened to me, and what will happen if anyone finds out, is sinking in. I hear the air roaring in my ears with every breath I take. I reckon we should be hitting the road, not shifting stoves around.

'What for?' I say. 'I don't understand.'

Rona puts her hard face on and grits her teeth.

'Kyle, every second counts. I need you to help me. Now.'

I still feel like screaming, but the desperation in her voice gets me moving. I throw my clothes on. Working together, we walk the stove back and lever up its hearthstone. Hidden in a hollow beneath this, smothered in bugwebs, is something wrapped in an oil-stained rag and a small electronic device.

More secrets Rona has kept from me.

'What's all this?' I ask.

She picks the device up, blows the worst of the dust off and powers it up.

'My old comm. Hoped I'd never have to use this.'

Amazingly — because it looks like it's been down there for ages — the communicator beeps and boots up. Looking satisfied, Rona powers it down, then buries it in her healer basket. The other rag-wrapped thing, she pockets. The shape of it and the weight dragging her jacket down all say blaster to me.

'Where'd you get tech like that?' I say.

Either she doesn't hear me or pretends not to.

'See if you can put the burner back the way it was,' she says. 'I have to go out now. You bolt the door behind me and let nobody in. Okay?'

I shrug. 'Where are you going?'

Rona frowns. 'I'll check my other patients, then call some old friends of mine from a lifetime ago. With luck, they'll be able to help us.'

'But if they find out I'm a —'

I stop myself from saying 'twist' just in time, as Rona glares at me. 'Trust me,' she says. 'I'll be back quick as I can.'

Last thing she does is stick some fresh dressings on me. I whine, saying I don't need them now, but she insists, telling me it's a precaution. She heads off then, her healer basket on its strap over her shoulder. I bolt the door behind her, like she said, open the shutters a crack and watch her trudge away, head down and back bent, along the track towards the other farmsteads.

She glances back once, but doesn't wave.

I get that, but only later. Why wave to someone who's supposedly dying?

*

Now I'm on my own, my thoughts run riot. I mean, how do you handle finding out that you're evil and a monster? The bane of Wrath. A foul caricature of humanity, like that High Slayer Morana woman said at the Peace Fair.

Don't ask me – I haven't got any answers. All I've got is a fever of questions and a lump of dread in my stomach.

After a while, I start thinking that bolting the door behind Rona wasn't such a slick idea after all. What if Fod comes back? Or somebody else pops round looking for Rona? Won't it look suspicious if the door's bolted and Rona doesn't answer? It's not like I can let them in; I'm supposed to be dying. Maybe it'd be better if I unbolted the damn thing, hunkered down under my sheets and took my chances.

Yeah right. And hope if I get a visitor they're not too curious.

In the end I chicken out and leave the door bolted.

The day limps by. The sun goes down and still there's no sign of Rona coming back. I'm on my bed, hugging my knees, moaning and trying not to puke. I stare at where my wounds were and more questions hammer inside my head.

What am I? Who am I? How can this be?

Thing is – I don't *feel* evil. Okay, I look at my skin and I see twist, but I'm still me, Kyle. Unless the becoming evil thing happens later? When I was little, I once stuffed my face with some mushrooms I found. Their purple was all over my face when Rona caught me. She went mental, terrified I'd eaten poisonous ones. I sat there, cringing and crying, wondering when the poison would kill me.

That's what this feels like now. An evil within, waiting to possess me.

You're *human*, Rona said. But she would, wouldn't she?

I'm so busy feeling sorry for myself, I don't hear the footsteps. The knock at the door is only a tap, but I nearly die of fright. I cower, wondering if it's Jude at last, or Fod again, before I hear Rona's whisper telling me it's only her. I draw the bolts back and open the door. She slips inside past me. In the glow from the tubes, I glimpse some colour back in her face. She looks tired but satisfied.

'You got hold of your friends?' I ask her.

She nods and smiles at me. 'Everything's going to be all right.'

'How come?'

'We need to be ready tomorrow,' is all she'll say.

I throw more questions at her — like who are these friends of hers and how come I've never heard of them before? — but she's not in a talking mood. And when I wake the next morning, after a long night of tossing and turning and dreams I can't remember, I find her gone again. There's a note waiting on the kitchen table. In her loopy scrawl, it tells me she'll be back very late, that there's food in the cool store, and to put together a day pack with my trail gear and be ready to go. Bolt the door, the note says, and don't let anyone in, no matter what they say.

That means Judith too is double underlined.

A second day of waiting stretches out into forever. A thousand times I shrink inside, sure I hear footsteps again on the path. I endlessly pack and repack my rucksack. In the end, I lie on my bed, Rona's rusty old hunting blade beside me.

What's Rona up to?

Where will we be going?

I stare at my little fingers. How can I be a twist?

Questions, questions. No bogging answers. It's doing my head in.

The room gets darker and darker and so does my mood. Through the cracks in the shutters I see the sun set again, but still no sign of Rona. I'm going out of my mind with being lonely and frightened and not having anybody to talk to.

As the glowtubes flicker on, I think of Jude.

I miss her. And that's when the thought strays into my head . . .

I just have to say goodbye to Jude. I know it's mad, but I can't clear off forever and leave her lonely and thinking I'm burnt to a black, charred crisp. Rona will kill me, but Jude's not just my girl, she's my only real friend.

The Flint farmstead is ten klicks away. It's cloudy, so neither the little dogmoon or the bigmoon to shed any light, but I find my way easy enough. Should do – I've worn a groove in this trail these past few months. A rain shower rattles through, but that's good. Less chance of anyone else being out. It feels great to be outside, breathing fresh air deep into my lungs. My skin tingles with the damp and the moving. With every step I take, I start to feel stronger.

Only . . . what's causing that? I shiver.

To cheer myself up, I think about how Jude and I got together last winter. I was over at her father's place, fixing his threshing machine. This curly-haired girl, about my age, was chopping firewood – I couldn't take my eyes off her. When I asked her name, she gave me this lopsided smile, said it was Jude, and asked me mine. I teased her, told her she was proper handy with an axe for a girl. She teased me right back, said I'd fix her dad's thresher a lot quicker if I quit staring.

We've been together ever since.

I don't know if I love Jude or if she loves me. All I know is, Jude's the only person, other than Rona, who smiles when she sees me. And I need to hold her one last time.

As I creep into the farmstead, their dog Bram woofs off a few half-hearted barks and rattles his chain, but he knows my Kyle stink and soon shuts up. Across the yard, the loaf-like outline of the thatched house appears out of the darkness. No lights are on. They're all in bed already. As the only daughter, Jude has a sleeping place to herself in the lean-to at the far end. I tiptoe round there and do the soft *tap-tappety-tap-tap* at her window that tells her it's me. Soon as I hear the telltale creak of her floorboards, I scuttle off to wait in the hay barn.

Jude takes her time.

Long enough for me to worry she's not coming. Or telling her father.

Finally, she slips inside the barn to join me. I flick on the solitary glowtube and see she's alone, a threadbare work jacket thrown on over her night stuff.

She scrunches her face up against the light.

'Is that really you, Kyle?'

'In the flesh, or what's left of it.'

I open my arms out to her and hold my breath.

'It *is* you!' she says. She comes running, throws her arms round me and buries her face into my bandaged neck. I'm so relieved, I hoist her up off her feet and spin her around. When I put her down again, she smiles up at me.

But as I go to kiss her, she pulls away.

'I don't get it,' she says, looking confused. Her chin wobbles. 'The last thing Rona told us was that you were close to —'

'I'm tougher than I look.'

Jude gives me her slow-nod sceptical look. 'What's going on?'

'I'll tell you later, but first things first.' I pull her closer, slip my hands under her jacket and feel how she's still lovely and warm from her bed.

'Ew! You're all cold and wet,' she laughs.

I kiss her and she kisses me back, pressing herself against me. Her hands are at the back of my neck now, pulling my head down so she can reach me. How it happens I'll never know, but she knocks one dressing off. It's only loosely taped on, more for show than anything, and comes away with a slight sucking sound.

'Oh my Saviour, I'm sorry.' Jude pulls back, her eyes big with concern. We both glance down at the bandage lying in the straw. 'Did I hurt you?'

'No, I'm fine.' I try to turn away, to stop her seeing, but I'm too slow.

I feel her go rigid. 'Kyle!'

With the toe of my boot, I scuff uncertainly at the straw. When I look up, I've made up my mind. I can't just say goodbye. It's mad, but all the horror, the fear and loneliness, I can't keep it inside — I need to tell her. Maybe if I can make Jude understand that I'm still me, everything will be all right again.

I sit her down on a hay bale. 'I can trust you, can't I?'

She nods stiffly, but I see her wondering.

'Don't be scared,' I say.

I unbutton my shirt. One by one, I peel off the rest of Rona's dressings and show Jude how my wounds have almost completely healed. I hold her tight when her eyes flood with panic. I shush her and stroke her curly hair.

She's petrified, trembling like a newborn lamb.

'It's not what you think,' I say.

Thank the Saviour she doesn't scream, but when I relax my grip, anxious not to hurt her, she makes a break for it and I have to grab her again.

'Jude, stop. I'm not going to hurt you.'

A long time goes by like this. I do everything I can to calm her. I whisper she has no reason to fear me. Her mouth opens and closes, but no words come out, only a low moan. It's an ugly feeling, me making her skin crawl. Not that I can blame her. She sees my unnatural healing and that means only one thing – human on the outside, inside a monster. No wonder she's terrified.

'Let – go – of – me,' she says.

This time when I release her she cringes, but doesn't run. She won't let me touch her again, but she looks able to listen. Quickly, I make up some crap about Rona finding an ancient wonder drug in her medchest.

Jude stares as I babble on, her chest heaving, until I run out of words. She knows I'm lying, I can tell.

'If anybody sees you like this,' she says shakily, 'you *are* dead. They won't listen; they'll kill you. And Rona too. You know that, don't you?'

'Uh-huh,' I say. What else is there to say?

We sit there, in the circle of light, the darkness crushing in on us. I try to read her face, but there are too many shadows. On the way here, I had so much I wanted to say to her. Now, it all seems so pointless. My impossible healing shouts more loudly than any words can.

'What will you do?' she says.

I hesitate, wondering what I should tell her.

'We're going away, to someplace nobody knows us. We'll be okay.'

'Going away? Where?'

'I don't know. But that's why I came, to say goodbye.'

Tears shine in Jude's eyes now.

'It's too late for that,' she says, very quietly.

'What's *that* mean?' I say.

But she won't look at me and I get it now – she thinks I'm gone already.

'You're wrong,' I say. 'I know what it looks like, but I don't feel any different inside. I'm the same as ever, I just heal faster. I'm not evil, Jude, not even bad!'

I try to smile and reach for her hand, but she snatches it away.

'Don't touch me!'

I curse and she flinches, like she thinks I'm going to rip her head off or something. Next thing, she's on her feet and backing away. I scramble after her, sensing she's about to run. And I can't help it, I'm angry now.

'Look, this isn't *my* fault!'

She trips over something in the muck and straw.

I swear I only grab her so she doesn't fall backwards, but she gasps loudly and I'm sure she'll scream. Without thinking, I clamp my hand over her mouth. She flails against me, tries to push me away, but I'm too strong. Her eyes bulge.

I pull my hand away, brace myself.

'You said you wouldn't hurt me,' she sobs.

I shake my head and try to get a grip on my temper. 'I'm sorry. I didn't mean to. But you mustn't scream. If your father finds us here, sees me like this, then it's like you said – I'm dead. And so is Rona. You don't want that, do you?'

She stares at me, but says nothing. Which says it all.

'You won't tell, will you?'

Jude shakes her head, but I see her little finger trace the Sign of One. I'm so stunned, I let go of her. She gives this huge gulp and darts to the side door. Beyond the spill of light, I hear her fumbling at the latch and her ragged breathing.

The door creaks open, then bangs shut behind her.

The drizzle eases as I make it home. The nearly full bigmoon finds a gap in the clouds and paints our shack silver, nestled in our herb and vegetable gardens. I'm wondering if this is the last time I'll ever see it like this, when I notice the sliver of light sneaking out from under the door. Oh great, that's all I need. Rona's back already, probably waiting behind the door with a hatchet.

I bang inside, slam the door behind me, determined to make no excuses.

'Look, I don't care. You can't keep me –'

Rona looks up from stuffing something into my backpack. Her glare could stop a charging fourhorn.

'Where the hell have you been, Kyle?' she growls.

And that's when I see we have a visitor.

She's sitting, her legs stretched out, in the chair by the stove.

Those leathers, the long white dreads, the teardrop tattoo, her dark green eyes. . .

My mouth drops open. So does hers.

'You!' we both say.

Windjammer girl launches herself to her feet.

'No way. I'm not flying this scumbag anywhere,' she says to Rona.

Rona looks from me to the girl and her eyes go wide.

'What? You *know* each other?'

8
I SAY SOME TERRIBLE THINGS

I shrug. The windjammer girl stands there all twitching and snarling. I wonder if she has that nasty little flamer on her. What did that bald bloke call her? Oh yeah, Sky. A stupid, made-up kind of name if you ask me.

She grabs her rain jacket off the back of the chair.

'No way. I'm out of here.'

She steps around me, but hasn't reckoned on Rona, who puts her back to the door to block it. I've never seen my mother look more fierce.

And that's saying something.

'Where do you think you're going?' she snaps.

The girl hesitates. She scowls, looks me up and down. 'Not him,' she says, spitting the words. 'You don't understand.'

Rona groans. She runs her hands through her hair in obvious frustration. 'Show her,' she says to me.

'Show her what?' I say, confused.

'Your dressings, Kyle, take them off. Show Sky your healing.'

My collar is still turned up against the rain, so Rona can't see they're gone already. 'Are you out of your mind?'

'Just do as I say!'

I throw my hands up. If Rona asked me to sing 'Oh, My Saviour', all twenty verses, I couldn't be more gobsmacked. Show this stranger my twist healing? Yeah, sure. Why not? For the second time this evening, I unbutton my shirt.

Rona twitches, seeing my already bare neck and chest.

The girl's eyes narrow as they flicker over what's left of my wounds. She purses her mouth as if choking poison down. I expect her to scream or make a run for it like Jude. Instead, she just frowns, as if she's seen this before.

'Blaster burns, that what you said?'

'A week ago, low power maybe, but point-blank range,' says Rona, all healer matter-of-fact now. 'He was in a terrible state, but now look at him.'

Sky darts one last venomous look at me, then throws Rona a little nod.

'*O-kay* then,' she says, sounding half-strangled.

'Okay,' echoes Rona. 'Good.'

Whatever they've agreed, it looks like it's on again.

'Will somebody *please* tell me what the hell is going on?' I say.

Rona ignores me. She marches over to the table and starts stuffing my backpack again. She's got her back to me, but I can tell from how stiff it is and the way she's punching the gear in, she's furious.

Well, I don't care. I'm angry too. At her – at Jude – at the whole world.

'Off you go,' she says to me, handing me my pack with a grunt. 'Follow Sky; she knows the way. I'll join you later, soon as I'm done here.'

'No.' I sling the pack back on to the table.

'Oh, don't *you* start,' Rona says, her voice rising.

'This is crazy! I'm not going anywhere,' I say. My voice wobbles. I see the windjammer girl out of the corner of my eye, sneering. 'I've had it with not knowing what's going on. I'm staying right here until you tell me everything.'

Rona twitches. 'We haven't got time for this, Kyle.'

I shake my head and stare at the floor until I hear my mother's sigh.

'Sky,' she says, 'maybe you could give us a minute?'

I look up now. The girl stares at Rona, then at me. I see the hostility, but something else too. Curiosity? Maybe, but a blink and it's gone. She shrugs her jacket on over her thin shoulders. 'Whatever, but remember we ain't got all night.'

The door bangs shut behind her.

Silence. My heart thrashing, my head thumping. Neither of us able to look the other in the eye. I feel numb and empty inside.

'Sit down,' Rona says at last. 'And button your shirt.'

I do as she says. She sits opposite me and sighs again. My heart tries to batter through my ribs, but I stay quiet. I don't want sighs – I want answers.

'Please tell me you didn't go see Jude.' she says.

I roll my eyes. She curses, making me jump, but then takes my hand.

'Listen, I've sorted us a trip out of here on that girl's windjammer, no questions asked, to somewhere safe. I can't imagine how you know each other, but she can be trusted. You must do as she says though. Promise me that.'

'Fine,' I say through gritted teeth.

'Good. That's good,' says Rona.

She glances at the closed door, as if she can see through the wood to Sky waiting impatiently outside.

I pull my hand away. 'Why is this happening to me?'

'It's too long a story,' she says, with a tired shake of her head. 'Try and be sensible, Kyle. I'll tell you everything later, I promise you I will.'

Try and be sensible?

Oh sure. Turns out I'm the bane of Wrath.

A monster so awful that I make my girlfriend's skin crawl.

I smash my fist on to the table, sending stuff flying. I jump up, sweep my backpack to the floor, kick my chair across the room. 'This is all *your* fragging fault! You should have told me. You should've stopped this happening. You –'

And I say some terrible things.

Rona doesn't flinch, just watches me as I rage and stamp about. When I stop, panting and helpless, she's there to gather me in her arms. She pulls me close. I sense then how she's trying to be strong for both of us.

'I'm sorry,' I whisper, ashamed.

'So am I,' she says. She pulls back and does her best to smile, but her eyes are shiny with sadness. 'More sorry than you can ever know.' She dabs at her eyes with a rag.

I feel a stab of guilt. I've seen her bleak before, but never cry.

'When you were little,' she says, 'I told myself the less you knew about your past, the better it would be. Life's tough enough, I thought.' She clicks her tongue. 'When you got older, I think I'd just got into the habit of keeping secrets.'

73

She takes my hands again. This time I don't pull away.

'Right or wrong, everything I did, I did for you. You must know that.'

A tear escapes down her face, drips off her chin onto my wrist.

'I didn't mean those things I said,' I tell her.

'I know,' she says. 'Kyle, you're frightened and you're confused. With everything that's happened to you, I can't blame you for being angry. And we all say things we regret when we're angry. It's only . . . human.'

'You're sure I'm not a monster?'

'Kyle, you're no monster,' she says, looking me in the eye. 'Believe me.'

I think about that caged creature I saw at the Peace Fair.

'But what am I then?'

She gives her head a little shake. 'Just a boy who heals quickly. And maybe you're stronger and faster than other boys. Different – that's all. No twisted blood. Not evil. On any other world, it wouldn't be a curse, it'd be a blessing.'

I'm shocked. 'Isn't that heresy?'

'Heresy? Hah, that's what they'd like you to think.'

She leads me back to the table and puts her hands to her cheeks, which drags her skin down so taut she looks a hundred years old. 'You must understand, this whole rotten world is built on lies. Our so-called Saviour is the biggest liar of all. Nothing is what it seems, not even me. But the biggest lie of all is that kids like you will grow up to be monsters. Whatever happens, never believe that.' She sighs. 'Just listen to me, droning on all self-righteous about lies. I may not have lied to you, Kyle, but I've hidden the truth and that's just as wicked. I've been a fool.'

I reach over and cover her cold fingers with my warm ones.

'So tell me the truth.'

Rona shifts uneasily, looks past me, at something that isn't in the room.

'The truth? The truth is that you're in great danger now, Kyle. And not only because of *what* you are, but because of *who* you are.'

'Huh?' I say, not sure I heard this right.

But Rona doesn't explain. Instead she throws her head back and stares up at the ceiling. I look too. For one mad second, I half expect to see her secrets carved into the rough-hewn rafters, but all I see are bugwebs and shadows.

'Okay,' I say, fighting to keep frustration out of my voice, 'when I asked if you knew about me being different, you said you weren't sure. You said something else like *there was always a chance it was me*. What did you mean by that?'

I squeeze her hand, until she looks at me.

'Even as a healer I couldn't tell,' she says, her voice a whisper. 'After you shrugged off the swamp pox, I thought it likely. But I wasn't sure until a few days ago. You see, Kyle —' She hesitates, a vein squirming at her temple. 'I suppose deep down I'd always hoped that it wasn't you, that it was your brother.'

My next heartbeat is a long time coming. 'My brother?'

More tears wriggle down her face. 'Your identical twin. Colm.'

I stand up so fast, my vision goes all blurry.

'*What?* I have a *brother*?'

Rona reaches for me, but I recoil.

'Kyle,' she pleads.

The door bangs open. Sky sticks her head inside, looking real tense.

'We've got company!'

Somehow, Rona beats me to the door. I'm trying to peer past her when her whole body stiffens. I hear her sudden intake of breath. When she turns round, I see she's bitten her lip so hard it's bleeding. I squeeze past and look outside. In the distance, I see a column of flaming torches, slowly winding its way towards us.

No three ways about it – it's a lynch mob.

'Oh, Jude,' I groan. 'What the hell have you done?'

'Time to go,' hisses Sky.

Rona runs, grabs my parka and my daypack and hurls them at me.

'Don't stand there!' she yells. 'Get out by the back window.'

She rips open a cupboard and grabs a plastic container. Stunned, I watch as she tears the cap off and starts sloshing liquid over walls and floor.

I know that stink – it's surgical spirit.

'I'm not leaving you,' I shout.

Rona throws the empty container down. 'I'll catch up with you at the old landing ground. Now please, Kyle, do as I say for once. And hurry!'

What old landing ground?

The girl starts hauling me away, but I shrug her off.

'Don't be an idiot,' she says.

Next thing I know, Rona is shaking me.

'Kyle, there's a gun in your pack. Don't be scared to use it if you have to. We *do* still have friends out there, more than you know. Sky will take us to them; we'll be safe there. I love you. Now, get moving! I'll follow as soon as I can.'

She crushes her lips to my cheek, then shoves me away.

I want to say, 'I love you too.'

But a sudden gust of wind rattles the shutters, bringing with it the sound of men's voices, baying for twist blood. And they're shouting my name.

It's like I feel rope around my neck already.

I throw myself out of the window after the girl. I run and run and don't look back until a *whoosh* sound overtakes me. I stop then, bent over and panting after the steep climb. Way below me a red and orange fireball leaps high into the night sky. The torches of the lynch mob scatter. I hear angry cries. I think maybe I see a figure flit from the back of the blazing shack and dodge through leaping shadows. Only I can't see anything but flames now as Sky appears beside me, gasping.

'Rona knows what she's doing,' I tell her. Tell myself.

'Good,' she says, sounding disgusted. 'But you don't. Where do you think you're going? The landing ground's up *this* way.'

She stomps away off to my left and the darkness swallows her.

PART TWO
ON THE RUN

9
WAITING

When the sun finally drags itself up in the west, bathing the world in watery dayshine, I reckon I've done enough running. I've never come this way on any of my hunting trips, so have only the vaguest idea where we are – someplace high in the mountains north of Freshwater. Half an hour ago, in pitch-darkness, the trail crossed over a ridge. We've been descending ever since.

Sky's ahead of me, limping along and not looking back.

It's been a hell of a night getting up here, cold and hard and scary. How we weren't stalked and gobbled by gibbercats or nightrunners, I'll never know.

With a curse, I ease the pack from my aching shoulders. My stomach rumbles, so I find a rock to sit on, take a drink from my canteen and open the pack. Knowing Rona, she'll have packed food. Sure enough, first thing I find is a bag of nuts and berries. I start munching. Below me, the trail switchbacks down to a plateau and what looks like an abandoned landing ground. The grass runway is overgrown. There's a barn with a water tower leaning against it, and some fallen-down shacks. At one end of the runway, I see what must be the steam winch, with its boiler, smokestack and cable drums. But what I don't see is any windjammer. I have another dig in the pack then, looking for the gun Rona said was in there.

It's at the bottom, still wrapped in its oily rag.

'No way,' I say, when I unwrap it.

I'd hoped for a blaster or a flamer, something lethal. But no, this is some ancient slug-thrower from the Long Ago on Earth. A quick fiddle and I get the cylinder thing in the middle to fall open. More disappointment. Three rusty bullets, three empty chambers. It's not even fully loaded. Just great. The whole world wants me dead and Rona gives me a weapon that will probably blow up in my face if I shoot it. I try aiming it, but it's so heavy it wobbles all over the place.

Sky turns and slogs back up the trail to me.

Quickly, I stuff the old gun back into my pack. If I'm tired, Sky looks destroyed. Despite it still being chilly enough up here for me to be glad of the parka Rona made me take, sweat is running down the girl's face. Those painted bars under her eyes are all smudged, dripping down into her hollow cheeks.

'What the frag are you doing?' she says, looking mad as hell.

'Oh, we're talking now?' I say.

The whole night, she's pretty much ignored me. A few times, I asked her where we were going – the most I ever got back was a grunted 'up'.

I fake-smile. 'Want some nuts?'

Her dark eyes blaze. For a second, I think she'll knock them from my hand.

'Stuff your face later,' she snaps. 'We need to keep moving.'

I shake my head. 'This is as far as I go.'

'Don't be stupid.'

'I'm waiting here for Rona.'

Sky surprises me. I expect her to bite my head off, but she doesn't. 'You'll be waiting a long time,' she says softly.

I shrug. Sure, I know what she's thinking – I've thought it too. My head is thumping from thinking it. Maybe Rona's dead, or captured.

'I'll take that chance,' I say.

Her scowl comes back. 'I don't think so. You promised your mother you'd do what I tell you. And I'm telling you to move.'

I stand up so quick that she takes a step back.

'Yeah?' I say. 'So tell me how come I don't see a windjammer? If you're leading me into some sort of trap, I'll kill you.'

'See that?' she says, sneering and pointing. 'That's camouflage.'

There's a weird cross-shaped mound covered in scrub at the other end of the runway from the winch. Now that I know where to look, I see the windjammer.

'Okay,' I say, feeling stupid. 'But what about Rona?'

'What about her? She knows where this place is and how to get here. We've got loads to do to get ready for take-off. If you help, it'll get done faster.'

'And you won't go without her?'

'We'll wait as long as we can.' With that, she sets off down the trail again.

After a quick think, I hoist my pack and chase after her.

'Hey, what do you mean, loads to do?'

'Look at the state of everything,' she says, over her shoulder. 'We took a hell of a risk landing here. If we can't get the winch going, then –'

She shrugs, but I get it. No winch, no flight, and we're stuck here.

'I never knew about this place,' I say.

She spits. 'You don't seem to know much about anything.'

I'm fishing for a comeback when a loud bang sends birds screeching and flapping into the air. I duck, sure we're being shot at, only to see smoke billow from the chimney of the winch. A man leaps from the cab and staggers away, beating at his windjammer leathers. I'm a long way away, but he looks familiar.

We reach the plateau and the path comes out behind the old barn we saw from the ridge. Sky hurries round it, towards the still-smoking winch.

'Wait here,' she says.

Fine by me. This is close enough.

Thought so — the man covered in soot and scorch marks is that massive bald guy who pulled Sky off me at the Fair, a lifetime ago. Even from here, I see he's very red in the face. Sky marches straight up to him and starts shouting. She waves her arms and then points at me. Not good. I wonder if I should run.

He glances at me, but doesn't seem interested.

Next thing I know, Sky's on her way back, pinch-lipped and angry.

'Not going to introduce us?' I say as she stalks past.

She stops, and definitely thinks about punching me. 'His name's Chane. And I'd stay out of his way if I were you. You'd better come with me.'

I follow her the length of the runway.

'Help me clear this,' she says.

Coarse netting is draped over the windjammer's hull and wings, foliage woven in to break up its outline. We pull the greenery clear, then haul the netting off. I help her to fold it. While she's stowing it, I stare nervously.

'You're sure this thing flies?'

Sky gives a short laugh. 'How do you think we got here?'

I look more closely and wish I hadn't.

The windjammer looks like an enormous metal bug. Where I expected sleek, the body of the machine is fat and round. The hull is a patchwork of battered metal panels, many stained orange-brown with rust. The wings are thick and stubby.

My heart sinks. 'Who sold you this scrap? You should get your money back.'

'Ha ha.' Sky reaches up and strokes the hull. 'She may be ancient, but she's still the finest jammer on Wrath. We call her *Rockpolisher*.'

I open my mouth, then shut it again. Don't want to know.

'Could Chane use any help?' I say later, after another winch explosion.

'Don't make me laugh,' says Sky.

Annoyed, I wander off to the barn. Inside I find an old cable-retrieve tractor rusting away, roughly the same as the ones we plough with back in Freshwater. The barn's roof has kept the worst of the weather off it. There are even some mouldy old lumps of coal left in its hopper. Getting my hands dirty working on it is a relief and it takes my mind off Rona and Jude. All it needs is a patch for a leaking high-pressure line and a fill of water, before I light the firebox. Pressure builds nicely. She rattles like a box of nails when I crash her into gear, but goes okay.

Who's laughing now?

They both come running, gobs open, as I drive her out of the barn.

'How'd you fix that?' bellows Chane.

'It's what I do,' I shout back.

See, Rona heals people – I heal stuff. That's how we put food on the table. Or how we used to, I mean. I peer up through the smoke and steam at the hillside trail we came along, but nothing moves. What the hell's keeping her?

'Why didn't you say you're a tech?' demands Sky.

How badly I want to say she didn't ask me. I don't though.

An hour later, Chane and me get the winch going. It's a punch-the-air moment, but scary too. Even at idle, the winch's boiler runs at far higher pressure than the tractor, but it's much rustier. Some of the vortex-multiplier pipes look so knackered I swear I could crush them with my bare hands. We both step back as it starts. It coughs and splutters, but keeps *chug-chugging* away.

'She won't last long at full revs,' I say.

'No problem,' says Chane. He slaps my back, nearly knocks me over. 'She only has to last a few seconds – that'll get us off the ground.'

I can't decide if he's joking or mad. Or both.

We use the tractor to pull the cable out from the winch to the windjammer. I watch, fascinated, as Chane unhooks the looped end of the cable and attaches it to a quick-release hook set into the jammer's belly. We're all set now. I know roughly how this works, even if I've never actually seen it. It's like flying a kite – the winch winds the cable in at full power and hauls us into the air.

I think that's how it goes anyway.

When I look up, I see Sky standing at the edge of the plateau. She's holding a small device above her head and staring at it. I wander over. One boot-length behind her is the cliff edge, a drop that makes my palms go all sweaty.

'What you doing?' I ask.

'Checking the wind speed,' she says, chewing her lip.

And that's when I notice how calm it is, no breath of wind on my cheek.

In the wind-scoured Barrenlands, that's weird.

Chane joins us. For such a big man, he moves quietly.

'No wind, no ridge lift,' he says. 'Our lift-cells give buoyancy, but to soar we need updraughts from wind hitting the cliff. Launch now and it's a one-way trip down to the valley floor.' He grins, showing me teeth green and rotten from chewing shadeweed. 'Don't worry. Wind'll be back, soon as the day warms up.' He stomps off then and starts checking all the windjammer's control surfaces.

Sky holds the instrument up again. Still nothing.

'It wasn't my fault, you know,' I say.

'What wasn't?'

'That twist. At the fair, when you clobbered me. They made me do it.'

She looks at me. '*Who* made you?'

'Nash and the rest. My mates. They ganged up on me.'

'And poor little Kyle couldn't say no.'

I shift uneasily. 'I wanted to, but they'd have beaten me up.'

'Right,' she says, staring at me. 'Better to zap the twist than risk a kicking?'

'Like you wouldn't.'

'No,' she sneers. 'I wouldn't.'

She throws me the wind meter, lifts her left hand to her mouth, makes sure I'm watching, then sinks her teeth into the flesh of her wrist. With a grunt, she pulls her head back *and starts peeling her skin off*. It comes away with a rubbery sound. I've skinned countless rabbits, but I still groan seeing this. One last tug and the skin hangs from her mouth, a fully-formed, inside-out hand. She holds her hands up and wiggles her fingers. Right hand, five of them. Left hand, only four.

No little finger – a stump where it should be. The indelible mark of the ident.

My hand twitches, but I stop myself from making the Sign of One. I stare at the glove – thin, skin-coloured rubber, the fake little finger padded and stitched to sit next to the next finger along. Cunning, that.

Without a word, she tucks it into a pocket.

I shiver. Sky's a scab. She'll have watched her twist sister die.

'Look, I still feel bad about it,' I say.

'Oh, I bet you do. Especially now you could end up in that cage with your mates paying to hurt you.' She points at the wind meter in my hand. 'Shout out if you see twenty on the gauge. Sustained, not gusts.'

She turns and limps away.

'We all have to survive,' I shout after her, but she doesn't look back.

Just then, I feel a tiny kiss of wind on my cheek, but when I hold the wind meter up, the little spinner thing can hardly be bothered to turn. It'll come sooner or later, so says Chane. Yeah? Well, I'll take sooner if that's okay. . .

Two hours later, the wind has picked up like Chane said it would, the steam winch is up to pressure and he wants to launch. I've yelled at him until I'm hoarse, but as far as he's concerned, he's already risked his precious *Rockpolisher* enough.

'We can't go,' I say again. 'I don't care what Rona told Sky. I'm not going anywhere until she gets here. You can't just leave her behind.'

But he's not having it; says I can stay if I want, but he's out of here.

It's Sky who finally persuades Chane to accept a compromise. I get to run back up to the ridge and take one last look, in case Rona is close. If there's no sign of her, I come straight back. We launch out of here, and that's that.

Sky follows me up the hill. At the top we stand there and peer down at the track that leads up from Freshwater.

Nothing doing. The trail is empty.

'I'm sorry,' she says. 'We have to go now.'

'I can't,' I say. 'I don't care what happens. I'm not going without Rona.'

Sky grabs me by the arm. 'Don't be a fool. It's a tough call, but Chane's right. We've got a long way to go and dayshine is wasting. Look, Kyle, if your mother was coming, she'd have been here hours ago. I don't think –'

I shrug her off. 'Don't think what?'

'Your shack went up in flames so fast. She won't have got out.'

'No way. I saw her.'

'You saw what you wanted to see.'

I'm about to contradict her when I glimpse movement on the trail.

'Look,' I say, excited. 'Here she is. I told you –'

Only it isn't Rona.

Two men step out from trees on to the trail, a long way below us. A dog pulls one of them along. Their faces, round under their hats, look up at us. Dog man, who could be one of the Fergusons, points his pulse rifle up in the air.

I see the green flash and hear the thump.

The hunter's signal – prey spotted.

10
CAPTURED

I'm so stunned, I stand there gawping until I hear Sky crashing her way back down the overgrown trail and realise she's cleared off without me. Instinct kicks in then, or maybe it's just fear and being alone. I throw myself after her. Branches lash at me as I run, but all I feel is guilt. Rona wouldn't leave *me* behind . . .

I catch Sky up, but she waves me past. 'Tell Chane we've got company!'

Only he doesn't need to be told, likely having heard the shot. When I reach the plateau, I see the pilot's already hauling himself into the open cockpit.

'Changed your mind?' he says as I scramble in after him.

I gulp air and tell him a search party from Freshwater has tracked us. He grunts, then orders me to strap myself into a jump seat at the back. I'm still fumbling with the buckle when Sky arrives, panting and wheezing. Even as she's strapping into her co-pilot seat, the canopy hisses down. I finally get my buckle done and watch Chane's thick fingers dance across the screen before him.

Lights flicker off and on. The lift-cells spool up with a loud whine.

'Controls full and free,' he chants. He stirs his control column and the windjammer comes alive under us. 'Instruments all green, lift-cells stable, trim set for take-off, canopy closed and locked. We're go for launch.'

I've got an awful taste in my mouth, like I'm going to puke. I lean forward and peer anxiously up at the ridge. No sign of those two scouts yet, but how much longer? One hit from their pulse rifles and we'll be going nowhere.

Come on! Come on!

Nothing happens. We stay rooted to the ground.

'What's the problem?' says Chane.

I see sweat trickling down the back of the man's bull neck.

'Can't get remote on the winch,' says Sky, calm as you like. 'Give me a second. I'll reboot.' She's punching stuff into a drop-down screen. Red spreads all over it, like a rash. Now it goes blank. Oh great, she's broken it.

The screen comes back, covered in green. Sky makes a happy noise. 'Okay. Taking up slack now.'

I look up the field. Black smoke belches from the winch and its drum starts to turn. I see the cable snaking backwards through the grass.

'Cable's live,' says Sky.

I take a deep breath and hold it – *we're going to make it*.

An alarm screeches. A different panel lights up red. Sky pulls it closer and curses. 'Aerial contact. Fast. Incoming.'

'Full power!' shouts Chane.

Sky slides her finger all the way forward on the winch control. I see and hear answering smoke and roaring from the winch. Our windjammer lurches as the cable snatches taut and starts pulling us. Slowly, we pick up speed.

A shadow hammers past low overhead.

We all pull our necks down into our shoulders, even Chane. There's a crackle of air being torn apart, a flash and a bang that sounds like thunder. The winch disappears in a massive explosion of smoke and flame.

'No!' shouts somebody. It's me.

The sky starts raining mangled iron. Above the smoke, a matt-black windjammer pulls out of its dive and banks left into a steep turn.

'Slayers!' shouts Sky.

The smoke drifts downwind and the winch is gone. We rumble to a halt.

'Well, that shot the fraggin' fox,' growls Chane.

He smashes his fist into the panel in front of him, cracking the display. Everything goes quieter as the lift-cells start spinning down.

'What do we do now?' I say, my voice shrill.

'Get the hell out,' says Sky.

She hammers a red button and the canopy hisses upwards. Her straps go flying and she vaults out of the cockpit.

'Here they come again,' says Chane, heaving himself up from his seat.

I follow his gaze. The Slayer windjammer is diving down at us, already so close I can see the scorched muzzles of its wing guns. I tear at my straps, frantically trying to free myself, but the buckle jams. I'm about to scream for help when Sky reappears. She reaches in, whacks the buckle and it falls open.

'What are you *doing*?' she shouts.

I grab my pack and throw myself after her, but I'm only half out as the Slayer warplane whistles past overhead again. Something rips at my hair and clothes. I think they've hit us, but it's only wind blast. Relief quickly turns to horror as I see bombs tumbling from the warplane's underbelly. I duck, like that's going to help, only to see them miss and fall behind our windjammer.

They don't explode, which is weird.

'Looks like the Slayers mean to take us alive,' growls Chane.

Only for a second do I think this is a good thing.

I crouch beside Sky on the hull and hoist my pack on to my shoulders.

'Let's run for it,' I say, but nobody's listening.

Sky peers back to where the bombs fell and curses. 'Spyders!'

'How many?' says Chane.

'Three.' The flamer appears in Sky's hand.

I stand and look too – and bite back a shriek. I see now why the ball-shaped bombs didn't go off. They aren't bombs, but some sort of robot fighting machines. I watch in horror as each uncurls a whole bunch of long metal legs, stands up and gives itself a kind of big wet-dog shake. Four yellow eyes gleam in a line across the top of what I guess is a head as they come scuttling towards us. Even from here, I hear the ugly *clack-clackety-clack* their feet make.

'What the hell –?'

Chane clambers aft to my jump seat. He rips a locker open and pulls out an enormous pulse rifle, the biggest I've ever seen. 'Get the kid out of here,' he shouts at Sky, pulling the mag out to check it. 'I'll cover you.'

'But —' says Sky. Her face goes slack, then hard. Hard like rock.

Chane slams the magazine home. 'Move.'

'You heard him,' she yells at me.

She lets go, slides down the curved hull on her bottom and drops to the ground. I'm so close behind, you couldn't slip a shadow between us. As we take off running, I hear the heavy *thump, thump* of Chane's rifle as he opens fire behind us. The heavy pack bangs into my back, slowing me down. As I pump my arms it feels like I'm tearing my new skin, but I grit my teeth and keep running. I risk a glance back, but can't see the spyders because *Rockpolisher* is in the way. What I *do* see is the Slayer windjammer sweeping in to land, undercarriage dangling. If Chane shoots at it, either he misses or its armour is too strong.

It settles on to the runway ahead of us.

'This way!' Sky shouts.

She swerves left, runs towards the old barn.

Even as we dive inside, Chane's pulse rifle quits firing. Both of us stop and swap stares. I stick my head back out to look. The big man is still in the cockpit, but he's dropped his rifle. It almost looks like he's fighting with himself. I don't get it, until I see the shiny spyder legs wrap around him and pull him down.

He screams and blood sprays from his mouth.

Sky grabs hold of my parka hood and yanks me back inside.

'We need to keep moving,' she hisses, her face contorted.

I nod, hardly able to breathe. I can't think — all I can do is follow her.

We hustle through the dark interior, both of us breathing hard, heading for the back wall where an old door lies half fallen in. Beyond, fifty metres away, I see trees and hillside. Between the trunks is waist-high razor grass. Nasty stuff, cuts you to shreds, but beggars can't be choosers – it's cover.

Clack-clackety-clack.

A spyder scuttles into the barn. It pauses on the threshold, half in dayshine, half in shadow, yellow eyes glowing brightly in its silver body. We both take a step back. It rears up and waves its front legs about, as if probing the air to feel where we are. This close it's even bigger than I thought, taller than I am. I pray it won't see us in the shadows, but now it gathers itself, compressing its leg pistons.

'Watch out!' Sky shouts as it launches itself.

It all happens so fast. One moment the spyder is hurtling towards us through the air – the next it collides with some old farm junk hanging in the shadows from the barn's rafters, flips upside down and crashes to the dirt floor.

It flails about, trying to right itself.

Sky doesn't hesitate – she dashes back and flames it.

Even crouching some metres away, I wince at the blast of heat. A torrent of flame spits from the stubby barrel, lighting up the barn with a crackling glare. I shield my eyes with my fingers, like she's doing as she plays the flames over the writhing machine. It curls up and stops thrashing. She squeezes off a few blasts at the barn itself. The old timbers, grey and bone-dry, go up with a *whoosh!* Black smoke, thick and choking, billows towards the roof.

Sky stalks past me, sweat streaming down her face.

I go after her as she scrambles out over the door, but my foot goes through the rotten wood. For a terrifying few seconds I think I'm stuck and about to burn to death, but I manage to pull clear. Sky stops and glares at me.

Her eyes go wide.

I look back into the inferno and the spyder is up again. Its body is battered and charred. One eye is dull, several legs trail behind it, but it's dragging itself after us through the flames. It's hissing now, like it's furious.

I cry out and stagger backwards.

'Run, you *idiot!*' shouts Sky.

I turn to run, but the spyder launches itself and drags me down.

My daypack saves me – it's that the spyder has hold of. As I hit the ground, one of the straps tears, the heavy pack shoots over my head and the spyder goes with it. I yank my other arm free, jump up and run for my life.

Sky's on her way back, but sees this and runs too.

I break right. Two of us, only one of it.

It goes after her.

Damaged it might be, but it's still quicker than Sky who's limping worse than ever. I see there's no way she'll reach the razor grass in time.

'It's catching you, Sky,' I yell. 'Torch it!'

Sky spins round and points the flamer. But now she's backing up, not looking where she's going, and she trips over a rock and falls. Bounces straight back up, but the spyder slams into her and knocks her down again.

And I should just keep going. It's not my fault Sky's slower than me. But I see the flamer go flying out of the girl's hand – and I see where it lands.

I run and pick it up.

Sky's kicking and screaming. The spyder is all over her,

wrapping her up in its legs, squirting sticky stuff all over her, some sort of web.

'Burn it off me!' Sky screams.

I aim the flamer, but there's no way – not without torching her.

'I can't,' I say, helpless.

Even fighting for her life, she manages a glare.

'Do it! I won't – *ugh* – be – taken – alive.'

She's sobbing now, her face livid with effort. I see the terrible pleading in her eyes and know she means it. But I can't kill her, not in cold blood. I drop the flamer, grab a metal leg and pull. I pull so hard I see spots in front of my eyes.

When the leg suddenly gives, I go flying backwards.

I struggle back up, but I'm too slow. The spyder pops some kind of syringe thing out of its head and stings Sky. She screams, then goes limp.

And now I hear shouts behind me.

Next thing, there's this blue-white flash and it's like an angry bull fourhorn has kicked me. I topple forward, but can't move my hands to break my fall. Can't even close my eyes as the ground comes up and smashes into me.

My nose makes a nasty crunching sound.

More pain now. Lots more pain.

I lie there, face down, blood bubbling from my broken nose, in complete muscle-lock. I can breathe, but only barely. I can't even scream. All I can do is watch as the spyder unwraps itself from Sky and drags itself away. Somebody turns me over on to my back. I glimpse the burning barn, a massive column of thick black smoke streaming upwards. A Slayer's helmeted face peers down.

'Do we need this one alive?' she calls out.

Another Slayer steps into view, a disruptor tube clipped under his pulse rifle's barrel. 'You heard what the Commandant said. No killing today.' He slings his weapon, bends for a good look at me. 'Check the girl. I think it stung her.'

The first Slayer heads off.

'She'll live,' she calls, seconds later. 'I gave her anti-sting.'

The second Slayer stands up, looks around and beckons to someone.

'Commandant!' he yells. 'We got them.'

And I want to curl up and die, but have to settle for howling inside my head.

11
IN THE SLAYER WARPLANE

Looking up from flat on my back, Commandant Morana seems impossibly tall. Gone is that figure-hugging dress uniform from the Fair. She's wearing a standard Slayer helmet now, together with matt-black body armour, shoulders and breastplate sculpted into big pretend muscles. I fight to squeeze my eyes shut and make her disappear, but I can't. She crouches over me and slides her visor up. And if I could wince, I would. This close, the woman's face looks even more cruel.

Sky was right, I get that now, with a sick feeling of dread. I should've pulled the trigger when she told me to, then turned the flamer on myself.

'Well,' Morana hisses. 'What have we caught here?'

Her body armour creaks as she bends down, peels a glove off and strokes my cheek, her fingers cold and lingering. Somehow, I manage a groan. She smiles, then does something to my nose so the shattered bits grind together.

The pain is so hot and blinding, I almost pass out.

When I can see again, she's licking blood from her fingers. My blood. She leans in even closer. Her lips brush my ear and I feel her wet breath on me. 'Interesting, isn't it? Your kind heals so much quicker and yet you still feel our pain.'

I say nothing of course, my tongue locked as solid as the rest of me. Anyway, what's there to say?

She rips my ID tag from my neck and stands up.

'You. Unlock him.'

A Slayer hurries forward. He pats me down and takes away Rona's hunting knife, before pressing a small device into my throat. This clicks, then pricks me. Not long after, I can move again. But I just lie there, clutching my nose.

'What do you call yourself?' Morana says, hardly glancing at my tag before pocketing it. She must know it's a fake.

I take too long to answer and her boot slams into my ribs.

'Kyle,' I gasp, covering up.

'That's better,' she says. 'Now tell me, Kyle – who has been sheltering a nasty little twist like you all these years, in defiance of the Saviour's law?'

I shake my head. 'Nobody. I live by myself.'

I've let Rona down once already by not waiting – I won't do it again.

Morana tut-tuts and bares her Saviour-perfect teeth at me.

'Don't lie to me, Kyle. I don't like liars. All lying will get you is more pain.'

At her nod, the Slayer who searched me steps up and swings his boot into me so hard I'm lifted off the ground. I cover up, only to get kicked again, so hard I'm sure he means to kill me. In desperation, I try and crawl away from him, but the other Slayer is waiting for me. She sticks her boot in almost as hard.

They kick me back and forth between them.

'That's enough,' says Morana.

The kicking stops at last. I'm lying there, clutching myself, wondering how many of my bones are broken, when a Slayer officer comes running up and salutes the High Slayer. 'Commandant, the rebel windjammer is secured,' he announces, darting a quick glance down at me. 'And we've heard from Freshwater on the comm. They say they've captured the woman who was hiding this twist.'

Can't help it – I let a sob slip out.

My stomach lurches. I'm torn, glad Rona's still alive, but appalled she's a prisoner too. Morana nods and slowly pulls her glove back on. The Slayer officer shifts his boots, like he's got more to say, but wishes he hadn't.

'What is it?' she snaps.

'Commandant, I told them you want the woman alive for interrogation, but the preacher type – the one who called us in – wants to string her up. Kept raving on and on about some Reaper attack and her having to pay the price.'

Fod! You bastard. You always hated Rona.

For a second, I think the High Slayer will explode.

'Remind him who he's dealing with.'

'I did, Commandant, but the man's mad. Reckons he runs things down there, even started cursing me. We lost contact. They aren't answering now.'

'Deliberate, no doubt,' says Morana. She takes a deep breath, then looks thoughtful. 'A shame, but not the end of Wrath – we have the twist.' She pokes me with her boot. 'We can't wait here though. That smoke is marking our position; we risk being caught on the ground ourselves by another rebel windjammer.'

She glances down at me. 'You lied, Kyle. You'll regret that.'

I cringe from her boot, my head pounding with fear.

'I'm sorry!' My mouth fills with blood and I have to spit it out. 'But it's me who's twisted. I'm the monster. Please, tell them to let my mother go. It's not her fault. She wasn't harbouring me. She just didn't know; neither of us did.'

Morana's lip curls. 'It doesn't work like that.'

Behind me, the barn roof collapses with a thump. Dimly, I hear the crackling as flames leap higher into the sky. A blast of heat rolls over me.

The officer squints up at the sky. 'Commandant, what are your orders?'

'Take a squad,' Morana says. 'Get down there as fast as you can. Seize the woman prisoner, or at least recover her body. Either way, I want to see her. And find the comm unit she used to contact these rebels; that could prove useful. As soon as we're airborne, I'll call for a transport to extract you.'

'And if the Barrenlanders give us trouble?'

Morana shrugs, a vicious smile lurking around her full lips. 'Even if they don't, round them up and kill them. I want nobody left alive. You hear me?'

The officer nods, like it's no big deal, and hurries off.

'You can't do that!' I shout.

'Really?' sneers Morana. She turns to the other Slayers. 'Take both prisoners on board and tell the flight crew to prepare for immediate self-launch.'

Without another word, she walks away, heading towards the cliff edge.

One of the Slayers gestures with his pulse rifle.

'You heard her. On your feet, twist.'

As I lever myself up, I glance at the razor grass. Ten metres, maybe less.

The Slayer grins under his visor. 'Try it. I'll shoot the legs from under you before you're halfway. That'll take some healing, even for you.'

I do my best to glare at him like Sky would, but he doesn't blink.

Another Slayer picks up Sky and pretty much throws her at me. I grunt as I catch her, but there's no great weight to the girl. I give her a hoist and settle her better in my arms. The web stuff is mainly around her arms and legs and isn't sticky now, but has set tight and feels like wire. Her greasy white dreads hang down as her head flops back. She looks really young without her scowl.

'I'm sorry I didn't kill you,' I whisper.

They march us away, past the still-blazing remains of the barn.

Chane's dead. His body is on the grass below his *Rockpolisher*. Even from here, I see the bloody hole ripped in his chest, big enough to put my hand in. The kind of hole a spyder's spiked foot would make.

My Slayer escort jabs me with his rifle. 'Keep moving, or that'll be you.'

I stumble on, sweat streaming down my face, mixing with blood. We're about halfway to the Slayer warplane when Sky stirs in my arms and starts mumbling and groaning. Her dark eyes flicker open. Suddenly, she squirms so hard that I drop her. She can't know what she's doing because she rolls into a big clump of razor grass. By the time I manage to pull her out of it, she's a bloody mess.

'Now who's the idiot?' I say, taking a breather.

My Slayer isn't happy. 'Pick her up. Drop her again, I'll shoot you both.'

I groan. Sky seems out of it again and I struggle to lift her. When that Slayer did it, he made it look easy, but he's a full-grown man. In the end, I only manage it by lifting her up against me, then squatting down and letting her fall and drape herself across my shoulders.

Only to get a hell of a fright!

The Slayers don't see – my body's in their way – but Sky gives my hand several urgent squeezes.

She's not unconscious, she's faking.

I stagger on, breathless with wondering what she's up to.

Behind my back, I feel her working away at something. I hear a snap and her sharp intake of breath, like's she's hurt herself. But whatever she's doing, she doesn't let pain stop her. She slips something into my jacket pocket.

By the time we reach the Slayer warplane she's gone limp again.

This windjammer is much bigger than I thought, twice the size of Sky's *Rockpolisher*, but I don't get time to study it because the Slayers grab me and shove me towards an open hatch, just aft of the stub-wing. I'm made to hand Sky up to more waiting Slayers, then I wait to see what they want me to do.

A Slayer woman steps in front of me.

'Hands together, twist, behind your back.'

I do as she says, wondering how on Wrath she expects me to climb inside the warplane if she ties my hands behind my back. She grins, then smashes the butt of her rifle into my stomach. I double up, retching and gasping for air.

And feel myself lifted up.

By the time I can breathe again I'm lying beside Sky, inside the warplane. Her eyes are open and she's glaring at me.

'Hey, look up!'

I wince into a flash as another Slayer images us.

This done, they drag us towards the rear of the aircraft and what looks like a small cargo area. The Slayer dragging Sky sees that she's conscious now. He hauls her to her feet, slams her against the hull and leers into her face.

'Yeah, we'll have fun with you later, you filthy little scab,' he says.

Sky spits in his face.

He curses, steps back and slaps her. Twice. Hard.

She freaks out and launches herself at him. I hear this sickening *crack* as she headbutts him in the jaw. They both go down, her on top. Sky's got no chance though, her hands and feet still wrapped in spyder web. More Slayers come running. They haul her off him and use the stocks of their rifles to subdue her.

They beat her so bad, I have to look away.

She's hardly moving as they lash her to a pipe that runs along the hull.

'You going to give us trouble too?' a Slayer asks me.

'Nuh-uh. Not me.' I shake my head.

They haul me opposite Sky and force me to my knees. Behind my back, they jam my right arm down behind another pipe then lash my wrists together below it so I'm going nowhere. They almost tear my arms from my shoulders doing this, and make sure to pull the cord so tight that it bites deep into my skin.

One Slayer grunts, as if surprised.

'Hey, look, it's got all its fingers,' he says. He pulls my sleeve up. 'No old Cutting stripes neither. You sure this is the twist we're after?'

'Boss seems sure,' says the other Slayer.

She squats down, yanks my head up and gets right in my face. I groan, not because she's grabbed a fistful of my hair, but because I see my bloody mask of a face reflected in her visor. My nose is bent and swollen and cut across the top. Fresh blood streams like thick red snot from my nostrils and down my chin.

I'm so messed up, I hardly recognise myself.

'How come you still got all your fingers, twist?' she asks.

'Good question,' I say.

I don't know why — it just comes out. Maybe Sky is watching and I want to let her know I can act tough too.

Only that's all it is — an act. Inside, I'm sick with fear.

12
HATCH CLOSED AND LOCKED

Slayer woman smiles at her mates. 'How about we cut it and make sure?'

'Leave it be,' growls a Slayer officer. He elbows her out of his way, leans in and checks I'm properly tied. 'Okay, let's move out. Commandant wants us ready for launch as soon as possible. You –' he nods at a Slayer trooper, 'stay behind on guard, the rest of you give me a hand with these bottles.'

They leave me alone. I take a deep, shuddering breath.

We've got a saying in the Barrens – *If you ain't dead, you're still alive.*

The Slayers go forward and manhandle two large cylinders out of the loading hatch we came in through. Our guard sits in a jump seat beside the hatch, pulse rifle across his lap. He glances our way, but seems more interested in rolling a smoke and watching whatever's going on outside. A few metres past him an opening in the bulkhead leads to another compartment. Beyond this bright dayshine streams in through the canopy over the warplane's flight deck.

The last dayshine I'll ever see?

My backpack is on the deck near the guard's feet. Inside is that rusty old gun Rona gave me. I never even got a chance to fire it, see if it works.

Opposite me, Sky wheezes and coughs out a big gob of blood. She grits her teeth and slowly raises her head to look at me. I suck my teeth, seeing how beaten up she looks. Her thin face is all lumpy, covered in red blotches and flecked with blood. Her left eye is bloodshot and half closed, her lower lip torn.

'Next time I tell you to kill me,' she mumbles, 'do it!'

She winces and coughs up more blood. Our guard laughs. And even though I'm scared, I can't stomach this.

'Can't you see she's hurt? She needs help.'

The Slayer stands up. 'Shut up, twist. Don't make me come back there.'

'Leave it,' hisses Sky.

I bite my lip, stare at the deck plates until he sits down again. When I look up, I see Sky staring at me. She looks so mad at me, I'm almost glad she's tied up.

'This is all your fraggin' fault,' she whispers.

I flinch, but say nothing. What can I say? She's right.

I hang my head. The only sound now is banging and clattering from work going on outside the warplane. My broken nose throbs like crazy. My heart mad-thumps inside me. Guilt corners me and gives me a real kicking.

If only I hadn't defied Rona to go to the Fair.

If only I hadn't selfishly risked everything to say goodbye to Jude.

If only I'd let Chane launch when he'd wanted to.

Alone. That's how I feel right now. More alone than I've ever been before.

'Did you see what happened to Chane?' whispers Sky. 'Is he –'

She swallows, tries again, but all she manages is a choking sound.

I glance at our Slayer guard, but he's not watching. With all the noise outside, if we keep our voices down, he shouldn't hear us.

'He's dead, Sky. I'm sorry. One of those spyder things got him.'

I tell her then about Morana's orders – how everybody I know is to die. And I feel so awful that I clutch at a sudden wild idea. Maybe this is only another of my nightmares. I'll wake up in my bed soon and Rona will kill herself laughing when I tell her about it. I squeeze my eyes tight shut.

But when I open them again – I'm still here.

There's shouting outside and our guard jumps to his feet. The Slayer officer clambers inside, closely followed by his troopers. They clatter into the forward compartment and start strapping into jump seats. Commandant Morana pulls herself aboard last, lithe as a cat. She glances at us, then heads all the way forward to the flight deck. The guard bangs the hatch shut and swings a lever.

'Hatch closed and locked!' He racks his rifle, and straps himself in too.

'Hey, what's going on?' I whisper to Sky.

'What's it look like?'

I must have a face full of puzzled because she scowls.

'They're going to launch.'

I twitch. 'How? They blew the winch up.'

'Slayer warplanes don't *need* a winch.' Sky tosses her head, sending her dreads flying, and peers towards the flight deck. 'You saw those big tubes they hauled outside? Light-and-fly, that's what we call them. Rocket-assisted take-off.'

I look too and see the pilot flick a switch.

Whump! Whump!

Along the roof of the hull, the feeble glowstrips flicker.

My knees tingle as the lift-cells start spinning up. These Slayer units clearly have way more grunt than the *Rockpolisher*'s tired old lifters. Everything starts rattling and vibrating. The thrumming rises to a loud whine then rises again to a high-pitched whistle. And I feel this weird lightness, as gravity lets go.

A warning klaxon howls.

'Brace yourself, Kyle!' Sky shouts. 'This'll —'

The rockets fire with a deafening roar. Outside, through a small and badly scratched plastic panel, I see billowing smoke. Solid-looking flame spears and crackles past. Even through the hull, I feel the blistering heat. The warplane accelerates forward violently and I'm thrown sideways, my tied arms almost wrenched out of their sockets. Everything goes blurry and confused, but I think I see the floor tilt up as we're hurled skywards. Suddenly, it's like a dozen men sit on my chest. Each breath is a battle. I cry out, but even I can't hear me. The roaring and shaking goes on and on and on. Then just when I think I can't stand it any more, the rockets quit firing. Everything goes relatively quiet and smooth again.

Wind whistles past outside and I feel light again.

I strain towards the plastic panel and peer through it. No grass. No ground either. Smoke whips past from the dead rockets. Lots of blue sky.

We're flying. Flying!

The pilot rolls us hard right and I see we're not high, maybe only a hundred metres above the plateau. The abandoned *Rockpolisher* flashes past below us and I glimpse Chane's body still stretched beside it. I cry out then as the warplane suddenly pitches into a steep dive. Without the slightest hesitation, our pilot dives us straight off the plateau's cliff edge, pulls up into a swooping left turn, then levels out a few metres below the top. And even a grubber like me can tell we're soaring now. It's like I feel this giant kick in the seat of my pants. We shoot upwards and the cliff seems to fall away below us. Some instrument in the cockpit starts bleeping like mad. Metal creaks and complains. We turn steeply, away from the cliff, and hang in the lift. Then back the other way. Turn and climb, climb and turn.

I have to close my eyes. Either that or puke my guts into my lap.

'You can look now,' sneers Sky, a long time later.

It's okay for her, she's used to windjamming.

But when I do open my eyes, I see we're proper high now, flying straight and level. This I reckon I can handle. We're leaving the plateau behind. Already it looks so small I struggle to pick it out. Jagged mountains, deep valleys with rivers twisting through them, all are laid out beneath us like a tri-D chart.

Who'd have thought the Barrenlands could look so beautiful?

But that's not what rips my breath away. The steep launch has slid my rucksack nearly the whole length of the compartment back towards me. It's wedged under a jump seat. If only my hands were free, I'm sure I could reach it before the guard could stop me. I give my wrists a hopeful tug, but the Slayer who tied me knew what he was doing and the pipe feels like it's solidly attached.

And now I remember: Sky put something in my pocket.

A quick look at our guard. Good. He's busy lighting another smoke.

I squirm around until I can get my fingers under the flap of my pocket and inside. *Frag!* Something viciously sharp slices into my fingertip. I curse, grit my teeth and reach in again, more careful this time. My trembling fingers close on something small. Not a knife, but nearly as good as. Razor grass.

When I look up, Sky is staring at me again.

It's not much, a blink-and-you-miss-it twitch of her lips, but she smiles.

13
CUTTING LOOSE

Prime. Like most Barrenlanders, I've only heard of it, never been there. All Rona would tell me was it was 'a long way away, but not nearly far enough'. It's the original landing site, from when Wrath became a dump world. Sky reckons that's where they're taking us because the Slayers have their headquarters and stronghold there. Inside the fortress, the Saviour lives in his palace, built — so the wordweavers love to tell us — from the hulls of the dropships that dumped us here, its glittering metal walls polished daily to a mirror shine by his conquered enemies.

I don't know about that, but Prime's also supposed to be where the biggest shanty town on Wrath is, a vast human swamp called the Blight.

Once we reach Prime, Sky says, there's no escape.

That's why, in whispers, we've come up with a plan. Well, *she* has. Sky reckons it's better to die fighting now than screaming later in some dark room. She says we should cut ourselves loose and make a break for it when we land for the night. Only problem is, cutting ourselves loose is taking forever. We're tied with some synthetic cord, which feels like rope, but is harder than steel. And the whole time we're sawing away we have to pretend like we're slumped here, hopeless and doing nothing, so the guard doesn't see. Several times I nearly drop the razor grass. Several more times I almost give up, sure I'm wasting my time. I've sliced myself so often I've lost count and now my fingers are cramping up.

I don't mean to groan out loud, but I do.

'What?' says Sky. Her pale face is slick and shiny with sweat.

I shake my head. 'This is hopeless.'

'Hopeless?' says Sky, looking disgusted. 'Hope is for losers, for people who are soft in the head. Don't waste time hoping, just keep cutting.'

I stare at her. 'But if you haven't got hope you've got nothing.'

'Who says?' she sneers.

Rona says. But there's no way I'm telling Sky that.

'So what do *you* believe in?'

Sky tosses her head. 'Hate. Revenge.'

'No talking back there,' growls our Slayer guard.

No problem, boss. Suits me.

While I'm sawing away, my mind wanders. I find myself thinking about Sky. What must life have been like for her, born an ident and ending up a scab? Her little finger hacked off at birth. Her parents forced to hand her over almost as soon as she could walk. Growing up in the camps, all the time wondering is it me who's twisted or my sister? Who'll die, who'll be spared? And then, each year, the ordeal of Cutting and Unwrapping. Until one day it turns out she's the scab and gets her life back. Only first she has to watch as her twin sister is hung by the neck.

It must be like watching yourself die. How sick is that?

No wonder Sky believes in hate and revenge.

See even scabs aren't spared, not really. Hardly any families take them back. The disgrace is too great and nobody trusts them. The few scabs I've come across were always the lowest of the low, good for nothing but the worst jobs. Most end up slaving in the Blight. Some, so they say, go run with Reapers.

I take a break and stare at Sky's white dreads, thinking how I'm sure some of the Reapers who hit us by the river wore their hair that same ropey way.

'How'd a scab like you end up as jammer crew?' I whisper.

Sky doesn't answer, just scowls.

Okay, so maybe I could have put that better . . .

For the hundredth time, I gauge the distance to my pack. To the gun. I haven't told Sky about the gun yet. I still wonder if the thing's capable of firing its last three bullets. But it might be, and it's the only weapon we've got.

'Keep sawing,' Sky hisses, making me jump.

'Tell you what — I'll saw through my wrist. It'll be quicker.'

She glares. 'It might come to that.'

I look at her, not sure if she's being serious. 'How long have we got?'

'Three hours, maybe four. I can't be sure.'

I peer outside through the scratched plastic panel. A tree-covered ridge slides past below the warplane's wing. Jagged, snow-swept peaks rear up in the background, but don't look familiar. Have we left the Barrens already? The sun is well below its highest. We've been in the air two hours at least.

'You're sure we'll land before Prime?'

'Yes. Like I said already.'

'Tell me again.'

Sky curses under her breath. This needing me kills her, I can tell.

'For the last time,' she whispers, her teeth gritted, 'it's eighteen hundred klicks to Prime. We did it in three days once, but this thing's got better glide speed than our old *Rockpolisher*, so let's say two more days of ridge-running. *If* this westerly keeps blowing and *if* we don't hit bad weather. It *could* take longer.'

Eighteen hundred klicks!

I didn't think Wrath's moons were that far away . . .

'There's a trader way station,' she continues, 'on the border of the southern Barrenlands. Tranquility Junction. It's a busy one because three windjammer ridge routes meet there. I reckon we'll be stopping the night there.'

She looks me in the eye, licks her torn lip. 'You'd better be ready.'

'I'll be ready all right,' I say. 'Will *you*?'

Sky bends her head slowly left and then right, like she's stretching kinks out of it. If she had a tail, I reckon it would be lashing now.

'I was born ready,' she says.

I'm pulling my wrists apart, straining to open up my cut in the rope, when it suddenly parts and I can't help doing this great big stupid twitch. Out of the corner of my eye I see our guard looking. I freeze, look down, hoping he can't see how badly I'm shaking. He goes back to cleaning his rifle and I breathe again.

Sky screws her face up into a *what* are *you doing?* look.

'I'm loose,' I whisper, licking my dry lips.

'Well, don't go waving your arms about,' she whispers back, glaring as usual. No 'well done' or anything, but then what did I expect?

Behind my back, I flex my cramped fingers, trying to get the blood flowing again. It's agony. But imagining my fingers round Sky's neck helps.

'So how are *you* doing?' I ask her.

Her turn to twitch now. She gives me this slow head-shake and glances down. In the half-light back here, I see the sliver of razor grass lying on the deck by her legs in a puddle of blood. She's dropped it and it's out of her reach.

Sky meets my stare and shrugs. 'It's down to you then.'

Not long now until we land. It's getting gloomy outside as the sun sinks lower or the mountains get higher, but Sky says she knows where we are now. This Tranquility place, she reckons, is only a dive away into the next valley upwind. That's why our pilot is beating back and forth along this ridge, slowly working us up high enough so we can safely clear the high ground in the way.

The air's getting colder or I'm more scared – I can't stop shaking.

It's murder holding on to this pipe, pretending I'm still tied to it. I can't feel my arms, I've been in this position so long. My nose has started itching too, and not being able to scratch it is hell. Worst thing is, I'm busting. I need a piss so bad the small of my back's hurting. You don't get that in the wordweavers' tells, the hero wetting himself, but I will if we don't land soon.

'Watch out!' hisses Sky.

I hear them too. Bootsteps entering our compartment.

It's the High Slayer Morana woman, ducking through the open hatch in the bulkhead between us and the flight deck. I feel even colder now. Our guard jumps up, but she waves at him to stay put and makes her way back to us.

'Kyle,' she says. She rolls my name round her mouth, stretching it out, as if she's tasting it. 'Are you behaving yourself back there?'

I study the grid pattern of the metal deck and say nothing. My heart starts thumping so hard it hurts. I hear her boots coming closer, the creak of her body armour as she squats down before me. Her breath ruffles my hair.

'Look at me when I'm talking to you.'

I look up, but only as far as her chin. No way am I looking that woman in the eye. Somehow I know if I did, she'd be able to tell I'm untied. She smiles, reaches out and caresses my battered face again, brushing my cheek and my nose.

I jerk backwards, away from her, and bang my head.

'Leave him alone, bitch!' shouts Sky.

Morana ignores her. She takes my chin, forces my face up to the light and peers at me. 'Incredible really. Mere hours since you broke your nose, but already I sense that you don't feel much pain. Perhaps some itching, am I right?'

She flicks my itchy nose. Painful, but not agony.

I shrug. The way she's squinting, I reckon her seeing's not so good.

'That's not *normal*, is it, Kyle?' she says.

Can't help it – I shake my head.

She sighs. 'A symptom of the evil twisting inside you. I hear you were at Deep Six's Fair, so you will have seen our captive twist. Not the most pleasant fate, I'm sure you'll agree. However, if you tell us who your contacts are –'

Behind her back, Sky shakes her head at me. 'Don't tell her anything.'

I come close to crying then, I feel so sorry for myself.

The Morana woman leans even closer. 'Don't listen to the scab, listen to *me*. Tell us what we want to know, Kyle, and we'll help you. We can cure you.'

My breath whooshes out of me. 'There's a cure?'

'Cure him?' jeers Sky. 'How? By hanging him, like you hung my sister?'

Morana laughs, a dry rattle full of malice. 'Your scab girlfriend, she's quite the fierce young warrior isn't she, Kyle?' She reaches up and fusses with my hair, as if tidying it. 'Awful manners, however, but we have cures for that too.' Without warning, her fingers tighten in my hair and she slams my head into the hull.

I glare at Sky as warm blood trickles down the back of my neck.

If she's sorry she doesn't show it. All I get is scowled at.

'You know what *I'm* wondering?' says Morana. She waits until I shake my head. 'I'm wondering why your rebel friends would scramble a windjammer all the way out here to the Barrenlands just to rescue a hideout twist like you.'

'I don't know,' I say quickly, not wanting to have my head slammed again.

She stares at me some more. Then, to my relief and surprise, her fingers let go their grip on my hair and suddenly the woman is all smiles again.

'Let's start again,' she says. 'Shall we, Kyle?'

I watch, confused, wondering, as she produces a cloth and wets it from a water bottle. She leans in and starts swabbing the encrusted blood off my face. Not roughly like I expect, but gently, as if she's trying not to hurt me. 'Isn't that better?'

Behind her back, Sky frowns a big warning look at me.

When she's done with cleaning up my face, Morana sits back on her haunches and peers at me again. 'There now. You look much –'

She gives a big start and then frowns, almost as if she *knows* me.

I didn't think I could be any more scared, but I am now.

So scared, I can't help glancing past her at my pack, to check it's still wedged under the jump-seat. It is. But Morana's no fool and sees me looking.

'That your bag, is it?' she says, getting up.

I watch in horror as she fishes the pack out and starts rooting through it.

The old gun. Our last hope. Maybe our *only* hope.

With a roar, I throw myself at the High Slayer, knocking her down and grabbing the pack. Thrusting my hand inside, I feel frantically for the pistol. But even as my fingers close on it, Morana starts yelling and hauling me back towards her. I jackknife around, smash the gun into her face until she lets go.

'Kyle!' Sky screams. 'Look out!'

The Slayers in the forward compartment are unstrapping. The guard by the hatch is pointing his rifle at me, but doesn't shoot, maybe afraid of hitting Morana. I take quick aim at him, but as I pull the trigger, she claws at my arm.

There's an ear-splitting bang and the pistol slams back hard into my hand.

I shoot the deck though, not the man.

Sparks fly. Lights flicker off, come back on red.

The warplane lurches viciously left, sending everybody flying.

Morana lets go, or is torn off me.

From the flight deck, I hear alarms and lots of shouting.

'LIFT-CELL FAILURE,' chants a robot voice.

And now I smell smoke. A moment later, I see it, thick and grey and ugly, crawling up out of the slots in the deck gratings. *Oh, what have I done?*

Outside, through the plastic panel, I glimpse rocks rushing up towards us.

14
CRASH

The crash seems to go on and on and on forever. An enormous impact, the warplane slamming down, skidding, bouncing up again, cartwheeling madly. Me being thrown about, bouncing off things. Seeing the hull tear open in front of my eyes. An avalanche of dirt and stones lashing at me. The noise is insane – a terrible screeching as metal twists and tears apart, so loud it's like someone is hacksawing into my skull. Then a very hard stop as we smash into something.

I feel myself go flying through the air.

Maybe I'm knocked out because everything goes pitch-black for a while. When I can see again, I'm lying on my back on the ceiling. Except that the ceiling is now the floor.

Nothing moves except for some dangling cables. These flick about, showering me with sparks, crackling and spitting like they're angry. A chill wind moans its way inside through holes torn in the hull. Hot metal ticks as it cools. It looks like a bomb's gone off in here. Buckled deck plates hang down from the upside-down floor, showing the warplane's ribs. Lockers have burst open, spilling their contents. Our Slayer guard lies face down in a pool of spreading blood. Lying curled up around me, like Jude used to, is a female Slayer. Stone dead, her neck broken, maybe by me landing on her. I lash out and shove her awful stillness away.

I sit up, shake the dizzy out of my head and peer around.

A flock of mountain bluebirds wheel past outside, hooting loudly, startled from their roosting by our crash. That's when I realise most of the forward half of the warplane has been torn off beyond the bulkhead and is lying further down the rocky slope we've crashed on. It looks way more crushed than our tail section. Back here, one Slayer hangs upside down, still strapped into his jump seat. Three others lie scattered about. One looks dead, but the others are stirring.

That's when I realise I've dropped the gun.

I'm scrabbling about, desperately looking for it, when I hear cursing. It's Sky, still tied and webbed, but thrashing about trying to free herself. Blood streams down her face from a cut on her forehead. 'Help me!' she yells.

Every nerve in my body screams run and leave her, but I can't.

I find a shard of hard plastic, scramble over to Sky and saw at the rope binding her. Nothing doing – I'm hardly scratching the stuff. I could scream with frustration. This will take ages, time we haven't got! I glance around and see one of the injured Slayers pulling himself up on to his hands and knees.

'No use,' groans Sky. 'Save yourself. Run.'

But now I realise what a gom I'm being. I hurl the useless plastic away, scramble over to the dead guard and drag his pulse rifle out from where it's pinned beneath him. When I squeeze the bloody grip it powers straight up. With a sob of relief, I fight my way back to Sky.

'Are you mad?' she says, staring.

For once I'm way ahead of her. I fire up the plasma lance under the rifle's barrel and its golden blade shimmers into life. 'Hold still!' I tell her. I slash her hands and feet loose from the spyder stuff, then move on to the rope.

Only for her to gasp and stare behind me.

I spin round, to see the High Slayer burst upwards from where she's been buried beneath a tangled mess of seat foam, cables and other rubbish. How my heart doesn't stop beating then I'll never know. She lurches to her feet, her face a blood-streaked mask from where I smacked her with Rona's gun. With a howl of rage, she staggers towards us, her long arms outstretched.

Stops dead though as I raise the rifle.

I'm shaking so bad, the gunsight leaps around all over her chest.

We stare at each other for what feels like forever.

'Waste the bitch!' Sky shouts.

The pulse rifle's trigger presses into my fingertip. Tempting me.

Morana's lip curls. 'What? Too scared?'

'I'm *not* evil,' I shout.

But she just turns away, her cloak swirling behind her. The hatch has torn open in the crash. She clambers over to it and drops down outside.

All I do is watch her go, helpless.

'Idiot!' Sky snaps.

She grabs the rifle, nearly slicing my head off with the live blade. Elbowing me out of her way, she goes after Morana. I watch as she peeks outside, only to pull her head back in fast as a blaster shot whacks the hull real close. She leans out again and snaps a few shots off in return, but curses so I figure she's missed.

'Don't stand there gawping,' she yells. 'Let's go!'

'Wait!' I see my backpack half buried under some debris near me. I throw myself at it with a big 'Yes!' and haul it clear. Meanwhile, the Slayer who's made it to his knees fumbles a handgun from its holster. Sky sees him, lunges forward and sticks him. He gives this rattling groan, clutches at the smoking bayonet, then topples backwards. Sky grunts, pulls the blade free and moves on.

She guts the Slayer still trapped in his seat.

'Stop! You don't need to do that,' I shout at her, sickened.

But she won't be stopped. She sticks the remaining Slayers before powering the blade down. 'Better dead than coming after us,' she says, scowling.

She finds my old slug-thrower and chucks it to me.

There's a breathless moment then. We stand there, glaring at each other amid all the wreckage and the carnage. It's bitterly cold and Sky's quick breaths shoot out as little explosions of mist. I blink first, so she leads.

'Stay close,' she tells me. 'And keep your gommer head down.'

I follow her as she shuffles through what's left of the forward compartment. We crouch in the jagged shadows where the hull has torn apart. She gives me this urgent look and points. I grit my teeth and nod. There's a tree-choked gully not too far away; reach that and we should be able to creep away from the crash site without being seen. She sketches some sign in the air, jumps down and starts running. I throw myself after her, pack in one hand, gun in the other.

Running for my life – it's what I do now!

We're seen. I hear shouts. I don't know if it's Morana, or Slayer survivors in the forward part of the wreck, but I see green flashes and hear the dull thumps as someone opens fire on us. Dirt geysers up to my right.

Sky cries out and goes down.

I stuff my pistol into a pocket, haul her back to her feet. 'Are you hit?'

She shakes her head, but she's limping much worse now.

More shots buzz overhead, ripping the air apart, and we both duck. Ahead of us is a waist-high clump of ferns. I scramble across the rocks, staying as low as I can, and dive full-length into their cover. A second later, Sky lands on top of me, crushing my face into the soil. She doesn't wait to see if I'm hurt, just clambers over me, all sharp elbows and sharper knees.

I curse, roll over and risk a peek back.

Crap! Slayers heading our way. Four, counting Morana.

I'm about to shout out when Sky comes crawling back. She shoves me aside, kneels up, takes careful aim and fires. One Slayer falls, the rest scatter.

'That'll slow them down,' she says, grinning.

Then she's off again, crawling so quickly through the ferns I can hardly keep up with her, even though she's carrying the heavy pulse rifle. We slip and slide down into the dark gully. And here, finally, we catch a break. What's left of the river that carved this rocky channel is still dribbling away at the bottom. The water's freezing, only deep enough to cover my boots, but it offers us a way through dense brush which would otherwise be impossible. It'll hide our tracks too.

We wade in and splash off into the gloom.

The gully plunges deeper as we descend, until granite walls tower high above us, leaning in and choking off the last of the dayshine. It's so dark down here at the narrow bottom that we have to feel our way. It gets steeper too. Not long after we're climbing down the bank, not walking but clinging on to tree trunks and lowering ourselves down hand over hand. The water is white and fast-moving now, hissing treacherously past. Sky slips and accidentally kicks some rocks loose.

They sound like they fall a long way.

I'm thinking we've screwed up big time, until I see twilight ahead. We scramble round a pillar of rock and the gorge suddenly opens out on to the top of a much gentler slope. In the gathering dusk, I see rushing water tumble down a low waterfall and disappear underground into a misty chasm. Way below us, details vague in the darkness, is a barren-looking valley.

'Oh great,' pants Sky. 'What do we do now?'

I wince up at the purple sky, the first few stars winking, and try to think. All that's left of the sun is a crimson glow picking out jagged peaks to the east. The dogmoon is up already, but it's only a crescent and won't give us much light. Even here, still tucked half inside the gully's shelter, the cold and bitter wind which brought us here whines about our heads. With no clouds, it'll get colder. Much colder.

'Wait here,' I tell her.

I scramble back up the gully until I can't hear the waterfall. I listen then, hard as I can, mouth open, heart pounding. Nothing, no sounds of any Slayers coming after us, only the gurgle and splash of the tumbling stream. I tear at my trousers and finally empty my tortured bladder, pissing into the stream to leave no trace. I'm buttoning up, swaying with relief, when I hear the scratching sound. I look up. Dark shapes flit from rock to rock high above me, impossibly sure-footed.

Oh crap! That's all we need . . .

I scramble back down fast, to find Sky leaning over with her hands on her knees, as if she's going to be sick. In the gloom, her face seems even grimmer than usual as she looks up.

'What's the rush?' she says. 'We got company?'

'Yeah, you could say that.'

On cue, somewhere above us, a dreadful screech tears the darkness apart.

'What on Wrath is *that*?' says Sky. Even she sounds scared.

'Nightrunners. We need to find shelter. And fast.'

'Why?' she says, brandishing the pulse rifle at me. 'We've got this.'

'You ever seen a nightrunner?'

She shrugs. 'No.'

I grit my teeth at her. 'Well take it from me then, shooting them only makes them angry. These things are half the size of a fourhorn, a hundred times as nasty and they hunt in packs. And they're not fussy; they'd even eat *you*.' I peer down the slope and see some stubby, wind-bent trees that look familiar. Longthorns? Hard to be sure it's so dark now, but I remember an old trader once telling Rona a story about them. If they are longthorns, we might still have a chance.

'Come on!' I grab Sky's arm to get her moving.

Bad move. She lashes out. I lose my footing and fall, taking her with me. We both go crashing down, slipping and sliding down the moss-slick rocks beside the waterfall. We're damn lucky not to end up in the underground river. Next thing I know, I'm flat on my back on soft earth. Winded, but otherwise unhurt. Gingerly, I pick myself up and go to where Sky lies in a heap. I'm so mad, I'm tempted to kick her, but I'll save that for later. There's no time now. 'Are you okay?'

She curses and it takes her a hell of a long time to get up.

'My leg,' she groans, her chest heaving. 'It's broken.'

Horrified, I take a quick look back at the cliffs either side of the split in the rock we came down. They're alive now with the scurrying of black shapes. Closer behind us, another screeching howl lifts into the darkness.

'Can you still walk?' I say, anxiously.

'Just about. But no thanks to you, you gommer,' she says, unslinging her pulse rifle.

15
HEALING AND DEALING

We make it down to the trees, me helping Sky to lurch along. And they *are* longthorns, I see that now, the cruel, finger-length barbs sticking out and glinting in the dim moonglow. Relieved, I drop my pack and feel for the shiner I know is in one of the side pockets. I fumble it out and dial it for red light.

'You'll give our position away!' says Sky.

'Tough. I need to see what I'm doing. Hand me the rifle.'

She backs into me, almost pushing me into the thorns. 'I don't think so.'

I glance back over my shoulder and wish I hadn't. The nightrunner pack is coming after us. Dozens of dark shapes slink down the hillside towards us on their bellies. Their luminous eyes reflect the glow of the shiner.

'The bayonet,' I say. 'Quick! I've got an idea.'

Sky unclips it from under the rifle's barrel and passes it to me.

'Better be a good one,' she says, cool as you like.

I grit my teeth, power up the blade and get to work. Hastily, I slash a small arch into the longthorn's foliage near the ground. Then I hold my breath and, before I can think too hard about it, drive my arm into the smoking cut. Countless thorns rip through my parka sleeve like it isn't there, tearing into my skin. I can't help crying out, the pain's so fierce, but being eaten alive will hurt more. I turn the blade sideways and start slashing. Six more times I have to do this before I can pull a solid plug of thorns out and the blade lights up the longthorn's hollow inside.

Sky elbows me. 'You about done there?'

I look where her rifle is pointing. The shaggy bulk of a nightrunner crouches just beyond the spill of shiner light, jaws gaping at us. Others watch from close behind it.

'Sky, get inside!'

For once, she doesn't argue. She slips past me, grabs my backpack and wriggles into the hole. The nightrunner lunges, but backs off fast when I yell and wave the shimmering plasma blade in its face. 'Don't like that, huh?'

Only for the blade to flicker and fade away.

I stare in disbelief and waste precious seconds thumbing the power switch.

Nothing doing. Dead.

Like me, if I stay out here any longer.

I hurl the useless thing at the nightrunner's head. This distracts it long enough for me to toss the shiner into the tunnel and follow it feet first. I'm reaching back for the plug, to block the hole, when the creature pounces and rips it from my grasp. I squirm frantically backwards, deeper inside the longthorn. The nightrunner thrusts its wrinkled black snout in after me, but its body is too big to follow. Drool-covered fangs snap at my face. I cry out, sure I'm done for, but suddenly Sky is there and jams the pulse rifle's muzzle past the fangs, right into the creature's gob. She pulls the trigger; there's a flash and a bang. Fur and flesh and brain go flying.

The thing doesn't die, but at least it backs off.

'Thanks,' I gasp, as we both wriggle away from the hole.

Outside, I hear a sudden orgy of snarling and growling and slobbering.

'What's happening?' says Sky, scrunching her face up.

'Sounds like its mates are eating it.'

I grab the shiner and hold it up. In the dim red light I see it's like a cave inside here, the longthorn's trunk a twisted pillar of heartwood in the middle. Overhead, not quite high enough for me to stand up, branches stick out and drape down to the ground on all sides, weaving together to form a solid-looking wall.

No thorns inside, like the old trader man said.

I scramble to put the trunk between me and the creatures outside. Sky's braver. She plants her back against the trunk and covers the tunnel with her rifle.

'Think they're all too big?' she says.

Heart pounding, I stare at the hole. 'We'll soon know.'

Even as I say this, another huge nightrunner tries to smash its way inside. It gets its head in and thrashes about, snapping at us and scaring the crap out of me. The savage longthorns do their job though, and it howls and backs out. This happens three more times before they seem to give up. Only now I hear snuffling.

'Trying to find another way in,' I tell Sky.

She winces. 'Relentless little gommers, ain't they?'

I pull the pistol from my pocket and cast the shiner around, heart in my mouth, looking for any gaps in the tree's defences, but there's nothing obvious.

Not too long afterwards, everything goes quiet.

'Maybe they've gone?' Sky mutters.

I shake my head, creep towards the hole and toss a stick outside. Soon as it hits the ground it's pounced on. I scramble back, away from all the growling and snarling outside, and pull a face at Sky. 'Uh, no. Didn't think so.'

She groans, clutching her leg. 'So we're stuck here?'

I shrug. 'They'll clear off when it gets light. And there's one good thing – while they're out there, we won't have to worry about Slayers coming after us.'

Even inside this shelter it's cold to the bone. To warm us I get a small fire going. There's plenty of dead wood lying about. I make tinder from some worm-eaten bits and show Sky the hunter trick of shorting the pulse-rifle magazine into it to spark it to life. The fire's smoky as hell, but cheers us up.

It might keep the nightrunners out too.

We share some trail mix from my pack and half the water.

Now I have to do something about the thorns still stuck in me, which are driving me mad. Some are so deep I have to dig them out with my teeth. They're barbed too and each takes a chunk of flesh with it. I moan and curse until I find a small medbag Rona packed for me and smear green painsucker mix over the wounds, which helps. I'm pulling my shredded parka back on when I happen to look round. Sky's watching me . . . waist-deep in my sleep bag.

'Hey, no way,' I say. 'That's *my* bag.'

Her leathers lie beside her on the ground. In the flickering firelight I see her stick-thin arms, blotchy and red from the beating she took, a sweat-stained undershirt that might've been white once, and some weird charm thing hanging on a cord around her neck. On her left forearm I see the stripes of old scars.

Three cuts from three Peace Fairs, I guess.

'Don't panic,' she says, sneering. 'You can have your smelly bag back if you fix my leg. I'm just trying to stay warm.'

'Look, I'm sorry,' I say. 'I'm no healer. I fix mech stuff.'

What I don't say is: *If your leg's really broke, then you're dead already.*

She sighs and points with the rifle.

And now I see her leg lying between us in the leaf-strewn dirt.

I make a stupid kind of sputtering sound as a whole bunch of questions all come tumbling out of my mouth at the same time and trip over themselves.

First the glove, now this. Is any of her for real?

'I don't think there's too much wrong with it,' says Sky. 'A short maybe.'

Wrong. Everything's wrong. And I'm sick of surprises.

I look more closely and see what it is now: a powered brace that clamps over her real leg and strengthens it. At a guess, it's been put together from some scavved and stripped lightweight bot legs. Clever. Slick bit of welding too.

'Where'd you get this from?'

'Can you fix it?'

I dial the shiner brighter and study it. 'Maybe.'

Sky scowls. 'Thought you said you fixed mech stuff?'

I scowl back at her. 'And I do. But I use tools. You see any tools here?'

Neither of us says anything for a long while after that.

Outside, in the distance, something chatters then screeches. Hunter or hunted, I can't tell. I shiver and throw more wood on the fire. Sparks fly up. They dart about like my thoughts, only my thoughts are darker. Like, is Rona still alive or did that scumbag Fod string her up before the Slayers got down there to stop him? And if there's a cure for twists, like that Morana woman said, why do they hang them at the Peace Fair? More questions to add to all the rest. I give myself a shake, tell myself I've got more immediate things to worry about, like what the hell do we do now? We got lucky, but come morning, any Slayers left alive will be after us again.

I look up from my swirling thoughts, wondering what Sky knows.

'So you're some sort of rebel then?' I ask her.

Sky doesn't say anything, but she pulls up the sleeve of her undershirt and shows me her shoulder. Her P-for-pureblood scab brand is still there, but tattooed over with a black handprint, the little finger done in red. It figures. The symbol of Gemini, the ident resistance movement. I've only seen it once before, sun-bleached and faded on the door of an old barn when I was little and we were on one of our moves. Rona wouldn't tell me what it was, but somebody else must have.

'I thought that was all over years ago,' I say. 'I heard —'

'Heard what?' she interrupts. 'That Gemini is nothing more than a bunch of wrinkly old twist survivors from the war, clinging on in the mountains and occasionally making trouble?' She shakes her head, sending her dreads flying. 'Not any more. We're stronger, united and organised now. And guess what — we're not just idents. Loads of non-ident purebloods have joined us. Won't be long before we're ready to take on the Saviour and his Slayer thugs and smash them!'

She's almost shouting. I wave at her to shut up.

'Okay, okay,' I say. 'So you're Gemini. But why help me?'

Sky snorts, but at least she keeps her voice down now. 'We're always looking to help idents who've escaped from camps, or the occasional nublood hideout like you, who's been found out. It's just part of what Gemini does, that's all.'

'*Nublood?*'

She winces and dabs at her split lip.

'What you are. Slayers call you a twist; we call you nublood.'

Nublood then, not twisted blood. Great. Whatever.

'That Morana woman,' I say. 'She seemed surprised that you came to get me.'

Sky shrugs. 'We got Rona's call and we were close by.'

My head is banging, but I see the hesitation before her it-was-no-big-deal shrug. She's hiding something, I'm sure of it. Outside I hear the distant *rat-a-tat* of a rockpecker. It's as if the noise hammers free the suspicion inside me.

'My mum, is she Gemini too?'

Sky rolls her eyes. 'No idea. She didn't tell you?'

'If she did, I wouldn't be asking you.'

I look away. So many things Rona didn't tell me. So many secrets.

Another long and awkward silence stretches out between us, with just the hissing and crackling of the fire to listen to, until I happen to look up from the dirt and catch Sky pawing at her battered mouth again.

'Want me to take a look at that?'

She shakes her head. 'I'll live. What about fixing my leg brace?'

I glance at it, still lying there. 'Later. Listen, Sky, I'm no healer like Rona, but I could clean that cut up and take the pain away. The last thing we need now is it getting infected and you coming down with a blood-fever.'

She glares at me, but says nothing.

I get up, tear a rag from my undershirt and wet it.

Soon as I go near her face with it however, she snatches it off me. But at least she uses it to do the cleaning herself. And thorough too, which must hurt.

Lesson learnt. I open the painsucker jar and hold it out.

'Stick it on and it's goodbye pain. Your left eye could maybe use some too.'

She sniffs the green paste and looks uncertain.

'It's good stuff – Rona treated my blaster burns with it.'

Gingerly, she tries a little. Then, as it quickly works its magic, some more.

'That's . . . amazing,' she says, glancing up at me.

My turn to shrug now. 'Yeah. Rona's full of amazing. I just hope –'

But I don't say it. She *won't* be okay; how could she be?

Sky hands me back the painsucker jar.

'Listen, about us coming to pick you up,' she says. 'It *was* a bit weird. See, HQ hauled us off an important mission, more important than you can possibly imagine. Blew the whole thing off for you. Code red, all risks justified.'

She shakes her head and looks ready to spit, as if disgusted.

My heart sinks. 'But why would they do that?'

'How should I know? Me and Chane, we just follow orders.'

For a second, I think I see Sky's green eyes go all shiny.

'I'm sorry about your friend,' I say.

'Don't be sorry,' she says. 'Just be worth dying for.'

Oh right. How am I supposed to be that?

I grab a stick and give the fire a poke, to get it going again. Code red. Important mission. My head spins; it's all just too much to take in.

'We should talk about what we do tomorrow, when it gets light,' Sky says.

The way she says this, I know she's got an idea. 'Go on then.'

She nods. 'That windjammer way station I told you about, Tranquility Junction, it can't be too far from here. If we follow this valley south we can't miss it.'

I stare at her. 'And how does that help us?'

'We make Tranquility, we can hop a ride out.'

Hop a ride out. Takes me a tired second before I get what she's suggesting. Like Prime, I've only ever heard of this hopping rides on windjammers, never seen it done. Freeriding. Scratching. Completely illegal, it's got loads of names, but they all mean the same thing. Wrath's a world of wind and ridges. Windjammer freighters run the ridges, shipping trade goods between the bigger settlements. Freeriders sneak aboard when they stop overnight at way stations and duck off when they land at the next. It saves weeks of walking or riding and sounds like fun.

Mad though. Get caught and you're dead.

'You can if you like,' I say. 'I'm going back for Rona.'

Sky throws her hands up, glares at me like I've just farted.

'*What?* Are you out of your mind? Have you any idea how far away Freshwater is now? We were in the air five hours minimum. You saw the terrain we flew over. That's a month's hiking at least and Slayers will be hunting you the whole way. And even if by some miracle you did find your way back, Rona won't be there. You heard what that High Slayer said.' She drags her fingers through her dreads and scowls at me. 'Look, I'm sorry, Kyle, but that's how it is. You know how to get around and survive in this backcountry, and I can get us out of it. Together we stand a chance. But if we split up now, we're both dead.'

Her words sting, mainly because I know she's right.

'I should never have left Rona behind.'

I'm expecting more eye-rolling from Sky, but she shakes her head.

'Look, it's hard, but you did what your mother wanted. And she also told you to do what I say. You gave her your word, remember?'

I twitch, but what can I say? I did.

A branch hisses and flares up in the fire, making the shadows leap about.

'After your whatever Junction, where then?'

Sky grimaces. 'One thing at a time, huh? But the idea would be to hook back up with Gemini. You could join the resistance and become a fighter.'

I almost laugh. 'Why the hell would I want to do that?'

She bares her still bloodstained teeth at me.

'If you don't know,' she sneers, 'I ain't going to tell you. Figure it out.'

Just then there's more nightrunner snuffling and growling outside, but it seems like they've given up. None try to smash their way inside.

Next thing, Sky's stifling a yawn.

'Enough talk,' she says, squirming deeper into my sleep bag. 'If they're not going to eat us, then I'm getting some sleep. You can take first watch.'

'No way. You said you'd give me my bag back.'

She throws me the pulse rifle.

'You said you'd fix my leg. And you've got your parka.'

I can't believe this, but I'm suddenly too tired to argue with her. Especially when I think back to how she gutted those Slayers after the crash.

'Fine,' I tell her. 'Keep my bag. You're welcome to it.'

Yeah. And all the bugs in it that I was going to smoke out over the fire.

Without tools, only firelight and a hand-held shiner to see by, it takes me a lot of peering and prising and cursing, as well as half the long, cold night, to fix that damn leg brace thing of hers. In the end, I only manage it by stripping down the pulse rifle and using the stock as a lever to unjam the battered knee joint. Even then it won't power up until, almost by chance, I feel a frayed cable tucked away that's causing an electrical short. Twisting the wires back together is so fiddly with cold hands it does my head in, but I manage it after more cursing and another struggle. But how to keep it from coming apart again? Finally, I hit on the idea of using another of Rona's healer pastes, the one she calls her liquid skin, to secure and insulate it. Used to cover wounds and keep them clean, it sets slow and it's waterproof.

Not sure that my mother would approve, but hey . . .

Anyway, I'm waiting for the stuff to set, thinking bleak

thoughts about Jude, her fingers twitching the Sign of One after seeing my unnatural healing, and how she betrayed me, when I glance round and catch Sky watching me.

Not scowling or glaring. Solemn. Wondering.

Or maybe it's the dim shiner light and my tired eyes.

'What?' I say, a bit startled.

'So can you fix it or can't you?' she says, and her scowl comes back.

'I'm doing my best.'

She grunts and rolls over so she faces away.

Not long after that, I power up the leg brace and it stays powered up. I reckon I can't do any more. Time for some rest now, if I can. I prod Sky with my boot, figuring to wake her to keep watch, but she just mumbles something, clearly fast asleep. And what's the point anyway? It's not like there's anything sneaky about nightrunners, and it's been a long while since I heard them stirring outside. Hopefully they've cleared off back to their cliff lairs. I pull my hood up and lie down as close to the glowing embers of the fire as I dare.

Sleep doesn't claim me, it crushes me.

16
MAKING TRACKS

I wake up, cold and stiff, the ground rock hard under me. Hot, stinking breath hisses into my face. Slobber drips across my cheek. When I open my eyes, I'm staring up at the wrinkling snout of a nightrunner, showing me its fangs. Its rumbling growl is like thunder in my ears. It lunges, but I roll aside and —

And wake up for real this time, shaking.

I stare about wildly in the dim red shiner light. Just me and Sky. No sign of any nightrunner. It was a dream. I sob with relief and rub my eyes. Frag it! Even sleep is out to get me now. The thunder is real though and rumbles again. Outside, it sounds like it's blowing a gale and heavy rain lashes our longthorn shelter.

I glance at the fire, but it's long gone to ashes.

Sky groans, making me jump. Seems I'm not the only one tormented by bad dreams. I watch as she tosses and turns, her shut eyes twitching. She groans again and starts muttering stuff. Nonsense mostly, nothing I can follow.

But one word leaps out, she says it so often.

Tarn. A name maybe?

After a while I curl up again, but daren't close my eyes.

I stare at the black hole that leads outside and listen to the storm raging. When I was little I'd always sleep with my sheet pulled up over my neck, so monsters couldn't suck my blood. Sometimes I'd wake in the darkness to find I'd thrown the sheet off. I'd be so scared and scramble to cover my neck again. Stupid kiddy stuff. Like some thin sheet could stop monsters. Still, I wish I had one now.

I find the pulse rifle and curl up again round it.

The storm soon blows past. I sleep despite myself and this time my dreams leave me alone. It's still quite dark outside when I wake again, but birds are singing already. I get up, stretch, and poke Sky with the rifle. Next thing I know, she's somehow grabbed it off me and I'm looking down its barrel.

'Your leg brace should work now,' I say, making sure I don't blink.

She yawns at me and lowers the rifle.

'Next time, call my name. Less chance of being killed.'

I pick up the brace and chuck it at her. Not hard, but hard enough.

'Give it a go,' I tell her. 'We should hit the road.'

Sky checks out the brace eagerly, but then gives me this weird look.

'What's the matter?' I say.

'Turn your back,' she says. 'Don't look.'

I shrug, surprised, but do as she says. For a while anyway, until curiosity gets the better of me. I dart a glance back. And feel guilty. The leg she's pulling the brace on to is all white, horribly scarred and shrivelled. I look away quickly and wait until I hear her zipping her leathers up before I turn round. She hauls herself back to her feet using the longthorn trunk. I go to help her, but she waves me away crossly. Feeling through her leathers, she powers the brace up.

There's this nasty crunching sound and she groans, in obvious pain.

'What's the matter?' I say anxiously.

'Nothing,' she says, teeth gritted. '*Ay-ay-ay*. It always grips hard at first.' She shuffles about some, then nods. 'Yeah, it's working okay.'

No thanks for the fix or anything. Course not.

I'm cursing under my breath when she stops and looks at me.

'Who taught you to fix mech stuff like this? Your dad?'

'Taught myself. He died before I was born. What's it matter to you?'

'Just asking, that's all.' She looks away quick.

And I feel bad for snapping, wondering if scabs like Sky like to hear about other people's families. Not that I know much. All Rona ever told me about my father was that he was no good and we were all a whole load better off without him.

Sky says nothing, just shrugs.

'Listen,' I say, 'I don't know how long my fix will last.'

At first I don't think she hears. She turns away, grabs her rain jacket, struggles into it and pulls the collar up against the cold. Only then does she look at me, and I'm treated to that little blink-and-you-miss-it smile of hers again.

'This is Wrath,' she says. 'Who knows anything?'

I pack my gear, then do the throwing the stick outside trick again. This time nothing pounces. Sky still has the rifle, so gets to poke her head out first. She looks around, then scrambles outside. I don't hear her being torn apart, so I follow. There's a few distant and dismal-sounding yowls and an ugly mess of blood and fur where the creature Sky shot was gobbled, but that's the only trace of our nightrunner friends. I'm hoping they're back in their dens already, bellies full. To the west, the coming dawn pinks the sky. No sign of Slayers neither; no lights moving about up on the cliffs. With any luck, they've been gobbled too.

I find the plasma lance, on the ground where I threw it. It starts recharging as soon as Sky clips it into the rifle. A green light winks above the mag.

It's so cold the ground crunches underfoot as we set off down the hill.

Moving before the sun's fully up is a risk, but it pays off. Nothing comes chasing after us as we clatter down the scree-covered slope. The sun claws its way above the peaks and mist rises up from the valley bottom to swallow us in its swirling greyness. It's soon so thick we have to slow down, for fear of losing each other or turning an ankle. I'm putting my pistol away, figuring we're well hidden from any watchers, when a tall shape looms out of the gloom.

'Who's there?' hisses Sky, aiming her rifle.

Fortunately, she doesn't fire. It's only a venomberry tree, thin and gnarled, its roots snaking into a crack in the rocky outcrop it stands on.

'Let's take a break,' I gasp. 'Have a drink.'

Sky doesn't argue, so I know it's scared the crap out of her too. I dig out my canteen, take a sip and hand it over.

'No wonder you guys call this place the Barrens,' she says.

She's right. This valley is about as bleak as it gets. It reminds me of one of my mother's favourite sayings – that nowhere is as nowhere as the Barrenlands.

Rona. I feel sick wondering what's happening to her.

'At least rocks tell no tales,' I say.

Sky stares at me, so I explain. 'We're not leaving any tracks.'

'How do you live out here?' she says.

I shrug. 'We don't. We die mainly. How's your leg?'

She swigs some water, coughs, then tosses the canteen back to me. 'Fine so far. It's the rest of me that's destroyed.'

I'm not surprised she's struggling after that beating she took yesterday. Was it only yesterday? I'm impressed she can stand, let alone walk.

'How come nothing's biting *you*?' she says, cursing and scratching.

'They must prefer girl blood.'

All morning, Sky's been tearing at herself. At first I was glad, figuring it served her right for grabbing my sleep bag, but now I feel bad.

I hear something. 'What was that?'

We both listen out. If anybody's following us, we should hear them. It's impossible to move across these loose rocks without making a hell of a clattering noise. But there's nothing, only the gentle muttering of the wind.

Which reminds me. 'Who's Tarn? Your twin sister?'

Sky scowls at me. 'Who told you that?'

'You did. In your sleep. You were calling her name.'

I think she's going to snarl at me, but she just nods and looks grim. She climbs back to her feet, snatches up the rifle and stumbles off into the mist.

I scramble after her, feeling even guiltier.

'I'm sorry. I was just curious.'

Sky won't look at me. Serves me right, me and my big gob.

She stops so suddenly I nearly run into her.

'My sister's name *is* Tarn,' she says. 'Not was. *Is*. Okay?'

'Okay,' I say. 'And my brother's name is Colm. I think.'

It sounds so weird coming out of my mouth.

Sky frowns. 'You *think*?'

'I didn't know. I only found out about him just before we ran.'

She winces, then slowly holds her mutilated left hand out in a fist. I go to bump fists, but she pulls away.

'Always the left, stump to stump.'

I swap hands and she bumps me.

'In the camps, we call it bumping stumps,' she says. 'Guards hated it.'

'But I've got all my fingers.'

Sky shrugs. 'We'll take care of that later.'

'You're kidding?' I look, but her battered face is unreadable.

By the time our mist cover burns off, we're in among the scrubby marsh pines that choke the valley floor. Above us, the sun is high in the sky and it's starting to get warm, even in the shade. I don't know about Sky, but my head feels all tight and I'm choking with thirst. We stop again, but my water canteen's empty.

'There's a river here somewhere,' I tell her. 'We can fill the canteen when we find it.'

I glance back the way we came and bite my lip.

'What's up?' says Sky.

'The ground's getting boggy. We're leaving tracks.'

'So what? By the time anybody finds them, we'll be long gone.'

'You think? I've got a better idea.'

I sniff the air, then follow my nose. The tree is a sort of low-hanging fir. Rona would know its name, but I don't remember. Its long, resin-filled needles are what I'm after. I get Sky to unclip and hand me the rifle's plasma lance, power its golden blade up and hack the fan-like ends off some of the branches.

'What's that *stink*?' she says, holding her nose.

'Fierce, isn't it?' I say. 'Imagine what it does to tracker dogs.'

She watches as I lash some branches underneath each of my boots. Eyes streaming, I stomp around with them, like I'm wearing snowshoes. I show how I can walk across the same marshy ground as her, but leave no tracks.

'You should see yourself,' she says.

And now she laughs, a pleasant tinkling laugh that doesn't fit her at all. I stomp about some more, taking bigger, wilder steps. She laughs even louder, but this mustn't do her battered body any favours and she ends up coughing.

'You're crazy, you are,' she says, after she gets her breath back. 'We're never going to be able to hike all the way to Tranquility like this.'

'Only till we get to the river.'

She's so useless at tying her footpads on I end up doing it for her.

'Look at your hands,' she says. 'Hardly a scratch.'

I can't help twitching, still not used to how fast I heal. Sky's right — the cuts and tears from razor grass and longthorn are nearly gone. The pain too. All I feel is a slight itching. When I flex my fingers, they're stiff, but that's about it. With everything else on my mind, I hadn't noticed.

'How's my nose?' I ask her, feeling it. It doesn't hurt, it's stopped itching and I can breathe through it again. 'Is it bent?'

This sets Sky off laughing and coughing again.

'Give me a break. The whole world is out to kill you and you're worried about your looks.'

I go all hot as she studies me, mock serious, her head on one side.

'I just want to know how bad it is.'

She sighs. 'It looks straight to me. Happy now?'

With that, she turns and stomps off ahead of me, deeper into the forest.

It's soon harder going, the trees crowding closer. Fortunately, we stumble across what looks like a swamptrotter trail. I tell Sky to keep her pulse rifle ready, in case I'm right, and we follow this. It should lead to the river.

'It's weird,' I say, as we creep along. 'Last night, as soon as I pulled a longthorn out, the wound stopped hurting. It's as if I'm healing even quicker now.'

Sky flicks a bug off her face and nods.

'You will be. That's the way it works. The nublood changes start after you hit breeding age, but only slowly. But if you get injured, it's like the hurting speeds everything up. All the changes start happening faster then.'

I stop. 'What do you mean, *all* the changes?'

We're in the middle of a small clearing. Sky stops too, looks me up and down, then picks up a broken tree branch from the trail and throws it to me. 'Break that in half.'

'Why?'

'Just see if you can do it.'

I weigh the branch in my hands. It's hardwood, easily half as thick again as my wrist. There's no way I should be able to break it. All my life I've been skinny and wished I was bigger and stronger, but I don't wish that any more. If I break it, it's because I've got twisted blood. And I don't need reminding about that . . .

'No.' I hurl the branch away and stalk off across the clearing.

I only walk a handful of steps though, before I hear a kind of low droning noise. I look round and see Sky's face. She hears it too. She squints upwards and, a second later, points. My heart gives a big, scared thump. Slipping across the sky high above us, following a street of dark-bottomed clouds, is a windjammer.

We race back to the cover of the trees.

'Slayers?' I whisper.

Sky nods and chews her lip. 'It's Slayer all right. A transport out of Tranquility, I reckon. Too fat for a warplane. Looks like it's heading for the crash site.'

'Will they have seen us?'

'Doubt it. They're high and didn't alter course.'

I follow her as she makes her way round the edge of the clearing. From the far side, we can see the windjammer, while staying hidden in the trees.

'See that?' says Sky, her voice excited.

I do. A flare wobbles up into the sky from the clifftop, thick white smoke trailing it. Crap. Looks like the Slayers survived the night.

Shading my eyes, I watch the windjammer bank into a turn.

'They've spotted the flare.'

The transport flies towards the smoke, before circling just short of the cliffs. I'm wondering why, when I see dots tumble from its belly. Seconds later, white circles blossom above each dot. As they get bigger, I see what the dots are and my heart sinks. Slayer reinforcements, floating down like seeds.

'How are they doing that?' I ask Sky.

She mutters something, then: 'It's old tech – they're called parachutes. We use them for emergencies. Jump, count to three and pull. They let you down soft.'

I grab my pack and sling it over my shoulder. We move out.

'Think they'll come after us?'

'Not yet,' Sky says. 'They'll secure the wreck and haul Morana and any other survivors back to Tranquility. Their only way out is walking, the same as –'

We both spin round at the hiss and crackle.

Close behind us, a second flare spits and wriggles its way up into the sky.

I gasp. 'That's less than a klick away.'

Sky looks at me accusingly, then unslings her pulse rifle.

'So much for covering our tracks.'

'No way could they have followed us,' I say angrily.

'Really?' she says, glancing up at the sky.

High above us, the Slayer transport whines its way upwind of the fast-dropping flare. More dots tumble from the machine's belly and drift down towards us under their parachutes. Most are Slayers, but some are spyders. Without a word, we both kick off our now useless footpads and run for our lives.

17
CROSSING OVER

We crouch down in the cover of a last few trees, sweating and staring. Ahead of us the river is narrow and fast-flowing, milky blue-white from mountain glaciers far upstream. Boulders stick up here and there, squabbled and foamed over by white water. Both banks are littered with the sun-bleached trunks of fallen trees, washed down in the floods after the spring thaw. Across the wild water, the other side of the valley climbs steeply to a high ridge that leans against the sky.

It's a forbidding sight, and the end of our running.

Sky points across the river, up to a faraway dip in the skyline. 'Tranquility's up there, for what it's worth.'

I hardly hear her, my head's pounding so hard. We were so careful to cover our tracks. How have the Slayers found us so quickly?

Beside me, Sky scans the far bank through the pulse rifle's scope. 'It looks clear over there,' she says.

I fill the air with curses. 'The rifle! It's got a tracker.'

Sky looks at me wide-eyed, then at the rifle.

I point out the green light winking above the mag. The few

old pulse rifles we had in Freshwater don't do this. I'm such a fool. I'd thought it was a charging indicator.

'We'll have to ditch it.'

Sky looks doubtful, but I'm sure.

'Right now,' I tell her, 'Morana will be looking at a dot on a cleverbox screen with our range and bearing. That's how she's tracked us, it must be!'

'You want to throw our only real weapon away?'

'We've no choice.'

'Great,' she groans. 'That's just great.'

I reach for the rifle, but Sky knocks my hand away.

Her face, slick with sweat, goes all sly. 'Wait. Let me think.'

I throw my hands up. 'Wait? Every second we wait, they're closing in.'

But I might as well be talking to myself. Sky isn't listening.

'Listen, it's time we got smart,' she says, grinning. 'Quick, go cut me some wood. We need to make something that floats, like a small raft.'

I think the strain is screwing with her. We've got minutes not hours. 'You want me to build us a raft?'

She rolls her eyes. 'Not for *us*, you donk, for the rifle!'

I get it now. We don't just dump the rifle, we send it on a journey.

It takes me about five frantic minutes of running about, cutting and weaving, to make a rough little raft of branches. By the time it's ready, Sky has stripped the rifle of useful stuff, like the scope, the plasma lance and the mag. She hands it over and I lash it on as secure as I can, using the stems of some tall waterweeds.

Sky chucks some greenery on to cover it.

I scuttle down to the water's edge and launch the raft, only to watch in dismay as it snags on a fallen tree. I think I'll have to wade out, but fortunately the current frees it and steers it safely out into mid-stream. Trembling with relief, I clatter back up the stony bank and race back to Sky. By the time I reach her, the raft is already sweeping around a bend in the river. 'That's a serious current!'

'Let's hope they figure we tried to cross and got swept away,' says Sky.

'I thought you don't believe in hope?'

My sneer is soon wiped from my face, however, as I hear crashing sounds coming from the swamptrotter trail behind us, the one we followed down here. Seconds later, disturbed birds thrash and screech their way into the air.

Sounds like the Slayers will be here any minute.

'Now what do we do?' whispers Sky.

'We'll have to hide.'

'Where?'

Anxiously, I look along the riverbank. Good cover, but impossible to move across the shingle without making an awful racket. We could try and force our way back through the trees, but that won't be any quieter. And the marsh pines are stunted and weedy, not worth climbing.

Only now I happen to look up. As luck would have it, we're crouching beneath a solitary manga tree. The trunk's bare low down, but higher up it's got loads of dense blue-green foliage.

It's a chance *if* we can get up it.

I look back at Sky and she nods. 'You go first.'

Slinging my pack, I leap for the lowest branch, only just making it on my third try. Pulling myself up on to it takes all my upper-body strength. When I look down, I see Sky peering up at me. I see too that there's no way she'll be able to climb up like I did, not with her being shorter than me and having a bad leg.

'Back up,' I whisper down. 'I'll jump down and give you a boost.'

It's too late though. I hear a voice shouting orders. High Slayer Morana!

Sky shakes her head. 'You'll have to lift me.'

'Don't be mad. Look at me – no way can I do that.'

But she won't take no for an answer, backs off, takes a run up and jumps. I have to throw myself flat on the branch and make a despairing grab. Somehow, we manage to catch each other's hand, but that still leaves her flailing around beneath me, her weight almost pulling my right arm out of its socket.

Her pale face peers up at me, her eyes wide.

'What are you waiting for?' she says through her teeth. 'Pull me up.'

So I give it a go, but she's too heavy.

'I can't!' I pant at her.

'You call *that* trying?' Sky's swollen lip curls at me.

A glance back at the mouth of the trail and I see dayshine glinting off metal and hear the *thump-thump-thump* of Slayer boots. Fear chokes me, but so does anger and frustration. In desperation I suck in a big breath, close my eyes and yank Sky up as hard as I can, screaming inside, straining every fibre of my being.

Next thing I know, I'm on my feet on the branch.

And Sky's clinging to me.

All I can do is stare at her, my gob open.

'Want to live? Then keep climbing,' she hisses, before

scrambling past me and hauling herself higher up the tree, way more agile than I'd have thought.

I give myself a shake and pull myself up after her.

Not a moment too soon either, as Slayers spill out into the clearing below us.

Like I thought, it's Morana and half a dozen of her Slayer goons. They advance on the river in short rushes, one fire team covering another. From up here looking down, all I see are their matt-black helmets and shoulders, their pulse rifles sticking out in front of them. A gust of wind rattles through the leaves around us, swaying the branches. When they don't find us, the High Slayer shouts more orders. Two Slayers clatter down the stony riverbank, only to hurry back and report finding my tracks leading to the water, from when I launched the raft.

'Don't tell me where he *was*,' she screeches at them. 'Tell me where he is *now*!'

Sweat trickles down my face, but it's so precarious up here I don't dare lift a finger. We're clinging on beside each other in a fork of the tree, but we're so high I swear the branch is bending under our weight. And now we're stuck up here I see all the holes in what seemed such thick foliage from the ground.

If the Slayers look up, they're bound to see us.

'Great idea this was,' whispers Sky.

I stare down at my hands that pulled her up here, an impossible dead lift. It's as if the leaf-stained dayshine plays tricks with my eyes. Just for a second, I could swear I'm looking at scarred, claw-like hands, like that caged twist had. Panic grips me, but the shadows shift and I blink and I see my hands again, the same as ever, crooked fingers and chipped, chewed fingernails. I shake my head and give my bicep a quick squeeze, but that feels the same too, no stronger.

I look up and Sky gives me a sad-looking smile.

'Stronger, faster, better at healing. You see why people hate you.'

But I'm still so stunned that I hardly hear her. I hear Rona instead, her voice miserable and urgent. *On any other world it wouldn't be a curse, it'd be a blessing.* I remember too how I managed to pull that spyder's leg off Sky.

No three ways about it — there's monster in me.

Another Slayer runs up, clutching some sort of hand-held device. He goes to show it to Morana, but she snatches it off him before stalking down to the riverbank. I watch, holding my breath as she holds it up and studies it's screen.

Her head snaps up and now she's looking downriver.

Beside me, Sky pumps her fist in delight. 'Looks like she's bought it!'

How long do we wait before we climb back down the tree? Are the Slayers really gone or hiding like nightrunners, waiting to pounce? That's what's so slanky about hiding — sooner or later you have to crawl out and face your fear. Next time I'll just keep running. At least with running you're doing something.

'We can't stay here forever,' whispers Sky.

She's right. How long before they discover our trick?

The sun's a good hour lower in the sky since the Slayers took off along the riverbank after the rifle. All this time I've been straining my ears, listening for noises that don't fit, but all I hear is wind and birds singing.

They must be gone. Must be.

Still, my sweat-damp back cringes on the climb down.

I drop the last few metres to the ground and crouch, heart trying to smash its way out through my ribs. Nobody shoots me. No Slayer leaps from cover and yells at me to put my hands up. A startled animal scuttles away through the undergrowth and scares the crap out of me, but that's the worst that happens.

We're alive, for a little longer – I'll settle for that.

I'm turning around to give Sky a hand down, when she jumps from a hell of a height, way higher than I'd dare, and thumps to the ground next to me.

Stunned, I watch as she straightens up. 'How'd you do that?'

She shrugs, clearly unhurt. 'Amped up my leg brace.'

I stare at her in disbelief. 'So why didn't you do that to jump *up* then?'

'Didn't need to, did I?' She grins and brushes off a few twigs caught in her jumpsuit. 'That was great. I've always wanted to climb a tree. Not many trees in ident camps, and climbing them was forbidden. You'd get shot.'

'You made me pull you up deliberately?'

'I knew you could do it if you put your back into it.'

'You're crazy, you are.'

She laughs at me. 'You're stronger than you thought. Is that so bad?'

'The whole world wants me dead,' I growl. 'I call that bad.'

She says nothing, just rolls her eyes.

There's a handy-sized stone at my feet. I boot it away.

'I don't want to be stronger. I just want to go back to being human!'

'You *are* human. And is being pureblood so great?'

Sky turns her back on me and walks off a few stiff-legged steps. I hear her mutter something under her breath, like I get to heal anyway. And now I remember last night in the longthorn, looking when she'd asked me not to and seeing that ruined leg of hers. Yet here's me moaning, when by rights I should either be dead or missing half my jaw if it wasn't for my nublood. In my head, it's like I see Rona glaring at me. No way am I admitting it, but maybe Sky's got a point.

'We should get going again,' I say to her back.

She glances around at me. 'We should. You still got that old gun?'

I take the pistol out of my parka pocket and check it, as if by wanting them badly enough more bullets might somehow appear. But no such luck — still only two bullets left. Both are rustier than Sky's old windjammer.

'I'll take that.' Sky goes to grab it off me, but I don't let her.

'No way. Get your own gun.'

She gives me a look. 'Fine. You can take point then.'

I figure this means I get to lead. 'Whatever.'

We crawl away through the scrubgrass towards the riverbank.

Downstream to the east, the way the Slayers went, the river soon jags right around a rocky outcrop lightly covered in trees. Sky uses the scope to make sure nobody's on watch there. Satisfied we're in the clear I lead off again, but the opposite way, upstream and west. Sky protests, pointing out this takes us away from Tranquility. I tell her that from up the tree I saw the river open out this way.

'So what if it opens out?' she says.

I sigh. 'It'll be shallower where it's wider, easier to ford.'

We pick our way along the riverbank, staying close to the trees in case we need to dive for cover. As I thought, the river soon opens out and slows down and it's not long before I see what I'm looking for. A gap smashed through the trees, a muddy trail leading down to the water. On the far bank, something similar. I point it out, but can't help shivering.

'What's the matter?' says Sky.

'Nothing. Look, if animals ford the river here, then so can we.'

The milky river water still hustles past, but isn't as frantic white as before.

'Will your fix to my leg be okay in the water?'

'We'll soon find out,' I say, wading in.

She makes a *yeah, that's real funny* face and follows me in.

'With luck, this'll kill the bugs eating me,' she says.

The water is so cold I nearly cry out and my teeth chatter. One slip . . . but I wont think about that. Only it's hard not to. Soon I'm up to my armpits and have to hoist my pack above my head to keep it dry. Under my feet, the bottom is weedy and treacherous. The whole time, a fierce current is dragging at my legs. How I keep wading, I don't know, but suddenly I see I'm almost across. I glance back to see how Sky's getting on. And that's when I see the splashes as several long, glistening bodies slide down the bank into the water. *Leatherheads!* Half lizard, half water snake, massive jaws stuffed full of bone-crunching teeth. Horrified, I'm shouting a warning to Sky when something snags my foot. I go down. Instantly my world turns all green and white and confused. The shock of freezing water on my face punches all my breath out of me. I thrash like crazy, coughing and spluttering, struggling to get my head above water, but I can't — I can't even tell which way is up.

I feel myself picked up and whirled away by the current.

A dark shape spears towards me and I scream as jaws sink into my arm.

But it's not a lizard — it's Sky.

'Hold on to me!' she yells, pulling me to my feet.

I throw my arms round her. I don't know how she does it, but she half drags, half carries me the rest of the way across the river. My pack comes too, the strap still looped over my shoulder. We haul ourselves out on to the far bank and scramble to higher ground. All I can do then is lie there, retching up river water, staring helplessly as V-shaped ripples converge towards us. But Sky's warrior blood is up now. She screams something, snatches up a fist-sized stone and hurls it at the lizards. And another. The third finds its mark. I glimpse a snapping jaw full of yellow teeth. A powerful reptilian tail thrashes the water into foam. That gets me back on my feet. I heave rocks at them too, as hard and fast as I can.

The ripples fade away and the river calms again.

We turn and run, and keep running until we can't run any more.

'Are there any creatures out here,' gasps Sky, head down, hands on her knees, when we eventually stop, 'that *don't* want to eat us?'

We're both wet through and dripping.

'Not many,' I admit, throwing myself down on my back.

Maybe it's the fright I've just had, but a feeling of utter

helplessness hits me then, so hard I nearly cry out. Sky must hear the sob in my voice because she limps over and gazes down at me. 'What's the matter? Are you hurting?'

I can't meet her look; it's almost like she cares.

And that *does* hurt, because it reminds me. Everyone who cared about me is either dead already or will be soon. Rona. Jude. Even those few kids who'd nod to me and not throw stones. All dead because of me. Because of what I am.

'You should've left me for the lizards,' I say miserably.

'Don't kid yourself, Kyle,' Sky says, frowning. 'It was the pack I was saving.'

She's trying to cheer me up, but it won't work.

'It's me the Slayers want,' I say. 'We should split up. I'll lead them away from Tranquility and you'll have a chance. No point us both getting caught.'

Sky sighs. 'Don't suppose you filled the water bottle?'

'Did you hear what I just said?'

'I did. But you're talking crap, so I'm not listening. We should go.'

'I'm talking sense.'

'No, you're not, you're feeling sorry for yourself.'

'Well, screw you, Sky. Enough people have died because of me.'

Sky laughs at me. Actually laughs.

I jump up, fists clenched. 'What's so funny?'

'You are, Kyle. You talk like you're the only person who's ever lost somebody. Well, I'm the scab, remember. I watched my sister die, or so I thought. Either way, I lost her. But you –'

She stops, swallows, goes red in the face.

Like she's kicking herself for letting something big slip.

My fury melts away and I look at her curiously. 'Or so you thought? What do you mean by that?'

'Nothing,' she says, too quickly. 'Doesn't matter. Look, we've come all this fraggin' way and you're not giving up now!'

She shoulders the pack and limps off again.

'And quit whining,' she mutters, or something like that.

I grind my teeth at her back, but in the end I grab my dripping pack and follow. It's what Rona would want.

18
GOING HOBO

Sky and me have hardly spoken since the river crossing. Here we are now, on our bellies in the dark, peering down through scrub at the windjammer way-station she calls Tranquility Junction. A storm howled through earlier and it's still lashing down rain, so even though we dried out some as we climbed up here we're sopping wet again. Sky reckons it's doing us a favour, keeping the bulls inside their huts. Bulls are what she calls guards – this freeriding thing has its own weird kind of talk. And it turns out hopping windjammers, which sounded so exciting, is mostly lurking about outside fences, watching and waiting, then waiting some more.

'So, what was that about your sister?' I whisper to Sky, rubbing my cold hands together to try and get some feeling back into them.

Sky looks up from the scope, then hands it over. But if she heard what I said about her sister she doesn't let on.

'I reckon our ride out is the grain freighter over there beside the hangar,' she says. 'See the big transport windjammer with the red V-tail?'

I peer through the scope. 'The lit-up one?'

'Looks like they're prepping it for launch, don't you think?'

A gang of people are working beneath it, but I can't tell what they're doing.

'Where will it be going?'

'Who cares? I don't. Anywhere's better than here.'

Lightning cracks the night sky, showing me bulging purple clouds. On its heels comes an ear-splitting crash of thunder. We wriggle back into the shelter of some blackwood trees. The rain drums on the broad leaves above us, but the ground is dry. My empty stomach gives this embarrassing rumble, so I dig out the last few crumbs of Rona's trail mix. Sky turns her nose up, so I scoff her share.

'More for me then. Your loss.'

In the next flash of lightning I catch her fingering the teardrop inked below her eye and wonder. 'That tattoo something to do with your sister, is it?'

She sighs as if the weight of Wrath rests on her shoulders, then nods.

'Nine months ago,' she says, shivering, 'I was sure Tarn was dead. I'd stood there and watched her hang. Only then this Slayer transport crashes on its way back to Prime from the Fair at Whim Creek. One of our recon teams finds it before the Slayers do. They figure they'll scav some Slayer tech, maybe a few pulse rifles. Instead they find a survivor, a terribly burnt boy. And he –'

An animal wails in the far distance, making us both jump.

'What's this got to do with your sister?' I say.

Sky takes a deep breath. 'Everything, if you listen. The boy's an ident, still in that stupid smock they make us wear to the

167

Peace Fair. He keeps raving on about how Purification is this big lie and crying for his brother. It takes them a while to get him to make sense, but they figure out he's nublood – which is why he's still clinging on. They get some water into him. He tells the recon guys the executions were faked, staged for the benefit of the crowd. And he should know. He was a healer and squealer. He was one of the idents they pretended to hang!'

I can't see her face, but I know she's staring at me.

'Faked?' I say, incredulous. 'But that's impossible. I saw them hang.'

'Did you? Or did you just *think* you did?'

This is too mind-blowing. I have to get up and prowl about. Lightning flares. I glimpse Sky's face, those dark eyes of hers, all excited now and full of wanting me to believe. I feel as if I could fall into them and never hit bottom.

'You didn't see them die,' she says. 'Think about it – all you saw was them falling through the trapdoor, then a rope twitching about.'

And she's right. That *is* all I saw. It sounds mad, but I believe her.

My legs start shaking. I have to sit down again.

'They found the rest of his nublood mates in the wreck,' she says, her voice sad now, 'all past talking, burnt to a crisp. Only this one poor kid was thrown clear. Me and Chane, we extracted the recon guys in the *Rockpolisher*. That's how I got to hear about it. But I knew anyway – somehow I'd always known Tarn wasn't dead.'

It's haunting, listening to Sky's disembodied whisper.

'But why?' I say, wincing into the darkness.

'We don't know, not yet.'

'Was that why you and Chane were at Deep Six?'

'Uh-huh. That was the mission I told you about. We low quoted for a cargo-carry in and out of the Fair, then hung about. And it was right there staring us in the face. That kid was right. All those executions, but no bodies. No big pit, no burning, nothing. And a Slayer transport lifts off two days after the Fair. We never saw it load, so it must have been done sneaky and overnight. We take off after it, but that's when *you* happened.' She makes no effort to hide the disgust in her voice.

I don't know what to say so keep my mouth shut.

'You still there?' says Sky.

'I think so,' I say, pinching myself.

A week ago it all seemed so straightforward. Idents are bad and twists are worse. Mark them, take them, test them. Kill the twist, save the pureblood. A law put in place by our benevolent Saviour to save us from another war, while sparing the innocent twin. But if nubloods like me really *aren't* evil, and the killing is all a sham so they can be spirited away, what's it all about?

None of it makes any sense that my thick head can puzzle out.

'What happened to the boy?'

'He didn't make it,' Sky says, and sighs again. 'Slayers swarmed from every direction, looking for the crashed transport. We had to scramble the hell out of there. It was close; we were very lucky to get clear.'

'And a crippled boy would only slow you down.'

'His information was too important. We had to get it back to Gemini.'

'So you killed him.'

Sky twitches. 'We spared the kid from more suffering.'

Dawn in only a few minutes. Time to hop a windjammer or die trying.

'I feel sick,' I tell Sky.

'And I wish we still had that rifle,' she says.

I watch as she produces a tube from one of her pockets and carefully daubs on the thick bars under her eyes that mark her out as windjammer crew.

'Why bother with that?' I ask her.

'Because,' she says.

We move out, crawling on our bellies through the still-wet scrubgrass. Below us, the base is starting to stir. I hear muffled hammering and see the flick-flicker of a welder coming from the furthest of three squat, fabric-covered hangars, where Sky says they service the flying machines. Over to our right, in a pool of arc light, men are loading crates into another windjammer. I hardly glance at them – it's the dark figures in the watchtowers that squeeze my insides.

Slayers. I try not to think what will happen if they spot us.

A rusty old razor-wire fence is our first problem, but Sky finds an animal scrape underneath it, big enough for us to wriggle through. She goes to head straight for our V-tailed transport, but I haul her back by her foot.

'Let go!' she hisses, twisting round.

'You sure you've done this before?' I whisper. 'Listen.'

Under one of the towers a dog greets the sun with a howl. Last night's storm is long gone, but the breeze it left behind shivers the leaves in the trees.

'Go that way and we'll be upwind. He'll sniff you.'

'So which way then?'

I peer through the waving grass and give my lip a chewing. I'm so nervous, my thinking just turns to mush. And Sky is glaring at me now. Which doesn't help. At all.

Come on, Kyle! You've stalked skittish black-tails, how hard can this be?

And now I think I see a route. 'Follow me.'

I lead us on a long crawl round the overgrown foot of the fence until we're downwind of the dog and looking at the back of this long building, with no windows but several shuttered loading bays. I'm chewing my nails, wondering how the hell we're going to cross the dozen metres of open ground that still separate us without being seen, when I hear a loud bang. Loads of shouting and swearing come from the direction of the transport windjammer being loaded.

'Move!' I bolt across.

Hopefully, Slayer sentries are still human enough to like gawping.

Must be, because nobody shouts.

'Smell that?' whispers Sky beside me, back to the wall.

'All I smell is oil and smoke.'

'That's windjammer stink – our way out of here.'

Next thing she flashes me that lovely ghost of a smile again. My heart's thrashing like crazy, I'm so scared, but I swear Sky's enjoying all this. At least we're in among the buildings now and spoilt for good cover. She leads and we cut right through the centre of Tranquility to get to where the V-tailed transport is parked up, winding our way between hangars and huts and workshops so there's no way the sentries in the towers can see us. Even so, we still nearly come unstuck. As we're walking past a door, it suddenly opens, spilling light, smoke, the stench of stale beer and a whole bunch of people. I glimpse hard faces and windjammer leathers.

There's no time to run, no place to hide.

Suddenly Sky's hanging off me, laughing and chatting away.

'Seriously, you should've seen his face . . .'

I'm so stunned I freeze and stumble, but she drags me along.

'Keep walking, you big gom,' she hisses. 'Make it look like I'm your girl.'

Finally I get it and sling my arm round her shoulders.

'No need to pull my head off,' she mutters.

She lets rip now with more rough laughter, grabs my other arm and folds it round her waist so I can't go for my gun even if I wanted to. Every nerve in my body is screaming run, but somehow I force myself not to. I just hope that in the shadows they won't notice our ripped clothes and beaten-up faces.

That hope thing again – I can't help myself.

'Slow. Don't hurry,' Sky whispers. 'Like you belong.'

The windjammer crews hurry past us. One older man, more lines on his face than a chart, looks and scowls. Sky stares back at him, bold as dayshine, until he looks away. The rest ignore us, too busy laughing and chatting. And maybe the relief goes to my head. I start to enjoy myself and give Sky's waist a squeeze.

Mistake. I get elbowed in the ribs. Hard.

'Do that again,' she hisses at me, 'and I'll kill you myself.'

Only some more people are coming the other way now,

traders by the look of them, so she has to go back to pretending to be my drunk girlfriend.

Soon as we're on our own she pulls away from me.

'No kiss then?' I growl, rubbing my side.

The look Sky gives me – I'm glad she doesn't have that rifle any more.

And I'm suddenly fed up again, a bitter taste in my mouth. Holding Sky, even if it was only pretend, reminds me of holding Jude and the good times we had together. Okay, so she ran to her father and betrayed me and Rona, and that's still raw enough to stab at me, but the poor girl's dead now. Because of me.

I guess I just feel guilty and mixed-up about that.

Sky heads off again and I trail after her. We take more care, listening for movement in the huts before we tiptoe past them, avoiding any with lights on inside. At one point we spot a Slayer patrol, but they march past without seeing us. Finally, from the shelter of a steam tractor, I see our ride ahead of us. The last few metres of open ground is so well lit it make us both wince, until I spot a ditch, little more than a fold in the ground. And our luck holds. One last heart-in-my-gob crawl and we're looking up at the transport's mud-splattered underbelly.

If there's a hatch I can't see it. 'Now what?'

'Watch and learn,' says Sky.

I follow as she scuttles to the far side of the jammer, away from the watchtowers. A quick look about and she ducks out from underneath, scrambles on to the wing first, then along the curved hull. I hold my breath and go after her.

The morning dayshine is getting brighter every minute.

'This is mad,' I say. 'We'll be seen.'

Sky ignores me. Several big, shutter-like hatches are built into the hull, for loading cargo through. She tries the first one, but it's locked. No kidding. I mean, what did she expect?

'Give me something to jemmy with,' she says. 'And that shiner of yours.'

I glance at the secure-looking hatches. 'You'll never jemmy these open.'

She curses at me. 'Shut up. I know what I'm doing.'

Reluctantly I root through my pack until I find a small multi-tool and hand it over, along with the shiner. Then I clamber up to the top of the hull and take a quick peek about. My breath shoots out of me and I slide back down.

'People are coming!'

'What kind of people?' she says crossly.

'I reckon it could be the crew.'

'Relax. We'll be inside long before they get here.'

Using my multi-tool, she prises open a small panel next to the hatch. As she flashes the shiner inside, I glimpse tangled wires. Sky curses, not looking so cocky now. Frantically I slide along the hull, testing the other hatches. I know it's hopeless – if one is locked they'll all be – but I need to *do* something.

And the last one gives a bit when I try it.

'Sky! This one's not locked.'

She scrunches her face up like she doesn't believe it, but when I use more force and slide the hatch half open she quickly limps back to join me here. Inside the unlit cargo bay I can make out the vague shapes of sacks and crates.

'That's weird,' Sky says, still frowning.

No thanks or anything, but I'm getting used to that.

We both twitch at a series of loud clunks from somewhere inside the hull. Big power relays switching, I reckon. A second later the cockpit lights flicker on at the bow end of the windjammer as its systems start to come to life. From only a few metres away now, I hear the sleepy grumbling of the fast-approaching crew. Sky doesn't hesitate; she dives inside. I scramble in after her, reach up and wrestle the hatch shut. Pitch-darkness, my heart pounding like mad. At my feet, Sky flicks the shiner on and looks up at me. Her eyes go wide.

Something cold and metallic jams into the back of my neck.

And I don't have to see it to know it's a gun.

'This ride's already taken,' growls a deep voice.

19
OLD FRIENDS

I freeze. A hand pats me down, quickly finds the gun in my parka pocket and takes it, before shoving me down to the deck beside Sky. I roll over and find myself looking up at a home-made bolt gun in the fist of a young but fierce-looking man. A lammerjay feather sticks up out of his greasy hair. Half his ugly face is a bugweb tattoo, his left eye at its centre. Between some grain sacks at his back, two more faces peer out at us, both girls. One's fair-haired, sad-eyed and freckled, about the same age as Sky and me. The other's a dark-haired youngster.

'Put that gun away, you big gom,' Sky snarls at tattoo guy.

The older girl squirms out from behind the sacks. 'Sky! It's me, Fliss.'

Sky's mouth drops open. 'Fliss! No way!'

But both have to shut up now as we hear the crew clambering aboard.

'You checking the hatches, Ran?' a woman shouts.

'Yeah, yeah,' shouts a younger voice, closer, obviously bored.

Tattoo guy curses, puts the gun away and lunges past me to lean his weight on the inside of the hatch. Sky gives me this urgent look. We join him just in time as boots scrape the hull outside. Sky flicks the shiner off, plunging us into darkness. Whoever it is outside gives the hatch a half-hearted pull. With me and Sky and this other guy holding it, it doesn't move. The boots scrape to the next hatch along.

So *this* is what hopping windjammers is like.

Anyway, I'm glad when a little while later Sky thumbs the shiner back on and I can see again. But less glad when tattoo-guy gets in my face.

'Like I said, this ride's taken,' he growls, jabbing the bolt gun into me.

'Leave it out, Matty,' says the fair-haired girl, pulling him away. 'There's room for everybody in here. Sky and me, we go way back.'

'They could've led the bulls to us.'

'But they didn't, did they?'

Sky hangs up the shiner then goes and gives the Fliss girl a hug. After they step apart they bump stumps and that's when I see Fliss is a scab too.

I check Matty, but no, he's still got all ten.

Outside I hear the unmistakable rattle and whoosh of a steam tractor. Not long afterwards, the windjammer gives a big jerk under us. Our shadowy little world starts bouncing and swaying and I have to hang on for dear life.

'Hey, what's going on?'

'They're towing us to the drop ramp,' says Sky.

'The *what* ramp?'

'Your first time, is it?' says Fliss, grinning. 'Hopping jammers?'

There's no point denying it. 'Uh-huh.'

'I'm Fliss,' she says. 'The big lump is Matty. He's not so bad when you get to know him. And this mucky little darling is Wink, our good luck charm.'

She hauls the girl out from her hidey-hole in the sacks.

'Who are *you* guys?' Wink squeaks.

Sky does our introductions, just names, nothing more.

'You guys look messed up,' says Fliss.

'Road's been hard,' says Sky.

Matty still looks suspicious, especially of me.

We eye each other up, the way guys do here in the Barrenlands, to see who'd win a fight. Him, I reckon. The guy's not that much bigger than me, but with that tattooed face of his he looks a hell of a lot meaner. He opens his mouth to say something, but snaps it shut as our windjammer jolts to a halt. We all freeze and listen. Orders are shouted outside. A few moments later I hear the whine of our transport's lift-cells throttling up to full power and get that floaty feeling again. It's not long though before some muffled thumps come from underneath us, the lifters throttle back and the windjammer settles again, but nose down now.

A loud clanging sound, like metal jaws snapping shut, makes me jump.

'Clipping on,' says Fliss, like this means something.

'Any idea where she's headed?' asks Sky.

'Mills at Whitescar,' says Fliss. 'Must be, with this cargo.'

The others are all clinging on to stuff, so I do too, but nothing happens. We sit. And wait. And then wait some more.

Even Sky looks worried when we hear more shouting outside.

I can't help it – I have to know what's going on. I prise the hatch up a finger-width so I can peer outside. And nearly bite my tongue off. A pack of Slayers, the tall figure of High Slayer Morana at their head, are on a platform alongside us.

Morana's doing the shouting, at a fat, red-faced merchant.

'I want it searched again!' she yells.

The merchant wrings his hands and protests about delays and costs. My heart sinks. Sky takes a peek and curses.

Next thing, Morana plants a gloved hand in fatty's face, shoves him aside and stalks towards the nose of our windjammer. But even as she climbs aboard, one of the Slayers runs after her, salutes and hands over a comm unit. Morana snarls questions into it, then listens. I don't catch everything, but enough.

'They've found the rifle,' I whisper to Sky.

Morana jumps back down and leads her Slayers away at the double.

The red-faced merchant mutters something, then turns and yells in a language I don't understand. Men in grubby overalls scamper about, doing mysterious things. He watches, raises a pudgy index finger and twirls it above his head. The lift-cells throttle up again to max power. One last flourish of the finger, some more muffled thumps from underneath us and our windjammer slides forward, accelerating down some sort of ramp. A second later and it feels like we fall off a cliff, we're travelling so fast. I float up into the air. The hatch bangs shut as I let go.

I'm working on a scream when we level out.

Uummpphh! From weightless to massive heavy in the blink of an eye.

I slam down from head height on to the deck. By the time I can move, I sense we're flying. The others are all hanging on to cargo straps and grinning. Wink blows big snot bubbles, she's laughing so hard.

'You okay?' asks Fliss.

'He'll be fine,' says Sky. 'He landed on his head.'

They all kill themselves laughing. I don't care. All I'm thinking now is we've done it — we've got away.

The wordweavers, with their brightly painted faces and the big, glossy throat feathers of the lammerjay in their hair, come to the three valleys once in the spring and once in the autumn. They tag along with the traders' wagon trains for protection, and because they know Barrenlanders are more likely to part with credits when they're still hot in their hands after selling their wares. I loved their tales of wonder from faraway places or distant worlds. Storytelling, told by a fire under the stars, was the only thing I ever looked forward to. My favourite tells were the ones where the hero fights his way through impossible challenges, kills the villain and saves the girl he loves. I'd spend the long months, after they'd gone and before they came back, imagining myself as one of their badass heroes.

I remember this now, as I look at the feather in Matty's hair.

We're maybe an hour out of Tranquility, all of us sitting around inside of a kind of cave Matty made by restacking the grain sacks. It's dusty, stinks of rat shit and you can't stretch your legs out without kicking someone, but I'm not complaining. Nobody's going to find us in here — not without doing some serious looking anyway. Turns out Sky and Fliss were in the same ident camp, someplace called Ravenhole, but lost touch after they got out. Matty's been hopping jammers for years, since his wordweaver parents got wasted by Reapers. And it's not like we're mates now, but he's chilled enough to have handed me back my pistol. Wink isn't theirs, only some abandoned kid they found half dead a few months back.

And now they're staring at us, like it's our turn to do some talking.

I'm thinking we should lie or say nothing, when Sky – without so much as a glance at me – goes and tells them everything, starting with how I found out I'm nublood, her coming to get me, running from the lynch mob, the winch shot from under her windjammer, our capture, and finally our escape from the crashed Slayer warplane. She makes no secret of working for Gemini either. Even sour-faced Matty's gob is hanging open after she's done telling. No kidding. Sky says it all matter-of-fact, but it's a tale any half-starved wordweaver would be proud of.

I scowl at Sky, not happy, but she shrugs it back at me and nods towards Fliss, Matty and Wink. 'This is *their* ride. We have to be straight with them.'

Matty gets his mouth closed at last and stares at me. 'So you're why Tranquility was suddenly crawling with Slayers?'

I can't help wincing. 'Guess so.'

And now Sky goes on to tell them about the faked ident executions.

Matty curses. Fliss tries to say something, only for her words to drown in sobs. Wink sits in the middle, wide-eyed.

'You sure about this?' growls Matty, pulling Fliss close.

Sky ignores him, leans forward to take her friend's hand and squeeze it.

'Fliss, Tarn might still be alive, and Fleur too.'

I'm guessing Fleur must be Fliss's ident sister from their time in the camps.

The girl wipes her eyes and manages a weak smile.

'But I don't understand, Sky. Why would they do such a thing?'

Sky sighs. 'We don't know. Not yet.'

'Sure we do,' I say.

They all turn and stare at me, even little Wink.

'What are you on about?' says Sky.

My cheeks burn, but I know I'm right so she can sneer all she likes.

'It's exactly like when Rona torched our shack,' I tell them. 'She wanted preacher Fod and the rest to figure I was dead already, so they'd quit looking for me. The Slayers will be doing the same thing. They spare the twists for some secret reason then spirit them away so nobody comes sniffing after them.'

There's a stunned silence, which leaves me feeling pleased with myself. Even Sky can't help flashing me an impressed look.

'Makes sense,' she says, glancing at Fliss. 'But what I want to know is what really happened to our nublood sisters, and where they are now.'

'Nublood. That's what I meant,' I say quickly.

'But they believe nubloods are evil,' Fliss says. 'So *why* spare them?'

Sky takes a deep breath and leans back against the wall of sacks behind her. 'I hate to think.' She scowls and massages her bad leg, as if it's hurting her. 'But if we can find out *where* they are, I'm sure we'll find that out too.'

'Then what?' Matty says, narrow-eyed.

But it's like Sky catches herself now. She doesn't answer him.

Not much longer now to Whitescar, Matty reckons. I'm wondering how he can tell without peeking outside, but don't want to ask. Fliss must see the look on my face however. She tells me Matty's been hopping jammers so long he can follow the ridge routes by counting the turns. She points up to a crack in the hull plates back here, through which shines a tiny sliver of dayshine. It starts to slide around and I vaguely feel we're turning, although I couldn't say which way.

'Sometimes we have to drill a hole,' she says. 'Not often.'

I go back to cleaning my gun. A bit of sacking for rag, a drop of oil Fliss persuaded a grudging Matty to give me, and the old pistol looks better. Less rusty, more lethal. I spin the cylinder and lose myself in its metal purr.

'Can I play?' says Wink, coming over.

'No. It's not a toy.' But I cringe even as I say this. I sound just like Rona. I wonder if she's still alive and wondering about me.

The little girl gives me this big-eyed and grubby-faced pleading look. I try and shoo her away, but she's not easily shooed. 'P-lease, Kyle. P-lease.'

'Okay, but don't shoot us down like I did.'

I unload the bullets and hand it over. She grabs it with a giggle, scoots back to sit on her favourite sack. And aims it right at my head. *Psshooo! Psshooo!*

'That's gratitude for you, huh?' says Sky, laughing.

She's let Fliss help her patch up the worst of her cuts and bruises using my healer stuff and now looks almost like her old self again. Relaxed even. I wish I could relax, but I can't. These guys are all experienced freeriders; they know what happens when we get to Whitescar. I don't and they won't tell me.

'You'll see,' they keep saying, like it's funny.

Sky and Matty and Fliss put their heads together and start planning. To kill time, I set about polishing my last two precious bullets.

'Ever used a chute before?' Matty says to me a while later.

'A what?' I say, trying not to look too dumb.

He shows me this small and weird-looking pack thing, the size and shape of a rolled-up sleep bag. When I look closely, I see it's more complicated and comes with a webbing harness so that it can be strapped to your back. And now I get a sick feeling. The harness looks even more home-made than his bolt gun.

'Course he hasn't,' snorts Sky.

'Is this one of those things that floats you down gentle, like we saw before?' I say.

Sky swaps looks with Matty. 'Kind of, yeah.'

'Uh, what's "kind of" mean?'

My sick feeling gets so bad, I can feel bits of me shrinking.

'It's only a drogue chute,' Fliss explains. 'Half-size. Used to drop cargo pallets into places jammers can't land at. We scavenge them and fit the straps.'

'Half-size?' I gulp. 'What good's that?'

Matty gives me this jeering smile, like he's so tough. 'Slows you down a bit.'

'So you're only half dead when you hit the ground?'

'Do it right and you won't be hitting the ground,' Sky says.

They all bump fists and stumps. Even Wink.

'Huh?' I say. I can't help it.

'There's a swamp on final approach,' Fliss says. 'We'll drop into that.'

Oh great. More water to drown in.

'I'll take my chances after we land,' I say, trying to keep my voice from wobbling. 'We sneaked on here, we can sneak back off. Why not?'

Sky shakes her head, her white dreads flying.

'We got lucky back at Tranquility, Kyle. Look, all it takes is for one of Whitescar's bulls to see us and we're screwed again. Jumping's better.'

I think about this.

'Is this mine then?' I say, reaching for the chute.

But Matty laughs and pulls it away.

'We've only got three,' says Fliss. 'I'll share with Wink. Matty gets his own because he's a big lump. Sky gets to hang on to you on the way down.'

'Lucky me,' I mutter.

Sky bares her teeth at me. 'And watch your hands, Kyle, or you'll be dead before we hit the bog.'

20
LEAP OF FAITH

The wind shrieks and batters at us, makes it impossible to talk. As we climb outside, Matty signals for us to follow him along the top of the hull. When we're all out, he reaches down and kicks the hatch closed behind us. Fliss fiddles with the wires behind a panel and I feel a *clunk* as the hatch locks. With luck, nobody will ever know this jammer carried more than just grain from Tranquility. No going back now either.

I look down and frighten the hell out of myself.

Our jammer's skimming alongside a steep cliff face, which rears above us. I crank my neck back to see the top. Big mistake. Now I feel dizzy. Great big slabs of rock flash past our wingtip. Any closer and we'd be striking sparks.

Above the howl of the wind, I hear this groaning sound.

Takes a while to realise it's me making it.

Matty and Fliss clamber upwards, sure-footed as mountain goats. When they reach the flat spine at the top of the hull, they drop to their hands and knees and start crawling back towards the transport's tail section. Wink, tightly strapped to Fliss, gives us a cheerful wave, like Fliss is crawling across a yard, not clinging to a wind-lashed windjammer hull over a thousand metres in the air.

Our turn. Sky pinches me and shouts in my ear.

'Come on. Wink can do it, so can you.'

I suck a lungful of air, then crawl after them. There's nothing much to hang on to and it's brutal hard work because Sky's wearing the chute and so she's strapped to my back. I'm carrying her, as well as the pack on my chest.

If I slip before we're over the swamp, we're dead.

One good thing – at least like this, Sky can't see how scared I am.

The windjammer hits lift and banks into a turn. Feeling myself sliding off, I look around desperately for something to hang on to, but all I see is a gap between two buckled hull plates. I dive and wedge my fingers in, hard as I can.

Somehow, I hold on until we finish the climb.

Matty comes back. He drags me along to where Fliss and Wink are waiting. The hull slopes down here and we can shelter from the blasting wind.

'Soon as *I* jump, *you* jump!' he shouts.

'And don't pull too early,' Fliss shouts at Sky.

Sky will pop the chute, so my life's in her hands. Matty wants us all to open the chutes as low as possible, so we don't spend too long hanging about underneath the white and easy-to-see canopies. I don't like the sound of any of this.

'What if it doesn't open?' I ask Sky over my shoulder.

She laughs, her warm breath tickling my ear she's so close behind me. 'Well, I guess you get to break my fall.'

Great. Wish I hadn't asked.

Our windjammer wheels away from the cliff. An air brake

pops up from the wing and I feel pressure in my ears. We're going down now.

Sky gives my arm a squeeze. 'Relax. If this fouls up, it'll be quick.'

Way below, water glitters in the late dayshine.

Matty gives us a thumbs up, then flings himself off backwards without even looking. Gravity's a monster – one moment he's there, hair whipping round his head, the next it gets its claws into him and he's a tiny falling dot.

Fliss and Wink step off next and are gone.

I can't. I freeze, like I've been blasted by that Slayer muscle-lock.

'Jump!' yells Sky.

And I don't mean to, but suddenly we're tumbling through the air. I close my eyes and everything goes white. When I open them again, I'm looking up and the windjammer's a little insect now, crawling across the blue sky. Everything happens so bogging fast I don't have time to be scared. Sky must pull the release because suddenly I feel like I'm turned inside out. The straps holding me to her do their best to cut me in half. Next thing, I'm staring at my feet, dangling under me.

The ground comes up to meet us horribly fast.

'*Yeeeaaaaayyy!*' Sky screams in my ear.

I hate swamps like I hate water. Always have. They stink. They're full of bugs that bite and creatures that slither. Step in the wrong place and they suck you down.

Won't hear a bad word said about this swamp though.

We drop through some fern-like trees, which slow us down

some more, then dump us nice and gentle into some waist-deep, watery mud, where we thrash about until Sky manages to unclip herself from me. By the time we struggle out on to an island of higher ground, we're both covered head to foot in muck and swamp slime.

'I'm *never* doing that again,' I say, digging filth out of my ears.

'You should *see* yourself, Kyle,' says Sky.

I look round, and she's killing herself laughing at me.

'Like you look any better?'

She shakes her head, her green eyes shining, her hollow-cheeked and mud-spattered face still flushed from the rush of the jump. 'I've never seen anyone look so fed up as you do now,' she says. 'Not even me, and that's saying something.'

I glare at her, but this sets her off laughing even harder.

Suddenly, I'm roaring laughing too. And somehow we end up giving each other a big, wet, squelchy hug. We stagger back and forth like this for a precious few moments, laughing helplessly into each other, before Sky decides she's done being hugged and starts squirming. Only I'm not thinking straight and a tiny bit slow letting her go. She goes from squirming to shoving me in the chest. And I don't think she means to, but I go flying and splash down on my backside in the mud again. I sit there gritting my teeth for a good few seconds, feeling horribly embarrassed, before wincing up at her. I'm expecting one of her fiercest scowls, but instead she looks almost sorry. She even gives me a hand to get back up again.

But it's all a bit tense and awkward.

Sky hauls the chute out the water and starts wrestling it back into its bag. Waterlogged and heavy, it's a nightmare. I offer to help her with it, but she grunts at me that she can manage. After that I don't dare offer again, worried it'll sound like I think she's useless. I can't watch her struggling, so I turn my back and make a start on scraping the worst of the mud and slime off my clothes.

Next thing, Sky's chucking me the packed chute bag to carry. 'C'mon then. Let's go find the others.'

'How?' There are trees all around us, drooping little mossy things whose name I can never remember, but which flower the same day each year and spit the yellow seeds you chew to make headaches go away. They grow so boggin' thick down here I can't see much further than a few dozen metres in any direction.

'They dropped first, so they'll be upwind of us.'

She heads off that way.

I scramble after her. 'Hey, do you think anyone saw us?'

And now I *do* get scowled at. 'Saw what? There was nothing to see.'

Anybody else, I'd have to laugh. 'No, I mean d'you think our jump was seen?'

She shrugs. 'We opened low. I doubt it.'

'So we're in the clear?'

'For now maybe. Still not home and dry though.'

I'm so soaked, I can't imagine being dry again. And as for home, I can't think about that. As I slog along after Sky, the thought that we might be safe now, even if only for a while, is tough to get my head around. I feel suddenly tired.

It's like I daren't relax or fear will catch up with me.

Sky suddenly stops. 'You hear that?'

I listen, but hear nothing and shake my head.

Now, to my horror, Sky cups her hands round her mouth and calls. 'Fliss! Matty! Where are you?'

Not a shout, but still louder than I like. I'm so shocked, all I can do is stare at her, like are-you-out-of-your-mind?

'What?' She frowns. 'There's nobody here but us.'

With that, she calls them again, but louder.

It feels so weird after days of whispering, but I guess she's got a point. Anyway, not long after, Matty answers her call. We soon find each other. Fliss and Wink are already with him.

'What kept you guys?' he asks.

And I guess maybe we both look a bit startled.

Fliss gives us a look. 'You two okay?'

Even now, I can't stop my fingers twitching the Sign of One as I hear the 'two' word. They're swapping looks when Wink suddenly starts screaming.

Her face is bright red and terrified. 'Get it off me!'

She tears her coat off and claws at her back.

Fliss pulls Wink's shirt up. 'What the frag is *that*?'

Something big and wriggling is clamped to the poor child's back. A massive, sickly-white grub, thick as my arm. Even as we stare, the thing pulses and starts glistening pink. Matty sets his teeth and goes to pull it off her.

I knock him aside.

'Stop! Don't, you'll kill her. It's a megasucker.'

These things are mean. Try to pull one off, it squirts a gob full of poison into you. You swell up, go black and die roaring. Best thing is to grit your teeth and hope you've still got some blood left when it's done sucking.

Thing is though, Wink's too small and I've no time to explain.

'Sky, the rifle magazine. Quick!'

Fair play to her, she doesn't ask why, just hands it over.

It's a bit like lighting the fire. I jam the mag's contacts hard as I can into the creature's slimy skin until I hear a bang as the mag shorts out. Even megasuckers can't take a million volts of zap. It drops off Wink with an almost human sigh.

We all stand around, staring at it in disgust.

Until Sky stomps on it.

I'm telling them about the poison, Matty looking at me now like maybe I'm not such a donk after all, when Wink climbs up me and buries her snotty little face under my chin. I go to prise her off gentle, but nothing doing.

'Looks like you've made a friend,' says Fliss, smiling at me.

'You never know,' I say, glancing at Sky.

Not so much a friend as a shadow. Over the next few days, Wink sticks so close it's like having my own dark-haired leech following me. The only time I'm alone is when I'm hunting.

All of us are glad to be clear of the swamp. We spend one awful night there, listening to creepy splashes and thinking every itch is a megasucker. The next day we set off hiking cross-country, making for a place called Drakensburg. It's another big windjammer way station and junction. Matty says you can pretty much hop rides out of there to anywhere on Wrath. He also says the week it'll take to walk there isn't time wasted because the fuss of our escape will have died down. The bulls – who are pretty fierce there – will be getting careless again.

Suits me. Why push our luck now?

Sky's not happy. With her leg, she hates walking any distance.

She goes along with it though because she knows a Gemini contact based at some place called Haggletown, a short ridge run south of Drakensburg. She won't say who this is, only that if we hook up we're sorted.

Sorted. Whatever that means.

Anyway, we're here now, holed up in a cave five klicks west of the Drakensburg hub. We got here yesterday, footsore and hungry. Matty led us straight to it, says it's an old freerider hole in the wall. It's dry enough inside and a crack in the rock of the roof means we can have a fire at night. Compared to swamp and trail it's like paradise. I've spent the day hunting for food.

When I whistle that I'm back, Wink runs out of the cave.

'Hey, Kyle, what you got?'

'Not much.' Hailstorms made hunting tough. All I've bagged are a pair of scrawny young jumprats and a turkey lizard missing half its tail.

Wink wrinkles her nose. 'Is *that* all?'

She grabs them and ducks back into the cave. I follow her on my hands and knees. In the pale gleam from my shiner, I see Sky and Fliss in the shadows at the back, heads together and chatting. They shut up as soon as I crawl in. Fliss calls out a greeting, friendly enough, but Sky scrambles up and pushes past me.

'I'll check the traps,' she says and heads outside.

Wink gives me a *What's that about?* look.

I turn to Fliss, but she ducks my eye and gets busy skinning the rats.

I fling my useless home-made bow on to my sleep bag. 'This thing doesn't pull straight. I'll have to make another. Where's Matty?'

Fliss shrugs. 'Went to Drak to see what jammers are there.'

Out of the corner of my eye, I see Wink sneaking up on me. I turn and growl, but she just sticks her tongue out, grabs the bow and runs off to play with it.

Fliss laughs. 'Wink, be careful with that.'

'So you were in the same ident camp as Sky,' I say to her.

She rips the skin off the rat. 'For ten long years.'

'That why you're helping us?'

'Maybe.'

'What was it like?'

I wait until she sighs and puts the knife down.

'Did you know all ident camps are in mining towns?' she says. 'No? Well, they are. And guess who does the mining? We did. You start when you're four, working the vents in the pitch-dark. At six, you join the pulling gangs, hauling the ore wagons. At ten, if you're still alive, you start working the seams, picking and shovelling.'

In the shiner glow her eyes look through me to her past.

'We always worked in the same gang,' she continues. 'A roof prop failed. Sky saw it go and pushed me clear, but the rockfall caught her.'

'Is that what happened to her leg?'

'Uh-huh. Her leg got crushed so badly, it crippled her. Turned her hair white too, the shock or the pain. She had to spend the rest of her time in the camps hobbling about on some rubbish crutches I made.'

I think about this and wince. 'Must've been awful hard for her.'

Fliss sighs. It's a guilty-sounding sigh.

'We weren't the monsters in the camps, Kyle, the guards were. You cried, you got thrashed. Talked back, you got the lash. I've seen kids beaten to death. After Sky got hurt she couldn't hit her coal quota. We all took turns helping her so she got her food ration. We loved her so we were glad to, even though it was back-breaking work. But you've seen what Sky's like. She paid us back the only way she could, by taking our beatings. If we made mistakes, she'd say she'd done it.'

'And you let her?' I say, shocked.

'We couldn't stop her; even Tarn couldn't.'

'Tarn's her sister?'

Fliss nods. 'So that's how it was. Rough enough, I guess.'

Neither of us says much for a while. Fliss finishes skinning the rats and I rip the armour off the turkey lizard. We gut them while Wink plays at archery.

The better I know Sky, the more I wish that she'd stop scowling at me.

'You hooked up again then, after you got out?' I ask.

'Neither of us had family. I got out a year after Sky so I don't know how she got into freeriding. I was begging in the Blight. One day she comes swinging along, still on those sticks I made her. She spots me, says why don't I come with her for the ride? Beats being spat on, I figured. Been hopping jammers ever since. Thing is, Sky can't let go of what happened in the camps and losing her sister. She would take crazy chances. Kept going on and on about revenge. I don't blame her, but she was going to get me killed. One day I split. Missed her ever since.'

'So how come Sky ended up with . . . Gemini?'

'No idea,' says Fliss. 'You'd have to ask her that. Why don't you?'

My turn to sigh. 'You're kidding, right?'

Fliss gives me a lopsided smile now, like something's funny, but sad too.

'What?' I say. 'Sky hardly talks to me at all.'

'You don't know much about girls, do you, Kyle.'

'What's to know? You saw what happened just now – as soon as I show up here, she leaves.'

'She's checking the traps.'

'This late? You know there's no point until the morning.'

Fliss rolls her eyes. 'She's just shy, that's all.'

'Shy?' If she'd told me Sky was a Slayer spy, I'd be less gobsmacked.

She goes to say something else, but a whistle comes from outside the cave. Matty is already crawling inside before Wink can run out to meet him. He's all rain-soaked like me, his face shiny with excitement and news.

'A tramp windjammer with loose hatches is bound for Haggletown tomorrow morning,' he says, throwing his hood back. 'But look what I found.'

He pulls a crumpled piece of paper from his pocket, spreads it on the floor.

'That's you, isn't it?' squeaks Wink, delighted.

It is. A grainy image of me and my broken nose, Sky in the background. Across the top, WANTED, in big letters. Below, smaller writing describing what we're wearing, stuff like that.

And then some numbers. I'm no great reader, but I get the gist and almost choke.

Fifty thousand credits to anyone who squeals on us.

Anywhere on Wrath, that's a fortune!

21
DEBT PAID, TRADE MADE

'C'mon, Kyle,' Fliss says, 'it's not the end of the world. They were always going to put posters up. It's good news – means they don't know where you are.'

'Good news?' I say. 'I don't think so.'

'At least they want you alive.'

'Yeah, but only so they can have fun hanging me later.'

I go back to pacing about and feeling sick.

Seeing my face on that wanted poster was a nasty surprise, but it's the reward that's doing my head in and making me sweat. A barn full of credits for me, one lousy twist. This is scary and makes no kind of sense, even if I did make a Slayer windjammer crash. See, it's just way too big a reward. Most Barrenlanders I know would cheerfully sell out their own mother for a few hundred.

One thing's for sure, this will only make things worse for us.

I happen to look round and catch Matty watching me. The guy's got this narrow-eyed and thoughtful look on his bugweb-tattooed face, and I wonder if he's spending my fifty thousand blood credits in his head already. A second later and my heart almost stops as a breathless Sky comes crashing into the cave.

So much for whistling a warning like we'd agreed.

'Seen this?' says Matty, grabbing the poster and thrusting it at her.

But Sky hardly glances at it. 'You were seen,' she snarls.

'No way,' he spits. 'I was in and out like a ghost.'

Sky snorts, her angry eyes never once leaving Matty's face.

'I was up the hill and saw you running back in such a hurry to show us your poster. Guess you didn't have time to watch your tail. If you had, you'd have seen the two bulls following you. You've led them straight to us.'

Matty opens his mouth, twitches, closes it again.

'Where are they?' I say, horrified.

'I took care of one, but the other ran and I couldn't catch him.' Sky sucks her cheeks in then blows them out in a sigh. 'He'll have got a good look at me.'

'Oh, that's great,' I moan. 'So they'll know it's *us* then.'

Sky shrugs. 'For sure. The bull I killed had that poster on him.'

I stare at her, swaying on my feet in despair, feeling as crushed down now as if the roof of the cave had just fallen in on us. 'What do we do?'

Sky grabs my pack and chucks it at me.

'We run. What do you think?'

And now everybody starts yelling and shouting, even Wink.

Not Fliss though. She stands there like a rock in a river, calm while we rage around her. 'I've got an idea,' she says, and keeps saying it until we listen.

'What idea?' I say, clutching at the determined look on her face.

Next thing, she crouches down and beckons to Wink.

The girl runs to her. 'What's going on?'

'Wink, go outside. Shout if anyone comes.'

The little girl looks unsure, but does as she's told.

'Matty,' Fliss says as soon as Wink's gone, 'tell Sky about the ride.'

The guy has a face on him like he's been shot, but mutters through his teeth about the Haggletown-bound windjammer with its take-off set for tomorrow.

Sky rolls her eyes. 'So what? Drak will be on full alert now.'

Fliss swallows hard, reaches out and takes Sky's hand.

'It won't; the bulls will be too busy chasing Matty and me. You know how greedy they are. With a reward like that, none of them will want to stay behind to watch the windjammers. We'll lead them away and you can hop a ride out.'

Sky says nothing, but I see the way she squirms, as if in pain.

'You don't look anything like us,' I say to Fliss.

Fliss glances from me to Matty. 'That won't matter. All those credits, the dumb bulls will see what they want to see. We'll help them out by trading clothes.'

Matty stares back at her, his bugweb tattoo writhing as he scowls. But then he grits his teeth and nods.

'I screwed things up, I'll sort it,' he growls.

Fliss hugs him, gives him the kind of look I'd like a girl to give me one day.

'We can't ask you to do this,' says Sky, her voice fierce.

Can't we? I glare at her like she's mad.

I needn't worry. Turns out sad-eyed Fliss can do fierce too.

'So don't ask!' she snaps at Sky, her voice high and wild now.

'All those years in the camps you *never* asked anybody for anything, but you saved my neck then and we're going to save yours now, and that's all there is to it. You get back to Gemini and you find my sister. We're just a pair of lousy ridge rats, but you can change things. Now quit pulling faces and hand over your leathers.'

Sky chews at her lip. 'And what if they catch you?'

Fliss shrugs. 'They won't, but even if they do, so what? We're not you. We'll swear blind we only ran because we're freeriders and saw bulls coming. Worst that'll happen to us is we'll get a beating, and we can handle that.'

Even I don't think she can believe this.

I glance across at Sky. Her face, always so pale, is like chalk now. Half of me can't believe she's going to let her friend do this thing. Only half though. The chickenshit rest of me is hoping and praying that she will.

Sky curses and starts tearing her leathers off.

Matty shrugs off his dogskin coat and holds it out to me. He'll struggle to fit into my old parka, but that's his problem. I start emptying my pockets.

'Take Wink with you,' he says.

That straightens me up. I stare, but he's serious.

'She'll be safer,' he says. 'And we can move faster without her.'

I toss him my parka and pull his coat on. It's tight and stinks something awful.

'Are you *sure* you want to do this?' I say.

But Fliss just smiles at me. It's heartbreaking seeing how brave this girl is because I can see how scared she is behind that front she's putting on. Her hands are shaking so bad she struggles to do up the zips on Sky's leathers.

'Who's your contact in Haggletown?' Matty asks Sky.

Sky's got her back to me, pulling on Fliss's jacket, but I see her stiffen.

'Why do you want to know?' she says slowly.

Matty curses. 'Why do you think? After we lead your bulls away, we'll have to lie low for a while. I figure maybe Gemini could give us a hand afterwards, to catch up with you and Wink again. Or is that too much to ask, huh?'

Fliss says nothing, but looks uncomfortable.

'Sky, tell them, for Wrath's sake,' I say, terrified they'll change their mind.

Sky gives me the full scowl.

'His name's Efren,' she says, teeth gritted. 'A tavern master.'

Matty grunts, and I can breathe again.

'Sky, there's one more thing I'll need,' Fliss says.

'Anything,' Sky says, and I've never heard her voice so unsteady.

'They've been seen,' Sky says, peering through the scope from the pulse rifle.

I know. I hear shouting and see the green flashes.

We're high on the hill above the cave, flat on our bellies with a view down to where Matty and Fliss are leading the bulls away. They do it smart. No standing up and waving nonsense, just running, dumb and careless and scared.

Even from here I see the white dreads lashing about behind Fliss's head.

'They definitely think she's you,' I say.

I check on Wink. I'm crapping myself she'll scream and get us killed. But no. I guess the kid's learnt the hard way from running with Matty and Fliss. She's curled up in a little hollow behind us, doing that feral thing baby animals do straight out of the womb. Tell her to stay and be quiet, and she does it.

For a rag of a girl, she's good really.

'Right then,' says Sky, as the sounds of pursuit fade. 'Let's do this.'

She says it offhand enough, but I'm not fooled. I saw the way she and Fliss hugged and looked at each other when we said our goodbyes.

'Think they'll make it?' I say.

Sky doesn't answer. Which is answer enough, I guess.

As I follow her down the back of the hill I still can't get used to how changed she looks with the dreads gone and her white hair cropped so short. It's like I'm looking at a different girl, younger, a lot less tough. It was a brutal thing to watch, but Sky just sat there and didn't flinch once, even though she'd had those dreads since not long after she left the camp. Fliss did the hacking, using her sharpest skinning knife, and a decent job of tidying her up after, considering how little time she had. Clever too how Matty wove the severed strands into Fliss's hair so that she could wear them. Won't fool anyone up close, but it doesn't need to.

Sky glances back and catches me looking again.

I look away quick. Her dreads might be gone, but her temper isn't.

Half an hour later, as the sun sets, we swing around in a wide circle, sticking to forest where we can, and pick our way towards the Drakensburg landing site. Sky takes my pack and I carry Wink piggyback. I try to talk to her when we stop for a rest and a pee, but the girl's gone mute. She won't even look at me.

Don't know about Sky, but I feel sick with guilt.

Fliss was right about the bulls and the reward. We curl up for the night in the low spreading branches of a changi tree. Looking through the scope, all I keep seeing is more people streaming out of the base. Not all of them are bulls either. Looks to me like everyone with a dog or a gun is scrambling after that fifty thousand.

They disappear off in the direction of the cave.

'More the better,' Sky mutters. 'They'll trip each other up.'

It's going to be another long, cold night. Wink sobs herself to sleep after a while, but I can't settle. Neither can Sky. The small dogmoon rises, half full now, so bright it shimmers and paints the forest silver and blue. It would be beautiful if it wasn't for all the deep shadows, which could hide anything. Those nightrunners we ran into are not the only creatures to be scared of out here. For something to do, I climb higher up the tree until I can make out the dark hulks of the windjammers beyond the fence. There's dozens of them. In the moonshine, I've no way of telling which one Matty found out was bound for Haggletown.

Hopefully Sky can figure it out.

She's wrong – you *do* need hope. I do anyway.

I start to clamber back down, only to see a dark shape below me, hauling itself up hand over hand to join me. I back up and make room for Sky to perch. She pulls the scope out, scans around and gives a satisfied-sounding grunt.

'That's the jammer Matty was on about, by the wire.'

She hands me the scope. It's set on night-viz, so everything's painted different shades of green. I've no idea which jammer she means, they all look pretty much the same to me, but at least I don't see any Slayer transports. I thumb the scope to infrared and scan around us for signs of warm bodies. Nothing large enough to make me suck my teeth. The local wildlife is cutting us some slack anyway.

'You didn't know you were an ident?'

Sky's whisper floats out of the darkness, making me jump. She leans forward from the shadows and shrugs her hood back so I can see her face. Her voice is flat, but she looks at me all curious – maybe a bit sympathetic even.

I shiver. 'Did Rona tell you, or were you having a good listen outside?'

She shrugs, like *does it matter?*

'No,' I tell her, my cheeks burning. 'I didn't know.'

She nods, then holds her hand out for the scope. I hand it over.

'What's your twin's name again?' she asks.

'Colm.' Saying his name out loud still feels weird and uncomfortable.

'Do you think about him?'

'Why should I? Chances are he's dead.'

I so nearly add 'like your sister', but stop myself. I figure there's plenty enough hurt going around. And I'm lying too. Truth is, in between all the running, my brother's been crawling into my head a lot. And I keep having that nightmare, the one where I look up from the red altar cloth to see another me.

Colm, my scab brother. Me, the twist who heals.

Sky frowns up at the sky to where a band of stars is shining now, a trail of twinkling light arching across the heavens. 'You don't know he's dead,' she says, her voice a hoarse whisper. 'Maybe he's out there somewhere too, looking up at these same stars and wondering where *you* are. You ever think of that?'

I hadn't, but I do now. And shiver.

Then, hearing the weird longing in her voice, I get it. Sky's talking about my brother, but she's thinking about her sister, Tarn. For a long while we both just sit there, so close we're almost touching, but alone with our thoughts. I try fierce hard not to think about Fliss and Matty. Instead, I picture Rona, her greying hair, the worry lines around her eyes. I'm scared that if I don't do this I'll start to forget her.

But the wanted poster gets in the way of my remembering.

'Did you see that reward?' I ask her.

'What about it?'

'Ever seen a reward as big as that before?'

Sky yawns and shakes her head. 'Does look like they want you real bad.'

'Your face is on it too,' I point out.

'Yeah, but you're the one they want. The reward's for you.'

I swallow. 'Why so massive though? I don't get it.'

'Yeah, me neither.' She shrugs. 'And only paid if you're taken alive. That's weird too.' She reaches out, plucks one of the tree's leaves and starts fiddling with it.

Neither of us says much for a while after that.

I go back to thinking about Rona . . . and let out a little groan.

'What?' says Sky, throwing the leaf away.

'Nothing.' I lick my lips. 'Just a bit of cramp, that's all.'

She gives me a thin, sceptical smile. 'Yeah, cramp, that can be bad all right.'

I know she doesn't believe me, but there's no way I'm telling her what I'm thinking. See, I've remembered what Rona said to me before that lynch mob showed up, about my biggest danger not being *what* I am, but *who* I am. And I've remembered something else too – the way High Slayer Morana started and stared at me after she'd cleaned the blood off my face, almost as if she knew me from somewhere, even though she couldn't. Add to that her surprise at Gemini rebels sending a windjammer to collect me and now this heap of credits for a reward.

It all points one way – this isn't just about me being a twist.

Whatever's going on, it's much worse than that.

I get the fear bad then. Even before I found out I was a twist, I'd sometimes wake up in the dark, in a cold sweat, terrified of dying. It's the ending that terrifies me, the not *being* any more. I imagine a darkness going on forever, like that time I was drowning. I'm so scared, I'm trembling. I hope Sky doesn't feel it.

We climb down and find Wink asleep where we left her.

I must nod off myself because next thing Sky is shaking me. The sky's already light. Dawn can't be far away. I'm chilled, stiff all over and my mouth feels like a bird has nested in it. Wink stares down at me, big-eyed and solemn.

'Sky was right,' she says. 'You snore like a pig.'

'You're talking again?' I say. 'Good.'

'Time to go,' Sky hisses, and throws my pack at me again.

22
HAGGLETOWN

Hopping the tramp windjammer to Haggletown was so easy I could have done it on my own. We did the crawling under the wire and creeping about thing, but we could have marched through Drakensburg's main gate banging drums and got away with it, the place was so dead. Quiet as the grave, Rona would say. Even the guard towers didn't look manned. Fliss was right; reward fever had hit hard. And Matty wasn't kidding either when he said our jammer had 'loose' hatches. Talk about a wreck – the problem wasn't levering the jammer's battered hatch open, it was closing it again. The cargo was aromatic wood, so I stink of that now.

Sky reckons this is a big improvement.

Slipping off at Haggletown is simple enough too. After a hard landing, which feels more like a crash, we hear a steam tractor puff its way out to meet us. It tows us backwards down the runway. Fortunately, this windjammer crew seem keener on heading off for drinks and a good time than unloading wood. They stomp off, chatting loudly. We wait a sweaty few minutes, prise the hatch open on the far side of the jammer, slide down the hull and clear off into the cover of some bushes.

My heart's pumping like mad, but nobody shouts so it's looking good.

And I get my first view of Haggletown. It's nothing like I expected. It's not a town, it's a market. The landing ground is little more than a long strip of meadow, running down the middle of a steep-sided valley. This side, where we are, there's nothing but scrub, but the valley wall opposite us has been hacked into lots of rocky levels linked by ladders and narrow switchback paths. Each terrace is covered with a rash of tents and stalls and bellowing merchants. The higher the terrace, the bigger the tents, and the finer and more brightly dressed the hawkers. It reminds me of the Peace Fair on that first day we got there, only a lot smaller.

I pull the scope from my pack. First thing I zoom in on are the food stalls. My mouth fills with drool, I'm so hungry. One thing I don't see is any inn or tavern. I scan the whole place, top to bottom. The only building there is a small white-washed temple, its faded prayer flags snapping in the breeze.

'How do we find this Efren guy then?'

Sky shoots me a look, like I've reminded her of a bad memory.

'*We* don't. You stay here with Wink. I'll go find him.'

I don't like this and my stomach ties itself in knots with a sudden terror. In the Barrenlands I've maybe been some use to Sky. Now we're here, back in her world, how do I know she won't just clear off back to Gemini and leave me?

Or might she even be mad enough to go for that reward?

'No way,' I say. 'We stay together, that's the deal.'

'Yeah,' squeaks Wink behind me.

Poor kid, I'd almost forgotten her.

'What?' sneers Sky. 'Don't you trust me?'

I mimic her way of shrugging. 'I don't trust anyone.'

Sky argues, but it's not like she can stop us following her. In the end she gives in, on one condition – we wait until sundown. Which makes sense; the traders will be packing up then. Less people will be around to see us coming. And it'll be colder too, so we can have our hoods pulled up without looking suspicious.

Chances are that wanted poster will have beaten us here.

We burrow into the long grass and crush it down to make ourselves an invisible nest. It's pleasant at first. This valley must be much lower than Drakensburg and the high sun warms us as we lie there with our stomachs rumbling. After so long in chill mountain air I can feel myself thawing out.

Only then the bugs find us. They're fierce hungry too.

Something's wrong. Sky gets all nervous and fidgety. The few times I dare talk to her, she practically snarls at me. Even poor little Wink gets snapped at. Okay, so we're all tired and cross after a long day baking in the sun and being gobbled by bugs, but Sky doesn't do scared, so why the sudden mood?

And something else is odd. She keeps staring at this small grey windjammer parked up near us.

I ask her why, but only get glared at.

Anyway, the sun slid down behind the mountains an hour ago, plunging the valley into deep shadow and sucking the warmth out of the air. It's proper black-dark now, so we grab our stuff, pull our hoods up and head out. Above us, in the light from swinging lanterns, the merchants on the upper terraces are packing away their wares. On the lower levels, large fires are blazing, a crowd milling around them. A soft evening breeze wafts us the shrill of pipe music, raucous singing and the gob-slobbering smell of roasting meat. As we pick our way round a roped-off area full of goods wagons, sharp-eyed brats watch us go by.

'Why the party?' I ask Sky.

With her hood pulled up I hear her scowl more than see it. 'Local fools being separated from the few credits they earned selling their wares. The merchants own the bars, the liquor and the girls. That's how these places operate.'

'Clever.' I'd never thought about things like this before.

'You think?' Her voice is acid.

Bulked-up guards block the trail up. But we get lucky – a bunch of loud-mouthed traders get there just before we do. They're stopped, made to hand over all their weapons, then get patted down. Blasters and blades – and these guys have plenty – are locked up in a cage in exchange for a token. Meanwhile, Sky pulls me to one side. Blinded by the flames from their brazier, the guards don't spot us as we circle round. Fine, but all I see now is a cliff, twenty metres high.

'Now what do we do?' I whisper to Sky.

'You'll see,' she says.

Minutes later, I'm hauling myself up rusty spikes driven into the rock, Wink hanging on to my back. I almost rip my arms off getting to the top, but up there is a side trail, lightly used by the healthy look of the weeds. This winds its way up to the lowest terrace, where we take cover behind a fallen tree.

'Off you go,' Sky says to Wink.

In the flickering firelight, she shows the girl our wanted poster again.

'Yeah, yeah, you told me already,' says Wink.

Before Sky can say anything more, bold as you like, the little girl clambers over the log, hops down and races towards the fires and the crowd.

'You sure she'll be okay?' I ask Sky.

She grunts like this is a stupid question. 'We need to know.'

'That's not what I asked.'

I hate sending Wink off like this. Okay, so maybe nobody's looking for her, but it feels pretty slanky sending a six-year-old off alone into a dive like this. To give myself something to do, I pull my gun out and start cleaning it again.

'Put that thing away before it goes off,' says Sky.

I take a break from polishing. 'What's this Efren look like?'

Sky sighs, pulls her hood down and meets my stare.

'There is no Efren. I made him up.'

She says it extra slow, making sure I hear. And it's like this cold hand reaches into my lungs and rips every bit of breath out of me. 'You did *what*?'

'I couldn't tell them my contact's real name.'

'Why not?' I say, astonished.

'Oh, come on,' she says. 'Don't be so dumb, Kyle. If they're caught, they'll talk. I couldn't risk my contact.'

I hear the words. I know what they mean. But I can't believe them. 'So you lied to your friends. Even after they risked their necks to save us.'

'You *don't* understand,' she says, fierce now.

Oh, I understand all right. It's just I don't want Sky to be so ruthless.

But I don't want to die either.

'Okay, so who *are* we looking for here then?'

She rolls her eyes. 'You'll find out soon enough, won't you?'

I watch as she reaches into a pocket and pulls out that weird glove of hers, the flesh-coloured one with the fake little finger. Carefully, she wriggles her left hand into it, holds it up and adjusts it so even I can't tell it's not real.

'No scabs allowed in Haggletown,' she says.

At the sound of running feet, I spin round. It's Wink. I put the pistol away as she scrambles back over the log, her face shiny with excitement.

'That was *fun*! Look what I found.'

She throws me something, which jingles as I catch it. A purse full of credits.

'Where'd you get this?' I ask, trying to pull myself together.

Wink looks all innocent. 'Found it.'

'Sure, but did you *find* any posters?' snaps Sky.

'Nuh-uh,' says Wink, and shakes her head.

'Enough talk, let's go,' says Sky.

She pulls her hood up and heads off without looking back.

Jumping off a windjammer wasn't half so scary as diving into this crowd of strangers, hoping nobody recognises me and shouts. My skin crawls as I push past one old woman and she glances at me. Even if she hasn't seen the poster, I can't help worrying she'll somehow know I'm a twist. But she just shows me the one rotting tooth she has left and curses me for getting in her way.

I breathe a sigh of relief, keep my head down and hood up. Inside my coat pocket, I feel for my gun's trigger. With my free hand, I tow Wink after me.

We catch up with Sky and fall into step behind her.

'Hey, look at that,' I say, grabbing her arm.

She looks, then curses as she sees what I'm staring at. A whole goat carcass, roasting nicely over a crackling wood fire, a small boy slowly cranking the spit around. I can't drag my eyes away from the sizzling meat. Seems cruel to walk past it with an empty stomach and a full purse.

'Later,' hisses Sky, pulling away.

She grabs Wink and plunges down a path between tents. I take one last look, fill my nose with the sweet stink of roast and hurry after them.

To my surprise she waits for me.

'Listen,' she says, 'This place ain't the Blight, but it's rough enough. I need you to watch my back. And Wink, no more nicking stuff. Last thing we need now is some stupid grubber missing his purse and shouting his head off. Deal?'

Wink looks sulky, but nods. 'Deal.'

Sky turns to go, then hesitates. Her hood swings back. In the flickering shadows from the goat fire, I see her staring at me.

'Whatever you think of me,' she says, 'you must trust me.'

'Sure,' I say. Like I've got any choice now.

She sighs, then leads off, threading her way between tents and campfires. I follow, glad she knows where she's going. This place is a maze. Finally, she stops outside the biggest and dirtiest tent I've seen so far. Flaring braziers frame its entrance flap. Above, on a badly faded sign, I can just about make out a tankard of foaming ale and crudely painted dancing girls. From inside comes a roar of deep voices, the most tuneless singing I've ever heard and the sound of clapping.

Even out here, it stinks of smoke, stale beer, piss and puke.

'If he's anywhere, he'll be here,' says Sky, grimacing.

Hardly are the words out of her mouth when two stocky farmer types crash out of the tent, trading drunken punches. One trips and falls. The other kicks him in the head, then falls over too. They pick themselves up and stagger off, laughing.

'Tell you what, Sky,' I say. 'You find your pal. I'll wait out here with Wink.'

Sky bares her teeth. 'Don't think so. Give her your pack.'

I do as she says. Sky bends down, shouts something in Wink's ear, points, then pushes her towards the shelter of a nearby parked-up wagon. Next thing, before I know what she's doing, she grabs me and pulls me inside. If the noise and the stink outside were bad, inside they're eye-watering. A few glowtubes hang from the frame of the tent, but they're turned down so low it's almost as dark in here as outside. And you could slice the hookah smoke with a knife, it's so thick.

Just as well, I figure, swallowing nervously. There's stuff going on in here, especially on the low stage at the back, I'm not sure I want to see.

Not in front of Sky anyway.

She leans in and shouts in my ear. 'Stay close.'

I follow as she picks her way round the crowded benches, peering at people's faces in the half-light. Most are way too flushed with drink or drugs to notice or care about this, but not all. We start collecting suspicious glances.

I steer Sky towards a gap in the crowd at the bar.

'Let go,' she hisses, squirming.

'Stare at people like that,' I tell her, 'and you'll get us killed.'

She knows I'm right because she stops wriggling.

Behind the makeshift bar – a bunch of wooden crates stacked in a circle – a skinny kid with a face full of pox scars and a gob full of shadeweed chew slides over to serve us. His bloodshot eyes flicker over me to linger on Sky.

'What you'se havin'?' he asks, leering at her.

'A bottle of black ale each,' Sky mutters, like she's done this before.

He knocks the tops off two dusty bottles and hands them over. As I pay from Wink's stolen purse, Sky leans forward and asks him something. He nods. She asks him something else, but now he looks sly. Sky nudges me.

I fumble a credit out and toss it to him.

The boy sneers and jerks his head at the darkness to the right of the stage.

'Dern's over there, last I seen. What's left of him anyway.'

23
PICKING UP THE PIECES

Maybe my nublood eyes do gloom better than Sky's because I see the guy before she does. He's the drunk face down on a table, one arm flung out in front of him clutching an empty spirits bottle. He looks dead, but can't be. Dead guys don't snore that loud.

'Don't tell me,' I say, appalled. 'This pisshead's your contact.'

Sky pushes me aside, grabs the guy's long blond hair and hauls his head up. He's not old. Late twenties maybe. A good-looking face, but lived in. Underneath a battered and stained rain jacket I see he's wearing windjammer leathers.

'Murdo,' Sky hisses at him. 'Murdo Dern! Can you hear me?'

But the only thing that comes out of his mouth is a string of drool and a groan. She lets go of his hair and his head thumps back down on the table.

'Guess not then,' I jeer.

Sky curses, her face grim and pinched.

'We need him sober. You're the healer's son. Do something.'

I try tipping my beer over his head. Waste of beer. We take turns slapping his face. He flails a bit in pitiful self-defence, but that's all. In desperation I pay a serving girl to bring us scalding hot chai and we pour that down his throat.

He pukes over Sky's boots and that does the trick. At least now when we let go of him he doesn't face-plant again.

'Just let me die, won't you?' he groans, shaking, head in his hands. 'And can't you guys breathe more quietly – I've got bombs going off in my head.'

I fetch a candle so we can see better.

'Murdo,' says Sky, pulling his hands away. 'It's Sky. Remember me?'

He peers at her, obviously struggling to focus.

'Yeah, course I do,' he slurs. 'Get us a drink, will you?'

'We're wasting time here,' I say, twitching I'm so mad. 'If this loser's the best Gemini can do, I figure we're better off on our own. We should go.'

Sky glares and looks to see if anyone heard.

'Are you mad?' she hisses.

She's about to say something else when Murdo suddenly rears up and peers around, his face rigid with what looks to me like fear now.

'Hey, you guys ain't seen that nutter Skull or any of his goons?'

I glance at Sky, but she looks as confused as I am.

'We haven't seen them,' she tells him. 'Why? What've you done now, Murdo?'

'Nothin'. I was – just askin' that's all.'

Sky rolls her eyes at me. It's obvious the guy's lying. She lunges forward, grabs his wrists and gets right in his face. Heroic – I'm not sure I could do that. The man's breath stinks so bad it could stop Reapers in their tracks.

'Listen, Murdo. We need you to take us someplace, no questions asked.'

He squints at me bleary-eyed, then at Sky.

'Hop a jammer. I hear you're real good at doin' that.'

'It's not that simple,' says Sky.

'You got credits then?' he mumbles, still trying to look past her.

She shakes him until he looks at her.

'No credits, Murdo. It's for the cause,' she says. Lots of emphasis on *cause*.

He groans louder than ever. I think he's about to puke again, but instead he gives her a sly smile. 'Told you before, Sky. Don't talk to me about causes; they disagree with my mercenary nature. And don't ask me favours.'

I glimpse that ghost smile flicker across Sky's face again and feel jealous.

'Too late, Murdo,' she says. 'I'm asking.'

He curses and rubs at his red eyes.

'Yeah? Well here's the thing, Sky. I can't help you. I'm too busy.'

'Oh sure,' I can't help sneering, 'we see that.'

Sky waves at me to shut up, then does this big shrug. 'Okay, Murdo, tell you what, how about I go find this Skull guy and tell him you're here?'

This gets his attention. 'You wouldn't!'

'Want to bet?' I chip in.

Murdo scowls and thinks about this for a few seconds.

'Where do you want to go?' he says at last.

Sky looks around, checking she won't be overheard.

'Bastion.'

Amazing. This one little word clearly sobers Murdo up more than any amount of cold beer poured over his head, face-slapping or cups of steaming chai.

Only problem is, he goes even more shifty now.

'No such place. Only a rumour.'

Sky shakes her head. 'It's real. You've been there, so quit stalling.'

'Who told *you* that?'

The way he sputters this, even I can tell it must be true.

Sky stands up and stretches, like everything's settled. 'We saw your *Never Again* down on the landing field. She's still yours, isn't she?'

I picture that small, fast-looking grey windjammer Sky kept looking at.

'Why wouldn't she be?' he growls.

Sky smirks. 'How'd you lose the last one? Card game, right?'

'She's still mine,' Murdo says through his teeth.

He shows her a device on a cord around his neck. At a guess I'd say it's some sort of proximity key. Whatever it is, as soon as Sky sees it she leans in and snatches it from him, breaking the cord. Murdo tries to grab it back, but she ducks out of his reach. He struggles to get up, groans and slumps back down.

'Give me that,' he moans.

Sky shakes her head. 'How's your night flying?'

He belches. 'Like a bat, only better.'

'No way can this guy can fly anything, the state he's in,' I say.

'Who are you again?' says Murdo.

'Fly us to Bastion,' says Sky. 'I'll make it worth your while.'

The man's eyes light up now, blue and calculating. 'How worth my while?'

I watch the skin on Sky's face go taut.

'I'll tell you where the *Rockpolisher* is,' she says. 'She wasn't damaged, last we saw, but she's marooned. I'll give you half the salvage.'

'Full salvage,' says Murdo.

Sky doesn't blink. 'When do we leave?'

Murdo makes another attempt to struggle to his feet, fails again. 'Ugh. How about you guys come back tomorrow?' he says, groaning. 'It's like your boyfriend says, I don't feel too clever right now.'

I glance at Sky. 'What's this Bastion place you're on about?'

'Can't you give him something?' she says.

'Didn't you hear me?'

'I'll tell you later, okay? Not here.'

I glance around the bar at the rough-looking crowd and spot watching eyes flicking away from us. 'Okay,' I tell her, 'I'll be back in a minute.'

I scoot outside again, find Wink still hunkered down under the wagon.

'What's taking so long?' she whines as I raid my pack.

'It's complicated. I'll tell you later.'

I find the plastic bag of herbs in Rona's medkit, then hurry back inside. 'It doesn't taste half as bad as it looks,' I tell Murdo. It's healer tradition; Rona always told the same lie.

He pulls some awful faces, but chokes it down.

'What *is* that stuff?' Sky whispers, watching.

'Rona calls it hype,' I tell her. 'It's like adrenaline. He'll feel worse before he feels better, but after it kicks in he'll be bouncing off the walls.'

'Let's hope so.' Sky looks thoughtful for a few seconds. 'Listen, you'd better stay here with Murdo and keep an eye on him. I'll go fetch Wink and run back down to the *Never Again*. I can power her up and call for a winch-launch.'

'You know how to do that?' slurs Murdo.

'Sure. I night-launched out of here with Chane one time.'

Murdo nods. 'Chane. Yeah. How is the big lump?'

'He's dead. Slayers got him.'

'Shame. Chane was okay. Although what he ever saw in *you* . . .'

Sky stiffens and clenches her fists. I think she'll slug him, but she takes a deep breath and scowls at me instead. 'Kyle, soon as this useless gom can walk, bring him down the hill. If those guards stop you, just tell them he's too smashed to find his own way back to his jammer and you're helping him out.'

She sneers at Murdo. 'Act drunk. Shouldn't be too tough for you, huh?'

'See what I can do,' he says, looking sick now.

'Full salvage, remember,' says Sky.

As she turns to go, she leans in to me and whispers.

'Don't let him mess with you. If he needs persuading, use your gun.'

'Okay.' I nod, startled, wondering if she's serious, but she's already gone. When I look back, Murdo's eyes are bulging. He clutches his belly.

Frag it. All Rona's herbs look the same. I hope it's only hype I gave him and not something worse . . .

The longest twenty minutes of my life later, Murdo's on the

mend. There's colour back in his face, he's stopped shivering and his voice is less slurred.

But he wants one last drink before we head off.

'No,' I say. 'Sky's waiting. Let's go.'

'You ever flown a night winch-launch?' he says. 'No? Well, let me tell you, kid, you can't do it dry. One beer, for luck. Then we go, I promise.'

In my head I run through a whole bunch of wild ideas to get him moving. Most involve me beating him over the head with my gun and then slinging his unconscious body over my shoulder. Reluctantly, I buy him the beer.

'Hair of the dog,' he says, and knocks it back in one.

To be fair, it seems to do him some good. With a loud belch he staggers to his feet. It's not like he beats his chest or anything, but at least he's moving. I steer him round the bar and towards the tent flap. My nerves are pulled so tight inside me I can hardly walk myself, let alone help him.

'Quite some girl, Sky,' he says, stopping and staring at me.

I shrug, desperate to keep moving, aware of curious eyes watching us.

'What you doin', taggin' along with her?' he says.

'We're friends,' I snap. 'That's all.'

I shove Murdo to get him going again, hoping he doesn't try anything. We're so nearly at the tent's entrance now. A few more steps and we'll be outside.

'Sky doesn't have friends,' he mutters. 'Only people she uses.'

That's when I see people elbowing each other. Chairs scrape back from tables.

'Going somewhere, Dern?' growls an unfriendly voice.

Murdo stops so suddenly that I crash into him, which must look seriously dumb. 'Aw shit,' he says.

I peer past him and wish I hadn't.

Blocking our way is a huge, bullet-headed man in rich merchant's robes. He's incredibly fat, as wide as he is tall. His slab face is one big, freaky skull tattoo. And he doesn't mess about. He steps up and hammers a fist the size of a shovel into Murdo's face. Murdo reels back into me and we both go down.

I scramble up, but Murdo stays in a groaning heap on the dirt floor.

'Pick him up,' says the fat man.

Then I get it – this is the Skull guy Murdo was on about.

Two thugs bundle me aside and haul Murdo to his feet, twisting his arms behind his back so he can't defend himself. His head lolls forward. Blood streams from his mouth and down his chin. Skull punches him again, this time in the stomach, doubling him up. A growing crowd of watchers *ooh* and *aah*.

Behind me, I overhear a guy telling his mate what the deal is.

'Murdo's had it this time.'

'What'd he do?'

'Stuck a blade in some guy in a fight over a girl.'

'Killed the bloke?'

'Only slightly. Dead guy was family to Skull. He ain't happy.'

I reckon maybe the Skull guy hears all this too because he narrows his piggy eyes and glares around until the whispering and muttering stops. And now a wicked-looking blade appears in his hand, as if by magic.

'Any last words, Dern, before I skin you?'

Murdo starts coughing and can't stop. Gobs of red fly everywhere.

I'm holding my breath and quietly backing away, but that doesn't suit the bloodthirsty crowd. Watching one man die isn't enough entertainment.

Hard hands thrust me forward again.

'Who are *you*?' Skull rumbles.

'Just some kid,' Murdo gasps. 'I don't know him.'

I'm shaking so bad, people point and laugh.

Skull isn't laughing though. He stares down at me and shakes his head, making his jowls ripple.

'Seems like I saw your pretty-boy face somewhere before.'

I don't mean to run, but my legs take off and the rest of me is still attached, so goes after them. I don't get very far. Another of Skull's muscled-up thugs catches me, grabs me by the throat and slams me down on to a table.

'Boss, this is the kid from the wanted poster,' he calls.

'Outstanding,' says Skull, hefting the knife. 'Now, where was I?'

Maybe it's my head smashing into the wood, the impact knocking something loose inside my brain. Or maybe it's desperation. Anyway, one heartbeat I'm me, Kyle, scared and moaning with dread, the next . . . I'm possessed.

'NO!' I scream, at the top of my lungs.

The guy holding me isn't looking, sure I'm no threat.

I push him away to make room, then drive the heel of my hand into the side of his throat like Rona showed me. As hard as I can. He lets go and staggers backwards, eyes bulging. Skull's snake-fast for a big man, but I'm faster still. He swipes at me with his knife, but I knock it from his hand. Before his goons can react, I'm behind him, arm round his neck, jamming my pistol into his ear.

'Nobody move!' I shout. 'I'll blow his head off.'

With my thumb, I cock the gun.

'Don't shoot,' Skull squeals, waving his massive hands.

The watching crowd of people go berserk with hooting and yelling. I guess Skull isn't that popular. Sweat stings my eyes and I feel like I've swallowed a box of rusty nails.

'Let Dern go!' I shout, seeing him struggling.

Amazingly, the two guys holding him do as I tell them.

Murdo drops to his hands and knees. For one long, panicky second I worry he won't be able to get up again, but he grits his teeth and manages it.

'Nice one,' he wheezes, in between coughs.

'Let's get out of here,' I say, dragging Skull backwards.

'Wait,' says Murdo.

He ducks down, then pops up again, Skull's long blade in his hand.

'Don't!' I say, sure he means to carve himself some revenge.

Wrong. He waves it to make Skull's thugs take a few useful steps back. I make it out through the tent flap, feeling for every step, pulling Skull along, terrified I'll trip or screw up some other way. I look to see if I'm backing into more of his thugs, but those braziers blind me. All I can do is trust to luck.

'You're dead. Both of you!' rages Skull.

'You think?' Murdo follows us out, but pauses in the flap to shout. 'Don't anybody come after us or my mate blows some new holes in Skull's head.'

I figure we run then – *RUN, RUN, RUN* – but Murdo has other ideas. He tells me to wait and starts slashing furiously at guy ropes. A second later, I yell with delight as the whole front of the tent crumples to the ground.

Inside, people go crazy screaming. Tough.

'Now we go,' Murdo says, grinning.

I shove Skull away, but keep him covered with the pistol. The big man lumbers round and glares at us out of his tattooed skull eyes, panting horribly.

Murdo pulls me after him and we run for it.

But something, some instinct, makes me look back. I see Skull's arm dip then raise. And it's not only knives he keeps up those baggy merchant sleeves. He's clutching a small bolt gun now. 'Dern!' he roars, taking aim.

I don't mean to step in the way of the bolt; that's just what happens.

I hear this *phut* sound. It's like one of his bulked-up thugs punches me in the chest. I stay on my feet, but only just. And look down – to see a bolt sticking out of my chest. The pain. The pain. It's like someone's smashing my ribs with a hammer. I try to yank it out, but can't get a grip. It's slick with blood. My blood.

Time turns to mush. I think my next thumping heartbeat will never come.

And I feel so cheated, to die like this.

When I see Skull struggling to reload, I shoot him. In the head, like Murdo said we would. Pink and grey stuff comes flying out. He topples backwards.

Murdo shouts something, but I can't hear him.

I can't breathe either. And I'm blowing these bloody bubbles now. I'm so tired, more tired than I've ever been, but Murdo won't let me rest. He drags me down that hill, half carrying me. Cursing me and keeping me going.

Somehow, we make it to his windjammer.

There's a ramp down. Sky's there, beckoning, beckoning . . .

24
SANCTUARY

I'm on my back, bathed in red and looking up at twirling lights. I feel a throb of pain in my chest, but it's nothing really, as long as I stay still. It's quiet here. No more shouting and screaming, only the wind whispering. I feel sleepy.

Maybe being dead isn't so bad. Apart from not being able to breathe and lying in all this wet stuff.

I turn my head slowly, to see a very red Wink kneeling beside me, pressing a bloody bandage on to my chest, the bolt sticking out between her little fingers. She must see me looking because she squeals with delight.

And I get it now – I'm not done dying yet.

But I still can't breathe.

Sky's face appears above me, dark-eyed and worried-looking and red.

'He's hyperventilating,' she calls out.

I feel myself drifting away, but she shakes me until I look at her.

'Give him o-too,' shouts Murdo from somewhere.

Sky disappears. Wink lets go of the dressing and grabs my left hand.

'Please, Kyle, don't die,' she sobs.

'This should help,' says Sky, back again now.

She clamps a mask over my mouth and nose. I hear it hissing at me and immediately I'm not suffocating any more. I can't suck big lungfuls of air because I'd tear myself in half doing that, but if I take cautious sips at least I can breathe.

I give Sky a weary thumbs up.

She rocks back, tries to smile, but it it's more of a wince.

'Hang in there, grubber boy,' she says.

I look around and take it all in. I'm wedged in the gap behind a crew seat on a windjammer flight deck. Those winking lights above me are stars, seen through the canopy. Everything is lit up red so we don't burn our night vision. And the reason I feel all wet, I see now, is that I'm lying in a pool of my blood.

So much blood – is there any left inside me?

'Where are we?' I groan.

I know, sort of. I hear the whine and feel the deck shifting under me. But I just want to hear Sky say it.

'We're airborne,' she tells me. 'An hour out of Haggletown and headed to Bastion, Gemini's main base. They'll take care of you there.'

'We made it,' says Wink, squeezing my hand.

I'm in and out for the rest of that nightmare flight. Mostly out, which is a mercy, because each time I come to breathing gets tougher, even with o-too. All Sky can do is bang on at me to stay still so I don't rip myself up worse.

'I'm nublood,' I gasp, over and over. 'That means I'll heal, won't I?'

'You will, Kyle,' she says. 'You will.'

What she doesn't say, but I see in her eyes, is *unless you die first* . . .

I wake up one time and Murdo and Sky are arguing. I can't make much sense of it, but Sky sounds suspicious, like she doesn't trust him.

'Impossible,' she keeps saying. 'Bastion can't be *there*. I'd know.'

A cross-sounding Murdo tells her he couldn't care less what *she* thinks, that's where it is.

The next time I come to is after we've landed. Even then, I'm so half-dead and out of it I'm only vaguely aware what's going on. I force my eyes open, like this is the hardest trick in the world, only to be blinded by dayshine. Everything around me is blurry, skipping and sliding about. I squeeze them shut again.

Sometime later — could be minutes, could be years — I hear whispering.

'What? You're sure this is the guy?' Stuff like that.

Maybe I imagine it, but the whispers sound disappointed.

'Is this necessary?' Sky's voice. Unhappy.

Something soft is tied round my head, covering my eyes. A blindfold? Hands lay hold of me. I feel myself lifted and loaded.

Sky again, angry now. 'Careful! Can't you see he's hurt bad?'

Who's hurt? I think. *Oh yeah. Me.*

I try to open my eyes, but it's too hard. Inside my head, I'm falling, falling.

*

I'm dreaming again. Hope so because this woman in a soldier's uniform and wearing a white mask over her mouth freaks me out. Looks like I scare her too because she's looking down at me like she can't believe what she's seeing.

'He's awake!' Dimly, I recognise Sky's voice.

Scary woman frowns over her mask. 'He's fighting the sedative.'

'Is this Bastion?' I ask her.

My voice is slurred, like Murdo when we found him.

'Yes, Kyle,' says the woman, after a pause. 'This is Bastion's healing room.'

My head weighs a ton so it takes a hell of an effort to look about. More masked figures, Sky the only one not in uniform. Rough-hewn rock walls, shelves with jars and bottles on. Over me, bright lights shining down.

Healing room, I get it now. No wonder it stinks of Rona's antiseptic.

'You're safe now,' Sky says.

'Give him another shot?' asks one of the masks.

Scary woman nods. 'Double the dose. We'll need him out.'

And that's when I see the woman's hand. She's holding a bloody scalpel.

'What are you doing? What's going on?'

I fight to sit up, but I'm so weak. They push me back down.

'Relax, Kyle,' says Sky. She pulls her mask down so I can see her face and looks in more pain than I am. 'They're cutting the bolt out.'

Oh yeah, that bolt the Skull guy fired into me. I stop squirming.

Scary woman leans in and she doesn't look so scary now, more concerned. 'Kyle, listen. One of your lungs has collapsed and you've bled into the other. That's why you're having difficulty breathing. The bolt is lodged close to your heart, but I have to take it out before you'll heal. To do that, I'll need you to lie still.'

I cringe. How on Wrath am I supposed to do that?

'Can't you knock me out?'

The woman's mask wrinkles. Lines appear at the corner of her eyes. 'We're trying to. Your nublood is fighting us.'

She nods to an assistant and I feel a sting in my arm, like a stone-bug bite. Not long after a delicious warmth starts spreading through my veins. Panic claws at the back of my mind, but I'm too tired and it can't catch me. With my consciousness slipping away fast I search through the masks until I see Sky's face and cropped white hair. In case I don't wake up again, I want to look into her green eyes one last time. She gives me a little nod and chews on her lip, looking worried.

No tears or anything, but I see she cares.

Somehow, knowing this chases all my fears away.

I sit up, panting, heart thrashing, dripping sweat and shaking from being chased by hundreds of identical Moranas. A bad dream. Must be, because I'm sitting up in a dimly lit windowless room on a wooden bunk among tangled sheets and blankets thrown asunder. And I've not a stitch of clothing on.

I smell weird too. I'm all clean, like somebody's scrubbed me.

My chest itches, but only slightly. I go to scratch, then flinch as I remember the bolt sticking out of me and scary scalpel woman about to cut it out. But when I look down at myself, clutch and feel at my skin, there's nothing bad there.

No wound, not even a scar. I groan out loud.

Was being shot a nightmare too?

'Finally,' says a voice, sleepy but familiar.

Sky! Slumped in a chair by the door, her legs stretched out, like back in my shack.

She rubs her eyes, sits up and stretches. Only now do I notice she's traded Fliss's rags for the same kind of dull-brown soldier uniform as the masked woman who treated me wore. On her left sleeve she has an armband with the Gemini symbol of the black handprint, the little finger stitched in red, the match of the tattoo I once saw on her arm. A big yawn and she reaches for a switch. The room's glowtubes swell from dim to bright.

I scramble to cover my nakedness.

'How do you feel?' she says, that faint smile playing with her mouth.

'Fine,' I say warily. 'I guess.'

I peer down at my unmarked chest. Hard to believe.

When I look up again, Sky is on her feet.

'Kyle's awake now,' she says, speaking into a grid on the wall.

'How long was I out for?' I ask her.

'Best part of three days. They pumped loads of stuff into you, morning and evening, kept you knocked out so you'd heal even faster.'

'You been here the whole time, have you?'

I get shrugged at for asking this, but she doesn't answer.

'What happens now?' I say.

Sky comes closer. I think she might plonk herself down on the bed, but she hesitates. Gazes at me almost like I'm a stranger.

'Murdo told me you saved his life.'

I squirm, pleased but embarrassed, well aware that Skull's bolt found me, not the other way around. 'He's exaggerating. Where is he anyway?'

'Around somewhere. He keeps himself to himself.'

'So what's Bastion like?' I say, peering about.

She pulls a face. 'You'll soon see. Everybody here calls it the Hole.'

The cell – and that's what this is – is about four metres by two metres. No windows, one door, my bunk, the chair, a bucket toilet and a sink. The rough walls look to be cut from the same dark rock as the healing room.

Just then, I hear footsteps outside and the door bangs open. In hurries the healer woman who treated me. No mask this time, so a lot less scary. Two assistants follow her, both with blasters in shoulder holsters.

'Now,' healer woman says, marching up to me. 'How do you feel, Kyle?'

'Hungry,' I say. It's true – I'm starving.

'A good sign,' she says. 'We'll take care of that later.'

She reaches for my wrist, but I snatch it away. 'Who are you?'

'Yes, of course. My name is Scallon and I am the senior healer here at Bastion. Now that you're back with the living I need to run some simple tests to make sure you're fully recovered. It won't take long and there's nothing to be afraid of.'

I shoot a look at Sky, by the door now. She nods encouragement.

'What tests?' I ask nervously.

For the next few minutes Scallon pokes, prods, probes, scans, swabs, weighs and measures me. She sticks a needle in my arm and sucks blood out of me. I have to give other samples too, but luckily, Sky is gone by then. She even cuts me with that little scalpel of hers, a slice across the palm of my left hand. Every ten minutes, her assistants note down how much the wound heals. Finally, they tick the last box and the male assistant hands me a uniform jacket and trousers, the same as his and Sky's. They're roughly made, but warm, and better than stinking dogskin. No blaster or armband, however, which is a disappointment.

'Where are my old clothes?' I ask, pulling the new ones on.

The woman assistant snorts. 'Those old rags? I said we should burn them. But don't panic, we kept them for you in case you're ever allowed topside.'

'Topside? Where's that?'

But none of them will tell me. I figure I'll ask Sky when I see her next.

Anyway, they bring me food now. It's only some sort of thin and greasy meat and vegetable stew, but the fact is I can't remember the last time I had a proper meal so I grab the spoon and start stuffing my face.

'If you've finished,' says Scallon, wrinkling her nose as I lick the bowl, 'my comrades have some questions for you.'

'What kind of questions?' I say, deliberately picking at my teeth.

She looks at me, all hard and no messing.

'The kind, Kyle, that you'd do best to answer truthfully.'

For two long days, over and over, I tell Gemini my story. The Peace Fair, being blasted, my unlikely recovery and realising I'm a twist, Sky rescuing me, our capture by Morana, escaping from the crash, hopping windjammers until we find Murdo and him bringing us here. I tell it so many times I lose my voice.

And where does all this telling get me? Seems like nowhere.

It's as if they can't, or won't, believe me.

There are three of them: two men and one woman sitting behind a table.

I don't get a chair. I'm made stand in front of them, lit by a spotlight. They don't tell me their names. The men, who always sit either side of the woman, are ident brothers. The same greying hair over the same hard, wind-burnt faces.

Which is nublood, which is pure? Impossible to tell.

Even now, I can't take my eyes off them. Identical twins, comfortable with who they are. Older than Rona, clearly neither has manifested 'evil' like that caged monster at the Fair. The woman's younger. She has hawk eyes and asks the questions. If I stumble remembering, she's the one who pounces.

I just want the questions to stop.

This is day three. I feel so alone and confused.

I wish Sky was here, but I haven't seen her since that first day.

Sorted. That's what she told me we'd be after we hooked up with Gemini. I'd taken that and imagined a mountain hideout and a warm welcome from fierce-looking ident rebels. Not so much cheering, but lots of bumping stumps. Later I'd be handed my own pulse rifle and join their ranks in the fight against the Saviour and his Slayers. Not safe exactly, but at least somewhere I could feel like I belonged.

Only here I am and I feel more prisoner than sorted.

'Is there anything else you can tell us about Rona?' says the woman. Again.

I shake my head. Again.

'Answer the question,' growls one of the men.

'I've told you everything already. There's nothing else.'

I glance at the wall to my left where there's a grille set into an opening in the stone. Looks like it could be for ventilation, but I'm not fooled. I sense eyes watching from the darkness behind it, the same way I sense prey when I'm hunting. And all three of my interrogators have a plug in one ear, a white lead curling down into their collars. It's some sort of voice link, feeding them their stupid questions.

'Not even her surname?' This from the man on the left.

I chant my answers now, to irritate them.

'She called herself Rona the Healer. So I'm just Kyle, the Healer's son.'

Sometimes I talk to the grille. That *really* winds them up.

'You and your mother, always on the move,' says the woman. 'Didn't that strike you as odd?'

'No. In the Barrenlands, everybody's running from something. You don't ask.'

More hours of asks and answers.

Who are you, Kyle? What makes you special? Tell us.

And I don't get it. As far as I know I'm *not* special. Neither was Rona. It's like I keep trying to tell these guys – all I know is two weeks ago I was a nobody scraping a living in the Barrenlands. And now I'm one of *them*, a nublood, or a twist, call me what you like. But that's all I know. There's nothing else to tell. No, I don't know how Rona called them for help. No, she didn't tell me; she didn't have the chance and now she never will. No, I never knew I had a brother called Colm until Rona told me that last day. And no, no, no, I don't know why half the Slayer army is out looking for me now, in the biggest twist hunt ever seen on Wrath.

But cheers for telling me. As if I wasn't terrified already.

'What makes you think I know?' I shout back at them one time.

'We ask the questions, Kyle,' the woman says.

I so hate that. They hammer at me using my name. Kyle. Kyle. Kyle.

'Look, I don't know. I DON'T KNOW ANYTHING!'

25
MAN BEHIND THE GRILLE

The fourth morning I figure I'll make them drag me to the interrogation room. When I hear the door unlocking and opening, I don't get up. I roll over on the bed to face the wall and brace myself for a struggle. Futile I know, but at least it gives me some grim satisfaction. Only all that happens is somebody coughs. Not a clearing your throat kind of cough, more a polite *excuse me* cough.

Like the fool I am, I look round.

'Good morning, Kyle,' says the stranger in the doorway.

What's left of his hair is silvery white, as is his carefully trimmed beard. Around wire-framed glasses, he's got a fossil of a face, so deeply wrinkled it makes me think of soil cracked open after a drought. Over his combat fatigues he wears a simple grey cloak. He must be one of the oldest people I've ever met, yet his back's straighter than mine as he stands there silently, meeting my stare.

I can't help looking, but he's got all ten fingers.

There's something about him, a stillness that whispers of authority.

'Are you the man behind the grille?' I say.

He smiles. The smile looks real to me, but what do I know?

'My name's Ballard,' he says. 'Would you care to join me for some breakfast?'

He gestures toward the rock-walled corridor, lit up behind him. I hesitate, but breakfast sounds better than more questions I can't answer.

'Follow me then,' the man says, heading off.

I still sleep in my clothes, a Barrenlands habit tough to shake, so it's boots on and I'm good to go. Just as well. This Ballard guy doesn't hang about.

'Do I get more questions today?' I ask, catching up.

He glances back. 'Today you ask the questions. Breakfast first, however.'

I follow him along corridor after corridor. Several times we duck through hatches, as if sections of the base can be sealed off. We climb up-ramps to higher levels. The whole time, people hustle past us in both directions. Most wear combat fatigues, but a few wear the shabby, homespun clothes I'm used to. Nobody salutes or anything, but they nod at my elderly guide with obvious respect, and jump aside if necessary to let us past. Finally, we step into the largest room I've seen so far, packed with people sitting at trestle tables, stuffing their faces. It's noisy in here, full of the buzz of conversation, the clattering of knives and forks.

Across the room, Sky stands and waves.

I'm thinking maybe this Ballard guy eats at some special table, but he gives Sky a nod, heads across the room and slides on to the bench beside her. The only other space left is opposite her, so I scoot round and sit there.

'How's it going?' Sky says.

If she's any way pleased to see me, she forgets to tell her face. I shrug, not sure what to say to her.

'Eat,' says Ballard. 'We'll talk with full bellies.'

Breakfast is already there, waiting on a tray. A steaming bowl of some oatmeal-like stuff with lots of fruit on it, some of which I recognise. Wouldn't be my first choice, but it's hot, it slips down okay and doesn't fight back.

As I shovel it into me, I sneak a look around.

Loads of tough-looking faces, yet I can't hear a harsh word said. People are chatting away, smiling and laughing. Unbelievably, I see ident brothers and sisters sitting together, like this is no big deal. Even now my left hand can't help twitching the Sign of One – luckily, out of sight under the table. Soon as we're done eating, a boy brings us mugs of hot chai. Ballard leans towards me, elbows on the table, looking serious. My heart pounds as his watery old eyes bore into mine.

'It must have been hard,' he says, 'finding out your true nature as you did. Forced to flee from everything you know. Losing your mother. Fighting your way here with Sky's help, only for us to throw all these questions at you.'

His voice is gentle, but I know to keep my mouth shut.

'But you must understand, Kyle,' Ballard continues, sipping his chai, 'we needed to be absolutely sure that you are our friend and not our enemy.'

'And are you sure now?' asks Sky.

I think it, but she says it. Afraid of nothing, that girl.

Ballard nods and chuckles, seemingly amused by her impatience.

'As sure as we can be, I suppose. Although –'

'You said before that I could ask some questions,' I say, interrupting him.

'Yes I did. And I meant it.'

I take a deep breath. 'Okay, so what am I then?'

He takes his glasses off and pinches the bridge of his nose.

'Sadly, there's no simple answer to that question. We're a dump-world. We don't have access to the sophisticated med-tech we'd need to be sure. Without it, our best guess is that the increased numbers of ident births, together with our nublood advantages, are some form of alien reproductive strategy.'

Good job my gob's empty or I'd spit chai everywhere.

'Alien what?'

Ballard grimaces. 'Yes, I'm sorry. Perhaps I could have put that less bluntly. Kyle, tell me, have you ever heard tell of an extinct Earth bird called the cuckoo?'

I stare at him like he's mad, but he's serious.

'Cuckoos were devious,' he goes on. 'They laid their eggs into the nests of other bird species. Soon as the cuckoo chick hatched, it threw the original eggs out. The host birds couldn't tell, so raised the young cuckoo as if it was their own. Not quite what's happening here, but hopefully you get the idea.'

'So I'm *not* human. I'm some sort of alien cuckoo?'

Ballard shakes his head. 'No, no. You *are* human. A nearly exact copy, if you like, of your brother. Every bit as human, but something more too. Your nublood means you can heal faster, react quicker and so on. We can't be sure, but we believe that this physiological superiority is designed to give us an advantage in competing with our pureblood siblings. We're born identical so our host parents can't discriminate, but you're more likely than Colm to survive and breed.'

I don't know why I look at Sky as he says this, but I do.

She almost chokes on her chai.

'Well, that's what *we* believe anyway,' he says, putting his glasses back on.

My head spins, trying to make sense of this.

'So I'm *not* evil then.'

Ballard reaches out and grips my arm.

'No, Kyle, you're not evil. But surely you know that already.'

I pull away. 'Then why does the Saviour say I am?'

'Why? Because of a war. Because of fear. Mostly because it suits him. Fear is his most powerful weapon.'

'He's fraggin' mad,' blurts Sky.

Ballard sighs. 'You think so? Well, I fear you underestimate him.'

Sky blushes. I only believe that because I see it.

'Please,' I say, worried Ballard will stop talking. 'All we're told about the war was that twists tried to take over Wrath, but pures stopped them.'

Under the table I kick Sky to stay quiet.

'We fought to survive, not to take over Wrath,' says Ballard.

I stare, willing him to go on.

He clears his throat. 'You think it's rough now, Kyle, but it was impossible for the first landers, people like my parents. They stepped off the dropships with little more than the clothes they stood up in. For years their crops failed, not yet adapted to Wrath's climate and soil. Most starved. Then, suddenly, women started giving birth to identical twins. With so many children dying they think it's a miracle, more little hands to work the fields. Only years later do they discover the truth, that one of these twins is different – faster, stronger, quicker to heal. Unfortunately, desperation makes people quick to fear what is different. Fear leads to hate, hate breeds persecution. Unscrupulous people, like our so-called Saviour, preached that the suffering was *our* fault, that we were evil. People believed him, turned on us and that was his route to power. Who knows what he really believes? The fact is that like every tyrant, to hold on to his power he *needs* an enemy for his people to fear.'

Ballard pauses to wet his throat with chai. His hand shakes.

'And that's how the war started?' I say.

'Not only the war, but the lies and savagery that came after. Ident children reviled as evil, feared by everybody, including their parents. Forced to slave down mines in appalling conditions. Experimented on. Butchered like animals.'

'Or so we thought,' says Sky, half under her breath.

Ballard stands up. 'But enough of our grim history. I'm making you late. Your first training session is in ten minutes in the exercise area on level four. Sky will show you the way.'

She stands too and nods. 'Level four. Yes, sir.'

Not wanting to appear rude, I jump up as well. What training, I wonder?

'Train hard, Kyle, my young enigma,' Ballard says, frowning. 'I'll send for you soon. We'll talk about a mission we have in mind. Until then consider Bastion your new home. You're safe here among friends and your own kind.'

He turns and strides out of the dining hall.

'What mission?' I ask Sky.

She twitches and sticks her lower lip out. 'Don't ask me.'

As I follow Sky along more endless tunnel-like corridors, my heads thumps as I try to get it round this alien-inside-me stuff and Ballard's take on the Twist War. Not paying attention, I keep losing Sky and she has to chase after me.

'Wake up,' she snaps. 'You don't want to be late for training, believe me.'

I give up. Thinking will have to wait.

'Too busy to visit me then, were you?' I ask her.

She glances back. 'I asked to, but they wouldn't let me.'

'What's this training about?'

'You'll soon know.'

Only now do I see how fed up she looks.

'Hey, what's the matter?'

'Nothing,' she says. 'Hurry, will you?'

'Tell me.' I stop and stand, wait until she stomps back.

'Look,' she says, 'I should be back topside already, finding out about those fake executions, not hanging around this hole just so I can babysit you.'

I wonder if this is all that's bugging her.

'Any news of Fliss and Matty?'

She shakes her head.

'Well, how about Wink then? How's she doing?'

'Fine, but she hates it down here too. Apart from the food.'

'Down here?'

She rolls her eyes. 'We're underground. A disused mine, can't you tell?'

Underground? Of course we are. Rock walls, no windows anywhere in sight and the constant background swish of fans blowing fresh air around.

Sky heads off again. I have to run to catch up.

'You believe all that alien cuckoo stuff Ballard told us?'

'Sure, why not?'

'Did you know already?'

'Chane told me some of it. What's it matter?'

'You're kidding. Course it matters.'

She turns on me real quick, her eyes full of pain.

'Why? That's all just talk. What matters to *me* is that my sister's out there somewhere and Wrath knows what she's going through. Tarn needs me, but I can't help her because I'm stuck here. So don't tell me what matters, okay?'

'It was *your* idea we came here.' I'm grumpy myself now.

Sky ducks through a hatch and I follow.

Looks like we've arrived. A large chamber with padded walls and floor.

'You're late!' snarls the meanest-looking woman I've ever seen.

The young woman with a face that looks like it might have had a few bottles broken on it tells me her name is Seph. She explains her orders are to give me some basic training in unarmed combat. Worryingly, she has me take off my jacket and boots and throws me this plastic gumshield thing to stick in my mouth.

'We haven't got much time, Kyle, so pay attention.'

Paying attention to Seph is no problem.

Mean-looking she might be, but she strips her jacket off to reveal a sleeveless black undershirt at least one size too small.

While she's tying her long brown hair back, my eyes go for a little wander. Among other things, I take in the flat stomach and the muscles snaking about under the skin of her arms as she flexes them. She checks me out too, her grey eyes hard and confident.

'Done much fighting?' she asks.

I shrug and remember punching Nash. 'I can take care of myself.'

'We'll start by seeing what you got, shall we?'

I'm expecting her to square off against me. Instead she nods and it's Sky who steps in front of me, stripped down to her undershirt too, gumshield in. She winks and drops into a crouch, which must be some sort of fighting stance.

Got to say, it looks like she knows what she's doing.

'Try to hit her,' Seph tells me.

'Oh, no way,' I groan. 'You can't be serious?'

A smile plays around Seph's lips. 'What? Scared of girls, huh?'

I make a point of looking at Sky. 'Didn't used to be.'

Neither laughs. Sky hoists her eyebrows at me. She's looking forward to this, I can tell. I go to protest again, but at another nod from Seph, Sky suddenly jabs a punch at me that snaps my head right back and stings like hell. And just when everything's pretty much healed, I taste blood again.

'Hey,' I howl. 'It's me doing the hitting.'

'Well, get on with it then.'

'Your turn,' Seph says. 'C'mon, tough guy, see if you can hit her.'

Fine. I swing for Sky, but she ducks and makes me miss. Worse still, she spin-kicks me hard in the ribs as I go by. Makes me look a right gom.

'No, no, no,' Seph says, shaking her head.

Sky smirks at me, like *so what do you think of that?*

Only for Seph to shove her aside and take her place, dropping into the same fighting crouch, bouncing on the balls of her feet and beckoning to me.

'You call *that* trying, do you?' she says, her lip curling.

What with my mouth hurting and being embarrassed, I lose my temper and put some venom into punching the sneer off Seph's face. Yeah, right. I end up flat on my back on the mat with her frowning down at me.

Takes me a good few seconds to catch my breath and figure out that there's some pleased behind the frown.

'At least you're fast,' she says, offering me her hand.

Warily, I let her haul me back to my feet. 'Thanks. I think.'

'Thing is, Kyle, I can teach you how to fight. But are you a fighter? That's what matters.'

Can't help it, I glance at Sky. No help to be found there; she just raises her eyebrows at me again.

I shrug at Seph. 'Made it here, didn't I?'

She smiles, showing me a mouthful of broken teeth.

'Good answer. Right, now you try and stop *me* hitting *you.*'

26
ANSWERMAN

'Tell him about the distress call,' says Ballard, nodding at a bespectacled young red-haired soldier with several headphones tangled around his neck.

It's late in the third day since my combat training started. Instead of bunking down in one of the big dorms with the other fighters I'm still sleeping in that small windowless room, but at least now the door isn't locked. Sky came a few minutes ago and fetched me here to some sort of Gemini headquarters room. There's more scavved computer gear humming away here than I've ever seen. Charts, with lines and coloured marks on them that mean nothing to me, cover the rock walls. I do recognise one item pinned up – a crumpled wanted poster with that picture of me and Sky on it. Except for us, the redhead soldier and some armed guards, everybody in here looks awful senior. Soon as we walked in I sensed tension.

You should see the sour faces, as if they've been arguing.

That healer woman, Scallon, stares at me.

I guess I do look a mess. Every bone in my body feels like it's broken at least twice. I've got a bag of ice pressed to my jaw to try and keep the swelling down. Seph says my training's going fine, but I need to work more on my defence.

The redhead soldier clears his throat, obviously nervous. 'Sir?'

Ballard frowns. 'The distress call, Ness.'

The soldier glances my way, his face scrunched up and curious. 'Yeah, so when we picked up your call for immediate evac, it came in on an old, insecure channel so I wasn't sure if it was cool. But I ran the sender's squawk code against our systems and got a hit, only it came up as inactive.'

'A level-seven squawk,' growls a fierce-looking woman in a wheelchair.

My head was spinning when Ballard did the introductions, but I'm pretty sure this woman with no legs is called LeGuin and heads up Gemini's military operations. Now she stares at me expectantly, like I'm going to explain. She'll be waiting a while. I've no idea what the tech guy is on about.

'Thank you, Ness,' says Ballard.

He takes his glasses off, rubs his eyes and sighs deeply.

'What this means, Kyle, is your Rona used an obsolete call sign when she contacted us for help. Top priority, but that's all we know. You see it's only these last few years that Gemini has grown to become more than just some loosely organised resistance cells scattered across Wrath. Whoever issued that call sign to her, we lost contact with their cell long before we established this base and we have no way of finding out who they were, or even what Rona's role might have been. Of course we had hoped you could tell us more, but apparently you can't.'

He puts his glasses back on and regards me.

'Which leaves us with a problem. And that, Kyle, is you.'

I hold my breath and stare at the rush matting beneath my feet, wishing it would swallow me. Oh great. Most of Wrath is sure I'm evil and wants to kill me, and now Gemini – most of whom are my own kind – think I'm a problem.

'Our dilemma,' says LeGuin, wheeling to face me, 'is that you are bringing too much heat down on us. All over Wrath, Slayers are kicking down doors and rounding up Gemini suspects, hunting for you. It's making it impossible for our forces to operate. And right now, we could do without that!'

Ballard grimaces, stands up and starts pacing about. 'Sheltering you is hurting Gemini, hurting our cause. We need to know you're worth it, Kyle.'

'And why they want you so badly,' says LeGuin.

'You *must* understand,' says Ballard. 'There's too much at stake.'

I glance up to see them all staring at me. No sympathy now, more like cold calculation. I start to shake, dreading where this is going.

'Look, I told you. I don't know anything.'

'That's not good enough!' shouts LeGuin, banging the arm of her chair with her fist.

Others mutter agreement, but Ballard holds his hand up for quiet.

'Of course,' he says, looking thoughtful, 'there are others who suggest you may be less of a problem and more of an opportunity.'

'Huh?' I say, or something like that. I'm way too scared and confused to string words together.

Weirdly, I'm sure Ballard glances at Sky.

She takes the same sudden interest in the floor as I had done.

'Either way,' Ballard continues, 'there'll be a good reason why you're so sought after by the Slayers. We must find that out, by whatever means possible.'

He nods past me towards the back of the room. I swivel round to see one of the guards open the door, beckon, then step aside as Murdo Dern walks in.

'You told me you could help,' Ballard says. 'How?'

Murdo takes his time, chewing at something and looking around. 'You want answers round here,' he drawls at last, 'you go see the Answerman.'

LeGuin wheels away in disgust. 'Ridiculous!'

Murdo shrugs. 'I showed him the wanted poster. He says he knows.'

'And he'll tell us for a price?' Ballard says, frowning.

'There's always a price,' Murdo says. 'And he'll only tell Kyle. Says it's the kid's business and nobody else's. He's awkward like that, the Answerman.'

LeGuin snorts. 'This is madness!'

Ballard pulls at his beard. 'Perhaps. But I fear we've no choice.'

'Tell me again who this weirdo is,' Sky says, as we pick our way through the slum.

'He's the Answerman,' Murdo says, frowning. 'You'll see.'

There are five of us. Me, Sky and Murdo walking together. Trailing close behind us are two hard-eyed young fighters LeGuin insisted tag along so I'm not tempted to do a runner. Who'd have thought it? Turns out 'topside' is the sprawling shanty town of the Blight. Bastion is buried deep beneath this maze of plywood, corrugated iron and sun-bleached plastic. Sky says the Slayers know a rebel base is down here somewhere under their noses, but they also know any attempt to fight their way into the tangle of the Blight would result in fierce casualties.

We're all back in our rough old clothes. Matty's old dogskin jacket has a hood and I've pulled it up. Sky's wearing a shoulder-length black wig, greasy and wild-looking. Her teardrop tattoo is hidden under make-up and she's painted round her eyes to make them darker. I can't stop staring at her.

Anyway, here we are squeezing down a path between little huts built so close together that hardly any light penetrates. I constantly have to watch where I'm putting my feet – it's like walking through a cross between a rubbish tip and an open sewer. And it's back-itching creepy too. Wary eyes watch us from the shadows and I'm sure we're being followed. From what little Rona told me, I expected the squalor and filth, but what surprises me is the amount of industry I see. Many hovels seem both dwelling place *and* factory. I've seen the glow and felt the heat of several forges. The stench of tanning leather hangs in the air.

We duck underneath a washing line and step out on to a roadway, maybe three metres across. Skinny Blight-dwellers scurry by. Others stagger past, backs bent under massive loads. I look up and am glad for my hood. Looming above us on a hillside are the stone walls of Prime, Wrath's first and last city. Inside these walls, even higher still, I glimpse the shining metal towers of a fortress.

My chest tightens up. The Saviour. Up there, less than a klick away.

'Don't worry,' says Murdo, seeing my long face.

I look down. Maybe, I figure, if I can't see them, they can't see me.

Soon we cross over what once must have been a river and follow its creeping brown ooze as it winds through an even mangier part of the Blight. The filthy water is full of rubbish and the heads of swimming scavenger brats.

And I thought life was hard in the Barrens.

Even though it stinks so bad up here that you have to breathe through your gob or puke, it's still good to feel dirt under my feet and look up at blue sky and white clouds. Only now does it hit me how trapped I've felt being underground.

'How come he knows about me?' I ask Murdo for the hundredth time.

'He's the Answerman. He knows everythin'.'

'What's to stop him turning us in for the reward?' asks Sky.

'Yeah,' I say. 'How can we trust him?'

I can think of fifty thousand reasons why we shouldn't.

Murdo stops and rags sweat off his face. 'Relax. The Answerman's no fool. He knows if he messes with Gemini he'll end up floating face-down in this river, with Blight kids fighting over the meat on his bones.'

I shiver. There's me, thinking we were the good guys. But all this talk of credits and buying stuff reminds me.

'So how *do* we pay him?'

'Yeah, well,' says Murdo, glancing at me. 'You hear rumours.'

'What rumours?' chorus me and Sky.

Murdo shrugs, turns and points along the river.

I follow his finger and there's the tallest and craziest construction I've seen so far. Four leaning storeys of rusty corrugated iron, each piled carelessly one above the other with no respect for gravity, getting smaller as they climb. A pole sticks out of the topmost shack. At the end of it, a broken sign swings and creaks in the breeze.

NSWERMAN, it reads, in sun-bleached red letters.

'I'll wait here,' says Murdo.

'The Answerman is expecting you,' says the blaster-carrying heavy at the entrance.

He searches me and takes my pistol away, then Sky, but she isn't carrying. He waves a pudgy, four-fingered hand at stairs leading up into darkness. A fat scab in the starving Blight. The answers business must be booming.

I head up the steps while I've still got a shred of nerve left in me.

Sky goes to follow, but the guy blocks her.

'You stay here, darling,' he says. 'Keep me company.'

'We see him together,' I say. 'Or we walk.'

He scowls and mutters something into his wrist, it looks like. Something buzzes in his ear, he scowls even harder and lets Sky past to join me. At the top of the stairs is a heavy wooden door. As I go to knock, it swings inwards.

We both recoil as light and hot air blast us.

'Don't let the cold in,' a voice screeches. 'Enter, enter.'

I follow Sky in, blinking after the gloom of the stairs. No sooner are we inside than the door slams shut behind us. Two more hulking bodyguards, stripped to the waist, sweat running down their hairy barrel chests, encourage us forward.

We get our first look at the owner of the voice.

Got to hand it to Sky, she stands her ground. Not me. I step back.

It's the man's blue rabbit eyes that freak me out, bulging out of his narrow head, twice the size of any eyes I've ever seen. He's Ballard-old, I can tell from his blotchy face and caved-in cheeks. His skin looks weird – almost like yellow plastic pulled tight and shiny over his skull. A few greasy hairs straggle down past his ears. Despite the fierce heat he's bundled ankle to chin in a fur coat, collar up. He's sitting on a couch and sucking the pipe of a bubbling hookah. Thick grey smoke dribbles from his ancient slit of a mouth. He fidgets and the guards shove us closer.

'So you're the Answerman?' Sky says.

'Child, I am many things.' His head wobbles back and forth, looking from Sky to me, never staying still. 'I am secrets. I am discretion. I am the knower of knowledge and, yes, I am the Answerman. Answers are my slaves and chattels. I hunt them and trap them. Only for the *right* price do I set them free again.'

He takes another big pull from the hookah.

'Now,' he says, blowing a smoke ring at me, 'who are *you*?'

'That's what I want to know,' I say.

I don't mean to sound so smart-arse; that's just how it comes out.

The Answerman cackles and thumps his leg.

'You want me to tell you who you are? Is that your question?'

Spiders of sweat crawl down my forehead and into my eyes, stinging them.

'I guess so,' I say, struggling to think.

The Answerman frowns, makes a show of looking confused.

'But your mercenary friend Dern told me you wanted to know why Slayers are hunting you.'

'Who cares?' Sky snaps. 'It'll be the same answer.'

'I care, child. I will only answer one question, so which is it to be?'

Sky scowls my way, like it's *me* who's being awkward.

'Who am I?' I say slowly.

The Answerman smiles, showing us his rotting brown teeth in a kind of triumphant leer. Seeing this, and the knowing look in those horrible bulging eyes of his, my heart skips several beats. He has the answer all right.

Sky shifts beside me and I sense her impatience.

'So you going to tell us or what?'

He smirks at her now. 'Patience. We must first agree my price.'

The way he says 'price', hissing the word, his tongue flicking out after it like a snake's, makes me shiver with disgust. I get this cold, sick feeling in my guts. He licks his lips. My sick feeling starts working its way higher.

'We've got credits,' I say, gulping. 'We can pay.'

Our escorts outside are carrying them, but no way is it fifty thousand.

'What would I do with money?' he says, gesturing left and right.

And I take in the room for the first time. Up until now, it's as if I've been at the bottom of a well, peering up and seeing this sinister old man looking down, but now I see the room is a jungle of junk. In places it's stacked all the way from the floorboards to the rafters. It makes no sense; everything is jumbled up. Machine parts rub oily shoulders with bolts of woven fabric and rest on crates full of rotten vegetables. Fine rugs are rolled up on top of crude earthenware pots. The worst are the cages containing birds and animals, all of them strangely quiet.

I'm thinking barter now. Maybe he'll settle for the gun?

'What nobody wishes to give,' he says. 'This is the Answerman's price.'

Huh? But now I see he isn't showing me the rubbish. He's pointing at stuff hanging from a cord that runs all round the room. At first glance I think I'm looking at bits of meat drying on a line. But then I look more closely.

Bile fills my mouth and I gag. Sky gasps.

Fingers. Toes. Ears. Noses.

Something that looks like it could've once been somebody's tongue.

27
TRUTH

'You *don't* have to do this,' says Sky, looking at me like I'm mad. Behind us, I hear the slap and hiss of a blade being sharpened on a leather strop.

'I want my answer first,' I say, staring at the Answerman.

He wriggles, then shrugs. 'As you wish.'

I watch as he reaches behind his couch for a large cleverbox. Weird thing is, I'm not so much scared as numb. Suddenly, nothing else matters apart from finding out the truth, *my* truth. All my life, I've known Rona wasn't telling me stuff, but I always pushed this to the back of my mind. I guess I'm good at doing that – why deal when you can just not think? But now the need to know is an ache swelling inside me, like I've got gutworms.

'Did you hear me?' whispers Sky.

'I heard,' I whisper back. 'But I've got to know.'

The Answerman sticks on some thick-lensed glasses, which make his already bulging eyeballs look even more likely to burst. He glances over them, then takes his time swiping through screens on the box, as if reminding himself.

'Who do *you* think you are, Kyle?' he says at last.

'No idea,' I say, thrown. 'A nobody from the Barrenlands.'

He hands me the cleverbox. 'A nobody? I don't think so.'

On the screen is another me, although maybe a year or two younger, the image a little grainy and blurred as if taken from a distance or in a hurry. But this other me has cropped hair and he's wearing a matt-black Slayer uniform.

Sky reaches out to me, but I shake her hand off. Blood roars in my ears.

The Answerman rocks back on his couch, laughing a little dry laugh. 'That picture was taken some eighteen months ago,' he tells me, 'up in the fortress during one of the Saviour's beloved and interminable ceremonics. The resemblance, I think you'll agree, is unmistakable. Your twin, in his Slayer finery.'

'Colm,' I gasp. 'That's . . . my brother, Colm?'

'No way!' Sky says, looking past me at the screen.

But how could Colm, a scab ident, be a Slayer? Surely that's not right.

Except . . . now I remember High Slayer Morana's shocked frown, her staring down at me as if she knew me from somewhere. Well, what if it wasn't me she recognised, but Colm? If my brother *is* a Slayer, then she *would* know him!

I shiver despite the heat as it starts to make chilling sense.

Taking a closer look at the image I spot a claw-like hand resting on my brother's shoulder, but whether in friendship or for support I can't tell. Annoyingly, the hand's owner is just out of the shot. 'Who's that next to him?' I say.

'Who indeed?' says the Answerman. 'But first let me tell you a story.'

'We're not paying for stories,' hisses Sky.

The Answerman scowls. 'Stories often prove truer than facts.'

'Let's hear it,' I say, trembling.

He nods and settles back on to his couch. 'A good few years ago, fifteen or more, our beloved Saviour was very nearly killed in what we were all told was a rebel assassination attempt.' Silent laughter rocks the man. 'Kyle, if answers are my business, secrets are my lifeblood. Lies such as this are how I sniff them out. This, by the way, is another service I provide. Secrets are such heavy things to carry and people are weak. They come to me, I unburden them, I soothe –'

'We haven't got all day,' says Sky, scowling.

The Answerman giggles and takes another suck from his hookah. 'Haven't we? Well, not long after, whispers went round the palace that the wounding was nothing to do with rebels. That the Saviour had been shot with his own gun by a pregnant mistress, a slave girl from the Blight.'

He stares at me, mouth hanging open.

'I don't see what that's got to do with me,' I say.

My voice sounds all buzzy, as if it's coming from outside me.

'Don't you?' he says. 'This slave girl, she flees back to the Blight. She must be sheltered by somebody because it takes the Slayers over a year to hunt her down. Even then they only find her because of an informer. A snatch squad is sent in to fetch her, but the girl kills herself rather than be taken prisoner.'

He peers at me again, but I do my blank face.

'The Slayers found one infant clinging to her dead body,' he continues. 'They brought the child back to Prime. Her bastard son by the Saviour.'

A cold fist inside me squeezes my heart.

Sky reaches for my hand again and this time I'm glad.

The Answerman takes a long drag, then blows the smoke into my face. 'Your ident brother,' he says, tapping the cleverbox screen with a smoke-yellowed finger, 'is the boy they brought back, but all grown up now.'

The cleverbox drops from my nerveless fingers and bounces off the floor.

'You're lying!' I shout, reeling backwards.

The bodyguards grab me and thrust me forward again.

Sky still has hold of my hand and she gives it a squeeze now as I stand there swaying on my feet, sick with horror and disbelief. 'A story to make a wordweaver weep for sure,' she jeers, 'but how do we know if any of it is true?'

The weird little man bares his stump-teeth at her.

'I deal in truths, not lies,' he spits. 'Ask anyone in the Blight.' His eyes bulge even more horribly and flick from Sky to me. 'Yet should you still doubt, you might ask yourself why Slayers are turning Wrath upside down even as we speak, hunting for you? Why do they offer a reward of fifty thousand credits for your capture, but only if you are taken alive? Oh yes, I know all about this. And how else could your ident brother come to be wearing the Slayer black? Ask yourself that!'

Each question feels like a nail hammered into my head.

The Saviour is my father. And Rona . . . isn't my mother.

In desperation I glance at Sky, but even she's quit with her jeering now.

'So,' the Answerman says, a flamer appearing in his hand, 'you have your answer, even if you don't much like the taste of it.

Count yourself lucky you weren't there to be caught with your brother because the rebels had split you up. They do that, you know; the best way to hide twins is to separate them. But now it's time for my payment. Given you're an ident, a little finger I think. Don't you?'

I'm numb, but not numb enough. I moan with fear.

Sky squeezes my hand again, but a bodyguard hauls her away. The other bodyguard grabs me and marches me over to a low table on which sits a stained wooden chopping block and a mallet. 'Kneel down,' he orders.

When I don't instantly obey he kicks my legs from under me and expertly forces me down to my knees, like he's done this a thousand times before. He stretches my left hand out, palm down on the wood, and prises my fingers apart. The Answerman joins him now, a wood-chisel in his hand. He tests its edge with his thumb, lines the blade up carefully, feeling for the gap between my knuckle and finger bone. I squeeze my eyes shut as he raises the mallet, but I hear the *swish* as he swings it and the *thud* as it smashes into the hilt of the chisel, sending the razor-sharp blade slicing through my skin, bone and sinew.

I cry out, but hardly feel any pain.

Foolishly, I open my eyes. And stare in disbelief at my ruined hand.

The shape of it is all wrong now. Blood pumps out bright red against the wood. My severed little finger lies there on the block, curled up like a dead dirtworm. Next thing I know, Sky is binding the wound with a scrap of rag.

Then the searing pain hits and I stagger and almost pass out.

'You happy now?' Sky shouts.

Muddled by the shock and the pain, I think she's shouting at me, but then dimly I realise she's yelling at the Answerman.

'Get them out of here,' he tells his bodyguards.

He holds his trophy up to a light, turns it this way and that, admires it.

And I puke now, all over his fancy hand-knotted rugs.

Sky half drags me outside and down the stairs. The cold air smashes into my lungs and wakes me up a bit. Which helps, except now the pain from my severed little finger gets even worse, an agonising throb I can't run away from.

'What about my gun?' I say, clinging to Sky.

'Forget it,' she says crossly. 'We're not going back.'

Murdo comes running to meet us. When he sees me clutching my hand wrapped in its bloody rag he curses and looks disgusted, but unsurprised. He goes to help support me, but Sky snarls at him. She's shaking, she's so mad.

'How could you, Murdo? All that talk of rumours. You *knew* his price, didn't you?'

He backs up out of range of her fists, palms spread.

'Spin down,' he says, wincing. 'Did sicko give you your answer?'

I sigh and nod.

'Not the answer you wanted?' he says.

'We'll talk later,' snaps Sky. 'He needs to get back to Bastion for treatment.'

'I'll live. Can't you just leave me alone?' I moan.

'Don't talk stupid, Kyle,' Murdo says. 'You wouldn't last ten minutes here. And you're hosing blood out – we need to get that stopped fast.'

I look and he's right. The rag around my fist is dripping blood.

He produces a laser-knife, fires up its green blade and dials max power.

'Take that rag off,' he tells Sky, 'then hold him still.'

She clicks her tongue, but does as Murdo says. It feels like she pulls the rest of my fingers off with the rag. I look away as he presses the fizzing blade to the rent where my finger used to be. Agony spikes up my arm, like giant needles being rammed through my veins. I hear sizzling and smell my flesh burning.

I tear my hand away, sobbing. But the job's done; the bleeding's stopped.

'What do *you* want?' says Sky, looking around.

Through tears, I see our two hard-eyed shadows, Ballard's fighters are back.

'We'll take it from here,' says the woman.

'It?' says Sky furiously. 'He's got a name, you know.'

'Whatever,' says the guy. 'Let's go.'

'At least that scumbag took it off cleanly,' says Scallon, clicking her tongue.

Sky and me are back in Bastion's healing chamber where Scallon is dressing my wounded hand. She chased Ballard's two guards outside. Murdo went with them. I can hear him now, loudly chatting up the female fighter. Scallon tried to make Sky leave too, but Sky made it clear with curses she was staying. She's taken the black wig off now and is busy at a sink scrubbing the paint off her face.

When Scallon's done she offers me some pills for the pain,

but I say no. Truth is the pain is already much less and anyway I need it. I treasure each and every throb, because they grab hold of me and stop me thinking.

I don't want to think about who I am. And who Rona isn't.

Scallon frowns. 'You're both stubborn, aren't you? Made for each other. I have other casualties to check on. While I'm gone, try not to break anything.'

She leaves, closing the hatch after her and locking it.

Sky gets up and limps about the small chamber. A long silence stretches out between us until she suddenly stops and looks at me kind of sideways.

'I shouldn't have let you do it,' she mutters.

'What's done is done,' I tell her. 'That's what Rona always used to say.'

Rona. My voice catches in my throat and chokes me.

While Scallon was patching me up I managed to fight off the dark thoughts, but they come muscling back now. Finding out my brother's some kind of Slayer and that I'm probably the Saviour's son is sick and scary and unreal. But what troubles me the worst is thinking about Rona, the one constant in my life.

'Nothing is what it seems, not even me,' I moan.

I glance up and Sky is staring at me. I wince into those dark green eyes of hers that have scowled at me so often, but they shine with sympathy now.

And I sense something shift between us.

'Rona said that before you showed up,' I explain. 'She tried to tell me she wasn't my mother.'

'She's still your mother,' Sky says, taking a step towards me.

I take a deep breath. 'Maybe.'

Sky shakes her head at me, so hard it would have sent her old dreads flying.

'No maybe about it. Come on, Kyle. You're hurt and not thinking straight. Whoever your real mother was, she had no choice but to split you and Colm up to hide you. Rona must have taken you in to save you. Can you imagine the guts she had to do that, knowing who you were? Your whole life she fed you, sheltered and protected you. I hardly knew the woman, but there's no three ways about it – I saw she loved you as a son. She loved you so much she sacrificed herself so that we could get away. If that's not a mother, then I don't know what is!'

I swallow, close to tears. 'Fancy talk, but why didn't Rona tell me?'

'Maybe she meant to. Maybe you weren't ready to hear. How's your hand?'

'Sore as hell.' I admire Scallon's neat dressing. 'How's your leg?'

'Sore. All that walking topside.'

I shift along the treatment table to make space for her. She hesitates, gives me a shy smile, comes and sits next to me.

'Guess what?' she says, after a while.

'What?' I say, my heart racing.

'I bumped into some fighters here who aren't idents, but they had their little fingers chopped off anyway.'

I stare, but she's serious. 'That's mad. Why would they?'

'They said it was to show solidarity.'

'No. I mean why would non-idents fight for us?'

'Must believe in Gemini's cause, I guess.'

'And what cause is that?'

Sky shrugs and pulls a face. 'A Wrath where purebloods and nubloods live together in peace.'

Right. I try to imagine this, but all I see is that mob at the Peace Fair, open mouths shouting in blotchy faces.

Un-wrapping! Un-wrapping!

I shiver. Not a good memory.

Outside the door, I can hear Murdo still chatting away and a girl laughing. Why can't I be more like him? Instead, here I sit, tongue-tied and awkward.

'What you thinking about?' says Sky, startling me.

'Oh, just stupid stuff,' I say, picking at my dressing, another sigh getting away from me. 'Feeling sorry for myself mostly. You know, growing up in the Barrenlands was tough and we often went hungry, but at least I thought I knew what the deal was. I had Rona looking after me, so I was happy enough. And then I make this one lousy decision to go the Peace Fair. Next thing, boom, my life is wrecked. Turns out everything I thought I knew is one big illusion, lies piled on secrets piled on more lies. Even Rona's a lie, and now I'm this evil twist monster running for my life. You come along and give me hope, even though I know you hate the word. Somehow we make it here to Bastion where you say we'll be safe. And there's stupid me thinking this is great, I'll finally find out the truth and get some kind of life back. Sure enough, I get my answers. Ballard tells me *what* I am, the Answerman tells me *who* I am. But so much for thinking the truth would solve all my problems —'

I hesitate, aware that I'm babbling.

'It's just like I feel all hollow inside. You know?'

Sky sighs and nods. I look at her and see her chin tremble.

'I know that feeling,' she says. 'Like there's something missing. For me, it's when I try and picture my parents' faces.'

'You don't get to see them?'

'The day Tarn and I were taken, the Slayers killed them. They made us watch.'

I swallow hard. 'I'm sorry. That's just . . . awful.'

Sky runs a hand through her cropped hair.

'See, Mum and Dad knew the law, but wouldn't give us up. They hoped we wouldn't be found or we'd be forgotten. It was midwinter when the Slayers came for us. I remember the snow and the shouting, Tarn and me being dragged from our hut and bundled into a sled, my mother screaming. They burnt the hut with my parents, my brothers and my older sister still inside. Our mutt, Benji, chased the sled as they took us away. Tarn begged the Slayers to kill him too, so he wouldn't suffer. They just laughed, like it was funny. In the end, Benji couldn't run any more, just stood there in the snow, shaking and howling. That was the last we saw of him.' She stops and a tear trickles down her face. 'But you know the worst thing?'

I shake my head, choking tears back myself.

'All I see now,' she continues, 'is that stupid fraggin' dog. I can't see my mum or my dad, or my brothers and sister. They're all gone. How sick is that?'

'It's not your fault,' I tell her. 'You were too young.'

Hesitantly, I reach out to give her hand a sympathetic squeeze, much like Rona would often do for me. Only, gom that I am, I somehow forget I've just had my finger hacked off. No sooner do I lay my hand down on hers than an awful spasm of pain shoots up my arm. I snatch my hand back and curse.

Sky wipes her eyes with the back of her hand and starts laughing at me.

Crazy. But as the stinging fades, I find I'm laughing too.

28
CONSEQUENCES

When Scallon gets back, the hawk-eyed questioner woman is with her. She's still not smiling and friendly, but seems less cold now. And at least there's no light shone in my face as she asks us to take her through our encounter with the Answerman. Sky does most of the talking and answering for me, which I'm grateful for. I stick to nodding, mainly, when the woman looks at me or asks if I agree. She asks a few questions here and there, tapping our answers into a cleverbox while Scallon watches, arms folded and grim-faced. Only when Sky gets to the bit about Colm being the Saviour's bastard son and me being the other son, does the woman show emotion. She stares at me and curses under her breath. So does Scallon.

My cheeks burn. I figure I'm going to get a lot of this.

It takes the woman a good few seconds to pull herself together and start tapping this into her cleverbox.

Yeah? Well imagine how I feel.

Me and Sky, we're still sitting beside each other on the treatment table. She leans her shoulder against mine and keeps it there. I glance at her and she gives me a sad smile. Not long after – what more is there to tell? – the woman finishes with her questions and reads back to us what she calls our 'statement' so we can check it. Between us we correct a few small details until she's satisfied.

The woman stands up, still looking all thin-lipped and stunned. Before she leaves she swaps a few whispers with Scallon then orders us not to repeat a word of this to anyone else, under any circumstances. 'Do you understand?'

I can't help snorting. 'You think I'd want to?'

Sky nudges me. The woman scowls and goes to leave.

In the hatch she pauses to give me a searching kind of look. She opens her mouth and for a horrible moment I think she's going to tell me that she's sorry or something useless like that. But whatever it was, she shakes her head and keeps it to herself before continuing on her way, clutching her cleverbox.

A second later Murdo swings himself inside through the open hatch.

'Enough,' he says. 'What the kid needs now is a whisky!'

I don't get my whisky, no great shock since this is a rebel base and not one of the dives Murdo usually hangs out in. What I *do* get is a few more days of combat training and helping Scallon out, putting the little healing I learnt from Rona to good use. Better still, I get to spend more time with Sky that doesn't involve us trying to kick each other's heads in. Her leg brace is off somewhere being properly fixed so she's using a crutch. That means she gets to take a break from Seph.

The little free time we have, we hang out together and talk.

When I say talk, she listens mostly as I shoot my mouth off

and tell her stupid stories from growing up in the Barrens or heard from passing wordweavers. I love it when her face lights up and I hear her tinkling laugh.

But it can't last and even I know that.

I've been dreading being summoned back before Ballard and the others, to be told what will happen to me. So when Sky shows up this morning with a dark face on her instead of a smile, I already know what she'll say before she says it.

'They want to see you again, Kyle. I'm to take you there.'

'Any idea why?' I say, tasting bile.

'How would I know? Come on, they're waiting.'

She won't look at me, just turns and stomps away using her stick. What else can I do but grab my jacket and run after her?

As I follow Sky along tunnels I'm starting to recognise, people recognise me too now. The woman from our topside escort, the cute one Murdo's chasing, calls my name as she passes. She sticks her fist out and we bump stumps.

Bumping stumps: I can do that for real now. Almost makes me feel I belong.

We get to a guarded door without Sky saying hardly a single word to me. There she flashes me a taut smile, wishes me good luck and steps aside as the guards show me in. Ballard, whose title I now know is First Minister of the Revolutionary Council, is seated behind a large metal desk. Sitting either side of the desk are General LeGuin and Senior Healer Scallon. The room's like Ballard himself, neat and businesslike, nothing out of place. It's so cold in here I'm surprised my breath doesn't mist. As soon as I enter they stand, except LeGuin who wheels to face me.

I glance back at Sky, but the door closes behind me.

'Good morning, Kyle,' Scallon says. 'Please, take a seat.'

In the time it takes me to walk to the only empty chair and sit down, fear sucks all the spit out of my mouth. All their faces are so long and serious. Even LeGuin, who always looks as tough as old goat meat, seems unusually grim.

Ballard settles back into his chair and takes a deep breath. 'How are you?'

'Fine,' I croak.

'I hear your training is going well.'

I nod. Guess it must be; I no longer feel like one big bruise.

'Any problems with your hand?' asks Scallon.

'No.' I shake my head. It healed so fast even she was a little bit surprised, I think.

Ballard leans forward and regards me over his eyeglasses. 'Kyle, I've read the transcript of your trip to the Answerman. Our intelligence guys are satisfied that your personal link to the Saviour explains why you're being hunted.'

No shit. So tell me something I don't know.

I glance at Scallon sitting next to me, but she's careful to avoid my eye.

'Do you think —' I hesitate, unsure if I'm expected only to listen, but Ballard nods his permission. 'Do you think my — the Saviour, I mean — wants me caught so he can kill me? To cover up him having had ident children?'

I've talked it over and over with Sky and that's what we reckon.

Ballard swaps glances with LeGuin.

'It's possible,' he says, 'but we don't think so. You yourself said the High Slayer, Morana, insisted you were taken alive, and our comm intercepts confirm this.'

'So why then?' I say.

'We don't know, and there seems little to be gained by speculating.' He clears his throat. 'The real question is, what do we do with you?'

'I want to fight for Gemini,' I say quickly.

'Good,' he says. 'I'm sure Rona would be proud to hear you say that.'

'Was *she* Gemini?' I ask.

Ballard nods. 'We think she was a minder. Minders shelter fugitives and are issued with emergency squawk codes in case they need help.'

'Can we get to the point now?' LeGuin snarls.

Ballard frowns but nods agreement. 'Very well. Tell him then.'

'I believe you're aware,' LeGuin says, fixing me with her bleak gaze, 'of our discovery that the Peace Fair executions of nubloods are being faked. Yes?'

I swallow hard. 'Sky told me.'

LeGuin scowls, clearly unimpressed. 'This will be no merciful whim of the Saviour. He will want our children for something. Some purpose so appalling that even though they're considered evil, he cannot be seen to do it.'

'I dread to think,' Scallon mutters, shivering.

LeGuin wheels herself so close now that her chair bumps mine. 'But *you* can save them,' she says.

'What?' I say, leaning back. Has the woman gone crazy?

No. Ballard's nodding too. They all are!

'You,' LeGuin says, staring at me so fiercely that I flinch, 'are the key to discovering where these nublood children are being taken and what is happening to them. If you find that out for us, then maybe we can save them.'

'You're their best hope,' Ballard says.

'Their only hope,' Scallon says.

I try and get my brain round this, but it's too small.

'I don't understand. I mean, I get what you're saying about the executions being faked, but what's all that got to do with me?'

Wrong thing to say. The look on LeGuin's face, I think she'll explode.

Ballard holds his hand up though and she wheels herself away. 'This has *everything* to do with you, Kyle,' he says sternly. 'You yourself are nublood. Like it or not, you're part of this war now. Whatever the fate of these wretched children is, it will be yours too if we lose. You said yourself that you wanted to fight for Gemini; well this is how you can strike a meaningful blow.'

I squirm, hot and ashamed.

'I *do* want to fight. But how can I save those kids?'

'For Wrath's sake, just tell the boy,' Scallon says, wringing her hands.

Ballard and LeGuin swap a look I don't like. He nods to her.

'It's quite simple, Kyle,' she says.

And I know it's going to be bad because it's the first time she uses my name.

'The Slayers want you. We'll make sure they get you.'

I'm so shocked, I jump up. Scallon curses, stands too and gently pushes me back into my seat.

'You'll be carrying an implant,' she says. 'A homing beacon like the one in that rifle you ditched in the river. We think there's a good chance they'll take you to where these nublood children are being held. Once you're there, you dig the beacon out and power it up. LeGuin will send in fighters to get you all out.'

My next heartbeat is an awful long time coming.

'You can't be serious?'

'We've tried tracking the transports taking the children from the Fairs,' Ballard says with a sigh, 'but tracking them long distance without being spotted is next to impossible. If the Slayers suspect we're on to them, they'll move the children, or reinforce their defences, and our best chance will be lost.'

LeGuin nods. 'And the Fair season is already over for this year.'

I can't believe they can be so stupid. 'But if you hand me over they're bound to guess it's some sort of set-up.'

'They won't guess. One of their Blight informers will somehow find out where you're hiding. A Slayer snatch squad will be sent in, you will oblige by surrendering with no fuss and they'll congratulate themselves on your capture.'

'Yeah, and then hang me,' I jeer.

'It's risky,' Ballard says, gritting his teeth. 'Nobody's saying it isn't. And believe me, Kyle, I wish I didn't have to ask this of you. But it's a bold idea and a unique opportunity to save those children, one Gemini cannot afford to pass up.'

The man's a good actor or else I see real pain in his eyes.

On the way back from Ballard's office I notice the exercise area on level four is empty so I figure I'll take out my fear and frustration on the punchbag. In the end, of course, they made me agree to the mission, taking turns banging on at me, telling me their cause was my cause. Even Scallon. What choice did I have? None. LeGuin made it clear they'd implant me and hand me over whatever I said. You want our help and protection? You have to help us first. That was the deal. Saying yes was easier than saying no. It reminds me of when Nash pushed me into burning that twist at the Fair.

Feels as if I've come all this way and got nowhere.

So here I am, hands taped, punched out and hanging off the bag, when I hear Sky crutching her way awkwardly towards me across the mat.

I don't look round, too busy sulking.

Bastion was *her* idea. Sanctuary, she said. Death trap more like.

She doesn't speak, just turns me around, her cool hand pulling at my sweaty shoulder. Her crutch falls and slaps on the mat. To my surprise I feel her arms go round me, pulling me into an embrace. She buries her face in my neck.

'Hey!' I say. Or something equally dumb.

'Shut up,' she mumbles.

She sounds so wretched I can't stay mad, even if I wanted to. I slip my hands inside her open jacket and pull her closer, suddenly needing more than anything else to hold this strange, fierce girl and be held by her.

Only she pulls away now as someone enters the room.

We both look and there's Seph, halfway through the door. 'Hey, now I don't remember teaching him *that* move,' she says to Sky, grinning. She ducks back out before either of us can say anything and closes the door after her.

Sky winces at me and blushes. 'I bet she did too.'

'All Seph taught me,' I say, pulling her close again, 'was how to stop vicious windjammer girls knocking me down and waving flamers in my face.'

Her arms slide back round me.

'And this is how you do that – by crushing them?'

'Something like that.'

'You know, you're such a gom.'

I'm about to argue, but she shuts me up by kissing me.

I kiss her back, my heart thumping, but she pulls away sooner than I'd like. She half smiles in apology, but her green eyes look sad and troubled.

'Did I do something wrong?' I say.

'No. I just – look, pass me my stick, would you?'

All this time, I realise guiltily, she's been standing on her one good leg. While she holds on to me, I bend down, pick the crutch up and hand it back to her.

'You haven't got your brace thing back yet?'

She sticks the crutch back under her arm and lets out a big breath. 'They gave it back, all fixed up and working. But you know, it's nice to take a break from the pain of the thing always clutching at me. Without it, it's sometimes easier to pretend I'm the same as everybody else. Stupid, huh?'

'You're not the same.' I look at the floor. 'You're amazing.'

Soon as this is out of my mouth I feel so awkward I could shoot myself. Sky says nothing, but touches my cheek with her hand. She leads me over to a bench by the wall and motions for me to sit next to her. After a while she nudges me. I hold my breath and put my arm round her, and she snuggles into me again. Her warm breath tickles my neck.

'I hear you agreed to the mission,' she says.

Despite the thrill of Sky's shoulder and thigh pressed against mine, my thoughts flinch back to the mission. And I can't help it;

I cringe inside and start shaking. Fear is like longthorns stabbing me all over, making me weak.

She gives my taped hands a reassuring squeeze.

'I wish I could go instead of you.'

'Be my guest.'

I try to keep my voice light, but I can't help sighing.

There's so much dread inside me now it's impossible to keep it in. How I wish I was more like Sky – a natural-born fighter so hard that even the camps couldn't break her. All my life I've been scared. Scared of bullies like Nash. A coward, terrified of being found out. She'll never know what this feels like.

'You're braver than you think,' she says.

I stare at her, worried she can read my mind. Her eyes are closed.

And suddenly I'm mad again, like I was before she came in. Somehow her confidence tips me over the edge. Because I know it's misplaced – a belief in me I don't deserve and can never live up to. And it kills me.

'You're wrong,' I say sourly.

I get up, slam knuckle punches into the bag like Seph taught me.

When I look round again she's watching me, her eyes so big and dark I almost fancy I see myself reflected in them. Then I see something else too. Guilt.

She bites her lip. 'There's something I have to tell you.'

For a mad second, I forget about the mission. I figure Sky's about to tell me that she's already hooked up with some bloke somewhere. Only now I see how drawn she looks . . . and realisation rips through me like a blunt Reaper knife.

I gasp. 'This mission, it was *your* idea?'

She grits her teeth and nods. 'I'm sorry, Kyle. But we –'

'And you cuddling up to me all of a sudden, what's that? More sorry?'

This stings her. I see that.

'Is that what you think?' she says, her voice cold.

I don't know, but I do remember what Murdo said about her. *Sky doesn't have friends, only people she uses.*

And he's right. All this girl cares about is saving her twin sister. I should've known when she let Fliss and Matty sacrifice themselves to save us, and lied to them about her Haggletown contact. Sky's ruthless.

Gutted, I grab my gear and storm off.

And I don't look back.

29
DECISIONS

Most of that day I spend on my bunk back in my cell room, tossing and turning, sweating with fear. Either that or pacing about, hot one second, cold the next, almost like I've got that swamp-pox fever again. I should be helping Scallon out in the healing room, but there's no way. I can't face it. And fortunately, nobody comes to fetch me. When the bell sounds for midday meal, I ignore it.

My knuckles bleed from punching rock in frustration and despair.

I'm angry too, still raging at Sky for whispering ideas behind my back that will get me killed, and for stringing me along. Raging at myself for being such a gom and falling for her. All the girl cares about is her sister, and I *knew* that. But what rips me up the most is how small and helpless I feel. I've got less say over what happens to me than a windfall leaf in a storm. The Saviour and his Slayers want me captured alive, probably only so they can make a big show of executing me. Ballard, Sky and the rest, they just want to use me as some kind of secret weapon.

Nobody cares what *I* want or what happens to me.

I think about Rona, the only person who *did* care. I wish she was here. And wishing soon turns to wondering. Rona had her comm gear stashed for years, yet not once did she use it before she had to out of sheer desperation. Why not? I remember plenty of tough times before that when we could have used some help. Unless, knowing who I am, she figured I was safer with her than Gemini? I quit my pacing. That must be it. She had her orders, but *disobeyed* them. For me.

I'm still shaking, still scared, but I go hunting for Murdo.

Most evenings, soon as the lights dim, he's to be found propping up the counter of Bastion's mess area, nursing a glass of the foul watered-down excuse for beer they serve there. Only when I get to the mess there's no sign of him. The woman who serves the drinks says she hasn't seen him today. I'm about to walk when she winks and tells me she knows where he bunks down. Even with her directions this disused storage chamber still takes some finding and I only manage it when I eventually hear his tuneless whistling. Turns out I'm only just in time. He's on his knees, cramming his sleep bag into a bulging rucksack.

'Where are you going?' I say.

He finishes stuffing the pack, clips it closed, then looks round.

'Time's money in my game, kid. I've got Sky's abandoned windjammer to salvage; can't be hangin' around down here forever.' He stands up, swings the pack over his shoulder and grins at me. 'Hey, why so fed up?'

I know I shouldn't – Ballard and LeGuin made this crystal – but I tell him all about the mission, how I get implanted and handed over as some kind of bait.

And then I tell him how it was Sky's idea.

'Did tell you,' he says, shaking his head. 'That girl is nothin' but trouble.'

'Might as well kill myself and get it over with,' I say.

'Tell them you won't do it.'

'Easy for *you* to say.'

'Well, kid, I wish there was something I could do, but —'

He shrugs and goes to walk round me, but I step in front of him. 'Wait! You got to help me. You owe me.'

Murdo tilts his head to one side and fakes a puzzled face. 'I don't think so.'

'That Skull guy would've killed you if it wasn't for me.'

'True. And I flew you here. By my reckonin' that makes us quits.'

'No way. You got paid to do that!' I shout, furious now. 'Look, all I'm asking is to come with you in the *Never Again*. Just get me clear of the Blight, drop me off somewhere and then forget about me. No one needs ever know.'

He throws his hands up. 'No can do.'

'Why not?' I say, and even I can hear I'm whining.

'Look, Kyle, you're a good lad, but you don't know what you're askin'. Even I don't mess with Gemini. If you're so important, there's no way they'll let you clear off with me. You saw the security when we went to visit your mate the Answerman. Nobody leaves Bastion without clearance and an escort.'

I've thought of this on the way here.

'There must be some way to sneak out topside.'

Murdo shakes his head. 'Even the ventilation shafts have barriers, in case Slayers find them. I hear you need a special tag to unlock them.'

'So you're saying I'm stuck here?'

'No. What I'm sayin' is if you want to go topside you'll need a tag.'

He shoves past me now, no messing, but pauses in the doorway. 'Tell you what. It'll take me a day to prep the *Never Again* for launch. If you do get topside, the landing field is the old spaceport, a few klicks south of here. And that Maya girl I was foolin' around with? Look her up; she thinks you're cute.'

With that, he turns and ambles off.

Stunned, I step out of the room and stare after him. So much for thinking he would help me. All that loser cares about is credits and girls.

No wonder Sky doesn't think much of him.

I'm dragging myself back to my cell, numb with disappointment, when my brain finally catches up with what Murdo told me. That Maya girl led the topside patrol team that shadowed us. If anyone has an exit tag, it's her!

Hope stabs me, sudden and painful.

Only it's not like she'll hand it over, so how to get it off her?

But first I've got to find a possible route out. I wander the upper levels looking for ventilation pipes. Nobody pays any attention as long as I walk like I'm on my way somewhere. I follow small pipes until they merge and grow bigger. And finally, I find what I'm looking for – a pipe bending up into the ceiling. Above this must be a shaft to the surface. There's a ladder and an inspection hatch. My luck holds and nobody challenges me as I make my way back down the levels.

As I walk, another part of the puzzle falls into place.

I've hardly seen Wink since we got here. Bastion's a military base, so there are no other children. Seph told me they've got families topside in the Blight who'll look after her, but they're holding off while they try to find out what happened to Fliss and Matty. Meanwhile, I hear Wink is bunking down in the single women's dorm and being treated like a princess.

It's a bit embarrassing when I rock up there.

A few half-dressed women are lounging about inside, but no Sky.

They see me peering in, whistle and jeer. An older woman stalks over. When I ask to see Wink, she looks me up and down and tells me it's past the girl's bedtime.

'Come back at a more sensible time.'

I'm so nervous that I can't help laughing, which doesn't help. Only a few days ago Wink was living rough, hopping windjammers and throwing herself out of them. Poor thing, now she has to go to bed on time or else.

'Look, I'm on duty then,' I lie. 'Can't you just –'

Behind grumpy woman's back I see Wink tiptoeing towards us. She puts a finger to her lips and hides herself behind the open door. Somehow, I keep my face straight and mumble that I'll come back tomorrow. I wait round the corner.

Seconds later, Wink comes running.

Smiling, I crouch down, assuming she'll be pleased to see me. Only for her to shove me and nearly knock me over. Her face is blotchy and cross.

'Hey, quit that, Wink,' I say, fending her off.

'Why didn't you come sooner?' she says. 'You forgot all about me. I hate you!'

'I was hurt, then busy. Look, I'm sorry. I'm here now.'

I smile again, but she folds her arms across her chest and

looks at me down her nose, as if to say *don't waste my time with that smiling*.

'What do you want?' she says.

'Okay, you got me,' I say. 'I need you to steal something for me.'

'And why should I? Steal it yourself.'

She shrugs, still sulky, but her eyes go shiny. She's interested.

'I would,' I say. 'Only it's a girl who's got it and –'

'Got what? What is it?'

I tell her about Maya and her topside tag. I describe what it probably looks like, based on some others I've seen being used to unlock doors.

'Think you can get your paws on it?'

She shrugs. 'Easy. What'll you trade me for it?'

'Whatever you want.'

Suddenly, from the direction of the dormitory, I hear female laughter and the grumpy woman I talked to starts calling out Wink's name.

Wink glances round, then back at me.

'Matty'n'Fliss are dead,' she says. 'Aren't they?'

I crouch down and shake my head. 'We don't know that, Wink. Maybe they're lying low in some hole, you know, like we are. There's always hope.'

Her face goes sad and thoughtful.

'If you heard they *were* dead, you'd tell me?'

'Sure,' I say, not sure at all.

She nods, then turns and races back to her dormitory.

Another fearful night of tossing and turning and soaking my sheets with sweat. In my dreams I see those redhead Lynch girls again. They stare out at me accusingly through the bars of their cage as if they know I'm going to run away and let them down. Exhausted, I get up late and drag myself along to the mess for breakfast. One thing I'll miss is how well we're fed down here. I catch sight of myself in a polished metal panel and see this filled-out version of me, no bones sticking out now, fattened for the slaughter. My stomach knots with fear. I'm no way hungry, but it could be a while before I eat again, so I stuff my face anyway.

I wish I had some duties to fill the time between my combat training sessions with Seph. Anything, even scrubbing floors, would do. Doing nothing is killing me. I twitch when doors open or footsteps come up behind me. I keep expecting to be collected and have the implant done so I can be handed over.

What the hell is keeping Wink?

My question's answered when I return to my room after morning training, nursing a sore shoulder. Wink's sitting cross-legged on my bed, playing at soaring a crude wooden windjammer model back and forth over the messed-up sheets.

'Whatchathink?' she says, holding the toy up.

She looks incredibly smug.

I glance around, but nobody's about. 'Did you get it?'

'Course I did. I'm good, ain't I? Maya came back all sweaty from patrol. Went through her clothes while she was having a scrub.'

'And nobody saw you?'

Wink rolls her eyes and starts flying her toy again. '*Whoosh!*'

Somehow, I resist the urge to strangle her.

'Hand it over then,' I say, struggling to keep my voice calm.

But she shakes her head. 'Don't have it no more. Traded it for this.'

Her toy windjammer sails past my nose.

'You did what?' I shout.

'Keep it down,' says a familiar voice.

My whole body flinches. I look round and Sky's standing in the doorway, bleak-faced. Her crutch is gone, so she must have got her leg-brace back.

She flashes some plastic at me with a red 'T' stamped on it.

'This thing what you're looking for, Kyle, is it?'

Gob hanging open, I stare in disbelief at the tag in Sky's hand, my heart thumping, tasting bile. Last time I felt this crap, I had that Skull guy's bolt sticking out of my chest. A few more hours, that's all I'd needed to get away.

The unfairness of it all explodes inside me, chokes me.

'Give me the tag, Sky,' I say through my teeth.

'Why should I?' Sky says, stepping back out into the corridor.

'Because,' I say, but I follow her out.

She's alone. Course she is. Sky thinks she's so tough, and I'm only a loser to be used and sneered at.

'You-shoulda-visited-me,' Wink says, sing-song. 'Sky did.'

Sky nods at the door. I fumble behind me and close it.

'We need to talk,' she says.

'Fine. Give me the tag and we can talk all you like.'

She sniffs and gives me this look like she feels sorry for me.

That does it. I use all my nublood speed and make a grab for the tag. Almost get the boggin' thing too, but she twists away and even though I'm stronger she does something so agonising to my wrist that I cry out and have to let go.

'That what you call talking?' she snarls.

'Talk?' I say, massaging my wrist. 'Okay, let's talk about what happens to me if this mission goes wrong. Only what do you care? I'm not your precious sister, just some dumb kid from the Barrenlands, good for nothing but bait!'

'You're not dumb,' she says. 'But you *are* a fool.'

We stand there, glaring at each other.

Part of me wants to slide down the corridor's rock wall, sit with my back against it, my head in my hands, and moan about not wanting to die. A day ago, maybe I would have. But not now. I've made my mind up to live.

'I don't want to fight you, Sky,' I say. 'But I will.'

If she blinks I miss it. 'So what about those nublood children you saw at that Fair, Kyle? You don't care if they live or die, as long as you're okay?'

'That's *their* problem. Give me the damn tag.'

Sky's face crumples. I see disbelief and sadness. I'm still raging, but have to look away. Next thing, she curses. The tag lands on the floor by my boots.

'You'd better get moving,' she grates. 'Murdo won't wait.'

I empty my lungs in a shocked gasp and stare at her. 'What? He *told* you?'

She shakes her head. 'Just a guess.'

With that, she turns on her heel and limps away.

I bend and pick up the tag, my anger already melting away into a muddle of guilt and wanting her to understand.

'Wait! Sky! I didn't mean —'

But nothing doing; she keeps on walking.

'Come with me!' I call after her.

She stops now. Stands there stiffly for a few seconds before looking back over her shoulder at me, fierce-eyed and proud. 'No. I've got a war to fight.'

I'm so messed-up, I nearly change my mind about running.

Sky doesn't give me the chance though.

'Goodbye, Kyle,' she says, shaping my name with scorn.

I nod, too ashamed and too angry to say anything.

She sets off again and this time I don't waste my breath calling after her. I bang back inside my tiny little room, almost knocking the door off its hinges. I'm grabbing my stuff, a wide-eyed Wink watching me, when I hear Sky's shout.

'You know you can't run forever!'

She only shouts it once, but it echoes along the tunnel.

You know you can't run forever. Can't run forever. Can't run forever . . .

30
CHANGE OF PLAN

I clamber out of the vent into the shadow-filled and burnt-out ruins of what was once a storehouse. There I change into my old clothes and hide my Gemini stuff. Sky wasn't kidding about watching my back topside. Soon as I head out into the narrow lanes of the Blight I hear them scuttling after me, like human rats. Why do they take so long to attack? I tell myself they're as scared as I am, although I doubt that. Anyway, I find myself a rusty metal pipe. When they rush me, blades glinting in the dayshine, I'm all set and waiting. Three ragged kids, their faces filthy and hollow-cheeked. I mess one up pretty bad, but what else can I do?

They should've left me alone.

That's all I ever wanted – to be left alone.

I wave the bloody pipe at a second crew and they don't fancy it. Leathery faces watch from shack doorways, but nobody else bothers me. By looking how the shadows fall, I blunder my way south and clear of the shanty town.

Only a few klicks, Murdo said, but I figure it's more like ten. All over open ground too, with little or no cover on the way down to the plain. I hide out in a ditch and feed the bugs until it's dark. Then I get lucky – the bigmoon is up and full and shows me my way. There's a road, but I keep to the fields. The last few klicks I have to walk through knee-high grass, which sways around me in a warm night breeze. It's beautiful in the moonglow, almost like wading through a shallow and tickling silver lake, but my skin crawls. Each step I take blind, imagining hungry eyes watching me, predator snouts sniffing the blood spatter on my clothes. But at least I can't get lost. The old spaceport stands out below, a perfectly round black hole in the shimmering sea of grass. A few glowtubes twinkle through windows near the landing field, looking like a reflection of the sky above.

I reach the fence and see the squat shapes of windjammers beyond it.

Problem is this is no rust-gobbled and weak Barrenlands fence. This is a serious piece of chain-link mesh, solid and tall and well maintained. Even with the cutters I brought with me it takes ages and all my nublood strength to cut my way through it. One windjammer is some distance from the others. Light spills from its open loading ramp at the back. I creep towards it, wondering if it's the *Never Again*. Then I see Murdo sitting on the ramp, jug in one hand, cleverbox in the other. He's watching something on it, his lean face lit up by the flickering screen.

I stop creeping and walk forward.

'You took your time, kid,' he says, glancing round.

I don't know what to say, so I say nothing. He offers me his jug. My mouth's so dry I'm tempted, but one sniff and I shudder and hand the jug back to him.

Murdo squints at me. 'Is that blood? Are you hurt?'

I shake my head and tell him how I got jumped in the Blight.

He grunts, stares back down at the cleverbox.

'What happens now?' I say impatiently.

'We sit tight,' he says, not looking up. 'Tomorrow morning, we see if the weather's okay for a launch. If it is, we lift the hell out of here.'

'Think they'll come after me? Gemini, I mean.'

Murdo chuckles. 'What do *you* think?'

I can't help groaning.

'Don't worry, kid,' he says. 'It could always be worse.'

He tilts the cleverbox so I can see.

On the screen is a Slayer thumping his fist, his mouth working hard. Murdo pulls something from his ear and now I can hear what the man's saying. He's banging on about the Saviour's justice and crimes against purity.

'Is this the Saviour's broadcast?' I say, crouching. 'How'd you get that?'

Murdo grins. 'Easy. I'm a man of many wasted talents.'

In Prime and other big settlements I've heard they have screens showing this crap, day and night. The Barrenlands are too remote to get the signal.

One consolation of living there, Rona used to say.

As I listen, I realise this isn't just some routine rant – it's an announcement of a major public execution. Two nights from now, in Prime's main square. The image of the speaker fades, then re-forms to show a man's face, all broken and bleeding. He looks at the camera with dull and hopeless eyes, and knows he's dead. A woman's voice in the background tells us almost cheerfully that his crime is murder. Death by hanging. The next man, wild-haired, toothless and drooling, is a heretic. Death by boiling. A young boy, not much older than Wink, tears cleaning tracks down his grubby face, is a food thief. Death by stoning. And the list goes on.

What death have they planned for me?

The original Slayer presenter is back now. I'm thinking dark thoughts more than listening, but I catch something about the Barrenlands. 'What did he say?'

Murdo shrugs, but drags his finger across the screen. The image blurs backwards, then plays again. The man's voice quivers with outrage as he reports an insurgent atrocity, where all the men, women and children in a Barrenlands community of peaceful and law-abiding farmers were massacred.

'Isn't that where you're from?' says Murdo.

Frantically, I wave at him to shut up. The image changes, pans slowly across smoking ruins of shacks and farmsteads. Zooms in on bodies lying scattered in the dirt, many of them missing limbs, obviously hacked to pieces.

I shudder. This is Freshwater all right, the remains of it.

'. . . insurgents were pursued and destroyed, their ruthless leader captured.'

The picture dissolves again. This time when it re-forms it's showing a middle-aged woman's face, so bruised and swollen I almost don't know her.

Only of course I *do* know her.

It's Rona.

'Oh no, no,' I moan, clutching at my head.

*

It takes me half the night, blundering round the Blight, until I find the river of sludge. I use it to track back to the topside portal we used on my trip to the Answerman. Even then it's so well camouflaged I only know I'm outside the right shack when the cold metal of a gun barrel nestles itself behind my ear.

'Looking for something, Blighty?' growls a deep voice.

'Waste him,' a woman hisses.

'Don't shoot, I'm one of you!' I squeal, or something as pathetic.

Fortunately, when I look round I recognise the man with his finger on the pulse rifle's trigger. He's a Gemini fighter called Graf. We've chatted and bumped fists. He grabs me and forces my face up to the moonglow.

'Hang on, Sal, I know this guy!'

A shabby-looking woman follows her levelled rifle out of the darkness. She covers me while Graf makes me kneel, hands on my head, and searches me. He finds the plastic security tag and takes it off me.

The woman jabs me with her rifle. 'What you doing topside?'

I shake my head. 'Take me to Ballard.'

Out of the corner of my eye, I see them swap glances. Graf shrugs and the woman ducks back into the shack. She does a load of whispering into something before coming back out.

'Squad's on its way,' she tells him.

They settle down to wait, watching me over their gunsights.

I stare up at the star-filled sky until I find Sol, Earth's sun, where we're all supposed to have come from in the Long Ago. It looks dim and insignificant.

Maybe, I think, this is the last time I'll see it.

Do I really want to do this? Too late now anyway.

More Gemini fighters swarm out of the shack now and form a defensive screen. I'm grabbed and bundled inside, where a hatch gapes open in the floor. The trip back down into the guts of Bastion happens in a blur. As soon as we're safely underground they start firing questions at me, but I tell them I'll talk to Ballard and nobody else. It's the middle of the night topside so the corridor lights are dimmed. The few people we pass stare wide-eyed at the stony-faced escort marching me along. A door opens, I'm shoved through and it's locked behind me.

Ballard's office, only he's not here.

I don't get to sweat for long before the door crashes open.

A furious-looking LeGuin wheels herself in. Two guards follow her, close the door behind them and stand either side of it, watching. She glares up at me, her broad face red and twitching. 'You fool, have you any idea what you –'

'Rona's still alive!' I shout.

One of the guards grabs my shoulder. 'Shut up!'

I try to shrug the man off, sick of people telling me what to do and hunting me and trying to kill me. Rona's still alive, but she won't be much longer if I can't get these stupid people to listen. The man only grips me tighter, hurting me now. I lash out. Mistake. He ducks, then doubles me up with a punch. His buddy jumps me from behind, forcing my arms behind my back. I struggle, but both these guys are nublood too and way bigger than me.

'What's the meaning of this, LeGuin?'

They can't stop me looking and I see Ballard at the door.

'Let him go,' he orders the guards as he strides to his desk.

'Before we condemn the boy, perhaps we should hear what he has to say.'

'With all due disrespect, Ballard,' LeGuin growls, 'the boy's a security risk.'

Ballard sits, then shrugs. 'Even now?'

'He's dangerous.'

'I certainly hope so. He's going to need to be.'

LeGuin curses, and nods to the guards. They let go and step back.

'This better be good,' she mutters, wheeling herself away.

Ballard stares at me now, his lined face puzzled. 'Why did you run, Kyle?'

'I was scared.' I say, hanging my head.

'And yet here you are,' he says slowly. 'You've come back.'

I fix my toughest face on and look up at him. 'I changed my mind.'

'Go on,' he says, glancing at LeGuin.

'Stick that implant in me. I'll do your mission. But I want something in return. Rona's alive. You've got to save her!'

LeGuin snorts loudly, as if to say *see, I told you so.*

He frowns. 'How do you know she's alive?'

I tell them what I saw on the Saviour's broadcast.

'You're sure it was Rona?' Ballard says.

'I know my mother.'

He nods and then stands up. 'Very well. Let's get Ness here.'

Five minutes later and I'm telling the tech soldier about Murdo showing me the broadcast feed. He nods and says, 'Yeah, no problem,' goes off and comes back with some device, which shines a recording of the broadcast on the wall. He freezes Rona's battered face. It's not the cuts and bruises that sting my eyes with tears, it's how lost and empty she looks. Any fear I have left is swept away by rage. They haul in Sky next, who looks stunned to see me. She confirms it's Rona.

I dart a grateful look at her, but she blanks me.

She's escorted out.

Before Ballard or LeGuin can start talking again, I jump in.

'Look, I've got it all figured out. Your fighters hide in the crowd. When they start shooting, I grab Rona. We run, but I stay behind to get caught, like you wanted. I could maybe be shot in the leg, to make it look real.'

And we all get what we want . . .

I'm blown away when Ballard shakes his head. 'I don't think so, Kyle.'

'Why not?' I say, my voice a croak.

LeGuin sighs and counts the reasons off on her fingers.

'One, everyone there will be searched. Two, a big crowd, so masses of casualties in any firefight, mostly civilians. Three, Prime is a walled town, with guarded gates the only way in and out. Our fighters would be caught like rats in a barrel. Four, reprisals. The Slayers would think nothing of rounding up a hundred people and executing them one by one until we handed Rona back.'

'Rightly or wrongly,' Ballard says, 'people would blame Gemini. From what you've told us about Rona, I doubt she'd want that.'

'But –' I sway on my feet.

I was so sure they'd go for my plan. On the way back from the landing field I'd played it out in my head. I saw it all so clearly. Hard-faced rebel fighters throwing their hoods back and opening fire. Me snatching Rona from the gallows.

Only I see now it's just fantasy.

Ballard's right. Rona would hate the thought of people dying for her.

Sky's right too, was right all along. I *am* a fool.

I'm hauled outside then while Ballard and LeGuin discuss something. When I'm called back in, LeGuin still looks mad at me, but not *as* mad.

'There may be a way,' she says slowly, 'to save your mother.'

It's like being sucker-punched in my guts. 'How?'

'By trading you for her.'

I get so dizzy, I have to sit down.

Why didn't I think of this? It's so boggin' obvious! Only now it's like this hole opens inside me and fills with doubt.

'Won't they be suspicious?' I say.

Ballard shifts in his chair. 'Possibly not. Kyle, what we haven't told you is that, as part of their hunt for you, the Slayers have already rounded up hundreds of Gemini suspects and sympathisers. Publicly, as you saw, they claim they are executing criminals. Behind the scenes, they let it be known the arrests and executions will continue until we hand you over. Such mindless brutality, I'm afraid, is the Saviour's stock-in-trade.'

'Normally we wouldn't give in,' says LeGuin, scowling. 'We can't or our cause is too easily defeated. But –' She can't say it.

Ballard grimaces and finishes her sentence for her. 'But this time we feign weakness. We demand Rona to save face, as if doing you a last favour.'

They look at me, neither of them unkindly now.

I don't think, in case fear gets the better of me. I just nod.

PART THREE
ENDGAME

31
TRADE

Everything gets very real, very quickly. Too quickly for my thrashing heart. Not so many hours ago it was all talk, but now here I am crouched down inside a mud-built hut, topside in the western outskirts of the Blight. Outside, although I can't see it from here, is a large marketplace, deserted today. All around me are Gemini fighters, gripping their weapons tightly and looking tense. And these are only the ones I can see. Loads more are in hidden firing positions.

Won't be much longer until the trade. I run my fingers along my forearm again, feeling for the implant.

'Stop doing that,' nags Sky.

I try for a grin. 'Was it *this* arm Scallon stuck it in?'

She rolls her eyes at me. 'Ha ha.'

It still freaks me out how fast I heal these days. There's nothing, no scar tissue, no white mark even, to show where Scallon made the incision. Even she looked surprised at this afternoon's briefing, when she was telling me how to cut it out and which veins to avoid. Ness comes bustling up now, double-checking his tracker. He shows me the blinking dot on the screen, which is me. He can track the beacon while it's still buried in my arm, but says the signal will be an order of magnitude stronger if I cut the thing out. That's tech speak for it will shout a lot louder.

'Better out than in,' he says for the thousandth time.

I fight the urge to punch him. 'Got it.'

He peers at me, his magnified eyes doubtful, and wanders off again.

'I told you,' Sky whispers, gazing at me.

'Told me what?'

'You're braver than you think.'

I get a lump in my throat. 'Then how come I'm so scared?'

She shrugs. 'Chane said fighters who aren't scared are fools. The really brave fighters *are* scared to death, but they stand and fight anyway.'

I consider this. 'I'm both – scared *and* a fool.'

'You're just talented,' she says.

Sky's stayed in the background until now, but I'm glad she's here. I'm still hurting, but I reckon I understand her better now. She wants to find Tarn; I want to save Rona. We'll each do whatever it takes to get what we want.

Maybe we're not so different after all.

'I still don't get how I cut it out with no blade,' I say.

It. The beacon inside me. My only hope.

'Any old metal will do,' Sky says. 'Back in the camps, we made blades from all sorts of scavved metal. Just takes patience and lots of scraping to get an edge.'

I look into her eyes which have seen so much horror.

'Simple as that, huh?'

My voice wobbles up and down. I can't help it.

In the gloom, her hand seeks mine and gives it a squeeze.

And then we wait some more.

It's weird what I think about with my nerves so stretched; like how time messes with you. When I was a bored kid time dragged like an old man walking. Last night, with me dreading what the morning would bring, it seemed all I had to do was blink and hours went by. Now I'm here, just wanting this trade over and done with, and the seconds are crawling again. And I think about the fluff on my chin. Sergeant Havel is the leader of the Gemini tactical squad responsible for my handover. About Murdo's age, he's short, stocky and tough-looking, and I envy him his thick beard. Can't see myself living long enough to grow my own.

Havel's headset buzzes and chatters stuff into his ear.

'Here they come,' he growls. 'Keep it tight, everybody.'

He beckons for me and Sky to join him.

Dry-mouthed, I peer out at the marketplace through a slit cut into the mud wall and watch as three giant Slayer landcrawlers grind their way into the far end of the square, smoke belching from their exhaust stacks, blaster turrets swivelling back and forth, looking for targets. I've heard about these armoured vehicles, drawn imaginary versions when I was little, but never seen one for real before. They fan out, cut their engines and settle on to their tracks.

My heart sinks into the silence. So this is it . . .

'They're showing truce,' Havel says.

I see it too. A white flag flicks in the breeze above the middle crawler.

'And we're supposed to believe that?' sneers Sky.

Havel shrugs. 'I have my orders. Look, something's happening.'

A hatch opens in the hull of the crawler flying the flag and slowly unfurls in a series of jerks to form a ramp. Next thing, about a dozen heavily armed Slayers stream down it and spread out in front of the vehicle, taking up firing positions. Another Slayer, tall and slender, follows them out. She pulls her gloves off and strolls a few paces towards us. Dayshine glints off her ornate helmet.

Commandant Morana. High Slayer of the Barrenlands.

'Bring out the boy,' booms her amplified voice.

'Right, let's do this,' Havel says through his teeth. He glances around at his fighters. 'First sign of trouble I want smoke and covering fire. Got that?'

He gets nodded at. I hear a few good lucks called.

Sky gives me a hug now, pulls me so close that I can feel her heart beating in her chest as wildly as mine.

'We *will* come and get you,' she whispers.

I just hold her, and try hard to believe they will.

She pulls away. If I didn't know better, I'd swear her eyes were wet.

I hold out the letter that Scallon helped me scribble to Rona last night. In it, I thank her for all her love and kindness, for being a mother to me.

'Will you make sure Rona gets this?'

Sky takes it and nods.

I hold my left hand out to her and we bump stumps.

'Time to go, son,' says Havel, pulling a mask up to hide most of his face.

He heads off through the back door. I stumble after him, only vaguely aware of a similarly masked Seph, my combat instructor, bringing up the rear. After the gloom inside the hut, the dayshine stings my eyes, dazzling me. We keep our heads down and creep along a narrow path behind a wall. This twists and turns and brings us to the square, well away from the command post with its tunnel in the floor.

Havel curses, takes a deep breath and steps out into the glare.

Nothing bad happens. He beckons to me.

I hesitate, licking my lips, then lurch out beside him. Less than two hundred metres away, I see Morana turn and study us through a scope. The blaster turrets on the crawlers swivel smoothly round and point our way too.

'Not very friendly,' says Seph, at my side now.

'Where's Rona?' I say, peering, my head thumping.

'They're bringing her out now,' Havel says.

He's right. At Morana's signal, a hatch opens in the far-right crawler. Two Slayers emerge, supporting a woman between them. She shuffles along on legs that seem unwilling to obey her. Her shaven head hangs down and she only manages a few paces before collapsing. They grab her wrists, drag her forward.

One yanks her head up so we can see her face.

And it *is* Rona.

Without thinking, I go to run to her, but Seph holds me back.

'Wait,' she whispers. 'You sure it's her?'

I nod, not sure I can speak.

Havel mutters into his throat-mike. 'We've got positive identification. Moving out now.' Then to me: 'You first, nice and slow. No sudden moves.'

He and Seph click the safeties off their pulse rifles.

I hesitate, my legs shaking.

Seph puts her hand on my shoulder. 'We're right behind you, Kyle.'

She doesn't push me exactly, just helps me take the first step. And then she keeps her hand there for show, like taking this walk isn't my idea.

Ahead of us, Morana signals to the two Slayers.

They pace forward to meet us, carrying Rona between them, her bare feet dragging through the dust. I blink stinging sweat out of my eyes. My stomach feels like it's twisting itself inside out. With each step I keep expecting blaster beams to crackle out and cut me in half. Some mad thoughts chase themselves around my head – like I'm doing this heroic thing so there should be people cheering. But all I hear is blood pounding in my ears, our boots on the flagstones and the wind whistling and moaning on its way through empty market stalls.

'That's close enough,' says Havel.

He stops us just short of the marketplace's well, a hole in the ground with a low stone wall surrounding it. Rubbish from yesterday's market swirls round us in the breeze.

The Slayers dragging Rona halt at the far side of the well and drop her, like she's nothing but a piece of meat. Her head thumps on to the ground.

'You bastards!' I yell, rushing at them.

Seph hauls me back as the Slayers unsling their rifles.

'Contact,' Havel mutters, grabbing hold of me. His pulse rifle is settled on his hip, barrel pointing up, but his finger is curled around the trigger.

One Slayer beckons to me. 'You, come with us.'

Havel shakes his head. 'Not yet. First we check the woman's okay.'

'She'll live. Make it quick.'

Seph hustles forward, pulls some device from her satchel and starts scanning Rona. I squirm until Havel lets go and scramble to help. Up close I shiver as I see how horribly thin Rona is, the bruises from countless beatings, cuts on her scalp from being rough-shorn like a farm animal. We roll her gently on to her back. I cradle her head in my lap, my tears mixing with the blood on her face.

She *is* my mother. In every way that matters.

'Rona,' Seph says, her voice urgent. 'Did they give you anything?'

I guess she means poison.

Rona's eyes flicker open. She shakes her head. Then she sees me and her bloodshot eyes well up with a terrible sadness.

I try and smile. 'Hey, Mum. It's me.'

'Oh, Kyle,' she croaks. 'What *have* you done? They'll kill you.'

She looks past me and cringes, like a beaten dog.

'Enough bullshit! Let's go, twist.'

A shadow falls across us. I look up and see both Slayers standing over us, blocking the dayshine. One hauls me to my feet. The other shoves me, sending me stumbling towards the waiting Morana. Panic clutches at my throat. I want to run, but I force myself to walk. Rona's safe – I will not screw things up.

The Slayer shoves me again, even harder.

I look back and see Havel lifting Rona up in his arms.

Her shaved head falls back, like a baby's, as if she's lost consciousness again.

'Tell her I love her,' I yell.

'Hang tough, Kyle,' Seph calls, raising her fist in a salute.

That's when I hear a loud *ripping* sound. I only realise it's gunfire when Seph twitches and jerks like a rag doll, throws her arms out and falls down. Dust and stone fragments fly up around Havel and Rona. He drops her, flings himself on top of her and claws for his slung pulse rifle. I'm so stunned, I just stand there, gawping in disbelief. I hear a popping sound now. In front of me, there's a sudden line of flashes and bangs. A wall of oily smoke billows up and blocks my view.

'No!' I yell, finding my voice. 'Rona! Run!'

I go to run to her, but forget my Slayer escort. Something slams into the back of my neck and I go down. And stay down. I scream at my body to get up, but it isn't listening. All I can manage is to flop about, like a caught fish. Behind me, I hear the cough of the landcrawlers' engines starting, the bark of their exhausts. A second later, their heavy blasters open fire, slamming bolt after bolt of ravening golden plasma over my head and through the smoke. I hear the thumps of pulse rifles returning fire now, but they sound like children's toys by comparison.

I'm dragged backwards across the stones, helpless to resist.

Rona's dead. They're *all* dead. There's no way anybody could survive that murderous hail of blaster fire. Not stuck out in the open like they were.

One of the Slayers dragging me grunts and lets go.

He staggers, clutches his neck, then falls.

For one pathetic moment, that desperate space between

my heartbeats, I feel a surge of hope that Gemini are coming to get me. Stupid. The other Slayer keeps dragging me further away. Now I hear shouted orders. More Slayers hustle past and spread out to form a defensive line between us and the smoke.

It's done. I'm taken. Which is what Gemini wants.

Behind me, heavy tracks clank across the marketplace's flagstones. There's a screech of brakes and the reek of coal smoke and hot metal fills my nose. More hands grab me. They force my hands behind my back and bind them with some kind of cord, jerking it so tight that it bites into my skin. It's all I can do not to scream. I'm bundled through a hatch into the dark insides of one of the landcrawlers. The hatch bangs shut behind me. Dim lights flicker on and the deck under me sways as the machine starts moving again. My guards force me to my knees, grab my hair and force my head back.

Now I see who's in here with me. High Slayer Morana.

'Hello again, Kyle,' she says with a mocking smile full of malice. 'So much for your rebel friends sheltering you. I imagine it must have come as a nasty surprise when you learnt you were to be handed over. Now, where were we?'

'We made a deal,' I say, spitting the words. 'You said you'd spare Rona.'

The woman laughs. Delighted. Amused.

'She's a traitor. You didn't really think we'd let her go free?'

Gingerly, as if it hurts, she removes her helmet. Even now, weeks later, her harsh face shows signs of bruising from when I smacked her with the gun.

'You don't heal so good, do you?' I say.

It's not like I'm feeling suddenly brave or anything. I just *need* to lash out.

But she just shrugs. 'Your twist healing is a curse.'

I snarl Rona's words back at her. 'It's no curse, it's a blessing!'

'A blessing, is it?' Again that vicious, mocking smile. 'Well, perhaps it is in the right hands. But for you, Kyle, I will see to it personally that it really *is* a curse. You see, unfortunately, it gives you almost infinite potential for suffering.'

And now she shows me the gloves she's wearing. Studded fighting gloves. At her nod, the guards holding me let go and step back.

Whatever the Slayer stung me with, it's wearing off. I can just about move now, but nowhere near fast enough to get out of the way as she leans back then smashes me across the face with the back of her hand, spinning me round, knocking me down. I end up on the floor, groaning, blood spilling from my mouth. With my hands tied behind my back, all I can do is try and squirm away. I don't get far before the guards drag me back and up on to my knees again.

'Sadly, the Saviour has ordered me not to kill you,' Morana says. 'A shame, as I know some delightfully slow ways to kill twists. But I *can* hurt you.'

'You can't hurt me. Not any more, you can't,' I mumble, thinking of Rona.

The woman flexes her armoured fingers. 'You think?'

32
IN THE PALACE

They say you can't remember pain. It's true, you can't. Or at least I can't.

That's a mercy, I guess, but not enough of a mercy.

See, I was wrong. Morana *can* hurt me. And she does hurt me. And then keeps on and on hurting me, as if she can never get enough of listening to me scream and cry and beg. Oh yeah, I beg all right. I plead with her to kill me.

She hurts me, but doesn't break me. She's mad to know where Bastion is under the Blight, who the rebel leaders are and what they look like. But I keep all that knowing bottled up inside me. Ballard says I needn't, that I should squeal if that's what it takes to keep myself alive. But Morana took Rona from me and she won't be taking anything else. I'll die before I talk and sod the mission. I scream and whimper, but inside I'm picturing Rona, her sad face, her healer face, her tired-but-happy-sitting-by-the-fire face. Not letting her go. I won't lose her the way Sky lost her parents. Other times, I picture ways I'd like to kill Morana.

This one time, I manage to spit a gob-full of blood right in her face. I don't do this because I'm brave, I do it to provoke her so she'll end this. And she's tempted then. I see the longing in her eyes, her fingers twitching.

But the High Slayer obeys her orders.

Finally, reluctantly, she delivers me to the Saviour's Palace.

They drop me, naked apart from a metal collar, on to a cold floor. I'm still dripping wet from the water they blasted me with to scour all the blood and sweat and filth off me. I lie there, curled up like a newborn baby, spit dribbling from my mouth, gazing down at the black and white tiles under me, not sure if I could stand up even if I wanted to. Trying to remember who I am.

'Is this him?' rasps this weird voice, with a bubbling sound.

'It is, Your Benevolence,' says Morana.

Boots clatter behind me. I squirm round to see the Slayers who carried me here marching from the room. Morana is standing there, staring down at me.

Somehow, I find the strength to give her the finger.

More bubbling, then a wheezing chuckle. 'He has spirit.'

Morana scowls, but masks it with a smile. 'Too much for his own good.'

She stalks past me. I squirm round, watching her, conscious of my nakedness now as she steps up on to a dais to join an elderly man. Realisation sucks a gasp out of me. She addressed him as Benevolence. This must be the Saviour.

Only . . . what on Wrath has happened to him?

The Saviour I know from posters and that giant vid-screen at the Fair is old all right, but still ruddy-cheeked, broad-shouldered and strong; a man in his later years with long, flowing grey hair and a mouth full of white teeth. But this figure watching me is ancient, bent over and frail. A wispy-haired, shrivelled wreck of a man, hanging on long after the marrow has been sucked from his bones by age and suffering. A clear plastic mask covers his nose and mouth, and it's from this that the wet, sucking sound comes each time he fills his lungs. He turns to whisper something to Morana and I see other tubes sticking out from the back of his cloak. These snake across the floor and out of sight, red and yellow and brown liquids sliding through them. Almost makes me gag just looking at them.

Used up he might be, but I see menace in his damp eyes and shudder.

'Welcome home,' he wheezes.

Home. Is he mad?

'Acknowledge the Saviour,' Morana says, frowning.

I find what's left of my voice. 'And if I don't? You'll kill me?'

She opens her mouth, but this shrivelled version of the Saviour holds a hand up and she closes it again. He nods and she leaves his side, picks up a bundle of clothes and throws them so they hit me and fall to the floor. I stare at them, gather my strength, then pull them on. Slayer black. Thin. Nothing for my feet.

But they fit perfectly, as if Rona made them for me.

Morana stalks a wide circle round me now, looking me up and down. She's careful to stay out of my reach. Shame.

'There,' says the old man. 'Isn't that better?'

I shrug, like who cares? Not clever. The Saviour nods again. Morana smiles, shows me a device in her hand, jams her thumb down on a red button.

And I drop, clutching at my suddenly molten-hot collar.

'Manners,' she says. 'Now answer the question.'

She must take her thumb off the button because the burning goes away.

'Yes,' I sob, feeling my neck. Blisters are bubbling up already.

Her thumb hovers. 'Yes . . . Your Benevolence.'

'Yes, Your Benevolence,' I say quickly.

'Closer,' says the Saviour, beckoning me. 'Show me your face.'

I get up slow, making out I'm hurt worse than I am, and sneak a quick look around. The room's so vast, I've seen barns that would fit into it easy. A fancy whitewashed ceiling arches over me, held up by massive stone columns – it's got to be at least twenty metres high. Apart from a table laid for dining and some chairs on the platform, there's hardly any other furniture. The many doorways around the walls are minded by armed Slayer guards, all young women.

Nowhere to run to, nowhere to hide.

I stumble a few steps nearer to the dais, closely watched by Morana.

'Head up. Let your father see you,' she instructs.

I shudder, but do as she says.

The old man peers at me, then sighs deeply into his mask, as if satisfied.

'This is a great moment. It calls for celebration.'

He shuffles slowly to the far side of table, his tubes rustling after him. With much squeaking of plastic he settles himself on an ornate chair. Morana stalks round to take up a position behind him, her hand resting on his shoulder. Only then does she wave me forward. I take a seat in the empty chair opposite them.

'Eat,' the Saviour wheezes. 'You must build yourself up.'

A tiny part of me still wants to play the hero, to refuse my enemy's food. But who am I kidding? I'm no hero and my belly's so empty it hurts. And I've never seen so much food in all my life. Bowls of steaming soup, wooden platters buried under meats, cheeses and pickled vegetables. Plates of roast tubenose swimming in sauce, bowls of roast potatoes. Some grilled vegetables I don't recognise. Since Morana got her claws into me, I've had nothing to eat. Nothing to drink either, except for a few licks of foul water from the puddles on the floor after my morning spraying. I stuff my face. The Saviour leans back, watching me, but eating nothing himself. When I'm done, he hunches forward. 'How do you feel now?'

'Sick,' I mutter. No point lying.

He sighs breathily. 'No wonder, you eat like a pig. But that's not what I meant. Tell me, how does it feel to be restored to the bosom of your family?'

Even though I can't see it, I sense his sneer.

A hysterical laugh bubbles up inside me, but I choke it off.

'You're not my father,' I say. 'He's dead.'

I don't care what the Answerman told me. I can't – won't believe it.

Morana glances at the Saviour, thumb poised.

He shakes his head. 'Dead? No. Nearly, but not quite. You doubt, but when I was your age I looked much as you do now. The same thick hair, the same mouth and chin. Even now I think you can't deny where you come from.'

With that, he pulls his breathing mask aside. And he's right. I do see bits of my face hiding among all the sagging skin and the wrinkles. I squirm, trying not to let him see my disgust.

Facing the truth that this living-dead man *is* my father, that I *am* the son of the Saviour, is like sticking my hands into those longthorns again.

The Saviour pulls his mask back into place and takes several long and lingering pulls of whatever gas it's feeding him. Morana pouts at me over his shoulder and starts running her long fingers through what little hair he's got left.

'Now look what you've done,' she says. 'You –'

The Saviour cuts her off, his voice a painful-sounding croak.

'Despite the fact that you are a twist,' he pauses to shudder and suck some more of his gas, 'I am minded to spare you. And in return, you will help me.'

Spare me? My heart leaps. But then I remember Rona.

Nervously, I glance at Morana's hand. 'Why would I help you?'

He shrugs. 'Being difficult will only lead to more . . . unpleasantness.'

I try to swallow, but can't. My throat is still raw meat from screaming. I know, only too well, what he means by this.

'What do you want from me?'

'What,' he says, 'does any father want from his son?'

Baffled, I shake my head. Behind his mask, the Saviour starts to laugh. His shoulders heave up and down. His tubes rattle and squeak behind him.

'Your blood,' Morana says, smiling. 'That's what we want.'

I stare, horrified, unsure if I heard right.

The Saviour stops laughing and stares at me, his wet eyes glittering.

'My blood flows in your twisted veins,' he snarls. 'I want it back. You will serve me as your useless brother couldn't, and I shall be healed. A delicious irony, don't you think? Your mother, that scorned young slut, thought to kill me. Me, the Saviour of Wrath. She's why you see me like this, machines feeding me and scrubbing my blood to keep me alive. Yet now she will save me, through you!'

Healed? I gape up at him, confused, sure the man's out of his mind.

He snaps his age-twisted fingers at Morana.

Scowling behind his back, she pulls a gun from a holster at her hip and hands it to him over his shoulder. It's the ancient slug-thrower that Rona gave me. So much for the Answerman being worried about Gemini coming after him.

The Saviour stares at it for several long, bubbling breaths.

'My precious relic from the Long Ago,' he says at last. 'I was careless. Thought the drawer was locked. The bitch shot me with it and left me for dead.'

He glares from the gun to me, shaking visibly.

And now I feel my own rage boil up inside, thinking about this poor woman from the Blight who gave me life, and how terrified and desperate she must have been to take her own. 'A shame she didn't kill you then,' I growl.

His face darkens into a scowl and he aims the gun at me, his hand wobbling.

'Shall I shoot *you*, twist, so you know what it's like?'

I grit my teeth and say nothing.

'No?' he hisses. 'Where's your curiosity? It's only pain. With your twisted blood, if I take care where I shoot you, you'll live. And your gift means you will heal, unlike me now.

That's what you parasites are designed for after all.'

Loads of reasons I should keep my gob shut, but I can't.

'So my healing's a gift now, is it? Not a curse?'

He doesn't shoot, but this earns me another agonising writhe on the floor. I flop from my chair, clawing at my burning neck, whimpering like a baby.

'Enough,' says the Saviour. And the pain finally stops.

Slowly, I haul myself to my feet. I stand there, trembling, as he places the old revolver carefully back down on the white tablecloth. It's pitted metal looks brutal and out of place among the delicate china and cut glass. He spins it, but the barrel ends up pointing at him. Behind his mask, he clicks his tongue.

Slowly and painfully, he struggles back to his feet.

I eye the gun, but it's just too far away.

If I wasn't half dead maybe. But now I'd only get zapped.

'I tire of this farce, Morana,' he says, glaring at me and shuddering. 'Remove this creature from my sight. He disgusts me, as do all his monstrous kind.'

Morana bows. 'Shall I take him directly to the Facility?'

'Yes, yes, of course. Directly. Start work on him. I will join you there as soon as my latest treatment allows.'

'As you wish, Your Benevolence.'

Start work on me? Facility? I panic and make a dive for the gun. And down I go again, neck on fire, this time for longer. Much longer.

Vaguely, I'm aware of guards coming running.

I roll on to my back, thrashing about in agony as the High Slayer keeps her thumb planted. Just as I feel myself passing out,

I glimpse a boy's face wincing down at me from a balcony. Not hiding exactly, not trying to be seen either.

And I know who he is because his face is my face too . . .

33
THE FACILITY

Hours inside a chugging landcrawler, then a long windjammer flight with one stop overnight, that's what it takes them to cart me to this Facility place. Two full days, but that's a guess. I'm hooded the whole time, so I can't see or be seen. For this last stretch I'm lashed belly down across the hairy and swaying back of a pack yak. Even blind I can tell we're somewhere way up high now because it's fierce cold and the air breathes thin. But the strangest thing is the stink here, which is even more disgusting than the beast carrying me. The air reeks of rotten eggs.

My hood's pulled off, almost taking my ears with it. I blink tears from my eyes caused by the stink and the glare of dayshine. And what I see pulls a gasp out of me. Our trail crawls its way through a desolate landscape of snow and ice and rock, the bottom of a gigantic volcanic bowl. Here and there, smoke billows from cracks in the ground. On all sides, steep slopes climb back up to the jagged rim of the crater, gaps in the snow exposing patches of orange and yellow and red minerals. As we top a slight rise I twist round and see the landing field behind us, a long, ash-coloured runway scraped into the snow, windjammers scattered about. At the deepest point of the crater is an impossibly blue-green lake wreathed in steam.

'Welcome to the Facility, Kyle,' a fur-coat-wrapped Morana calls over from the fourhorn she's riding.

Her face is hidden behind a weird leather mask, her voice muffled through a canister thing where her mouth would be. But it's her all right. The long dark hair. The shimmering black nightrunner fur. The spidery way she carries herself. Her cold eyes regard me through the glass lenses.

All our Slayer escort wear the same masks.

Wish I did. My eyes are streaming and my throat's burning. I go to curse her, but only manage a groan.

Ahead of us, the trail mounts a plateau to head for a cluster of massive bubble-like domes. Some domes merge into one another, but others stand apart linked by covered walkways. And the Facility's domes aren't the only human-built structures here. Pitheads are dotted all about the crater floor. Our trail takes us past one of these rusting towers. The winding wheel is turning, but as my yak lumbers past it screeches and slows. A barred cage rises out of a hole in the ground.

It's crammed full of kids wearing filthy mining gear.

'Ah yes,' Morana says, 'our loyal workers.'

My yak picks this moment to do what yaks often do; it digs its hooves in and stops. I get to watch as masked Slayers emerge from a nearby shed. Rifles at the ready, they surround the cage as one of their number opens it. He's in no danger: these gaunt, half-dead kids are no threat. They stagger out, heads down, many having to be helped by their mates. Despite it being well below zero they're all barefoot like me, their ankles shackled. No protective masks for them.

To my horror I see several are coughing up blood. A girl is left behind in the cage, curled up on the floor and unmoving.

'What's wrong with them?' I say, appalled.

Morana glances at them and shrugs. 'Who cares? Some food and rest, most will be fine to go again tomorrow. You twists, you're so very cost-effective.'

Twists. All about my age or older. No youngsters.

I shudder, watching as they are herded away like animals. I shudder even harder as it suddenly hits me that I could be looking at what happens to the 'executed' nubloods. A second later I'm sure, because I recognise one of them, the boy whose tough-guy scab brother spat into the crowd at the Peace Fair and won me a credit by being the twist. Poor kid, he doesn't look so tough now. Eagerly, I look to see if any of the ident girls might be Sky's sister, Tarn, but no. It's disappointing, but there are dozens of pits and she could be working down any one of them.

A Slayer beats my yak until it yowls and starts moving again.

I hardly notice. I'm too busy remembering now what Fliss told me in that hole-in-the-wall cave near Drakensburg – about how ident camps are always located in mining towns, and how the Slayer camp guards put the ident prisoners to work down the mines from four years of age. As the complaining pack yak bumps and sways under me, it all starts to makes a sick and hideous sense at last.

Sky, she figured that as idents they were just slave labour.

But it was more than that, I get that now. I reckon they were being *trained* too, to one day work these mines.

*

I'm taken deep under one of the domes and dumped in a locked box of a cell that makes my room back at Bastion seem like paradise. Its bare floor and walls are made from some fancy grey substance I've never seen before. If I throw myself at it, it gives and I bounce off. No bed. In one corner a stinking hole in the floor. An unblinking, unbreakable camera lens watches me.

It takes me a while to get my thick head round what this all means. Morana doesn't want me killing myself. But at least it's warm here. I slowly thaw out and get a few hours alone to worry about what's going to happen next.

Armed guards come for me eventually. They drag me along to a kind of laboratory room full of the fanciest-looking tech gear I've ever seen. Slayer medics are waiting there. That's what they call themselves, medics, but even I can see that these guys are no healers. They peer at me over green masks covering their nose and mouths, as if they can't wait to start messing with me.

'Take your shirt off,' one of them orders.

'Why?' I say, sweating, petrified they'll find Ness's beacon in my arm.

He nods and my armed guards pounce and take it off for me.

They strap me down to a table and the medics start poking and prodding me, listening to my heart and my lungs, testing to see how healthy I am. I'm cringing the whole time, but Scallon buried the beacon deep and I needn't worry. They don't find it. On the trip here Morana left me alone mostly, so I've pretty much healed from the beatings she gave me. Anyway, the man in charge pronounces me ready.

It's only now, as a woman medic comes at me with this big,

nasty-looking valve and needle thing, that I panic and start struggling. Doesn't get me anywhere. The straps are tight and the guards collar-zap me until I quit. She shoves the needle into the wriggly vein on the back of my hand and tapes it on. It stings like hell. And now they plug me into this humming machine, which sucks blood out of me even faster than the megasucker grub thing that attacked poor little Wink. They drain so much blood out of me I'm wasted by the time I'm unplugged and unstrapped, hardly able to stand on my own as the guards lead me away.

Could be worse, I guess. I'm still alive and they give me a big feed afterwards. Then it's back to my cell to brood and fret until they come for me again. Days go by like this. The Slayer medics never find the beacon, but I took so many beatings off Morana I wouldn't be surprised if it's smashed. As for cutting it out, no chance. There's no way of getting my hands on metal, or sharpening it if I did.

It all sounded so boggin' simple back in Bastion.

The nights are the worst. I know I'm doomed and despair hunts me in the dark. I'll never get out of here. I'll end up a shrivelled sack of skin, all my blood drained out of me. To comfort myself, I take refuge in my thoughts. I picture Rona, her sad eyes staring up at me as I cradled her head in the market square. All those long years, risking her life to hide and protect me, never letting on. I picture Colm too, looking down on me from his hiding place in the Saviour's chamber. My pureblood twin brother. Remembering seeing him sends chills down my spine.

More than anything, I think about Sky.

I fight to stay angry at her for dreaming up this crazy

mission, but can't. I close my eyes and she's here with me: her cropped white hair, teardrop tattoo, green eyes flashing at me with real tears wetting them. I remember the feel of her cold hand squeezing mine, her bony hips sticking into me as we held each other.

I'm sorry, Sky. I'm letting you down. Letting everyone down.

Each morning, I scratch one more day survived into my cell wall. It takes ages, the surface is so tough, my nails so chewed. Thirteen scratches later I wake up knowing I'm waiting for a miracle that isn't going to happen.

In my head, it's like I hear Sky's whisper. 'Do something, you big gom!'

Easy for imaginary-her to say, but she's right. Deep down I know I need to at least try something before I go mad from loneliness and despair, like that caged and tortured twist I saw at the Peace Fair. But first I'll need a weapon.

Three scratches later, I realise I *am* the weapon.

And what's to lose really? They can punish me, but they can't kill me. Not if they want to keep sucking nublood out of my veins, they can't.

The next time they take me for my medic blood-letting, I act real pathetic, but take more of an interest in my surroundings. And I see how careless they're getting now, settling into a routine. It's been a while since I struggled. The four Slayer guards are bored, their weapons slung, when they should be watching me.

Next day, I see something else too. My chance. Sticking out of one of the senior medic's coat pocket is a scalpel.

Even though I'll be weaker, I wait until after they're done stealing my blood, figuring everybody will be even more relaxed by then. After they unstrap me, I drag myself off the table as if it's about all I can do to stand. I wait until the senior medic bustles past me before I pretend to stumble. And whether there's humanity left in the Slayer or it's just reflex, but he holds his hand out to steady me. I use all my nublood speed to pull him towards me and grab the scalpel. I've flicked the blade cover off and have it pricking my throat before the guards can react.

'Drop your guns or I'll slit my throat,' I yell at them.

The Slayer guards don't drop their weapons, but neither do they fire. Which is what I'm counting on. No Kyle, no more blood. One has the remote for my collar clipped to her belt. She slides her hand to it, but I'm looking for this.

'That won't stop me,' I growl at her.

I stick the scalpel deeper so it draws blood, let them know I'm serious.

Heart thrashing wildly, I start backing towards the door.

I'm just starting to hope when, at a nod from the senior medic, one of the Slayer guards shoots me right in the chest. I'm slammed backwards into the door and pinned there, foaming and twitching in agony as electric-blue sparks swarm all over me, feeling like I'm being turned inside out. The scalpel goes flying out of my hand. Only now do I see the guards' weapons aren't pulse rifles but shockers.

Last thing I think before I pass out is what a donk I am.

When I come to, I'm in a strange and freezing room, strapped down again, but this time on to some kind of bed thing on wheels. And I'm looking up at a stony-faced Morana. She's bundled up against the cold in her massively thick fur coat over her High Slayer uniform, her dark hair scraped tightly back and tied.

'You are being *very* tiresome,' she says.

I groan, sick with disappointment. 'So kill me then.'

'I wish I could, but as you've figured out by now, I can't. Not yet anyway. And I know this time you were only bleating on about killing yourself in a pitiful attempt to escape, but we can't have you really killing yourself either. Can we?'

She stares at me, like I'm less than nothing.

'If you let me go,' I jeer, 'I won't kill myself, I swear.'

She smiles at this, but it doesn't make it anywhere near her eyes.

'Enough of your nonsense.' She nods to some waiting Slayer medics. 'Stick him in a C-tank. Half power, no sedation.'

'Is that wise?' says one of them, a woman.

Morana shrugs. 'He thinks he's hard. Let's find out how hard.'

I'm wheeled away now, down a corridor and then across a vast, high-ceilinged hall containing hundreds of C-tanks arranged in neat rows. One of the Slayer medics wheeling me along seems to get a kick out of telling me exactly how the tanks work, but I don't listen because I know already. It's hard not to know because if you weren't born on Wrath this is how you were shipped across impossible gulfs of space to be dumped here. They're suspended-animation chambers, big freezers full of some fancy, supercooled soup called cryoxyplasma, or something like that. They stick you in and you drown – that's why they knock you out first – but the extreme cold means that you don't die. The trip out here takes years if you go cattle class, using finite-light-multiple drive, and you have to because there are no wormholes in this neck of the galaxy. Another reason Wrath was chosen to be a dump world. The guy takes even greater delight now in telling me there's a one-in-twenty chance I'll come out dribbling and brain-scrubbed after I'm thawed, and that's why only criminals, refugees and beasts are shipped FLM these days.

'That what happened to you, is it?' I mutter.

Most of the C-tanks in the hall are dark and open, but some are closed and frosted over, humming and whirring away, lights blinking. As I'm rolled past I see condensation dripping from these working tanks on to the white-tiled floor. A few Slayer medics wander about, clutching cleverboxes and checking stuff. My tank must be special however. It's in a dank, mouldy room on its own. The lid is already up, held open by gas struts either side. I make the mistake of looking inside and see it's full of a sparkling light-blue liquid with a mist rising up from it. The stuff writhes and crawls as if it's alive. Even metres away I can feel how icy cold it is.

My mortal fear of drowning takes over.

'Okay, okay,' I shout. 'I give in. I'll do whatever you want.'

I mean it too. My padded cell looks good now. They can have my blood.

'We're here now,' Morana says, catching up with us.

She nods at some watching Slayers wearing black rubber gloves that cover their arms up to their elbows. They unstrap me and grab hold of me.

'Strip him?' the biggest of them asks her, like he'd enjoy doing that.

'No,' she snaps, shivering. 'Just get on with it.'

I fight like crazy, but there's three of them and I'm still suffering from the effects of the shocker. They pick me up, kicking and cursing, hold me face up above the tank and drop me in. There's no splash; it's more like landing in freezing quicksand. I sink on my back into the liquid, slowly at first, then faster. I try and reach for the side of the tank, but I can't. It's as if the liquid grabs me and pulls me down. Desperately, I arch my head up, but the blue closes over me.

Horrified, I hold my breath.

I see Morana's blue, distorted face peering down at me.

The cold is so fierce, it burns me all over. I scream, wasting air, but all that comes out are bubbles. My seeing goes dark, my lungs burn. I squirm and strain and suffer, fighting against the urge to breathe. My craving for air is agony. If I could cry then, I would. I'm such a fool to think I could beat them.

The agony becomes too much. I can't help it. I breathe in.

The slimy liquid forces itself into my mouth and nose, choking me. I thrash around as its icy coldness slithers down my throat and floods my lungs. I die then, a thousand shuddering, drowning deaths, each more painful than the last. Only I can't be dead because I see the lid come down. And it starts to get colder. Much colder.

My bones shatter. My skin splits. That's what it feels like.

My seeing goes from blue to white as frost forms on the outside of the lid. And all the time, I'm drowning. Only this isn't like real drowning. Been there done that, and this is much worse. I'm like a frozen scream that goes on forever.

I pray for the release of unconsciousness.

But whoever I'm praying to doesn't listen to twists.

34
A TWIST OF FATE

I groan and open my eyes. I'm on the white-tiled floor, on my hands and knees, dripping into a spreading pool of light blue fluid. This is the third time I've been reanimated so they can suck more blood out of me. Or maybe the fourth. And it doesn't get easier. Thawing is worse than being frozen, like having molten metal pumped through my veins. And un-drowing is no fun either.

But this time I sense something's different.

Like I'm out of the tank, but the chamber lights are still dimmed. And when I look up, I see there's only one slightly built Slayer watching me, his helmet lying upside down on the floor by his feet. He makes the Sign of One.

No shit. I only just manage to stop myself making it back at him.

In the grainy image the Answerman showed me, he was a well-fed version of me with a military haircut. Now he's as thin as I am, his face drawn, hair wild, eyes baggy and tired-looking. He's twitchy too and can't stay still.

The boy on the Saviour's balcony. My brother.

'Kyle! Wake up!' he hisses, sounding just like me. 'Can you hear me?'

'Colm!' I sob, staring at him.

His face scrunches up.

'Colm?' he says. 'Yes, I prefer that.'

'Prefer it to what?'

'Tomas. The name the Saviour gave me.'

Takes me a few seconds, what with being half dead.

'Well, Rona told me your name was Colm, and she'd know.'

'She knew my . . . our mother?'

I shrug. 'She never said, but she must have done.'

My eyes adjust to the gloom and I see him more clearly now. And it's like being back in that nightmare again, the one I had about the two of us being unwrapped. We are seriously identical. His face is that bit lop-sided like mine and there's a matching gap between his front teeth. He's got the same fine brown hair.

His face is so pale though, he could be my ghost.

'Colm and Kyle,' he says with a sad smile.

Childish I know, but I meet his gaze. 'Kyle and Colm sounds better.'

'And Rona was the rebel woman you traded yourself for?'

Somehow, Colm saying her name while in Slayer uniform makes me angry.

'Why are you here?' I growl. 'What do you want?'

He doesn't answer, just winces.

I clamber up, only for a coughing fit to slam me back down again. I see the way my brother glances nervously at the chamber's closed door and struggle to cough quietly. Eventually I bring up more blue froth and can breathe again.

He comes over now and gives me a hand to stand up.

'I'm okay,' I say, wheezing, legs shaking, clutching at the tank for support.

He steps back quickly, as if frightened of me. Next thing I know, he pulls out this wicked-looking knife.

'What's that for?' I say warily.

He holds his left hand up, palm out towards me. Five fingers. No mark of the ident. And the way he holds the knife, he knows how to use it. I wonder what chance I have of taking it off him. But he just gives me that sad smile again, puts the knife on the floor and slides it over to me. Astonished, I snatch it up and stare at it in wonder. Its bone handle fits my palm like it belongs. The stiletto blade is razor-sharp, the balance perfect. A thrower. I glance from it to my left arm, where the beacon is. A flick of the wrist with this blade and I could cut it out.

I look up at my brother. 'I don't understand.'

Colm swallows. 'Your way out of here.'

Wild hope surges through me, but I clamp down on it. 'How come?'

Our eyes meet and in some mysterious twin way, it's like I step behind his eyes that are my eyes and into his head. Sadness floods into me. I'm crushed by his loneliness and despair, easily a match for my own.

'Use the knife to end your suffering,' he whispers.

I shiver, appalled. I get what he's saying now. All he's really offering me is a way to follow Rona into the longest dark.

Tears sting my eyes. So, this is it. This is how I make my end.

'Or —' he says.

I look up from my brooding.

He grits his teeth like I do. 'Or we see if we can fight our way out of here.'

I let go this massive breath I didn't know I was holding.

'You're a Slayer,' I say, staring at him. 'Why would you help me?'

He frowns. 'I have my reasons. Trust me.'

Thinking of Sky, I shake my head. 'No way. I'm done trusting anybody.'

'Then maybe this will persuade you,' he says. Colm slips his Slayer jacket off, drags his undershirt sleeve up and shows me his left arm. And I can't help flinching. From his wrist all the way up to his shoulder, it's a mass of scars.

'What happened?' I gasp.

He scowls as he pulls his sleeve back down.

'All Slayers are required to cut themselves once a year to show loyalty and as a test of their pureblood. As the Saviour's son, he told me I must be seen to demonstrate even higher virtue. Ever since I was ten years old I've had to cut myself once a month. Only of course it was all a lie, like everything else. All along, they were hoping my cuts would heal twist-fast. They knew I was an ident.'

'I don't get it. Why would they want you to be a . . . twist.'

'The same reason they were desperate to catch you.'

I shudder. 'Which is?'

'A few years ago, the medics found out by experimenting on idents that if you stick a twist's blood into his pureblood brother, for a while it will help the brother heal faster too. Blood-healing, they call it. They got all excited, thought they could heal the Saviour that way, or wounded Slayers. Problem is, it only works if the twist is closely related to the person getting the blood, like a brother or sister. Stick the twist's blood into anyone else and it's no good. It's incompatible.'

I think back to my audience in the Saviour's palace.

'And he's my . . .' Father. But I can't say it.

He nods. 'They're using your blood to heal him. And it's working.'

My mouth drops open and I curse.

'That's not all,' Colm says, grimacing. 'They've done other experiments. They're only waiting for your blood to make him strong enough to survive an operation. They'll give him your eyes first, then your lungs, your liver, kidneys and heart. They won't stop until there's nothing left of you worth having.'

I stare at him now in abject horror, my skin crawling.

'Are you sure? How do you know all this?'

He shrugs. 'I'm the Saviour's unwanted son. I come and go mostly as I please. Nobody looks at me, nobody sees me. I know more than I'm supposed to.'

I glance down at the knife I'm still clutching in my hand.

'Okay. But why would you risk your life for me?'

He frowns at me like I'm stupid.

'You call *this* a life?' He pats his left arm. 'Now they've got you, I'm not needed any more. You heard the Saviour – I'm useless. An embarrassment.'

I think about this. 'What will happen to you?'

Colm shrugs. 'I'll disappear. Morana will see to that.'

I remember how I felt Colm's loneliness and despair. Yeah, no wonder.

'How many guards out there?' I ask, glancing at the door.

He hesitates. 'Six. At least.'

'Armed?'

'What do you think?'

I groan. 'Why didn't you bring a gun?'

'They won't let me have one. I'm not even supposed to be here. I bribed them, but they still searched me. That blade's the best I could do.'

I glance down at the knife again, which seems to shrink before my eyes. Six armed guards, two of us, one blade.

Impossible odds. Unless . . .

'So do we fight then?' Colm says, his face grim.

I wave at him to shut him up. A wicked little worm of a thought is burrowing its way into my head. It's selfish and brutal, but clever too. So simple it just might work. Better chance anyway than fighting our way past six Slayers.

'I've got a better idea, Colm,' I say, slowly. 'But you're not going to like it.'

He gives me this look, like I'm mad.

So I tell him, turning my thought into tumbling words. . .

It can't be forty metres to where the Slayer sentries wait and watch from behind an iron fence across the tunnel, but walking there feels like it goes on forever. I'm so scared my legs shake and I keep stumbling. I've got Colm's knife up the sleeve of the Slayer uniform I'm wearing now, the tip of the blade pricking my fingers. Loosen my grip and it should drop into my hand. With every step I expect them to call out to me to stop, or a blaster beam to cut me in half. Instead, keys rattle and a Slayer officer unlocks the door in the fence. He opens it with an oil-starved screech and beckons for me to hurry. After I step through, he locks it behind me.

I keep going, head down, mouth shut, glad for Colm's helmet, his uniform buttoned all the way to hide the metal collar around my neck. We did our best to take it off, but it's locked somehow and I'm stuck with it. The tunnel leads on towards that big vault with all those other cryotanks, the way I came here.

The Slayer officer runs after me and grabs my arm.

'Not *that* way,' he says, his voice urgent.

He guides me towards a hatchway set into the tunnel wall, a few steps past their checkpoint. A Slayer trooper opens it for me and steps aside.

I don't argue; I go that way.

Behind my back I hear the officer cursing me. 'Who does he think he is?'

Steps spiral up. I take them three at a time.

The door slams below me and glowtubes flicker on automatically. When I look back I see I'm on my own. And that's how easy it is. The Slayers expected to see Tomas come out of my tank room. As far as they're concerned, he did.

That's the thing about idents – you can't tell us apart.

At the top of the steps is a landing. This leads to another metal access hatch with a wheel mounted on it. As I spin the wheel anticlockwise, latches slide back all around the edge of the hatch and I can pull it open. I slip through, close it behind me and bolt it so nobody can come after me. I glance around, my heart pounding, but there's nobody up here. I'm standing on this kind of gallery that runs high up around the main cryogenic hall, with hatches leading off it every few metres. There's an alcove in the wall a few metres away, stuffed full of shadows. I scuttle over and curl up inside, pull the uncomfortable Slayer helmet off and cradle my head in my hands. So far so good, but I badly need to catch my breath.

A good idea to stop shaking too, before I try and cut the beacon out. I won't be missed. Colm is seeing to that.

In a few hours the Slayer medic who checks the tank will wipe away the frost, glance in and see my frozen face still in there. He won't know he's looking at my twin, not me. That's the hope I cling to anyway as I sit here shivering. Before I tumbled Colm in, he let me knock him out using a trick Seph taught me, so he shouldn't be suffering the agonies I went through. Hope so, for his sake, as I'm not sure a pureblood could survive otherwise. It makes me groan out loud, just thinking what I've done to him. Maybe it would've made more sense if I'd cut the beacon out, shown Colm how it worked and given it to him to use. He knows his way around. There's no three ways about it — he'd stand a better chance of finding his way outside to send the signal. But could I *really* trust him? And, like he said himself, what if we couldn't stop my cut from bleeding? The medic might spot the blood in the tank, pull me out early and figure out what's going down.

Too many ifs, whats, mights and maybes.

Frag it! All this thinking is getting me nowhere and doing my head in. Time for some surgery.

I blink sweat out of my eyes and roll my sleeve up. Not a mark to be seen anywhere on my forearm, only some downy hairs and a scatter of freckles. I make a fist and squeeze. Veins bulge under the skin, but that's all I see.

Hard to believe salvation's buried there.

I tear a strip from my undershirt to use as a makeshift bandage. Then I feel for the slight lump, grit my teeth and push Colm's blade into my flesh. It hurts like hell. Blood spills out, but my first cut's not big enough. I curse and cut deeper, until I can get my finger all the way inside. And I feel something that isn't bone.

I dig out a small, blood-smeared white disc.

Trailing from it is a coiled aerial, looking like a mouse's tail.

Quick as I can, I wad cloth over my wound and bandage it tightly to stop the bleeding. I pop the beacon in my mouth and suck the blood off. Then I pull the aerial wire, gently like Ness told me to. He thought this was such a funny touch, the big gom. Only nothing happens, except that my heart sinks.

I count to ten, holding my breath. And see a tiny wink of green light.

My hand twitches so bad, I almost drop the bogging thing.

'Yes!' Another green flash. It's working.

No point punching the air – this was the easy bit.

I need to get the beacon outside the dome now, where its low power signal stands a chance of being picked up by Gemini's listening posts. Thing is, Colm told me this cryogenic area is cut deep into the rock under one of the domes. All the lefts and rights of how to get outside have already leaked out of my head.

Rona was right – I *never* listen.

But I guess if I keep heading upwards, that's a start.

I pull my sleeve down, stick my Slayer helmet on and clamber to my feet.

35
ONE LAST EFFORT

'Maintenance Shaft C Access — Authorised Personnel Only.'

Seven magic words. I chant them in my head like they're some kind of poem or spell. A hole in the roof of the tunnel, with a ladder inside it.

And I figure I'm authorised, by need.

I've been wandering about down here for ages and am more lost now than when I first left that walkway around the cryovault. A second ago I was cursing with frustration. The corridors all look the bogging same.

I take a breath, steady myself and peer up.

Maintenance Shaft C is secured by a rusty iron grating. Set into the rock wall under it is a panel, labelled *MaShC Access*. It's the kind of thing you wave a proximity pass at to unlock. Which I don't have. There's nobody around, so I wave my knife instead and prise the panel open. No chance. Too complicated.

I'll just have to do this using my nublood muscle.

I take a run up, jump and hang from the grating. It's locked, but when I pull myself up for a closer look I feel the tired metal give slightly. I drop back down, go scavenging and come back with a steel rod as long as my arm. Reaching up, I wedge it between the bars of the grating near the lock and lever it open. It's easy enough; the steel is stronger than the rusty iron, but shocking noisy. As the grate swings down its hinges make a screech so loud it could wake the dead.

I crouch, my heart slamming in my chest. But not for long, because Sky's back whispering in my head again. *Keep moving, you idiot!*

Jamming the steel bar into my belt, I jump up again and grab hold of the grating. Kicking my legs, I pull myself up into the shaft and on to the ladder. Soon as I'm all in, I lean back down, pull the grating up after me and hang there, shaking and panting into the darkness. There's no alarm, no shouts or sound of Slayer boots pounding rock towards me. Relieved, I start climbing, hand over hand. I pass crawlways branching off to either side. And I swear the shaft gets tighter the higher I climb, crushing in on me. Finally, I reach another grating. By pushing my face into this I see that the shaft ends in the corner of an unlit storeroom, little more than a cupboard. There's a door, ajar. Beyond is a much larger room.

I hold my breath and listen. Nothing.

This time around, I know what I'm doing. I take my Slayer jacket off and wrap it round the steel bar before I prise the lock open. And I've got better leverage this end, so I can ease the grating open more gently. The hinges still squeal, but only a dog or someone real close would hear it. Steel bar held ready I clamber out of the shaft, tiptoe to the door and peer into the larger room.

Here a few glowtubes have been left on. By their dim light I see tables and benches covered in scientific-looking instruments. My nose wrinkles at the sharp smell of acid and antiseptic and something nastier – the sickly smell of death and decay. It's some kind of medical lab. In the middle of the room stand several glass cylinders, taller than I am, full of dark liquid. I creep over and peer into the nearest, only to leap back with a horrified curse. A girl's body floats upright inside the cylinder, arms by her side, long red hair swirling about her face.

The Lynch girl from the Peace Fair. I'm sure it is.

I swear the girl's empty-looking eyes follow me as I edge away. I bump into a table behind me and recoil as I see the corpse on it, chest split wide open, the skin pinned back. Other benches are littered with similar butchery. Looks like Colm was right about what this sick Facility is for. He reckons the medics are experimenting on older nubloods, trying to figure out how to cut their powers out of them and transfer them to unrelated purebloods. Hand to my mouth I hurry past.

At the far side of the lab the whole wall is one big window sweeping down from ceiling to floor in a gentle arc. Through the curved plastiglass I see the night sky, both moons shining between wind-whipped clouds. It's chucking it down with snow outside, white flakes whirling past in the moonshine.

I flinch and duck down. Directly below me a bundled-up Slayer security patrol prowls past in the snow, two giant mastiffs hauling at their leads. This makes me think. I sigh and pull the beacon out of my pocket. It's still flashing. High above me I spot some vents, used to pull cooling air inside the dome during the summer. By climbing up on some storage cabinets I can reach one. It's fairly easy to lever it open and slip the beacon outside and, when I let the vent snap shut, it traps the end of the wire, holding the beacon with most of the aerial outside.

Okay, now to find a way outside for *me*.

Nothing doing. I do find ways outside, but they're all alarmed or guarded. By the time I find a balcony clinging to the outside of the dome, where night workers sneak out for a smoke, it's already too late. Dawn pinks the crater's rim and the snow looks like it's stopping. Run for it now and I won't get far.

It occurs to me to find Colm's room and hole up there, maybe pretend to be sick. Only I don't know where it is and it's not like I can ask. In the end I figure I should curl up inside that Maintenance Shaft C and just wait until Gemini hits the Facility. Even if they fail, maybe I can clear off in the confusion.

Heart in my mouth, I climb the levels back up to the lab and clamber back down into the shaft. Not a moment too soon. Even as I duck down and pull the grating over me I'm sure I hear people walking into the lab. Quietly as I can, I climb down until I think I'm about midway, then crawl into one of the many dark side passages so I can at least lie down. I toss and turn, but no way can I sleep. I keep waiting for an alarm to sound, when they find out it's Colm in the tank. Or maybe Colm's supposed to be somewhere right now and they're looking for him. Every noise I hear makes me jump, sure it's people searching for me.

Even when nothing happens, that's just as bad.

Maybe the beacon isn't working? Maybe it's fallen off and landed in the snow? Did I really see the green light blinking or did I just imagine it? Hours drag by in a squirming agony of not knowing what's going on.

One thing's for sure, no way can I do this again. I can't spend another day stuck in this tunnel. I'll take my chances on the run outside. At least then they'll have to catch me, not find me like a rat in a trap.

The last thing I remember thinking is how it's gone all quiet in the lab above me. No more whirring machines. No walking about, no chat. It's getting late. I mustn't close my eyes though in case I fall asleep.

Only, gom that I am, that's exactly what I do!

I wake up with a start and bang my head on the low roof. When I peer up the shaft, the grating at the top is in darkness. The lights must be switched off in the storeroom. I listen, my mouth hanging open. Not a sound.

I groan, sick with disbelief. How many hours of darkness have I wasted?

Quickly and as quietly as I can, I climb back up the ladder. Still no noise from above. Heart thumping so loud I think it's going to tear itself out of my chest, I lever the grating up and crawl out. Still no sound. From the open doorway I survey the lab. And freeze – there's a lamp still on at one bench and I hear a yawn. A medic is hunched over it, working away. The rest of the lab is in darkness.

With no way of knowing how much night I have left, I have to go for it.

I slip out of the storeroom and creep towards the lab's exit. But the dark isn't my friend. Halfway to the door I trip over an unseen cable. I don't fall, but I stumble and can't help making some noise. Not much, but enough.

'Who's there?'

The medic is on his feet, squinting in my direction.

Quickly, I duck behind a pillar. Only to hear a click and more glowtubes start flickering on overhead. The light shining down on me hurts.

I hear his boots coming closer.

'Show yourself!'

He knows I'm here. There's no point hiding, so I step out.

The medic curses and steps back.

'This lab's a restricted area,' he says. 'Do you have clearance?'

I glance up at the warning sign, the red letters, the skull symbol. 'I – I do.'

'Show me,' he says, his face suspicious.

'Okay.' I show him.

He looks up from the knife in my hand, his eyes wide with shock.

They go even wider as I snap the blade at him in an underhand throw. Seph would be proud. It takes him right in the throat, stopping his shout. He staggers back, clutching at the knife's hilt, blood dribbling from his mouth. I run and catch him as he falls, hold him down as he chokes the last of his life away.

Only after he's done dying, do I let go.

Another life I've taken. For a second, I think I'll puke.

I give myself a shake, remind myself of the grisly work he was doing, and drag his body to the storeroom. He's a big man and being dead doesn't change that. It takes some doing, but I push him head first into the shaft. For one gob-open, *this can't be happening* moment, I think he'll tumble the whole way down.

Luckily he wedges several metres from the bottom.

I hurry back into the lab and strain to listen as blood pounds in my ears.

Nothing. Not that I can hear anyway.

It takes me a few frantic seconds to figure out how to power down the laboratory lights. I switch off dead guy's bench light too. Darkness rushes in and now I can see outside. It's snowing again, and heavily. I grab a stained sheet off a table, careful not to look at what it covered, bundle it up and run. Two floors down the balcony is empty, its door swinging. I slip outside on to it. A bitter wind snatches my breath away. I cup my hand in front of my face, pretending to be a smoker while I look out for those dog patrols. But either the weather has driven them inside, or they've passed by already, or they're hidden by the blizzard.

Way below, up against the dome, is what looks like a snowdrift.

Better be or I'm dead.

I climb over the rail, hang from it . . . then let go.

Next thing, I'm tumbling and sliding down the curve of the dome. Dark plastiglass flashes past horribly quickly, only half-seen in the moonshine. In a panic, I flatten myself against the shiny surface, scrabbling frantically with my fingertips and trying to slow myself down. No chance – the plastiglass is slick with snow and ice. The lower I get, the steeper it gets, the faster I slide. A frame flashes past under me, bumping me. I grab at it, but miss. Suddenly, I'm falling free.

Falling and . . . *whomp!* . . . I hit something.

Soft and hard at the same time. Everything goes black.

Maybe I hit my head because for a while I'm sure I'm dead. It's easier than being alive anyway. Now I'm dead, I can stop caring. No Slayer can hurt me, or suck my blood. I can just lie here buried in the snow and make a start on rotting and being forgotten. Only then a dog starts barking in the distance.

And I realise, grudgingly, that I'm not dead. Not yet.

I fight my way out of the snowdrift that's saved me for one final effort. My sheet pulled around me as camouflage, I stumble off into the blizzard.

36
A GAME CALLED SCREAM

I make it out of the crater, but I don't make it down the mountain.

Back in Freshwater, to while away the long, dark evenings, Rona and I would take turns playing this stupid game called Scream. You start with a bunch of pegs sticking out of a wooden board. Each move, if you can jump one peg over its neighbour, you take the jumped peg away. The idea is to end up with the last peg sticking out of the middle hole. We called it Scream because it's impossible. Some games you get further than others, but you always end up screaming.

Seeing the electric fence is like that, only lethal. I'm out of moves. And I don't get to put the pegs back and start over.

Too destroyed to scream, I drop to my knees in the snow and stare. This fence is twice my height and buzzing with threat. A charred redhawk hangs off it near the top, feathers flapping in the wind, sparks flaring as it bangs the wire. Minutes later a Slayer patrol shows up. A whole bunch of them, all bug-eyed with night-vision goggles over their gas masks. I reckon this fence zone must be wired with motion or thermal sensors. I can't see hardly ten metres, yet their ghostly figures come straight to me out of the darkness and snow flurries, pulse rifles levelled.

'Going somewhere?' sneers their leader.

I glare up at her, too bone-tired and frozen to answer.

One of them reports finding me, speaking into a wrist-comm. 'Base, Echo patrol here. We've got a runner down at the fence, Sector Seven.'

I'm dragged to my feet. I struggle half-heartedly and my sheet rips off, revealing my Slayer uniform. I hear their curses. 'Shit! He's one of us!'

A light snaps on and shines into my face, blinding me.

Lots more cursing now, as they see who I am – or who they think I am.

The patrol leader calls in again. 'Base, you won't believe this, but runner is the Saviour's son. I say again, runner is the Saviour's son!'

I lash out and make a break for it.

Don't get very far however before there's a loud bang behind me. A weighted cord twists itself round my legs and yanks them from under me.

They strap me to some sort of sled and drag me back up the mountain. By the time we're back to the Facility, the sky's lightening again with morning. I'm so frozen – they can't be arsed to cover me – I have to be lifted from the sled. They carry me inside a dome and dump me on the floor. Next thing, heels click across the tiles towards me. I look up and shudder. High Slayer Morana. She glares down at me, her face all blotchy with rage.

'Pick the traitor up,' she orders.

I'm dragged to my feet, my arms twisted behind my back.

Morana prowls back and forth in front of me. All of a sudden, she steps in. Snake-fast, she rakes her long nails across my face.

I cry out, with shock and pain.

'You *disappoint* your father, Tomas,' she snarls. 'But not me. I knew you'd run one day. You've always been weak; it's in your mother's blood.'

I hang my head, try not to look surprised.

Tomas? She doesn't know . . .

Behind my back, I hide my left hand in my right.

My head's forced back up. The woman's eyes bore into mine accusingly.

'But why run now?' she says. 'Tell me!'

And I'm stuck, my mind a blank, no idea what Colm might say.

It's not a problem. Either Morana doesn't expect me to talk or she prefers her own answer. She startles me with a little hate-filled bark of a laugh, pulls back and looks at me sideways with a knowing smile.

'No, wait, don't tell me,' she says, her voice dripping sarcasm. 'The Saviour's lapdog son has finally seen the light. Was it watching that twist clone of yours that got you thinking at last?'

I grit my teeth and keep my twist mouth shut.

But now a frown chases the woman's smile away. 'You know, we found that medic you killed. I was surprised. To slay a man with a knife takes backbone, something we both know you don't have. Only . . . why *did* you kill him?'

When I don't answer, my arm's twisted so hard I gasp.

'We argued,' I lie.

Morana looks sceptical, but then shrugs.

'No matter. You've cut your own useless scab throat by

running and I will get my way at last – even your fool of a father won't protect you now.'

'What will happen to me?' I croak.

She trails her fingers across my face, making me flinch.

'Oh, I think a hanging, broadcast live on the feed. Wrath will watch you die, and you will remind them that no one, not even the Saviour's only son, is above the law.'

'No!' My bottled-up fear escapes and I start struggling like crazy.

The Slayers grunt with effort, struggling to hold on.

Morana jumps back, scowling.

'Control him!' she snarls. 'He's only a boy.'

More Slayers pile in now, but desperation and my nublood give me a strength that shocks even me. It takes five of them to wrestle me to the floor, and not before I hurt one or two of them. They return the favour, working me over brutally with fists and boots and rifle-butts until I quit fighting.

Morana's back, leaning over me, her eyes slitted and suspicious now.

'His left hand,' she says. 'Show me!'

I can do nothing – I'm too busy trying to breathe.

They prise my clenched fist open, show her I've only got four fingers. She rips my jacket open and the collar is still around my neck. Shock slackens and drains the blood from the High Slayer's face. She squeezes her eyes shut, tips her head back and sucks this long, furious breath in through her nose. I'm watching, fearful what she'll do next, when her eyes suddenly flick open again to stare at me.

The look she gives me, it's like being stabbed.

'How did you get out of the tank, Kyle?' she says through her teeth.

The beating I've taken makes me reckless. 'Go to hell.'

I get off lightly, considering. She kicks me a few times, but not in the head.

I'd thought High Slayer Morana knew everything there was to know about inflicting agony. I'm wrong again. Her Facility medics know way more.

She hands me over to them to get me to talk.

Whatever it takes, she says.

And I do talk, after a pitiful attempt to resist that lasts only minutes. Sobbing, I tell them how Colm and I traded places. They'd have found him anyway when they checked the tank, but that doesn't make it okay. I say the words. I give him up, as Jude once gave me up. And hate myself for being weak.

The medics are off somewhere now reporting to Morana. I'm lying here, strapped down on a table in some lab, fear and black despair chewing at me, dreading them coming back. On the next table over are dissected remains. I think it was a girl, but I haven't got the stomach to look too closely. Lift my head up and I can just about see my forearm where the wound I made cutting the beacon out is itching and healing well, but not yet gone completely. I glare at it, like this will somehow force it to heal even faster, but then let my head fall back, terrified they'll see me looking and put three and three together. I've already heard them muttering about it, but I'm hoping they'll think it's just something I picked up when I was captured.

Only what's the point of hoping anything?

Colm knows about the beacon. Chances are he'll squeal to save his neck. I groan out loud, knowing it's all over. I'll be butchered for spare parts, those nublood kids will slave down the mines until they die. And now I think of Sky. What would she think of what I've done? Not much. That hurts most of all.

The medics come back to peer at me over their little green masks. I'm cringing, expecting them to start making me scream again, but all that happens is one of them leans in and jabs something cold and sharp into me behind my ear.

There's a click and then . . .

Next thing I know, Slayers are rolling me off a hover-lifter on to the floor of an immense chamber, a domed roof arching over me. My Slayer uniform has been traded for the grey tunic and trousers the ident prisoners were wearing. Dazed, I lie where I've fallen until a kick encourages me to get up. Waiting for me here is the Saviour, Morana at his side. I hardly recognise the man, he looks so improved. Okay, he's still old, but the years don't bite him anything like as fiercely. He stands tall and straight-backed in his cloak and no horrible tubes stick out of him like before. Seems my nublood is doing the business.

He sees me staring and sneers, holds his hands out and shows himself off to me. 'Impressed, Kyle? Well you should be. This is thanks to you.'

Even his voice sounds stronger.

Only now do I see the gallows behind him, a metal frame with a pulley on a hook in the middle of its cross member, a rope hanging down with a noose on the end. Just like the one at the Peace Fair, where this nightmare started.

I look away quick. So I'm to hang after all.

Morana glides around her master towards me, all smiles now. But she doesn't fool me. I see the way the skin is pulled tight on her face.

'Patience, twist,' she says. 'Your brother will be here soon.'

And now I understand — I don't get to die so easy. The noose is for Colm. I've only been brought here to watch him hang.

At Morana's nod, my guards drag me on to this low, circular platform, let go and jump back. It starts humming and the air shimmers around me. Step off, no doubt the collar will zap me again. If there's any fight left in me I can't find it. I slump down in a heap. It's not long though before hydraulics hiss and I look up to see a glass-walled room rise slowly out of the floor in the centre of the chamber. Doors slide open. Slayers escort Colm out, shoving him along at gunpoint. His face is pale and bruised and tear-streaked, his eyes darting about. For clothes, he's wearing the same rough gear as the kids I saw back at the pithead.

When he sees the gallows, he stumbles. He opens his mouth to say something, but closes it as one of his Slayer escort forces him down to his knees. Slowly, I pull myself to my feet so he can see me too. He groans like he's been punched. I give him a nod. He pulls himself together enough to nod back at me.

The Saviour advances on him, shaking his head, his face grim.

'Here he is, my son the traitor,' he jeers, his face livid. He flings an arm out to point at me. 'You set this monster free deliberately, knowing I needed him to heal myself. You betrayed me. You betrayed your kind. Why, Tomas? Why?'

My brother sighs, but keeps looking at me. He even manages his sad smile.

Spit flies from the Saviour's mouth. 'Answer me!'

If it was me kneeling there facing the noose, I'd make up some crap, like wanting to see my twist brother out of curiosity, opening the lid of the tank for a look and being overpowered. Anything. But as we stare at each other, I see the set look on Colm's face and know he's way past wanting to save himself.

And I wonder. Maybe he *hasn't* squealed about the beacon.

'Kyle is no monster,' he says quietly.

'He is a twist!'

The Saviour roars this and makes the Sign of One.

I flinch, but Colm doesn't.

'He's human. Not evil, just different, and you know that. If anybody is a monster it's you, Father, with your lies and your cruelty.'

The Saviour draws himself up. 'Who are you to decide what is and isn't evil?'

'He traded himself to save the woman who raised him. Is that evil?'

'He did not. His Gemini allies traded him.'

'I gave him my knife. He could have killed me, but he didn't.'

'Yet you ended up left in the C-tank, while he fled.'

The Saviour glances round at me now, his sneering face so triumphant that I wonder then if he really does believe I'm evil.

'I mean, just *look* at him,' he says.

Why, I don't know, but despite all my pain I try and stand up straighter. Colm does look at me, long and hard, and I worry I see a flicker of doubt in his eyes.

But he shakes his head. 'All I see is my ident brother.'

I can't help smiling. Making sure he sees, I raise my clenched fist to him.

The Saviour stiffens. 'Enough, Tomas! Are you out of your mind?'

But my brother isn't done yet.

'No. And my name isn't Tomas . . . it's Colm.'

'We're wasting time, Your Benevolence,' snaps Morana.

The Saviour's expression hardens until he has a face on him like stone.

'I think perhaps we are,' he says. 'In any case I've heard enough. Sentiment can and will have no place here. The boy has failed me in so many ways and now he mocks our sacred fight for purity. We must make an example of him.'

He snaps his fingers at Colm's guards.

Just then, out of the corner of my eye, I think I catch a flash of something moving outside the dome. I glance up desperately through the clear roof panels arching over me. Whatever it was, a bird probably, it's gone now. All I see is sky, empty other than some towering clouds and the crescents of the bigmoon and its smaller dogmoon companion, lurking high up in the blue.

A sudden commotion draws my eyes back inside the chamber. The Slayers are dragging Colm towards the gallows, but he's digging his heels in, fighting and struggling like crazy. I lose it then and throw myself at the wall of shimmering air . . . only to stagger back clutching at my neck as my collar kicks in and burns me. By the time I can breathe again, they have the noose around my brother's neck and his mouth taped to shut him up. A big Slayer guard steps to the other end of the rope now and pulls it just tight enough so Colm has to stand on his tiptoes or else be strangled. Meanwhile, another group of Slayers are setting up what looks to me like vid-recording gear and a microphone. The Saviour is off by the wall of the dome with his back turned to all this, gazing outside. High Slayer Morana is having her hair and make-up fussed over by a woman assistant.

Guess she wants to look her best to viewers of the feed.

Poor Colm. There's no hole here for him to drop into when he's hanged. The watchers of the feed will get a gruesome show as he kicks his life away.

Sick, but no accident. They're sending a message.

Finally satisfied with her appearance, Morana stalks to her place between the camera and the gallows, enough off to one side so viewers will see both. After a sound check she starts spouting the usual crap about the Saviour's law and what happens to those foolish or mad enough to break it. But I'm not watching or listening. I'm looking at this twin brother of mine that I hardly know, who's about to swing for the crime of seeing through lies and trying to save me. His eyes shine at me over his taped mouth and he keeps blinking, but he can't blink away his fear.

I see that, but keep looking, trying to let him know that I'm with him all the way. It'll be terrible, like watching myself die, but I figure I owe him that at least.

By now Morana's worked herself up into quite a state, laying it on thick about finding a traitor in the midst of the Saviour's palace, as if she's overcome with outrage and shock, building up to the big reveal that it's the Saviour's son.

Behind me, a door slams open and I hear quick bootsteps.

Despite my best efforts, I can't help looking back. And wish I hadn't.

An excited-looking young Slayer officer, helmet tucked under his arm, is hurrying across the floor of the dome towards us. In his hand I see he's clutching a small white disc, the long wire attached to it flicking about.

My legs go weak. It's my beacon, its green light still flashing away.

Even though I know I betrayed him first, I can't help glaring at Colm as this last shred of hope is torn from me. But he looks me in the eye and shakes his head.

The Slayer officer skids to a halt, but hesitates. With Morana in mid-speech, it seems like he's reluctant to interrupt her. And I don't blame him. She flashes him a quick warning look, but continues talking to the camera.

The man grits his teeth and clears his throat.

Obviously distracted, she stops and snarls. 'What is it?'

He shows her the beacon. 'Sorry to disturb you, Commandant, but a worker found this device trapped in an air vent a few minutes ago.'

She peers at it. 'Is that blood?'

And now the Saviour marches over. The officer bows and starts to repeat his story. Before he can finish, the Saviour curses and knocks the beacon out of the man's hand. Then he brings his boot down, crushing it.

The green light flickers and goes out.

'You fools,' he snarls. 'This is the twist's doing!'

He points at me, his eyes furious with the promise of more pain.

Before anyone can react, sirens start to howl and wail. Several deafening blasts echo around the dome like thunder, and there's a terrible cracking sound as if the mountain itself is splitting asunder. I only just have time to throw my hands up to protect my face as the roof of the dome buckles inwards and explodes, showering me in a blizzard of sharp plastic fragments.

A small grey windjammer whines low overhead, wing guns blazing.

'*What kept you?*' I scream at the top of my lungs.

37
PAYBACK

All hell breaks loose. There's loads of shouting and screaming. I see the Saviour is down, a blood-spattered shard of plastiglass sticking out from the middle of his back. Several Slayers are hurt too. Only metres away, the big man who'd been holding Colm's rope staggers in circles, clutching the stump of his arm.

As the sirens wind themselves up into a too-late frenzy, I see more rebel windjammer gunships flash past low outside, blasts of energy pulsing from their wing guns. Our dome is hit again and again. Acrid grey smoke, thick and choking, billows up around me. Flames leap and lick at the smoke's grey underbelly, fanned by wind screeching inside through the gaping holes in the roof. Outside, beyond the smoke, I glimpse the Facility's defences waking up at last. Tower-mounted gun turrets swivel to track the attacking windjammers and open fire, hurling bolts of golden fire into the sky. One rebel windjammer is hit as it pulls up from its firing run. It cartwheels across the sky, trailing debris and smoke, before smashing into the dome next to us, turning it into a giant fireball.

Everybody cowers, stunned by the ferocity of the rebel

assault. Everybody except Morana, that is. Hips swaying, she walks to the nearest Slayer trooper, grabs his pulse rifle from him and rapid-fires it one-handed into the air.

The thumps and flashes get everyone's attention.

She thrusts the rifle back at the man.

'Take the Saviour to the hangar level! Get him a medic. The rest of you cowards, stop slinking on your bellies. Move to your defensive positions.'

Slayers unfreeze and scramble to do her bidding.

I hunker down on my little platform, trying to be invisible. And fail.

'And as for *you*, twist!' Morana snarls, stalking towards me. She stops, pulls my old pistol from her belt and takes aim, right between my eyes.

Can't help it – I squeeze my eyes shut.

Only there's no bang. No searing pain as a lead bullet smashes its way through my forehead.

In disbelief, cringing, I open my eyes again.

Morana smiles, thin-lipped and cruel. Turns and shoots Colm.

Hands bound behind his back, the noose still around his neck, my brother staggers. He looks down at the bloody hole blossoming in his chest before slowly crumpling to the floor. I can only watch as the rope, with no Slayer left holding it now, streams down and coils on top of him like a long brown snake.

Numb with horror, I drag my eyes back to Morana.

'What?' she says, her face all mocking. 'I couldn't shoot *you*, could I?'

Beyond the broken dome I'm dimly aware of the battle still raging noisily. Inside my head though, everything goes quiet and empty. Until my next heartbeat arrives with a sick thump. And suddenly rage explodes inside me, hot and fierce and desperate, filling me up, possessing me. Howling curses, not thinking, I charge at the shimmering barrier around my platform. The collar sinks its burning teeth into my neck again and the pain is so terrible that I end up on my knees.

Morana laughs. She actually laughs.

But I am the bane of Wrath, I will *NOT* be stopped.

I get up again. This time, I force myself to keep going, one agonising step at a time. Next moment I'm through the barrier and the collar is cooling.

'It's – only – pain,' I sob, lurching towards her.

Her eyes go wide with fear and she levels the gun at me.

'Stay back. I'll kill you if I have to and damn your twisted blood!'

I snarl at her, past words and past caring. All I want now is vengeance. I'm almost on her when she pulls the trigger, but the gun just clicks. She curses, pulls the trigger again and again and again, but it keeps on clicking.

Out of bullets. Colm stopped the last one.

She hurls the gun at me and turns to run. But she's too slow. Pureblood slow.

I knock her down, straddle her, get my nine fingers around her neck and squeeze while she thrashes under me, scratching at my face, trying to get her thumbs in my eyes. Her bodyguards come running now and rain blows down on my back with the stocks of their rifles, but I won't be stopped. I keep squeezing until finally one of them leans in, tags me with a disruptor and my muscles lock.

Still takes three of them to prise my hands from her neck.

She staggers back to her feet, coughing and choking, her hair falling loose across her face like a messy black shroud. One of her bodyguards leaps to help her, but she curses and shoves him away. Clutching her throat, her eyes wild, she glares down at me. 'I'll see you die roaring and screaming for this!'

Me, all I can do I stare my hate and loathing at her.

Outside, there's another massive explosion. Over Morana's shoulder I see a Facility gun tower has taken a direct hit from a rebel windjammer. The screech of tearing metal fills the air as it tips over and slowly collapses into the snow.

'Commandant, look!' shouts a Slayer.

Morana peers upwards through the broken canopy of the dome and stiffens. The way I'm lying, I can see too. Several fat-looking rebel windjammers slide past high overhead, the air below them pockmarked with parachutes, fighters dangling underneath them. And now I hear more yelling and shouting, the *tump-tump-tump* of pulse rifles being rapid-fired, the bang and crackle of blaster fire.

I strain to move, desperate to see what's happening. And something gives, so I can just about move my head.

Down on the crater floor, I see groups of white-smocked rebel fighters rise up from the snow and rush towards the domes, firing as they advance.

Morana barks orders, something about a refuge.

'What about this?' a Slayer officer says.

He jabs me in the cheek with the muzzle of his rifle, making it clear what he thinks.

Morana glares down at me again before holding a hand out

and snapping her fingers. The Slayer hands her a blaster and now I'm sure I'm done.

'Bring him with you.' Her voice is thick with regret.

Without another word she heads off, bodyguards screening her, firing up through the shattered roof. Two Slayers grab hold of me. They don't bother picking me up, just drag me along the floor after her, through the wreckage.

They drag me past Colm, so close we nearly touch.

I see my brother's not quite done with dying yet. Blood froths on his lips as he fights for each breath. He stares at me, his eyes bulging and frightened.

The front of his tunic is shiny and slick with blood.

'Kyle,' he says, his voice an agonised rattle.

But even if I could think of any words to comfort him in his last moments, I can't say them. Try as hard as I can, my voice is still muscle-locked.

They load me into that glass-walled room. The doors *swish* closed. We sink quickly, the dome's levels strobing past, until we plunge into a darker world of rock and start to slow. After we stop I'm dragged out along corridors and into some sort of control room. They dump me in a corner full of bugwebs.

This whole time I'm straining at the invisible bonds that hold me rigid. I picture Colm's eyes as he looks fearfully into the longest dark. I use the rage I feel to feed my strength. In some strange way I can't explain I let that *other* part of me which isn't human – is *more* than human – unlock me. And it works.

My muscles twitch and tingle. I can clench my fists.

I don't let on; I watch and wait.

Around me is frantic activity. I shift slightly, to get a better view.

Opposite me, medics are tending to the Saviour. He's propped up, but looks unconscious, his upper body swathed with bandages. A red tube runs down from a suspended bag and into the back of his hand. I see K written on the bag. K for Kyle. They're pumping more of my nublood into him to try and save him.

Other Slayers swarm about Morana.

She's standing in front of a bank of display screens, which show scenes of ferocious combat. The roar from the speakers is deafening. Hoarse voices shout orders over the screams of the wounded and dying. In the background, pulse rifles thump and the screens flare and overload as blaster beams crackle past. There's a rolling thunder of explosions as I watch well-drilled rebel fighters lob grenades then scuttle forward after them, guns blazing. Morana curses, flicks impatiently between scenes. I see now that the rebels have penetrated the domes. One monitor shows some Slayers backing away. Morana screams into a microphone, commanding them to stand and fight. They do, only to be cut down by blaster fire.

Seconds later, a rebel fighter looms into frame. She sees the Slayer camera because she looks up, flicks a middle finger and raises her rifle. It's a good job nobody's looking at me then because I can't help ducking.

The screen dissolves into hissing static.

Somewhere above us there's a massive explosion. The whole room shakes. Dust drifts down from cracks in the roof. A second later, the lights flicker off, plunging us into darkness. They come back on, but dimmer, and the monitors all stay dead. A voice alarm starts droning now, shrill and insistent.

'REFUGE PERIMETER BREACHED.'

Morana hurls the cleverbox she was using to switch the monitors and it shatters into a thousand plastic pieces on the floor. A white-faced Slayer officer approaches her now, his helmet gone, one arm bloodied and splinted. She glowers at him, her head swinging like a rock viper about to spit.

He swallows hard. 'The Facility is lost. We can't hold them.'

Morana raises her hands, makes claws out of them. I think the woman will hurl herself at him and scratch his eyes out, but she gathers herself and summons her cruel smile. 'That,' she says, her voice the lash of a whip, 'is unfortunate.'

Now that all the monitors are dead, it's so quiet in here I can almost hear her teeth grinding. Everyone left in the room falls silent, watching her.

She glares around at me. 'What are *you* looking at?'

I'm so tempted to say something, to jeer and crow at her that she's beaten. Fortunately, the Slayer officer saves me from giving myself away.

'Commandant, the escape craft is ready for launch.'

She turns on him with a scowl, but nods.

Everything happens so fast then. Morana rattles off new orders. The remaining Slayers, led by the injured officer, grab their weapons and hurry out. Slayer medics set off the opposite way, taking the Saviour with them on a hover-lifter. Morana supervises the hurried planting of explosive charges in the control room, then commands her bodyguards to fetch me. She heads off into a tunnel, flanked by the rest of her guards, and I'm dragged after her again. Fortunately, the Slayers are too busy watching out for rebel attackers to notice I'm not quite so rigid now.

This tunnel heads straight, then starts to climb.

Dayshine blinds me briefly as we emerge out on to a platform at the back of an enormous rocky chamber, hollowed into the face of the mountain. Five miniature matt-black Slayer windjammers sit here, at the top of inclined drop-ramps. But only two will be going anywhere, I see that straight away. In between them and the sky is the tangled and still-burning wreckage of a rebel windjammer that looks as if it's been deliberately crashed into the cave's entrance to try and block it.

On the floor of the cave there's a vicious gun battle going on, although there's so much blasting and smoke it's impossible to see exactly who's fighting who.

From up here on the platform I watch as Slayer medics finish lowering the Saviour to waiting hands inside one of the small windjammers. They slam the hatch closed behind him and leap clear. Seconds later a rocket flares into life and punches the little escape craft down its ramp. It narrowly misses the wrecked rebel windjammer before dropping out of sight outside, below the lip of the cave.

That leaves one more escape craft with room to get clear.

Morana's bodyguards fan out towards it. They start firing, but are cut down themselves by withering pulse rifle fire. *Tzziiip! Tzziiip!* Plasma-bolts fizz past, just missing me. One of the men dragging me is hit and goes down. The other keeps dragging me, but one-handed now as he returns fire with his pulse rifle.

Which is the chance I've been waiting for.

I grab his arm and pull, kicking his legs from under him. As he hits the floor I'm on him. I yank the blaster from the holster at his belt, ram it into his side, press the trigger and keep it pressed.

Soon as he goes limp I let go and leap to my feet. Only to stagger as a shooting pain almost takes my head off. At first I think I've stopped a pulse round, but it's Morana zapping me with the collar.

Next thing I know, the pain's fading, but she's got hold of me from behind and is using me as a shield. One of her arms clamps round my neck, forcing my head up and back. She jams the hot barrel of a blaster under my chin.

'Back off,' she yells, 'or I'll kill him.'

Dimly, I realise the shooting has stopped. Morana is talking to rebel fighters emerging from the smoke. A limping Sky is at their head, Murdo behind her.

'Let him go, bitch!' Sky snarls, scowling over her rifle's sights.

All I do is stare, dazed with shock at seeing her.

'Well, look who it is – Kyle's little scab girlfriend,' Morana says. She starts edging away, pulling me along with her towards the last escape craft.

'What did you call me?' Sky says.

I see her jaw tighten, the dangerous look on her face.

And then she shoots me.

Thump! I see this great big green flash and her rifle recoiling. There's a sudden tearing pain in my chest, like a Reaper's shoved a spear through me, and I'm spun round by the force of the blast. How I stay on my feet I'll never know, but Morana's not hanging off me any more. I watch her as she takes a few steps back, her eyes wide, legs all over the place. She hits the rock wall and slides down it into a heap, leaving a long bloody smear behind her.

I figure she's history. But no, the High Slayer must be half nightrunner or something. Hand shaking, snarling, she goes to raise her blaster again.

'Don't think so,' says Murdo, stepping round me.

I look away quick as he finishes her by emptying a whole clip into her.

Sky drops her rifle and throws herself at me.

'Kyle, are you okay?'

Shaking all over, I stare down at the burnt hole just under my collarbone and groan. 'No, of course I'm not all right. You fraggin' well shot me!'

Sky pulls back and gives me a pretend-scowl.

'She called me a scab. And I shot *through* you, that's all.'

I'm in too much pain to argue. Anyway, there's no time.

I struggle to free myself. 'I need a healer.'

Sky nods, yells 'Scallon!' at the top of her lungs, but won't let go.

Frantic now, I use the last of my strength to peel her off me. There's one thing I've still got to do – I just hope I'm not too late already.

'Colm. My brother saved me. I've got to save him now.'

38
A FINAL RECKONING

Fortunately, the few Slayers we meet as we make our way back up through the dome are medics, more interested in surrendering than fighting. Weird that, when you think we're supposed to be such monsters. Makes me think they know better. Anyway, there's so much wreckage in that topmost chamber, so many bodies scattered about, Slayer *and* rebel, it takes me ages to find Colm. His face is waxy and he looks horribly still. Terrified we're too late, I point him out to Scallon. She pushes me aside and kneels over him. I watch as she listens at his mouth, then feels for a pulse, before looking at the wound in his chest.

'How is he?' I ask her.

She bites her lip, gives me a sorry shake of her head. 'Still alive, but –'

'But what?' I yell. 'Do something!'

I take a step towards her, my head pounding.

'She would if she could,' Sky says softly, holding me back.

Scallon sighs. 'I'm sorry, Kyle. Your brother is hurt too badly. He's lung-shot, drowning in his own blood. There's nothing anybody can do for him now.'

Her words hit me so hard it's like being shot again.

Sky squeezes my arm until I look at her. 'Be with him, while you still can.'

Scallon shuffles round to make room and Sky pulls me down so we're both kneeling beside my brother. I'm so numb and broken I don't know what to do. Sky does however, takes Colm's cold-as-ice hand and folds it into mine.

Then she puts her arms around me and holds me.

Murdo is here now too, looking down and rubbing at his stubbled jaw.

After a while, Sky prompts me. 'Maybe he can still hear you?'

Gritting my teeth, I say Colm's name a few times, but get no response. It's almost a relief. I'm no good at words, never was and never will be. What should I say to him? Plead with him not to die on us? Tell him how brave he was, how proud I am to have him as a brother? Well I can't. Way I see it, no fancy words can help my brother now.

Instead, I ask Scallon for a cloth and water. When she brings it, I wet the cloth, dribble some water into Colm's mouth and wipe the bloody froth from his lips as gently as I can. I care for him, like Rona taught me.

When I least expect it, Colm's eyes flicker open.

He sees me, I'm sure. He groans. More blood spills from his mouth.

'He's trying to say something,' Sky says.

I lean closer, put my ear next to his lips. Even though he's so weak it's like an echo of a whisper, I catch it. And rock back on my haunches, stunned.

'What'd he say?' Sky asks.

'We're family,' I tell her. 'He said *we're family*!'

I stare around and get mostly sympathetic looks back, apart from Murdo who looks at me like I'm mad. I guess I do look wild-eyed and manic.

'We're *blood* family!' I focus on Scallon. 'There's a way I can save him.'

The healer woman frowns, but says nothing.

'You heard what she said, Kyle,' Sky says. 'He's too far gone.'

I know Sky only means well, but I can't help glaring at her. It hurts like crazy, with my badly wounded shoulder, but I tear my Slayer jacket off. I drag the sleeve of my undershirt up and tap the veins in my wrist at Scallon.

'My blood. We need to get some into Colm. Quickly! Before it's too late.'

'How will *that* help?' Scallon says, her frown deepening.

Frantically, tripping over the words in my rush, I tell her what I've found out as a prisoner here. How the only reason the Saviour wanted me found was so that my blood could be harvested to heal him. How, as twins, blood family, my nublood should be able to heal Colm too. I go to show them the marks the needles left in my hand, only they've already healed and gone.

She still looks doubtful.

Using all my speed, I grab Scallon's blaster and turn it on her. 'Look, just do it!'

'Put that gun down, Kyle,' snaps Murdo. 'This is mad.'

'Is it?' Sky spits. 'What've we got to lose?'

Scallon hesitates, but takes a deep breath and starts rooting through her medbag. She produces a field-dressing, slaps it on to Colm's chest wound and gets Sky to scoot round the other side of him so she can hold it in place.

'Lie down then, next to your brother,' she orders.

I throw the blaster to the watching Murdo and do as she says.

Scallon mutters to herself, still not happy, as she grabs a rubber tube and some savage-looking needles and starts plugging them all together.

'Sure about this?' says Sky, staring down at me.

I grimace up at her. 'I hope so.'

'Stay still.' Scallon whips off her belt and ties it tightly around my bicep. Next thing, with no warning, she cuts a slit in my wrist with a scalpel. She fishes around inside, pulls out a big vein or artery and plunges one of the needles into it.

A second needle she slides more gently into Colm's arm.

The rubber tube linking us pulses.

It's working. Sky gives me a big thumbs up.

I lie back, squeeze my eyes shut and listen to my heart thumping. In between the thumps, I can feel my healing nublood pump out of me and into Colm.

Weird. I've always wanted a brother, but only know that now.

A few minutes later and Scallon pulls the needle out of my arm. I protest, but she tells me I've already given Colm as much blood as I can afford to give.

'I'll dress that wound of yours now,' she says.

I wave her away. 'Is my blood working? How is he?'

'No change yet,' she says with a sigh. 'He's still with us though.'

I struggle up. A quick look at Colm and apart from a fresh

dressing Scallon has taped on I'd say he looks worse than when we first got here — even more pale and waxy and still. I have to look real close to make sure he's still breathing.

Scallon won't look at me. She busies herself with tidying up.

'Hey, least you tried,' Murdo says, then mutters something about not wanting to miss out on the best scavenging. Next thing, he's gone.

If I've any hope left, it drains out of me now like my useless nublood did. What a fool I was to think I could save Colm.

'It's too early to tell, that's all,' Sky says.

She stands watching us, hands red with Colm's blood, a strained expression on her face like something is chewing at her. She tries to smile, but fails.

Her glance flickers past me and outside the dome.

And I get it now and feel guilty.

Here she is sticking with me, when her own sister might be down one of the mines out there, or strapped to a bench in one of those sick laboratories.

'Go look for Tarn,' I tell her. 'We're okay here.'

Sky hesitates, but only for an instant. 'Come and help me?'

I shake my head. 'I'd better stay here.'

She nods. 'I'll be at the landing strip then. Any kids we find, we'll be loading them there to fly them out. I'll see you down there.'

With that, Sky's off too. I watch and wonder, but she doesn't look back.

Scallon is done with taking no for an answer from me and starts fussing over me like poor Rona would. She makes me take something for the pain and then dresses my wounds from where

Sky shot me and the burns under my collar. One of the rebel fighters guarding us is handy with locks and after a bit of a struggle she manages to break the collar off me. I take great pleasure in stamping on the hateful thing and smashing it. Meanwhile, outside in the distance I see rebel windjammers swooping in to land. It looks and sounds to me like the fighting is over.

Suddenly, Scallon makes me jump by cursing loudly.

I glance back to see her holding Colm's wrist and feeling his pulse, a wide-eyed look of disbelief stretching her face. She leans in, puts her ear to the dressing on his chest and takes a listen to his breathing, careless of all the blood.

'That's impossible,' she says, snapping upright.

'What? What's impossible?' I say.

She stares at me. 'A minute ago, your brother's heartbeat was faint and irregular. It's still not great, but it's definitely a lot stronger. And his breathing is much better too, I can hardly hear any bubbling. It's almost as if he's –'

'Healing?' I say, interrupting her. 'Could he be healing?'

A smile spreads across Scallon's face. 'You know what? I think he is.'

Down at the landing strip it's a madhouse of shouting with Gemini fighters running about and rescue teams bringing in stumbling gangs of stunned-looking and tearful kids, mostly still barefoot and in their filthy mining gear. The rebel windjammers that landed have their ramps down already and the shivering kids are being helped inside. Some captured Slayer transports are also being pressed into service. I wander about, thankful for the warm jacket Scallon lent me, looking mainly for Sky, but also keeping an eye out for her sister. I figure I'll know Tarn when I see her. Black-as-night hair, Sky told me, like hers was before her leg got hurt. Sharp face, green eyes and a scowl. Nothing doing though; I don't see either of them.

For a better view, I clamber up on to an abandoned steam tractor and try to spot Sky's shock of white hair, but I still can't see her. What I do glimpse is a woman tending some wounded who looks a lot like Rona from the back, which chokes me up with missing her. I'm about to jump down and check if Sky's inside one of the windjammers when a fighter I know from Bastion jogs past.

'Hey, Cobie. It's me, Kyle. You seen Sky around?'

He stops, peers up at me and pulls a thinking face. 'Yeah. Think so.'

I grit my teeth at him. 'Where?'

'Thataways, off by that crashed jammer.'

Finally. Without stopping to thank him, I leap down and set off at the best run I can manage the way he pointed, ducking and dodging through a line of nublood kids milling about waiting to be loaded. And begin to worry. The wrecked windjammer is a good hundred metres away, smoke still billowing from its tangled metal skeleton. Why's Sky over there instead of looking for Tarn?

I get closer and my worry turns to dread.

Sky's on her knees in the snow with her back to me, head down. Obviously watching her, but standing a few metres apart, are three of the rescued nublood prisoners. They hear me coming and look. I see their long faces. And I fear the worst then, that she's found out her sister is dead.

'Sky!' I call out. 'Are you okay? What's happened?'

She flinches hearing me. She says nothing, sucks in a big sobbing breath then slowly hauls herself to her feet before turning to face me. Her face is the saddest I've ever seen it, her green eyes shining.

She swallows hard. 'How's Colm?' And I can't help it, I tell her. It's easier than asking.

'My blood worked! Scallon says Colm will be okay.' I even grin like a fool as I tell her how the healer woman swore out loud she was so surprised.

'Yeah?' Sky tries to look pleased.

I'm not fooled. I see the despair and desperation pulling at her face. And I tell myself that if she can be this brave then I have to be brave too.

'What about Tarn? Is she —?' But still, I can't say *dead*.

'What do *you* care?' says Sky.

Next thing, she curses and pushes past me. Only I don't let her. I take a chance, throw my arms around her and pull her close. For a second or three she struggles to pull free, but I hold on. I figure if Colm had died I'd want to be held.

And suddenly she's holding me tight.

After a while, I ask again about Tarn. But Sky's not ready to talk just yet. Instead she takes a breath, lifts her head from my shoulder and nods to the tallest of the watching kids.

This girl looks at me bleakly, her brown eyes narrowed. 'So Tarn was here at the Facility, working the mines like the rest of us. We were shift mates and good friends too. But a week or so ago she was taken away with a few other kids. That happens here sometimes. They haul you out of line and you're gone.'

'Gone where?' I shudder. 'The labs in the domes?'

'No. Not there. They were flown out.'

My spirits soar again. 'So Tarn could still be alive?'

The tall girl shrugs. 'Probably. We don't know why they took her or where. But the kids they take, they're always the best fighters.'

Sky pulls away and scowls. 'One lousy week ago, that's all. So close.'

And it *is* heart-breaking. Not just close, but cruel. I feel her pain and frustration. On the other hand . . .

'At least we know she's still alive. That's good, isn't it?'

Soon as it's out of my gob, I know it's a mistake.

'*Good?*' Now Sky is glaring at me.

I mumble a quick sorry.

'You really are a gom, Kyle,' she snarls. 'You know that?'

39
WIND STILL BLOWS

The windjammer's flight deck shifts under me, its tired metal creaking and complaining as we're jostled by rough air currents outside. I rub my blistered throat, glad to be free at last from that hateful Slayer collar, and stare through the canopy at the ridge we're running past. We're staying low on it, and I see some wind-bent trees. These flash past under our starboard wingtip, seemingly only metres away, a last few golden leaves clinging stubbornly to their branches. Winter has pounced on Wrath while I've been held prisoner.

The demolished Facility is an hour behind us. That was fun, watching the bombs drop and domes bursting apart. And, so far, no signs of pursuit.

Murdo glances back at us from the controls, looking thoroughly miserable.

'This thing flies like a dog,' he moans.

'What did you expect?' says Sky, beside me. 'It's a freighter.'

'So why make *me* fly her?'

'Because you're the best. Or so you keep telling us.'

This lumbering hulk of a transport is the biggest of the Slayer windjammers our fighters 'liberated' so we could fly everybody out. Behind our flight deck, crammed into its massive cargo hold, are well over a hundred nublood children. Most of them are chattering away excitedly at the top of their lungs. A few lucky ones have their shiny faces and noses pressed up against viewports, staring greedily at the ridges slipping by outside. But I see plenty – and not just youngsters – who sit too quietly, darting frightened glances around, their pale faces still wide-eyed and fearful.

Who can blame them, after what they've been through?

This lot were rescued from the mines. That's why so many look sickly and pale.

We'll maybe never know all the horrors that took place at the Facility, although we've taken pictures of the worst we could find and one day soon we'll show Wrath these images of butchered children and what real evil looks like. But we do know what the children were mining now – something called darkblende. Unimaginably valuable, it's toxic and highly radioactive. Murdo reckons it's seriously rare, found only on a handful of far-flung worlds and so nasty it's mined by robots. Only robots cost money and cut profits, while fast-healing twists are free. The mystery is what the Slayers use darkblende for, but I'll let others worry about that.

'How's the young hero's wound?' says Rona.

Hearing her voice still makes me jump. I turn to look at her, not quite sure I can believe she's here with me.

'Not too bad. Hardly hurts at all.'

Another lic, but after all the worrying she's done, I figure it's not the end of the world.

Turns out the woman I saw up to her elbows in healing back on the landing field didn't just look like Rona, it was actually her. She'd been looking out for me, but as soon as casualties from the fighting started streaming in they'd needed all the healers they could get. Rona being Rona, she couldn't say no.

When we found each other, I don't know who cried more.

Since then we've had little time to talk; she's been too busy looking after hurt fighters and kids, but Sky filled me in on what happened. Seems Ballard had known all along that the Slayers couldn't be trusted, and had planned for it. Sergeant Havel saved Rona by first shielding her then throwing her down the old well where we did the trade. A rebel team was standing by in the shallow water at the bottom and hauled her to safety along another tunnel. Sadly, neither Havel nor Seph made it.

In return, I've told Sky my adventures since I was exchanged. Most of them anyway. There's some stuff I'll never be able to talk about.

'How's Colm doing?' I ask Rona.

'Sleeping. He's fine. Scallon's amazed. So am I.'

Rona stares at me hard then, and not for the first time either.

'One thing I still don't understand,' she says. 'I mean, I know Colm's your brother, but he was raised a Slayer. How come he risked his life to help you?'

I shudder. 'Have you seen his arm?'

Rona pulls a face. 'I have. Who did that to him?'

'Yeah, what's that about?' Sky says.

I tell them, and how he'd seen through the Saviour's lies.

Even Sky, always so fierce and tough, looks a bit shocked.

'He was sort of under house arrest,' I say. 'They dragged him to the Facility on the same windjammer as me, then kept him there while they argued about what to do with him. That Morana woman wanted to get rid of him.'

I swallow, guiltily remembering my past whining at Rona about having to grow up out in the Barrenlands. Could've been a hell of a lot worse.

We all shut up for a while, thinking our thoughts.

Rona says I should be proud of myself and what I've done here. And I am, I guess, but it feels strange and hard to take in, because deep down I know how scared I was the whole time and how lucky I got. Somebody – Sky I reckon – has told the rescued children who I am. I keep catching them staring at me, whispering and nudging each other. Earlier, when we were loading them, some even came up and bumped stumps with me, tears in their eyes, for Wrath's sake.

'I regret not telling you more,' Rona says.

I shake my head. 'You did what you thought best.'

She smiles sadly, reaches out to touch my cheek as if to make sure I'm real.

'How does it feel? To have a twin brother?'

I glance at Sky, but she looks away.

'It's weird seeing my face, hearing him talk with my voice. But good.' I nudge Sky with my elbow. 'I'm better looking though, don't you think?'

Sky still won't look at me, but mutters I'm more of a fool anyway.

'You two stay here,' Rona says. 'I've got work to do.'

She smiles at us, clambers through the hatch and back into the hold.

'You didn't tell her then?' I say to Sky.

She shakes her head.

I watch her summon a smile, see the pain behind it.

'You got Rona back *and* your brother,' she says. 'I'm glad for you.'

'Tarn's alive,' I remind her. 'We'll find her.'

Sky nods, then leans in and lays her head on my shoulder.

I put my good arm round her and she lets me pull her closer. I feel so wretched for her. If this was one week earlier, Sky's twin sister might be here beside us.

Tarn and the other taken kids aren't the only ones missing either. That's the biggest mystery we're left chewing on. For sure, it was a mad scramble to hit the Facility and get out again before Slayer reinforcements could respond and trap us, but we don't think we left anybody behind. The latest count I heard says we're leaving with about two hundred and seventy rescued nublood kids. One hell of a result you'd think, but I've seen heads being shaken and a few glum faces amongst our Gemini fighters. The mutter going around has it that Ballard was hoping to rescue at least four times this number, based on his spies counting the number of ident children 'harvested' each year at the dozens and dozens of Peace Fairs scattered all across Wrath. This sort of takes the edge off our triumph.

Unlike Tarn, these other kids were never here to be rescued.

Did Ballard get his numbers wrong, or did some of them hang for real? Were they taken to another Facility somewhere else? If so, where? Nobody knows, but we've taken a few high-rank Slayer prisoners and maybe they'll tell us.

Wouldn't want to be wearing *their* boots, that's for sure.

I sigh and Sky glances up at me. Her dark green eyes are back to being bleak and fierce, and I'm glad we're on the same side.

'Thanks,' I say.

'For what?' she says. 'Shooting you?'

I laugh. 'For coming to get me. I thought I'd had it.'

'They'd never have killed you.'

'Maybe not. But some things are worse than dying, believe me.'

She winces. 'You think I don't know that?'

And what can I say to this? Nothing. So I don't.

The windjammer flies on and on, rain rattling the hull now. Outside, the wind still blows, birds still fly and the sun still sets in the east. I feel dazed, as if I'm waking from a bad dream. But a feel of my blistered throat, a glance down at my arm in a sling and my missing little finger, and I know it was all too horribly real. I stare outside as the night tightens in around us. Soon I can hardly see the tree-smothered ridges slipping past below. Murdo pulls on night-viz goggles. In the cargo bay, the nublood children mutter or sleep or stare about. Rona comes and smiles at us, whispers that Colm is doing fine, then goes away again.

Sky falls asleep, her head on my shoulder. Or maybe she just pretends to.

In the darkness, I see my reflection in the canopy. It's so weird. I look older and tougher. I don't look like the me I remember.

If anything, I swear I look more like my brother.

I can't help letting out a long breath with plenty of sob in it.

Finally, as we leave the Facility further and further behind, my insides slowly start unknotting themselves. The horrors and terrors of the last few months let go of me. Don't get me wrong,

I've still got plenty to be scared of, like Murdo smashing us into a mountain in the dark, or Slayer warplanes getting on our tail, or the backlash and war that seems certain to follow this raid. And of course there's the Saviour, whose escape craft got past our windjammers. Should he survive his injuries, his Slayers are sure to come looking for me again, for blood and revenge.

Only now, strangely, I feel I can live with these fears and dark thoughts. Why that is, I don't know. That's just how it is.

There are those who claim the gift of foreseeing, but I'm not one of them. I don't know what lies ahead – I don't even know where our rebel windjammers are heading tonight. But none of this matters, I decide. All that matters now is that I'm with the people I care for, and who care for me. And no point either in kidding myself that this is the end. It can't be. All we've done is win one small battle. It's the coming war we've got to win if we're to rid Wrath of the Saviour's lies and build a world like Sky said, where pureblood and nublood can live side by side.

But one thing's for sure – I'm done running.

From now on I fight.

Maybe I mutter this out loud because Sky looks up. She stretches like a cat, reaches up, twines her fingers in my hair and pulls my head down.

'Will you help me find Tarn?' she says.

I shrug and kiss her.

She kisses me back, then pulls away and fixes those green eyes of hers on me with a grave look that says, *Well, will you?*

Under this sling that Rona insists I wear, my healing wound itches like crazy.

'You want me to?' I say. 'Thought I was a gom.'

She half smiles, half scowls. 'You are. But we make a good team.'

So I nod. *Why not?* After all, she did save me from Morana. And if we do find Tarn, the chances are we'll find the rest of the missing kids too.

I'll make sure I watch my back though.

Sky holds her fist out . . . and we bump stumps on it.

Acknowledgements

In space, nobody can hear you say thanks. But we're not in space, so here goes . . .

Rona Laycock, who runs the Avening writing group that got me started story-telling again.

Anthony, Marty and the rest of the crew at early Aspect who worked so hard then set me free.

Julia Greene and Steve Voake from the Bath Spa MA in *Writing For Young Children*, who accepted me, then showed me what's possible these days in YA fiction. Also my fellow MAers, Pat, Helenka, Nicola, Ekwy, Sarah, Kim, Jemma and Cerianne, for their feedback, encouragement, laughs and teacakes.

The relentlessly generous Lu Hersey, who whispered good things about me in my agent's ear and has been a constant source of encouragement ever since.

My remarkable literary agent, Ben Illis, who took a chance on me, is unfailingly genuine and enthusiastic and encouraging. Oh yeah, and fun and effective. If you ever want to hear someone talk with genuine passion about a book – listen to the Ben.

The wonderful Stella Paskins at Egmont UK for signing me up and turning my long-cherished dream of being a published author into reality, as well as for being a patient and talented editor.

And finally, last but not etc., my wife, Jana, without whose patience and support I would be lost. She lets me live my writer dream while the house and everything else falls down around us.

COMING IN 2017

Kyle and Sky are on the run again
as the quest for Sky's sister takes them

INTO THE
NO-ZONE